ℰ P

D0571681

OTHER BOOKS
BY THE SAME AUTHOR

Poetry

CHILDREN OF MORNINGSIDE

BUCK FEVER

SECOND WISDOM

Non-fiction

STOUT CORTEZ

PRIVATE VIRTUE, PUBLIC GOOD

SCIENCE VS. CRIME

FANTASTIC INTERIM

A SKELETON KEY TO FINNEGANS WAKE
[WITH JOSEPH CAMPBELL]

Fiction

THE PERFECT ROUND

THE
GREAT
SNOW

A Novel by

Henry Morton Robinson

SIMON AND SCHUSTER

New York, 1947

ALL RIGHTS RESERVED
INCLUDING THE RIGHT OF REPRODUCTION
IN WHOLE OR IN PART IN ANY FORM
COPYRIGHT, 1947, BY HENRY MORTON ROBINSON
PUBLISHED BY SIMON AND SCHUSTER, INC.
ROCKEFELLER CENTER, 1230 SIXTH AVENUE,
NEW YORK 20, N. Y.

FIFTH PRINTING

MANUFACTURED IN THE UNITED STATES OF AMERICA
AMERICAN BOOK–STRATFORD PRESS, INC., NEW YORK

FOR

Ellen, Hannele AND Tony

THE
GREAT
SNOW

CHAPTER 1

FROM HIS office window, higher by a thousand feet than the teeming harbor below, Ruston Cobb saw the first snowflake fall. It swirled out of a toneless February sky, careened past the chromium turrets of the Lawyers' Trust Building, and flattened itself against the windowpane scarcely six inches from Cobb's powder-gray eyes. He had been watching a school of freighters, loaded to the Plimsoll mark, assembling near the Jersey shore. His steep angle of vision made their decks seem flush with the putty-colored water, and, by an associative syntax growing richer and more compelling in his life of late, he found himself wondering about the margin of safety built into seagoing vessels. Prudentially wide, no doubt—the slide-rule chaps would see to that. Cobb made the customary beck to the engineering mind that kept the world afloat and right side up, then turned to gaze at the snowflake clinging to the windowpane.

Hexagonal and glistening, the flake reminded him of something deep in his unconscious. A milkweed filament? The compass-rose at the stern of the old *Gyrfalcon?* Very much like both of them the snowflake was. Reminiscent, too, in a curiously oblique way, of the crystal flacon of perfume he had given Nolla when they were first married. Yes, and of a certain six-pointed brooch sown with diamonds and seed pearls that his mother had always pinned to her high, wonderful bosom on grand occasions. In its starry design the snowflake suggested to Ruston Cobb the basic pattern into which all structures, natural and man made, fell.

"A new chip off the old universe," he said finally. As if dismayed by the idea, the snowflake lost its frail grip on solidity and went dribbling down the windowpane like any other drop of water headed back to sea.

"A new chip off the old universe." Cobb's casual thought about the snowflake contained precisely the mixture of logic and imagination that had made him, at forty-two, one of New York's outstanding patent lawyers. He was neither a scientist nor an inventor, but his grasp on technology was thorough and his talent for avoiding litigation quite extraordinary. The backlog of his business—and the whole world knew it after that $2,800,000 damage action in which he had successfully defended General Electronics against a growling pack of plaintiffs—was as patent counsel and consultant to a few great corporations. In handling the purchase of licenses or bargaining for assignments, he was the patent lawyer's lawyer, the chap who had written the books. (See Cobb on "Licenses," Cobb on "Assignments.") Worried corporation counsel, threatened by costly suits for infringement or contemplating a patent pool with shrewd competitors, knew that nothing was nearly so satisfactory as a little talk with that six-foot, quiet-baritoned nonpareil of the Federal Courts, Ruston Cobb, Esq., of Lufbery, Cobb and Bunting, Lawyers' Trust Building, New York City.

The snow was coming thicker now, tossed against the panes in windy handfuls. Cobb turned away from the window as a Sunday fisherman turns away from a trout pool. He sat down at his wide, moderately cluttered desk, picked up a sheaf of folders from the "Patent Applications" basket, and glanced at the preliminary reports attached to each. Today's grist was not promising; the bulk of the items were mere gadgets, impractical to use, unprofitable to make. He riffled through the drawings and blueprints, initialing and commenting briefly as he worked. Here was a golf club that made audible *tsk-tsk* noises when its owner dubbed a practice shot. Cobb grinned, then penciled, "Make search—RC." An electric oven

] 4 [

for baking synthetic gems. "Not new—RC." A refrigerating device for keeping skin surfaces at low temperatures, thus retarding the spread of bacteria in infections of the arm or leg. Hmm. Quite an idea. "Search carefully—RC."

Next on the pile was an automatic chessboard that would reproduce one hundred celebrated games from the masters merely by plugging an electric cord into a socket. "Each game a study in opening theory, mid-game strategy, and superlative ending technique." Cobb's devotion to chess (his father had taught him the game in childhood) led him to examine the application with more than ordinary interest. He read the descriptive material, then turned to the sketches for further light. What made the automatic chessboard tick? As far as he could discover, it worked on the old principle of the player-piano: if you wanted to study a Four Knights opening with a Scotch variation, you inserted a notched roll into a slot and watched the chessmen whiz about the board in the classic manner of Lasker vs. Capablanca. Damned ingenious—only the drawings didn't show how it was done. "Secrets not patentable," scribbled Cobb, then added, for his clerk's benefit, "Ask inventor to send in clearer drawings."

He came at length to a set of loosely typed sheets describing in detail a machine for casting gold and silver into small articles of jewelry. A light, involuntary tremor prickled Cobb's spine; the association was remote, but there it was. He picked up the first typewritten sheet and read:

"Molten gold is introduced into a steel flask. A motor spins the flask, and, by the operation of centrifugal force, the metal is thrown against the face of the desired mold. After five minutes of spinning, the finished objects are ready to be removed. This machine on its first trial cast eighty-six wedding rings."

Eighty-six wedding rings!

Cobb sat back in his chair and pondered the scheme. As always when in thought, he joined his hands behind his head, thumbs thrust

downward inside his collar. Many details of the machine were not
clear to him, but it was evident that the inventor had a fruitful idea.
Cobb's first step would be to determine whether a similar device had
already been patented. Possibly this ring caster merely adapted the
centrifuge principle already operative in, say, the cream separator or
the pipe-casting machine. Offhand, Cobb didn't know. Again, a patent might already have been issued to some jewelry manufacturer
who was keeping it off the market to protect the industry against a
glut of wedding rings. He made a notation: "Search carefully—RC."

Cobb let his mind stray from the mechanical aspects of the machine that could spin eighty-six wedding rings at a crack. He had
always supposed, though he had never really thought about it, that
these sacred bands were fashioned by hand, one at a time. That
wedding rings, circular symbols of sacrament and law, could be produced by belt-line methods didn't really surprise him. Nevertheless,
one would suppose . . . He glanced down at his own wedding ring,
the heavier counterpart of the one Nolla was wearing. With melancholy abstraction he slowly twisted it off his finger and held it in the
palm of his hand, as if to heft the ring's meaning in his life.

It gave Cobb no particular satisfaction to realize that he had been
faithful to the vows it symbolized. To the superbly naïve question
"Do you, Ruston, take this woman, Nolla, to have and to hold, for
better or worse, till death do you part?" he could still summon up
a loyal "I do." But the words were saltless in his mouth. And now,
as he weighed the ring in the cup of his hand, Cobb wondered
whether it counterbalanced the unexplored realms of pleasure and
experience he had renounced for its sake.

He put the ring back on his finger with the resigned helplessness
of a surgeon placing an old bandage over a wound he could not
cure. Yet if he were the hopeless surgeon, what of Nolla, the patient? Poor lost Nolla, gripped by a strange and unexpected darkness in the noon of life. True, there had been only one outbreak

thus far, but it would require all of Cobb's skill as a negotiator to stay the consequences of his wife's act.

From his pocket he drew a letter for the third time that morning. Impeccably typed on excellent bond, it bore the embossed crest of a great department store over the legend "Office of the President."

Dear Mr. Cobb:

I am in receipt of your note of February 16th requesting a personal interview. May I point out that, as far as our organization is concerned, we regard the incident as closed and can take no further action regarding it. Quite frankly, I do not see what purpose will be served by further discussion. But if it is within my power to set your mind at rest, I shall be happy to see you.

Will Friday, February 19th, at 12 noon, be a convenient hour? I would make it later but for the fact that I am leaving for the country directly after luncheon.

Sincerely yours,

Percival S. Richter

Courteous, discreet, noncommittal—just the kind of a document that Cobb himself would write in such a case. Dejectedly he put the letter into his pocket and turned once more to the pile of papers awaiting his initials. "Make search—RC." "Stay consequences—RC." "Till death do part—RC."

A buzzer whirred like a small tree toad inside the interoffice phone on Cobb's desk. He picked up the instrument, heard the operator's announcement: "Miss Deane calling." Then the too eager catch of Beryl's exciting voice. "Ruston?"

"Hello, Berry." A tiny crescendo of illicit gladness turned his words up at the end. "What gives?"

"Deane is taking to the open country this afternoon." A grape of pleasure broke under her tongue, trickled down her throat. "I'm driving up in my new Packard to spend the week end at your place. Thought you might like to squeeze in between us."

"Us? Must there always be an us?"

] 7 [

"Visiting a brother-in-law alone isn't much fun for a big girl of twenty-seven, so I'm bringing my fun with me."

"Who's the fun this time?"

"Edward Laimbeer, the painter. Dark and cryptic. Maybe you know him."

"Seen his stuff. Does Nolla know you're coming?"

"Naturally. I tell my married sister everything I do—especially when I plan to do it in her house."

A twinge bisected Cobb's larynx. He glanced at his wrist watch with a stalling-for-time maneuver. The pleasure of riding upcountry with Beryl was a considerable bait, but—no sense in tormenting oneself needlessly.

"Sorry, darling, the schedule's pretty full. I'm catching the three-thirty from Grand Central and wouldn't be able to get away a minute before that."

"Don't say I never asked you." The grape in Beryl's voice modulated to tartness of currant. "Well, hold dinner for us. We ought to be turning up a little after seven."

"Why so late? Driving by way of Minneapolis?"

Beryl was vaguely airy. "Oh, we may meet a Saint Bernard dog in the storm and sample his cunning little barrel. *Arrivederci.*" She hung up.

Cobb had the powerless feeling that Beryl was brimming toward one of her week-end benders and that he might as well command Niagara to flow the other way as to try to stop her. Why should he try? Beryl was old enough, big enough, smart enough to take care of herself. But as he turned to his papers he caught, as in a violet-colored mirror, a reflection of himself gazing at Beryl across a cozy table in a curtained roadhouse, leaning toward her, glass in hand, for their third drink in the late winter twilight. Words he had not used for years were bubbling out of him in a releasing surf, tumbling her beautiful head in a blurry tide. He knew that if he had said just now, "Cut Laimbeer. Come early; we'll make it a long ride together," she would have done it. But he would never say those words to Beryl in a winter twilight or any other time. He would continue to be circumspect and brotherly in her presence, and she would be mocking and provocative in his.

That was the way things were. Cobb gathered up his papers, arranged them in their folders, then crossed his office and knocked lightly on Ross Lufbery's door. Without waiting for Luff's "Come in!" he turned the knob and entered his partner's office. Lufbery, rubicund, bald, and excitable, was bellowing into his dictaphone; the effect was something like an anthill in eruption. Cobb, waiting till the last blast died away, laid the papers on Lufbery's desk.

"Batch of stuff from Butterworth and Larkin," he said. "Mostly junk—except one item. Centrifuge principle applied to non-ferrous metals. Might be useful to United Jewelers. After you've looked, let Riggs make a search."

"Fire-balloon optimism will strand you in the stratosphere one of these days," ribbed Lufbery. A pair of overactive adrenals gave his humor the subtlety of a freshman flag-rush. "If some chemical wizard came in here with a powder that made oranges taste like tits, or some other equally gracious boon to mankind, you'd give it that Dutchess County quick-freeze treatment of yours. I swear to Christ you would." Lufbery slapped the surface of his cluttered desk in six or seven places, as if searching for a document. "Here, let this whip up your lymph." He tossed an auditor's semiannual statement at his partner. "When you guzzle some of that old First National honey, maybe you'll feel better."

Cobb glanced incuriously at the statement. Nearly twice as much business as last year. Cash on Hand: $78,000. New Business: $180,000. Government Bonds: $120,000. Reserve for Taxes: $62,500. He nodded appreciatively but without zest. "Nice going, Ross. They can't stop us now."

"Can't stop us!" Lufbery's exophthalmic eyes popped with indignation. "Who in hell said anything about stopping us? My God, man, there isn't a patent outfit in Manhattan that can come within fifty thousand of that 'New Business' item alone. Taxes high, sure, but we're going to net sixty thousand apiece this year. 'Getting and spending, we lay waste our powers——' " He stopped short, like a cyclist jamming on a coaster brake. "Say, I want to talk to you about our new layout in the Hexagon Tower. Here, sit down. I'll show you the blueprints."

Lufbery pulled a set of plans from the top drawer, spread them on his desk. Cobb, gazing over his partner's shoulder, saw a six-sided ground plan bearing the legend "Proposed offices of Lufbery, Cobb & Bunting, 92nd Floor, Hexagon Tower. J. V. Remsen, Builder." He followed the tip of Lufbery's gold pencil as it demonstrated the unique features of the new layout. "All glass and Monel metal, one hundred per cent air-conditioned, express elevator, automatic shutters built right into the glass walls," explained Lufbery. "Not a shadow, draft, sound, tremor, or grain of dust in the whole damn building. It'll be like working in a nice cool vacuum right under the blue sky. Sweetest setup in New York, and the rent's only ten thousand more than we're paying for these old stables." Luff twisted his short neck to catch the expression on Cobb's face. "Now, don't dive through the window with enthusiasm," he grinned. "All I want is your signature on the lease."

Cobb strolled over to the window overlooking the North River and gazed out moodily at the sleety harbor below. Eight years of viewing the world from the seventy-first floor had given his eyes an accustomed slant, and he had no desire to change his perspective now. Cobb had always liked his gumwood-paneled offices, with the broad window sills and bronze door knobs. The thought of working in a hive-shaped glass and metal tower filled him with misgivings. He was sure he'd feel like a tadpole *in vitro* or like a wax-winged Icarus tempting the rays of the sun. Yet to say all this, or any of it, would lead only to horse-laughter and expletives. "Why, you troglodyte, you night crawler, you ingrown splinter on the banister of progress. . . ." That's what Luff would say, and, as far as the auditor's statement showed, he'd be right.

"Sure, I'll sign the lease, Luff," Cobb said finally.

Lufbery swiveled around, gazed questioningly at his partner. "What's the trouble, Rusty?"

Outside, snowclouds were scudding past like herds of unwashed sheep. A comfortable gasp of steam sighed from the valve in the radiator built into the window sill. Cobb wished that he could sigh like that and release the pressure mounting within him. If he could unburden himself to anyone, it would be to Luff—classmate, partner, friend. Luff, the surrogate older brother, the free one, unshackled in speech and morals—Luff would understand. But the valve stuck; the plug just wouldn't pull.

"It's the weather, I guess," Cobb said lamely. "The barometer's tumbling fast. We're in for a storm."

"At our age we should talk about the weather?" snapped Lufbery. "All right, it's going to snow. So I go to my little three-room suite in the Waldorf Towers, and you go to your little eighteen-room shack up the Hudson, and we turn the thermostat to a moderate seventy-two degrees Fahrenheit, and the long-horned winds rage, and we play gin rummy or go to bed—me with a Brazilian tornado from the Riobamba, and you with your wife, or a good book. Tough. Intolerable. Intolerably tough." Lufbery slapped some papers around on his desk waiting for Cobb to speak. "For God's sake, Rusty, what's eating you?"

Cobb wanted to take the letter out of his pocket and tell Lufbery about it. He could have told his friend about anything else in the world. But for Nolla's sake, he couldn't speak of this. He must be paralyzed, dumb. Wearily he faced his partner.

"Maybe I'll tell you Monday, Luff. I need the week end to think it over. But now, before that barometer hits bottom, I better get going."

Back in his own office, Cobb glanced at the clock, an electric ribbon winding horizontally past the illuminated dot of NOW. The NOW dot said 11:21. Cobb gathered up a handful of papers on his desk, tucked them into a flat brief case. Homework, thank God for homework. He put on his forty-dollar Homburg and tailor-made Chesterfield. Their fine black set off the ruddy color of his skin, accentuated the gray rufters where his hat rode his chestnut hair. Richter couldn't help seeing he was a solid citizen. From old habit he made a quarter genuflection, smiling, toward the desk that was the altar of his livelihood. Wasn't a hundred and eighty thousand dollars in new business worth a crook of the knee? *Humilitas deos placet.* Especially when one was going hat in hand to ask a favor of a man like Richter.

His secretary, the meek Miss Dunham with the no-color hair, put her head through the door. "Sorry, Mr. Cobb, but there's a gentleman here from the State Department."

"A courier?"

Miss Dunham shook a negative. "Higher, I'd say. Almost a—personage."

Cobb made a calculation involving time, distance, and the personage from the State Department. "Show him in."

A quietly important young man wearing the gray tie and striped pants of diplomatic usage entered Cobb's office, carrying a black leather satchel under his left arm. He removed a gray suede glove from his right hand, extended it a trifle too high.

"Grandgent's the name. Under Secretary Oliphant sent me," he said. His intelligent eye took in the fact that Cobb was about to leave the office. "I hope I'm not holding you up."

"Not at all. Won't you sit down? Unfortunately, I have a twelve-o'clock date, but there's still five or six minutes."

Grandgent sat on the edge of the proffered chair. "The matter's important but not necessarily tedious. Briefly, Secretary Oliphant has asked me to deliver in person the sketch and description of a device that the Department considers to be, well, to coin a phrase, dynamite." Grandgent manipulated the small combination lock on his satchel and drew out an oblong envelope sealed with three green-waxed blobs over red strings. "I can't tell you much more, except that the Department regards it as top-drawer confidential. The details are in this letter from my chief." He handed Cobb a smaller envelope bearing a State Department seal. "Mission completed," he said pleasantly, rising to go. "Oh yes, one thing more. The Under Secretary asked me to add that time is of the essence, and that he hopes to have your report for a Cabinet meeting Wednesday."

Cobb accompanied the junior diplomat to the door. "Considerate of you to serve it forth so promptly," he said, giving Grandgent his hand. "Please tell your chief that I'll deliver my opinion in person at his convenience early next week."

The NOW dot flashed 11:35 as Cobb tucked the two envelopes into his brief case, picked up his Homburg for the second time, and started for the elevator. Fifteen minutes later he was sitting in Percival Richter's anteroom—a decorator's dream of executive masculinity, constructed chiefly of space, good leather, and a few chaste prints. Successful as Cobb was, his own office seemed an artisan's workshop compared with this. How many hierarchies in the choir of success!

A male secretary entered. "Mr. Richter will see you now."

Percival S. Richter did not rise as Cobb entered the office, nor did he offer his hand as he indicated, with impersonal courtesy, a chair at some distance from his mercantile throne. P. S. Richter, last of the old school of great storekeepers, sat like a small but perfect diamond—hard, white, and flawless—behind a low Regency desk, in a room of fine but not overwhelming proportions. Abrasives of time and competition had not yet worn him down; he had the nostril of a man who, despite his years, could still cut cruelly when the buttons were off. He wore a turndown collar, polka-dot bow tie, starched cuffs with stiff-shanked cuff links of intaglio and gold; the white piping on his vest dated him as a beau of the early Wilson period. Richter's private morality was publicly unsmirched; like the elder Morgan, he believed that family doors were made to be closed and bolted from within. In addition to running a great store he had been a successful Wall Street manipulator, whose operations, unknown to the general press, were considered small masterpieces by the initiate. He had adapted the gambit of Zuckertort to his own uses and was considered a master in the use of rook and pawn.

"Colder than his note," thought Cobb. "Nolla hasn't a chance." Aloud, he said, "I value your kindness in seeing me, Mr. Richter." The sincerity of his opening was acknowledged by a two-inch nod from the department-store magnate.

"We—my wife and I," Cobb went on, "are much troubled by what has happened. Troubled and puzzled. It's the first time and, to my knowledge, the only time that Mrs. Cobb has ever done anything like this. She can't explain it; neither can I. But we're both positive that there will be no repetition."

"I quite believe you, Mr. Cobb," said Richter, matching the tips of his fingers in the manner of a lay cardinal. "And, I may add, quite off the record, of course, that these unexplainable actions are not at all uncommon. I'm speaking now not of professional—ah—er—operators but of well-placed women, indeed some of our best customers, who could afford to pay a thousand times over the price of the merchandise involved." Richter concluded his little lecture with a walrus sigh. "It is really very depressing."

Cobb, thoughtfully silent, was letting his perplexity plead for him on one plane while his character spoke to Richter on another, deeper level. He was trading, as he always did in any encounter, on the knowledge that his own indestructible goodness was his best argument and that it would influence Richter powerfully in granting the request he was about to make.

"When my wife was taken to your general manager's office," Cobb said, "she signed a statement of some kind. In her excited condition, she hasn't been able to recall the precise nature of the document."

"It was merely an acknowledgment that merchandise had been improperly taken from the store. The usual statement we require in such cases—nothing more."

Genuine tears, hot and sudden, sprang to Cobb's eyes. "It's that statement, Mr. Richter, that's troubling her. She's consumed by worry, sir. It's eating her up. She fears our son will find out. For her sake, for our son's sake, I appeal to you for the return of the confession she signed after—stealing that wretched ring." Cobb dashed the tears from his eyes. "As a responsible lawyer and an affectionate husband, I ask it, sir."

Almost irritably, Percival S. Richter shook his head. He had foreseen what would happen if he granted this interview, and, now that it was happening, he was annoyed.

"I'm sorry to refuse you, Mr. Cobb. But it's our unswerving policy never to return a signed statement of this nature. We believe that they act as a deterrent to future lapses. However, if it will comfort you or console your wife, I can tell you that these—confessions, to give them their proper name, are kept in a confidential vault, seen by no one but a trusted official. They are never referred to unless there is a—a repetition of the offense. Your wife can dismiss her fears; her act will never be known to her son or anyone else. It is, so to speak, locked in the innermost chamber of the corporate—and therefore, ha, ha, non-existent—heart."

Richter made a half-sideways turn to his desk, the favorite gesture of the executive indicating that an interview is over. "I regret that I cannot help you. Good day, Mr. Cobb."

Cobb's heat-making mechanism flared in a sudden draft of anger. For reasons that he recognized to be completely irrational, he could have killed the man. What did he mean by standing in judgment on Nolla? The canting hypocrite! Didn't Cobb know, along with everyone else, all about the notorious five-for-one split up of Richter and Dehn Preferred in 1937—a deal that netted its operators six or seven millions to the detriment of the common stockholders? Did anyone hold Richter's signed confession in the secret chambers of a corporate heart? Yet here was Nolla grinding her nerves to shreds over the pilfering of a nine-dollar bauble.

Cobb's expensive Homburg was being telescoped like an opera hat between his large hands. He rose, took a step forward, extensor muscles swelling, his eyes measuring the storekeeper for the punch. Unflinchingly, P. S. Richter glanced at him; years of dealing with angry victims had schooled him to despise their futility. He pressed a button with his toe; the male secretary opened the door.

Ninety seconds later Ruston Cobb, quite ill and very ashamed of himself, was dropping at the rate of eleven hundred feet a minute toward the street floor.

Straightening out his crushed hat, he jammed it onto his head and shouldered his way through the crowded aisles dense with women shoppers. A mixed reek of perfume, textiles, leather goods, and body odors struck the inner flares of his nostrils. He saw a swarm of women milling around under a "Special Sale" sign, pecking at the materials like hens at scattered corn. A flagrancy, unashamed and immoral, hung over the loaded counters, shrieking "Buy! Buy! Buy!" in a thousand sharps and flats. Bargains, special values, mark-downs, clearances, sales—anything to inflame the buying nerves and create appetites where no real hunger existed. Cobb passed the jewelry counter glittering with metallic temptations—bangles, clips, buckles, bracelets—rings!

Poor Nolla.

Outside, the snow was swirling like a dotted-muslin curtain in a stiff wind. Fluffy bats of snow sponged some of the heat from Cobb's face and neck as he strode northward, dodging in and out along the crowded sidewalks like a broken-field runner. He needed quick muscular release for the accumulated poison of anger churning in his bloodstream and hoped to find it by walking. But his irritation was increased by the traffic delays at every corner and by the incessant bumping into people carrying bundles, leading children, or bucking the wind, head down. Seeing an empty cab at the curb, he made a quick decision to escape the herd and gain the privacy and solace of his club.

Corinthian, University, or Metro Athletic? Oh, the last. A workout, a soak in the steam room, an icy plunge in the pool, then a Martini, lunch—how he needed them all. "Metropolitan Athletic Club," he said to the driver.

Then, abruptly, he countermanded the order. "No!" Before Cobb could give himself up to club pleasures there was The Errand.

"De Golyer the Florist," he said, "Fifty-ninth and Fifth Avenue."

The taxi driver, hating his trade, his customer, and himself, stopped bonging a tired string of dental floss between his front teeth and slapped down his flag. The side glance of his inflamed eyes and the back of his greasy, flattened cap both said: "Make up your mind, mister." So hostile was the hackman's personality that it smote Cobb like a bad breath. He glanced at the license card on the front wall of the cab, saw the desperate fatigue in the broken visor of Benno Sussman's cap, the "screw-you-Jack" curl to his defeated lips. Cobb was not given to intimate exchanges with taxi drivers; he found them neither picturesque nor rewarding, and in his present agitation he was vastly uninterested in the ill temper of Benno Sussman. He did not know that Sussman had indurated hemorrhoids, a son in the delinquency court, a daughter with the thickest eyeglasses in Public School 41, and a wife under observation in Bellevue because she would not eat. Even if he had known all these things, Ruston Cobb would have limited his sympathy to a half-dollar tip. You simply couldn't go about the city suffering like someone out of Dostoevski. All Cobb wanted from Benno Sussman was a reasonably rapid ride and no prima-donna antics. He settled back on the synthetic-leather cushion and braced himself for a nerve-jangling progress uptown.

To soothe the tension in his throat and mouth—the backlash of his unuttered rage at Richter—he put a cigarette between his lips, snapped a patent lighter. No flame. The marvels of science. He fished in his pocket for a match. No matches. Ask Sussman? Not yet; let the poor devil get his cab navigating first. Unlighted cigarette between his lips, Cobb sucked at it like a baby tugging at a pacifier.

Midtown traffic was wretchedly jammed; the cab made barely a block in five minutes. A great quantity of snow from the last storm still lay in the streets like dirty maple sugar; ice from a preceding storm cropped out in dark, slaty veins. A crawling paralysis gripped the mid-city; vehicles designed to travel at eighty miles an hour crept along slower than ox carts. Trucks, busses, pedestrians, taxis, traffic cops—all seemed inextricably muddled, as if the wires in some central control tower had been crossed by a malignant hand. Horns, whistles, skid-chains, the roar of motors and human voices, went up in warring confusion, making a noise like a gigantic phonograph record played backward.

The melody of chaos!

God, for a match!

Benno Sussman's cab, inching up Broadway, crossed the tide-rip of Forty-second Street and bogged down in the traffic flats of Duffy Square. Strange thing, pinning a priest's name to the rump of the amusement district. Values mixed, somehow. Cobb saw the ornate marquee of a first-run movie palace, its electric lights announcing to snowy gloom that "Hot Lips" Tucker was there In Person, with his Sugar Sax and his Are-You-With-Us Boogie-Beaters. And on the same bill, in Radarcolor, that Hollywood Sextravaganza *Overnight Bag*. " 'Puts you on the Scream-Beam'—*N. Y. Post.*" Signs of the times burned neonish patterns through the snow. "Drink *Coco-Pinola.*" "Wear *Hi-Truss* Arches." "Keep Normal with *Choco-Lax.*" "Try *Gleem* for Teeth Hard to Briten." "Say *Bazo* to your local druggist."

Blue-lipped, furtive, a man handing out pink cards squirmed

down the alley between lines of stalled traffic. He shoved a card into the open slit of Sussman's cab window; it sailed into Cobb's lap.

NERVOUS? FIDGETY? BLUE?

Relax at Roseland Massage Parlors, Thirty Female **Masseurs**
in Attendance

Blonde, Titian, Brunette. Select your Favorite.

If You Like Her, That's *Your* Business
If She Likes You, That's *Her* Business

Open from 3 PM till midnight. Private Rooms. Tel. Traf 7-5597

With a touch of curious envy, Cobb wondered what kind of people patronized the Roseland Massage Parlors. Sussman, cursing his bread, bucked forward another block.

A barker in the uniform of a French spahi was rounding up customers in front of Pinsky's Burlesque. "Afternoon show about to begin. See Dora La Porte, Queen of the Strip-Teasers. This Week Only." With a swagger stick, the spahi slapped a life-sized poster photograph of Miss La Porte, bearing the caption, "The Most Beautiful Body on Broadway." The spahi's stick, like a pedagogue's ferule, returned again and again to the focal nub of interest, the projecting mammaries of Dora La Porte. Cobb, following the pointer's argument, saw Sussman's red-rimmed eyes gazing hungrily at Dora's voluptuous breasts as if he, too, a greasy, bearded baby, still yearned to be fed. Was this hunger never satisfied? Was this the solace men died dreaming of? Cobb passed his tongue over parched lips.

"Got a match, driver?"

Awakened from his feeding trance, Sussman looked around at his fare, grinned sheepishly. "Big enough to hang your hat on," he said, motioning with his head in the direction of Dora's bosom. He tossed a card of matches to Cobb. All members of the same club.

The spahi beat Dora's luscious façade with his stick. "Show about to begin—about to begin. . . ." Cobb lit his cigarette; the traffic moved on.

In soda fountains, lunch-hour crowds were gorging their tuna-fish specials when Cobb said, "Wait here," to Benno Sussman and plunged across the sidewalk toward the invisible-glass windows of De Golyer the Florist. A liveried doorman, family-retainer type, opened a chaste white portal and Cobb entered an oval-shaped interior with rose-taupe walls and chancel lighting effects. Crystal vases held roses in urbane arrangements; a funereal odor of narcissus lingered on the air.

The place had changed since Cobb's last visit; he looked around for the more or less familiar face of a salesperson named Heist (or was it Feist?) who had arranged this business in previous years. Not Heist but another was coming forward—a slender young man with cinnamon hair, wavy, and a gardenia in the lapel of his morning jacket. He looked like the second juvenile in a musical comedy; a hint of the contortionist was in his glide. Very remotely he reminded Cobb of someone. Who?

"May I serve you, sir?"

A type. Unexceptional. Still, not the type that Ruston Cobb would have wished for the business at hand.

"Is Mr. Heist about?"

"Mr.—Geist is out to lunch." The cinnamon-haired understudy was having his little hour at the footlights. "I shall be very glad——" *Moue,* very winning, testing audience.

Cobb brushed past the byplay with road-finger directness. "In past years on this date, Mr. Geist has made me a corsage of small pink roses and lily of the valley. I forget the name of the roses . . ."

"Sweetheart," breathed the understudy, giving an Armande intonation to the trade name of a flower. He made a discreet scribble on his pad. "I'm sure I'll be able to get it out for you, sir." Pique by inference. Mr. Geist not the only knowing fellow in this shop. Then, the light touch, pleasing to man-of-world performing sentimental devoir: "To whom is the corsage to be sent?"

"Send it," said Cobb, "to the Head Grounds Keeper, Cedar Lea Cemetery, with directions that it be placed on the grave of Sarah Ruston Cobb."

Struck as if by a turnip flung from the stalls, the understudy's cheek flamed to the color of his hair. A ghastly miscue. His hand went to his cinnamon coiffure; with trouper nerve he pulled himself together. Quick-change transposition of voice, reverence *forte* and uppermost, sympathy *pianissimo.* "Ah—thank you, sir."

Cobb turned to leave the shop.

"Have you a charge account, sir?" Awkward, most awkward.

"Ruston Cobb. Lawyers' Trust Building."

A fierce need to atone for his gaucheries, to be loved in spite of them, clamored in the young understudy, tempted him to desperate devices. He selected a white carnation from a crystal vase, broke the stem just below the calyx, and held out the flower with ingénue simplicity.

"A posy for your buttonhole, Mr. Cobb."

Cobb hated the word "posy" and he disliked this young cinnamon-coiffed clerk who had ruined the annual rite of the corsage. He did not want the carnation, resented it as an intrusion on his mother's memory. But he could not bring himself to hurt this anxious, pitiful creature.

"Why, thank you. Very thoughtful of you, I'm sure."

Deftly, the young man inserted the carnation in the buttonhole of Cobb's overcoat. As he leaned close, Cobb could see the flesh-colored make-up that covered the pimples on the understudy's face, smell the scent on his too wavy hair. Disgust tightened the muscles of Cobb's cheek; pity relaxed them.

"Thank you," he said again.

"Thank *you*," smiled the clerk. His curtain was going to be a success after all. Death's favorite odor, narcissus, wreathed him as he opened the door and let his audience out into the falling snow.

Benno Sussman was playing bong-bong on his front teeth with the same piece of dental floss when Cobb said, "Metropolitan Athletic Club." With better temper, though not as one leaping to the tabor's sound, the hackman butted three long blocks across-town, made an adroit turn, and pulled up in front of the club. From his pocket Cobb drew some loose bills, handed one to Sussman. The driver's stoatish glance traveled from the two dollars and forty cents on the clock to the five-dollar bill his passenger had just given him. Crisis of the tip. Silver or folding money? Less than a buck I shouldn't get from this goneph. . . .

"Give me back a dollar," said Cobb. Decent, not excessive. Just the proper evaluation of a good ride. A crumbweight of Sussman's rancor changed to admiration. These gonephs had it because they didn't toss it around.

Eager for the refuge of his club, Cobb walked briskly up the broad flagged steps, but the expected feeling of sanctuary eluded him as he entered the lobby. The Club foyer resembled a paddock ten minutes before the first race—crowded, noisy, restlessly expectant. The expectancy had the mixed flavor of business about to be combined with hospitality. Florid men wearing deftly draped suits would soon be sitting down to a not too small but very good steak, plying their guests and/or customers with aged whiskies or Martinis smoother than the curd, awaiting cordial warmth to rise till the interest-bearing talk could begin. To Cobb, the whole institution of the business lunch had always seemed vaguely immoral. Not that a client would be anybody's chump for a meal; still, a Trimalchian decadence clung about these midday orgies. One of these times the Club would install couches in the dining room.

He pushed through the lobby to the coat room, saluting three or four acquaintances in his passage. Two-hundred-pound Tim Kennedy would sell six carloads of cement at lunch today and uncork some really inimitable stories while wrapping up the parcel. Carbuncular Ed Griffiths would bid for the towel and uniform concession for the Dittler Hotels. A lavatory attendant at heart. Cobb avoided Clary Cuyler, whose cups and medals filled a whole cabinet in the trophy room. Would anyone believe that Cuyler had ever hurled that bulk of fat over a crossbar for the world's record high jump at Stockholm in 1924? And there was Monseigneur Riordan, secretary to the Cardinal, meeting for lunch with the ushers of Saint Patrick's. Some kind of drive, probably.

Politicians, contractors, promoters, concessionaires, substantial citizens, good fellows all, not exactly at the helm of things, perhaps, but at ease within the wheelhouse—or, more likely, privy to the purser's office. Not bad chaps, really. Give you the shirts off their backs, never sell you short, inquire after your wife and kids, swell losers in a card game, pleasant companions at the snooker table, grand to meet at Palm Beach or Saratoga, buy you two drinks to one, excellent credit at the bank and bar. Not wicked men, not stupid or contemptible men. Yet somehow not thoughtful or tender, or alive. Whizzing zeros, all velocity and no momentum, highly energized at the rim but numb at the axle.

He checked his coat and brief case, then walked toward the elevator that would take him to the gym. The locker room was almost empty; it was the hour of fork and napkin, and the Club athletes were preparing to test their strength with dead lifts of food and alcohol. Cobb was hungry, too, but even stronger was his mood for exercise and steam.

In shorts, sweatshirt, and woolen crew socks he entered the rowing room, fitted out with a variety of mechanical oars and outriggers. He thrust his stockinged toes into the footstraps of his favorite rowing machine, leaned forward till his armpits hollowed over his knees, then pulled back in the smooth power stroke of the veteran oarsman. Cobb had rowed all through college; "The perfect Number Two," Grantland Rice had called him after his boat had set a new river record at Poughkeepsie in 1927. Now the old virtuosity came flowing back in delicate patterns of skill and power. Perspiration began to glisten from his forehead. The live sweat of exercise streamed in rivulets down his back, scouring away the dead wax that clogs the pores of city men. Cobb rowed steadily for twenty minutes, gradually lifting his beat from thirty to thirty-six and finishing with a brief all-out spurt of forty. When he took his last stroke and lay puffing on his oar, his rage against Richter had dissolved in salt, water, and the lactic acid of muscular fatigue.

Now for the soothing steam. Naked as the man in the Zodiac, Cobb entered the spacious tiled baths, latterday triumphs over the poor works of Commodus and Caracalla. The huge oblong pool was filled with bacteria-tested, chlorine-protected water; batteries of faucets, hoses, and sprays lined the sides of the bath. Masseurs, chiropodists, and directors of colonic irrigation held themselves in readiness to rub, soak, douche, anoint, and massage their passive patrons. Cobb picked up a fluffy towel, big as a crib sheet, and opened the door of the steam room. The familiar gush of pine oil and ipecac—sovereign medicaments for the loosening of plugged bronchia—flooded the membranes of his nose and throat. Someone was softening up a cold. In the hot, faint fog, Cobb saw a paunchy member, pink and bald as a grotesque baby, stewing out the sins of yesterday's gullet, and alkalizing himself against today's excesses with a bottle of mineral water. A lank cadaver wearing a truss and straw slippers emerged from the vapor depths, peered at Cobb through parboiled eyes, and asked, "Have you seen Ed Houlihan around?"

A faceless voice deep in the fog answered, "He's up playing snooker."

"Uric acid," mumbled the truss wearer. "I bet Charlie Doyle's up there, too."

"That's right. Practicing for the tournament. They're going to nut you, Pop."

"The bastards." Straw slippers shuffled off.

Cobb spread his towel on a stone bench and stretched out in the delicious warmth. This was heaven. Relaxed waves purred from his diaphragm, rippled to the extremities of his soaking body. He closed his eyes and let himself swing in the hammock of uncaring. All thoughts, plans, and anxieties were wiped from the scribbled tablets of memory. Richter, Nolla, the stoat-faced taxi driver, the snookerish worry of the trussed man, and the inexplicit bastardy of Messrs. Houlihan and Doyle dripped away under the kneading caress of steam.

An exquisite pleasure like the first bubble of a seminal spring stirred within him, and a fantasy of fair women revolved in slow circuit around the stone bench. Their face, limbs, and breasts were those of Beryl Deane, summoning him with coryphee gestures into an unexplored grove. May was making into June, and the paths of the secret wood were ankle-deep in quiet. Now the white bodies became a cluster of birch trees in postures chaste but inviting. At last he stood before a single birch, a very queen of purity, crowned with a halo of green and silver. He pressed his lips against its cool bark; with open palm he stroked the fork of its satiny trunk and breathed a name joyous as a new dream yet heavy with burial griefs of old ones.

"Lucy."

A leaf quivered, fell, and, as it settled to the forest floor, Ruston Cobb knew that of all the leaves on all the boughs of mortal longing, none for him would ever take the place of this dead leaf.

CHAPTER 2

From a hidden console the Grand Central organist was offering a subdued voluntary to the Friday-afternoon throng of commuters as Cobb entered the great terminal. The bustle of the vast concourse always stimulated him. He loved the names of the trains on the announcement boards—*Wolverine, Merchants' Limited, Yankee Clipper*—and never ceased to marvel at the efficiency of the despatching system that routed so many passengers through the narrow funnel of trackage under Park Avenue. What a complex organization of wires, switches, and semaphores that system must be! The delicate and vulnerable throat of a city, packed with steel nerves of transport and communication. Imagine the choking sensation, thought Cobb, if catastrophe should grip this throat.

At the newsstand he stocked up with his usual homegoing supply of magazines, games, and assorted goodies for Nolla and Roddy. Copies of *Life* and *The New Yorker,* a carton of cigarettes for himself, and a box of chocolate peppermints for Nolla. What should he get for Roddy?

"Any new jigsaw puzzles?" he asked the change-slapping clerk behind the counter.

Rummaging among his merchandise, the clerk bobbed up with an oblong box. "All we got left, mister."

"What's the title?"

The six-handed merchandiser examined some printed matter on

the wrapper, boggled at an unfamiliar word. "Fal—con Hunt at Tudor Castle," he reported.

Last week it had been Noah's Ark. Roddy, a whiz at putting the pieces together, had probably tired of his week-old puzzle by now. "I'll take it," said Cobb.

"All fixed on razor blades?"

"All fixed, thank you."

"How about a billfold with a patent key holder? Got a special on it today."

Cobb shook his head and moved rapidly away in the direction of Track 32. Juggling his brief case and bundles he dug out his commutation ticket and presented it to the official at the brass gate. "Rhinecliff," he said, as if uttering a password.

"Rear car," nodded the gateman. All part of the week-end ritual. Cyclic, familiar, secure-making.

The train was filling up with Friday-afternoon regulars, but Cobb's favorite place was unoccupied. For years he had sat on the left-hand side of the car—the river side—a trifle abaft the center. With proprietary intent he hastened to it now, stowed his bundles and overcoat on the rack, and spread his magazines on the empty seat beside him. The first phase of the homegoing was over, and Cobb could patiently await the next. Fifty seconds behind schedule the gentle tug of the electric engine roused the coaches from their linked inertia, and they were soon sliding through the gloomy labyrinth under Park Avenue. Number 19 was on its way, northbound to Albany and points west!

Cutting a channel between banks of apartment houses, the train stopped at 125th Street. The edge of Cobb's window just grazed the edge of a weatherbeaten sign: "Hotel Rialto. Rooms $2.50. By the Week $12." He gazed westward down the long thoroughfare usually crowded with trucks and taxis; today it was strangely bare. No jostle of pedestrians, window shoppers, or pitchmen cluttered the sidewalks. Through flurrying veils of snow, Cobb could see a platoon of mounted police deployed in extended order, their bodies forward, their bridle hands held in readiness for the gallop. Broken glass and scattered goods from looted shops littered dirty humps of snow along the edge of the sidewalk. An overturned police car was being hauled away by a departmental crane, and a hatless Negro lay at the base of a fire plug.

Across this tableau of suppressed disorder an ambulance sped eastward on wheels of dubious mercy.

The red brick edge of the Metals and Miners Bank slowly cut the scene. Through a tangle of Harlem switches, the train rolled north-ward. Elbow on the car sill, Cobb gazed point-blank into the un-curtained rooms of black and total strangers; he saw their lumpy bedding, their broken-legged chairs, the sprawling sullenness of the men, and the harassed patience of women standing over frying pans at gas ranges, with children tugging at their skirts. He had seen all this before; he could not feel that the scene was a special visitation of God's wrath on the Negro poor. There was nothing new or special about the sagging clothesline strung between damp walls, the back yards filled with tin cans, or the desolate children lingering in the snowy streets. Poverty, whether suffered by Italian, Jew, Polack, Irish, or Negro was as old as—as old as Arkwright. Arkwright? Older. As old as Noah. Noah was an arkwright. Well, as old as Noah then. Was there caste in the Ark? Yes, even there. As a boy, Ruston Cobb had won a Bible-class medal for answering the tricky question, "How many animals of each kind did Noah take with him into the Ark?" The answer had been: Seven specimens each of the "clean" animals, but only two each of the "unclean."

How odd of God!

The train serpentined around the junction of the toylike Harlem and the majestic Hudson. Fish-shaped Manhattan lay behind; here was the true beginning of the long, calming pull upriver. More than ever Cobb needed that vista of the west bank—the mighty es-carpment of reddish rock, the timeless Palisades. Through the screen of snow he could dimly make out the gigantic wall rising sheer from the lead-colored water like a purgatorial cliff. As always, the vision soothed him with its outcrop of uncrumbling permanence and abiding strength.

The conductor, lifting Cobb's ticket, saluted him with two fingers of recognition. "Bad storm blowing up from the West," he said, as one oldtimer to another.

"Another blizzard?"

The old train man grinned, "We can take it," and passed on.

Cobb's eye leaped across the frozen Hudson to the squat Jersey hills, blue-white with accumulated snow. The river itself had been locked fast in ice since Thanksgiving—only a thin thread of channel open for oil-tankers. A January thaw had loosened the ice for a few days, but a drop in temperature had paralyzed it again in postures of high-piled anger along the river banks. And now another storm was hurtling in from the West.

Peering through the window at Harmon, Cobb saw a magnificent Mogul locomotive being detached from a long train it had drawn in from Buffalo—*The Cannon Ball,* three hours late. It was limping toward the roundhouse as if exhausted by the long battering run against the storm. A stole of sooty ermine covered its high iron shoulders; icicles hung from the cab and oil-spattered rime caked the driving mechanism. The engine reminded Cobb of a creature that had met and barely escaped from an adversary too heavy for it.

Warm in the overheated coach, Cobb traced in fancy the course of the approaching storm. Vancouver, Winnipeg, Chicago. It had whirled out of the northwest, gored the middle plains, and now was stampeding toward the cities by the sea. Futile assault. Again New York would shudder, choke for a day or two under the avalanche of snow. A few tenement dwellers would die in heatless rooms; the city would spend another million for snow removal while the Fire Commissioner worried, and commuters came late to work. But in the big apartment houses, superintendents would turn up the steam, battalions of the unemployed would clear the streets, the early March sun would swell the gutters with dirty freshets—and all would be as before, love, only sleep.

Cobb grinned at the fantasy he had worked up for himself. Why did rainy days—snowy days . . . ? Probably an accentuation of the survival urge. Doubtless some scientist had already written a paper: "The Influence of Inclement Weather on the Mating Habits of City Dwellers." He thought of Lufbery mixing a drink right now in the Waldorf Towers for that sultry Brazilian number. What a torso the girl had. Too much of the electric eel about her, but probably wonderful on a wide mattress.

Past the car window, familiar river marks—numbered canbuoys, wooded promontories, miniature coves and inlets—slipped like sketches from the pages of a snow-blown notebook. Every scene cried, "Remember?" and to each of them Cobb could answer, "Yes." While car wheels clicked, the lonely river unwound like a memory tape secretly notched with associations from childhood. Cobb had been born on its banks, fished in its summer-brown depths, skated on its winter-polished surface. He knew its creaming tide-rips and lofty hawk eyries; as a boy he had defied the one, robbed the other. No muskrat had been safe from his cunning traps; no squall could blow down his dinghy's sail. With his father's long glass watching him from the big window, he had careened his iceboat on a single runner down the wind. Brave, hazardous sport, until the day his mother had pleaded her fears against its danger. "Please, Ruston . . ." After that, no more iceboating. Obedience to the prayer in his mother's beautiful eyes was always more satisfying than any hairbreadth adventure by field or stream.

Into those eyes, long closed, he gazed, a boy again. A summer haze displaced the gray ice on the Hudson. They were aboard the *Gyrfalcon,* headed upriver for Lake Champlain. How luxurious a craft the fifty-foot steam cruiser had seemed, with its canopied afterdeck and brass-bound wheel. Not quite big enough to be called a yacht, the *Gyrfalcon* had a richly paneled cabin, curtained, ship-shape, and neat forward quarters for the crew. During lazy after-noons his sunburned father stood at the wheel, a white and gold yachting cap set rakishly on top of his close-cropped chestnut curls, the very picture of a Captain-King who never raised his voice except in laughter. Ruston had liked it best when his father said, "Take the wheel, son. Hug the buoys to Catskill. We'll tie up there for the night." Then the Captain-King would draw out a box of fine cigars from a mahogany locker, nip off the end with a gold clipper, push his yachting cap still further back on his curls, and sit down in the rattan deck chair beside Ruston's handsome mother. King of Strength and Queen of Beauty. The King would smoke; the Queen would embroider. They would look at each other privately.

"Steward," the Captain would say around five o'clock, "Ice up a magnum of the *Moet et Chandon*." From his mother's glass Ruston always took a double sip, breathing in the perfume from her bosom as he bent forward for his benison cup. No perfume since had ever been so exciting.

No perfume since? Not Lucy's?

Well——

The train passed a low structure on a moated island, a kind of imitation Rhine castle with medieval turrets and embrasures. Ban-nerman's Arsenal. A curious place. The *Gyrfalcon* had anchored there once, and old Bannerman himself had invited its passengers to inspect his strange establishment. The Arsenal was a storehouse of obsolete weapons and ammunition: Gatling guns, lever-action Rem-ingtons, old Springfields with pop-up breech mechanisms, field pieces from the Spanish-American War. The newest rifle in the shop had been a bolt-action Krag! Ruston Cobb's glimpse of the tumble-down castle made him glad that he had been alive to taste the world's flavor before 1914. No one who came later could ever know the bouquet of that lost era mixed of morning freshness, afternoon leisure, and the twilight glow of imported cigars. The old Arsenal was sadder than one of those crystal paper weights that made flurries of snow inside when you turned it over. What a simple age it had been when architecture mounted no higher than a Rhine castle, when a steam cruiser traveled at nine knots, and the deadliest weapon in the world was a bolt-action Krag.

Cobb closed his eyes the better to recapture the soothing color and aroma of the King and Queen world aboard the *Gyrfalcon*. That time before 1914—had it really been less desperate, not quite so fierce in invention, so ambitious in engineering? Or did the wine-dipped sponge of memory, squeezing out delicious liquors of remembrance, only make it seem so? Cobb was too tired to know. His head nodded; he drowsed. He turned over the crystal paper weight of memory and snowflakes fell around him as he hugged the buoys, marking the old channel.

"Rhinecliff!" cried the brakeman, rousing Cobb from his train nap, sweetest sleep of all. He collected his gear and walked, refreshed but still drowsy, onto the station ramp. There, in the falling snow, he saw Nolla waiting for him in their car.

*   *   *

"I always forget how pretty my wife is," laughed Cobb, kissing Nolla in the hollow under her cheekbone. Like a woman thinking about something else, she let her cheek rest against his lips and adjusted her beaver toque slightly after the kiss was over. A faint crosshatching of wrinkles lay at the outer corners of her violet eyes lighted by wicks turned up too high. Nolla's hair, originally syrup-colored and never very plentiful, was thinning now. Paler and finer than corn silk, it still pulled Cobb with a secret tug. In a way he was glad his wife did not rinse or treat it, yet this disregard for her own hair was symptomatic of Nolla's dwindling interest in the physical arts of allure. Clean-scrubbed, of course. Her devotion to soap and water bordered on the neurotic. But cosmetically she was

] 32 [

without pretense. Well, after eighteen years of marriage, what should a husband expect? Did men really want their wives to come out of jars and bottles? Conditioned by everything he had seen, read, heard, smelled, and touched since adolescence, Cobb was obliged to answer reluctantly, "Other things being equal—yes."

Other things being equal. What other things? Well, to name a few—sensitivity, character, *stuff*. Unquestionably Nolla had stuff that didn't come in jars. Ergo, she magnetized you and you loved her. In spite of everything, against everything. Against the dream and the hunger and the temptation and the boredom. For richer, for poorer; in sickness and in health. Just cast *that* on your centrifuge.

Unwilling to lay aside the first eagerness of greeting, Cobb gently bunted his wife away from the wheel, slid into the driver's seat, and made an exaggerated show of vigor in turning the car around. Inwardly he was preparing a selected diet of news to fill the question in Nolla's eyes.

"How's my Beaver Puss, *really?*" he began, laying one hand affectionately on Nolla's knee.

"All right, I guess."

"And Roddy—what's he been up to?"

"Oh, the usual. Playing with Semiramis. Doing his school work."

"Did he set out the traps?"

Nolla shook her head. "Snow's been too deep, he says."

"Then he hasn't used the taxidermy set I gave him?"

"How could he?"

Cobb repressed a wave of irritability. "How's he ever going to learn to stuff a muskrat if he never catches one?"

Nolla's voice distilled an old bitterness. "Why should he learn to stuff muskrats?"

"If you take *that* line, why should he do anything but sit around and play with that damn Siamese cat all day? Good God, here's a thirteen-year-old boy who does nothing but wind up a music box and scratch a cat's back far into the night. It's—unnatural."

"But it's Roddy."

Cobb dropped the subject, drove on in silence. Usually at this point he regaled Nolla with some *nougats choisis* from the week's candy box, but the post-Roddy atmosphere was too painful. He had just decided to snap out of it when Nolla spoke.

"Beryl's coming up this week end."

Cobb jiggled the wheels back into the rut. "Yes, I know; she called me. She's bringing a boy friend."

"Which one?"

"A man named Laimbeer, a painter." Cobb settled back for a comfortably objective discourse on the subject of Laimbeer. He enjoyed explaining things to Nolla. "This Edward Laimbeer," he began, "is, or rather was, a controversial figure in American painting. Made a terrific stir in the late thirties. Some collectors were mad for him; others could take him or leave him alone. I saw a show of his at some gallery or other, oh, ten years ago. Made you feel as though you were hearing *Tristan* in a telephone booth."

"An academician?"

"No, but not modern either. Had a peculiar dash and freshness. Something happened to him, though. Went dead all of a sudden."

"How old is he?"

"Thirty-eight—forty, maybe."

Nolla became the older sister. "Beryl ought to pick someone her age and settle down. Leaping from peak to peak is all very well for mountain goats, but——"

"Who ever heard of a mountain goat falling into a rut?" The windshield wiper clogged with an overload of snow, then started racing again. "She better get here early; the snow's really coming down. . . . What's for dinner?"

Sequence of boredom entered Nolla's recital. "Duckling, timbale of wild rice. I think Mrs. Rollefson made a lemon-meringue pie."

Cobb snapped on the headlights for the left-hand turn into the narrow macadam road that led to his house, a mile inland from the river. The corner always gave him the comfortable feeling of being on home terrain once more. One of the old family jokes was for him to say, "We could walk from here." He said it now, but Nolla contributed no responsive smile.

"Heard from Sicely this week?" he asked.

"Only a letter practically *demanding* fifty dollars for a new ski outfit. That child can ask for—and *get*—more things! You'll just have to refuse her this time, Ruston."

Cobb had never been able to refuse his daughter anything. But to placate Nolla, he made a show of being judicial. "What does she want a new ski rig for? Winter's almost over."

"A boy at Middlebury invited her up for the Carnival this week end."

"Did the high-minded Mrs. Langham approve?"

Nolla nodded. "For a principal that has a reputation for strictness, she seems to let the girls run wild."

"I wouldn't call a Middlebury carnival exactly bacchanalian." In the twilight a frightened rabbit leaped across the headlight beam. Cobb swerved slightly to avoid it, and Nolla gripped his arm with terrified fingers. Cobb soothed her with tenderness.

"Nolla, darling, it's only a rabbit. Why, sweetheart, you're all wrought up. Listen, dear"—he talked coaxingly—"the winter's getting us both down. Next week let's pull out for Florida, just you and me. A couple of weeks in the sun. Warm winds, palm fronds, hours together on the sand . . . "

She rested her head on his shoulder. "If we only could."

"We *can*. What's to prevent?"

"We couldn't leave Roddy."

"Hmm. Well, we could take him with us."

"But he's doing so well in school just now."

Cobb nipped his budding vexation. "He can take his books along.

Darling, you've *got* to make a break. Otherwise—otherwise I'll have a withered old stem of a wife on my hands, just at a time when I want her to be all blossomy and sweet."

Nolla's silence echoed: blossomy and sweet. Not ever for me again.

Through a stand of dark firs Cobb saw the lights of his home, handsomely glowing in the snow. He swung the car into the remodeled garage, formerly a barn, snapped off the lights, and took Nolla in his arms. She lay there passively while he kissed her eyes in the darkness. "Promise me you'll think about Florida, Noll," he said gently. "I want terribly to make love to you, with nothing else on our minds."

Timid waves of warmth swept over her; some of the stiffness in her lips dissolved under his kiss. "It's good to have you home," she whispered. "The days seem so—so barren without you."

"Why not come to New York with me, then?"

Nolla's tension returned. "The city frightens me. The stores—the counters."

"Damn the stores!" exploded Cobb. He could have bitten off his tongue with chagrin at having uttered the words, but now the damage was done. "They're a reek of decadence," he railed, hoping to sidetrack Nolla's next question.

She wasn't listening to her husband's indictment of the merchandising build-up. "Did you go into Richter and Dehn's?"

Too late now to lie or back out. "Yes, I had an appointment with Richter." The name was hard for him to say, harder for Nolla to hear. Her body vibrated like the head of a beaten drum.

"Did he see you?"

"Yes." Bluntness was quicker, kinder perhaps. "I asked Richter for that statement you signed."

Nolla was putting herself under a fearful form of nerve surgery. "Did you get it?"

"No. The swine said——"

Nolla's head fell brokenly into her hands. She slid away to the furthest corner of the seat.

"Dearest," cried Cobb, fighting for her soul, lonely and sick in the darkness, "it means nothing. The paper is locked in a vault. No one will ever see it. Or, if anyone ever did"—he offered her the shield of his disregard for the world's opinion—"what difference would it make?"

Nolla did not accept the proffered shield. Her voice was dry as a bleached bone. "I would die, I would kill myself," she said, "if Roddy ever found out."

Helplessly Cobb waited for Nolla's spasm of self-torment to pass. That she should care more for her son's opinion than his—that she should reject the completeness of his love and dread only the green judgment of a boy—were constant hurts in his life. Patiently he waited till her sobbing became lighter. Then she sat up.

"Go in first," she said. "I want to collect myself. Tell Roddy I'll be right in."

CHAPTER 3

A CLEAR SHEET of flame rose from the hickory logs in the huge field-stone fireplace of the living room. Roddy lay on the carpet with his head toward the flames, his eyes on the ceiling, Semiramis snuggled in the hollow of his arm. Some carved figures dangled from the tiny gallows of a marionette stage, and the tinkle of a Chopinesque valse, thin and nostalgic, came from the inlaid mahogany music box on the floor beside him. Over the boy's posture and countenance a Cyprian languor hung; fire light, fingering his golden hair, burnished an aureole about his head. Drowned in the sad melody of the music box, he did not hear his father come in.

Cobb, burly and snow-covered, stood watching the boy. As always, Roddy's beauty sponged away whatever irritation or disappointment the father felt because his son was not a woodsman.

"Hey, there!" cried Cobb. "Where's the reception committee?"

Roddy sat up, abruptly disturbing Semiramis' nap. He laid the cat down gently on the music box. "Go find a dish of mandrake milk," he advised her. Then, rising gracefully, he walked toward his father, both arms out.

"Hello, Daddy." He slipped one arm under his father's great-coat, kissed him on the cheek. "Where's Mother?"

"Coming right in." Cobb slid his fingers affectionately through the lad's hair. Too silky, too long. "Say," he said, "you're cheating the barber again. When you come to our city igloo"—he tried unsuccessfully to strike Lufbery's ribbing chord—"white man's barber give you six-bit haircut."

Roddy didn't spark to the proposal. Cobb was sorry he had made it. He took off his coat, hung it in the big closet under the staircase.

"How's school going?"

Roddy, anxiously peering out the window in the direction of the garage, said, "Oh, mixed, sort of."

"Algebra causing pain?"

"Uh-huh—quadratics throw me. Help me with them this week, will you, Father?" The boy was nibbling his fingernails nervously.

"Glad to, son." Cobb glanced at the thermostat beside the coat closet. It registered seventy-two degrees; he dialed it down to sixty-eight. "Did the oil come this week?"

Roddy's expression was that of a puzzled faun who has been asked by a tourist: Is there a good boarding house around here? "I—I don't know," he said. The sound of Nolla's steps in the front hall cleared his face. He ran to open the door for her, plucking up Semiramis from the music box on the way.

"Mother!" he cried, as though she had just returned from a trip around the Horn. "Were the roads bad? Semiramis and I were about to offer up a burnt mouse to Saint Christopher, weren't we, 'Miramis?" He looked at the gold watch on his frail wrist, a present from his father on his thirteenth birthday. "In another five minutes I'd have offered up Semiramis herself." He imitated a short-order cook in a Greek hash house, "On the fire—one tortoise-shell pussy on milka-toast."

Cobb, his back to the blazing logs, had to smile. His son's oral energy alternately fascinated and troubled him. The lad had undoubted talent for the stage; Nolla's relinquished gift of acting, heightened in the passage, had fallen on Roddy. If only the boy were heavier, more masculine, less wreathed with flowerets. If only he cared a little more for muskrats and not quite so much for Persian kittens.

Watching Nolla beam upon her son, Cobb tried to recall the picture they suggested. A picture somewise Greek: the knot of hair at the nape of Nolla's neck, the brooding curve of the neck itself, the matriarchal attitude of hand on shoulder. Mother of the Gracchi? No, that was Roman. Who then? Cobb's thought floated backward along a meandering stream. Jocasta . . . the Greek games at college. Nolla standing on a bare stage, reciting Sophocles' majestic lines. The murmurs, the applause. Together they had sat in the deserted amphitheater after the play. She was to be another Duse, a latter-day Bernhardt—but pure, noncommercial, no Broadway taint. And he would help her. No marriage yet. A year in Paris first. They would be lovers, of course—but delicate, spare, spiritual—oh, and true! As true as moss to springs, as wood to fire.

"Promise me now, upon this burning book, my heart, that never a commoner beat shall clog our pulse or chill our bloodstream with accustomed death." Nolla had said something like that. In French. Whenever her mood was rarefied, she loved to talk French.

"I promise, love. A kiss?"

"Just the cheek."

Jocasta Bernhardt, now wived to a patent lawyer.

Cobb felt the need of a stiff Bourbon before washing up for dinner. From the cellaret he took a silver-chained decanter, poured two ounces of whiskey for himself, a smaller drink for Nolla. He passed her the crystal jigger, courted her with his eyes across the top of his glass. "To our cruise," he said, swallowing the old liquor in a grateful gulp.

She sipped the whiskey, shivered slightly.

Looking at his wife's anxious face, Cobb wanted to take her upstairs, smooth out her forehead and her fears. But even while the wish was being recorded, he knew the reality would be unsatisfying, the depth withheld.

Just the cheek. Merely. A cruise about the coast——

"I must look into the kitchen," said Nolla. "Maggie's off today with a cold, and Mrs. Rollefson will have to serve dinner alone."

Roddy broke in with one of the doggerel rhymes that he was always tossing off:

> Grub cooked and served by Mrs. R.,
> That's no hardship, is it, Pa?

Cobb grinned; the kid was all right. By the spasm of displeasure crossing Nolla's face, he judged that she didn't like the words "grub" and "pa." Proud of Roddy's rhyming skill, she deplored his use of the vulgate. Rimbaud wouldn't use such language. . . .

She went into the kitchen, and Cobb poured himself another Bourbon. The excellent draft of the big fireplace sucked the flames cheerily upward; the good fire, two earned drinks, dinner ahead, Berry coming, and, more important than any of these, the corny humor of his son's verse—all combined to open the valves of contentment in Cobb's bloodstream. His house was warm, handsome, well lighted. A turbulent wind was hurling crisp flakes against the double windowpanes. "Let the blizzard rage," thought Cobb, "I and those I love are housed against it."

He tousled Roddy's hair with both hands, held him affectionately for a moment in a chancery headlock, then ran upstairs to change his clothes for dinner.

* * *

The tall clock revolving sun and moon in its face had just chimed seven when powerful headlights cut the snow-fog drifting across the lawn. Roddy ran to the window, saw a long-hooded car curving into the driveway.

"It's Beryl," he said excitedly. "I must play 'Czarina' on the music box for her." He cranked the handle of the little barrel organ, poised the indicator over Beryl's favorite piece, waiting till he should hear the front door open before releasing the player mechanism.

Nolla took a final glance around the room and made a little movement with her hand in the direction of her throat. A pleasant agitation fluttered there; it was always something of a triumph to watch Beryl enter this really good room, take a quick taste, and acknowledge its flavor with critical approval. Beryl might have that wonderful job with Bandlemann Sœurs, get four-color pictures of her clothes in *Vogue,* and take boats to Paris every six months. (That was what Nolla really envied.) But she didn't have a room like this, or a boy like Roddy, or a husband like Ruston. Unpurchasables. Even a success girl had to knuckle under at the moment of beholding them, and it was that first yielding flash of admiration from her younger sister that Nolla awaited so eagerly.

It came, grateful as always, the moment Beryl entered. Her electric blue eyes made a bright circuit of everything, from the Coromandel screen guarding the cabinet of bibelots to the perfect Aubusson rug before the fireplace. This trick of swift appraisal—not for price alone, though it figured in her calculations—gave Beryl her strength as a designer of women's clothes. She had a waxlike talent for receiving impressions of mood, tempo, and color, then projecting them in terms of fabric and fashions. It was a shining, highly surfaced talent, like the coated paper on which the designs were printed, giving off a brilliant light but no penetrating ray.

"If only she had a brain," Cobb had once said to his wife.

Now as she stood in the doorway, her chinchilla coat lightly powdered with snow, Beryl needed no better brains than those in her exquisitely modeled body and vital laughter. "The 'Czarina'! You *remembered!*" she cried to Roddy as the tinkly barrel-tune floated out in measures of a porcelain gavotte. She raised an imaginary vizard to her eyes, extended a snow-sprinkled arm in an invitation to the dance. Roddy, quick on the cue, trod a figure in courtly mimicry before he gave way to an excess of happiness and hugged his beautiful aunt. Beryl kissed his flushed cheekbones, high like Nolla's.

] 42 [

"You've got a perfect Scherbatoff for a son," she said, her arms around Nolla. "And the best-looking husband north of Sutton Place." Ruston bent down for her kiss; fur-borne warmth, excitingly perfumed, radiated from her body as her arms went around his neck. Cobb gauged her alcoholic content at four cocktails.

"Why didn't you ride up with us?" she chided. "Oh, Ed——" She turned to see Nolla greeting the bag-laden Laimbeer at the door. "Ed, this is my sister Nolla and her husband Ruston. It's all the family I have. Family, this is Edward Laimbeer."

Cobb crossed the room, extended his hand to the man standing silently in the doorway.

"Always wanted to meet you, Laimbeer," he said cordially. "Know your work, of course. What I've seen of it I like very much."

Laimbeer held out a heavy-nailed hand, almost as big as the hod of an automatic stoker. Without bad manners, he conveyed the impression that he really didn't care whether Cobb liked his work or not.

"Any trouble driving?" asked Cobb, making conversation as Laimbeer took off his foreign-looking overcoat, belted and very much worn.

"Beryl managed." Laimbeer's gaunt figure and leonine features gave him a vague resemblance to Lincoln at forty. A yellowish cast to skin and eyeballs hinted either a Balko-Levantine ancestry or an overdose of bile. The painter's craggy forehead was his most telling feature—a quite legible carbon of his feelings and state of mind. Its chief statement, made by three deep horizontal grooves, was one of desperate ennui, but Cobb saw also that the forehead was a kind of upper cymbal that could come clashing down upon his heavy eyebrows in reverberations of anger, contempt, and cruelty. Laimbeer suggested a gyroscope that has attained seeming stability by the speed and fury of its revolutions; troubled energy was at a standstill in his voice and eyes. Trying to imagine what the *soignée* Beryl found in this tormented bear rug of a man, Cobb came upon a good enough reason.

"Mother and Berry went upstairs to fix themselves," Roddy announced, as they came into the living room. While Cobb busied himself with cocktail setups and Roddy twisted a bit of wire around the neck of a damaged puppet, Laimbeer, huge hands rammed deep into the pockets of his frayed Norfolk jacket, wandered restlessly around the room as if hoping to find some object worthy of interest. His bilious eye flicked indifferently past the fine pieces of furniture (mostly reproductions of Phyfe and his adaptors) but paused critically at the various *articles de vertu*—faïence figurines, trays of semiprecious stones, and hand-tooled books that Nolla had arranged on shelves and tables. With the tactile curiosity of a man to whom all light-refracting surfaces are a challenge, he fingered the massive ivory and ebony pieces on the inlaid chess table, passed his hand caressingly over a time-blasted fragment of a Cretan bull. From a set of French poets bound in emerald calf he picked up the *Nuits* of de Musset, opened it with random unconcern, then drew together the declarative grooves on his forehead as if in pity, both for the poet and anyone who could be troubled by his dated melancholies.

At length, having made a circuit of the room, Laimbeer came quite close to Roddy and watched the boy repair his marionettes. He said nothing, did nothing, till Roddy inquired, "Do you know about puppets?"

"I made a set once. Did you make these?"

"No, Mother gave them to me. I just write plays for them."

"Will you be giving us a play this week end?" asked Cobb, popping cherries into Manhattan glasses.

"I'm working on one. Hope I have it ready by Sunday night." He gazed up earnestly at his father. "It's the best thing I ever did."

"The true artist," exclaimed Laimbeer approvingly. "When Picasso was asked, 'Which picture is your best?' he always answered, 'My last.' What's your play about?"

"Kings and queens."

"I wouldn't miss it," said Laimbeer. "The private life of kings and queens is something I've always been curious about."

Nolla and Beryl were coming down the curved staircase, their hands on the polished balustrade. The ten years' difference in their ages was dramatized in the descent—not wholly to Nolla's disadvantage. She was wearing a white hostess gown of Doric drape; extra care with lipstick, rouge, and hairdo gave her face the indented clarity of a beautifully printed page—an illuminated Psalter containing a ciphered message. Beryl's ruby-colored dress with gilt accessories was more like a folio binding, glowing with crimson and gold, created solely for the joy of handling. If only Nolla possessed Beryl's binding, thought Cobb. Or if Beryl's magnificent cover enclosed anything more than an alphabet of passion.

"Paintable?" he murmured to Laimbeer, with an upward inflection of his glance.

No response lighted the painter's overcast eye. "By others, perhaps, but it's not my style."

Cobb distinctly remembered seeing several female figures at Laimbeer's show. "There's a canvas of yours—I can't quite recall the name—" he started to say.

"First three drinks on the house!" cried Beryl, floating off the bottom stair with the buoyant motion of flame. Her tongue, red and darting, was visible as she spoke.

"Round one, coming up." Cobb handed her the tray of Manhattans. Their ruby glow, matching Berry's ensemble, made Nolla seem almost colorless by contrast. The sisters took their glasses in character; Nolla, crystal stem held close to her body, prim and vestal, while Beryl's bare arm was extended and her glass swung between her thumb and middle finger. As she lifted it, her eyes were on Laimbeer but her index fingernail pointed like a lacquered arrow at Cobb.

Taking up a stance before Beryl, Roddy asked, "May I have your cherry, please?"

"A mark of special attention," laughed Cobb. "He usually chisels it from Nolla." His wife's downcast lashes made him sorry he had said it.

Laimbeer came to Nolla's defense. "Imported melons . . ." he murmured, giving his words the intonation of a proverb.

"What's the rest of it?" asked Nolla curiously.

"Something from the Persian, probably." Beryl's remark cut like a dressmaker's shears. "Laimbeer's full of camel-driver lore. Well, let's hear it, Mahmud."

". . . cannot stand the frost."

Roddy flung his arms around his high-hipped aunt. "Berry isn't an imported melon at all," he said stoutly. "She's a long-stemmed poppy, that's what she is."

Cobb, watching his son in Beryl's hands, remembered a velvety-knobbed young deer he had once seen in a drop fall.

"*Dar*—ling!" cried Berry. "What a joy you're going to be when ——" She checked herself, bent over and kissed the boy impulsively. The movement brought her unconfined breasts directly into Cobb's line of vision.

Imported melons says it, he thought, collecting the glasses for another round. Only three setups this time; one cocktail was all Nolla could take. And make a note to skimp Beryl's refill; she was riding high enough already.

As he busied himself with the shaker, Mrs. Rollefson came in to announce dinner. Beryl gave an appreciative squeal when she saw the inimitable Biedermeier table set for five. Nolla's best crystal and silver were out; four tall candlesticks shed a subdued light over the service, and the drawn shades of the long French windows gave an intimate coziness to the severely formal décor.

A single dark landscape in a dull gold frame was centered above the lowboy at the further end of the room. Laimbeer glanced at it casually.

"The only painter England ever had," he said, addressing no one in particular.

"You like Constable?" asked Cobb.

"Half the time. The other half——" Laimbeer shrugged a huge shoulder.

Nettlement stirred Cobb. He had paid three thousand dollars for that Constable, and now this shaggy egotist tossed it off with a half shrug. "Whom do you like?" he inquired, a shade too blandly.

Laimbeer was beginning a good cocky-leeky soup. "Rouault. El Greco, perhaps."

"You can't put *them* in a dining room," objected Beryl.

"Who said anything about dining rooms? Our host asked me what painters I like, and I told him."

Cobb had to admit that Laimbeer was right and Beryl was wrong. But she persisted dangerously. Six drinks had made her captious.

"This Constable here—does it happen to fall into the half-time bracket that claims your fancy?"

Nolla's face was tense in the candlelight. "Berry!" she pleaded.

Using his spoon to good purpose, Laimbeer finished his soup. He dabbed his lips appreciatively with Nolla's fine napkin, then spoke directly to Cobb.

"Your Constable," he said, "is in the painter's clayey period. To expand my opinion, I'd have to examine it more closely in a better light." He picked up a crouton in his large hand, tossed it easily into his mouth. "But I can say this much——" His eyes moved tolerantly to Beryl's shoulders. "It's very acceptable as decoration. Yes, a fine example of dining-room art."

Cobb had to smile. Whether he agreed with Laimbeer or not, the man was curiously sincere. No lackey, and no boor either. And such

] 47 [

a neat buttoning up of an opponent's lip he hadn't seen in a long time. He noticed the vexed tightening of Beryl's large mouth. What, he wondered, was the nature of the feud between her and Laimbeer? Why had she bothered to bring him, if their conversation was to be a continual passage at arms, an unequal bicker in which she was always being worsted?

Their relationship reminded Cobb of a painful engagement between a couple that he had known long ago. Every evening, no matter where this unhappy pair chanced to be, they would exchange violent words ending in a scuffle of blows—she frankly trying to kick him in the groin, he prolonging the battle till she was exhausted, then smacking her in the face with his open hand, one, two, three, while she stood passively quiet, taking her medicine. A funny setup. Lalley, that was the chap's name. Cobb had once asked him why he carried on so unspeakably with the woman he intended to marry. Lalley had explained quite frankly, "Louise is a good Catholic. So am I. We can't go to bed together, so she lets me beat her up instead. I guess she likes it."

A masochistic quirk in Louise, no doubt, but here it was popping up again more subtly masked in Beryl. The desire to suffer, the need to be degraded, belittled, *punished* for something—weren't these the source and fountain of Beryl's unaccountable choices in her boy friends? How explain otherwise this yen for Laimbeer, most recent of a long line of preceding ineligibles. Ineligibles? Why, if it came to that, wasn't her nickering for Cobb himself merely another aspect of her will to be balked, rejected, hurt, knocked on her can?

"Come off the bottom, dear," said Nolla. Mrs. Rollefson was handing him the old-fashioned pewter trencher heaped with roast duckling. Cobb helped himself generously, then lifted the goblet of good New York claret beside his plate, seeking to catch Nolla's eye for the thankful libation that took the place of grace in this house. But her eye was elsewhere. She had lifted her own glass to

Roddy and was reciting the first line of a toast that would give him a chance to improvise a rhyming capper.

"Red wine, white snow . . ." she began.

"Climb a star and away we go," said Roddy promptly.

"White snow, wine red . . ."

"Sprinkle dreams on every bed."

"Bravo!" cried Laimbeer. "The lyric pipe, seldom heard above the clash of idol gears." He lifted his glass to Roddy and recited a couplet from de Musset's "La Nuit de Mai."

> "Poète, prends ton luth; le vin de la jeunesse
> Fermente cette nuit dans les veines de Dieu."

The painter's eyes left the boy's face and traveled down the candlelit table to Nolla. With a poised assurance that Cobb rarely saw in his wife, she lifted her glass to Laimbeer and took up his invitation with a sibylline smile.

> "Viens, tu souffres, ami. Quelque ennui solitaire
> Te ronge; quelque chose a gemi dans ton cœur? . . ."

Suppressed vibrations almost rang notes on the crystal goblets.

Snow sifted against the windowpanes, and a grieving wind rustled the leafless ivy on the trellis outside the dining room, as if in mourning for the broken lute, the lonely bed, and the crumbled tower.

CHAPTER 4

THE DINNER went off not badly but not too well. Faint burgees of conversation fluttered between Nolla and Laimbeer; brisker signals flashed from Beryl to Cobb and Roddy. Gradually the warmth of food and wine lapped the table, and, when Mrs. Rollefson brought in the dessert, even Laimbeer's shaggy reserve had a silkier finish. The candles, too, were doing their work on Nolla and Beryl, soothing the flush of the touch-too-ruby Deane and bringing out warmer glints in Nolla's hair and flesh tones. Cobb noticed that Laimbeer's glance turned often to Nolla's face, and through the painter's eyes he saw with fresh pleasure the delicately taut planes of her cheeks, chin, and forehead. Nolla was a sensitive tambour, stretched too tightly, perhaps, over a fragile frame, but responsive to a finger tap of thought or emotion. Beryl, by contrast, was more like a snare drum, demanding a stouter thumping from a more obvious pair of sticks.

With the coffee Cobb produced a box of Hoyo de Monterey, cabinet size. The ritual of the fine after-dinner cigar was one of his dearest pleasures, a clear inheritance from his father. So few men smoked good cigars these days. Would Laimbeer? He offered the painter a beautiful Havana, mouse-colored, silky-wrapped, lightly resilient under the pressure of lips and fingers. Laimbeer rolled it for a moment caressingly between his palms before nipping the end with strong yellowish teeth.

"Hoyo de Monterey," he murmured appreciatively, the winelike aroma awakening a special sense reserved for cigar smokers.

Cobb valued the painter's nice estimate of the fine tobacco. No slopping over of enthusiasm, merely the acceptance of a naturally good thing. Evenly, slowly Cobb lighted his own cigar, inhaled the rare bouquet, turning the ashy end inward after each puff so that the smoke could mount to his nostrils. A trick his father had taught him. He noted that Laimbeer went so far as to cup the burning end between his hands so as to waste nothing of the delicate aroma. A sensualist, but in a great tradition.

Now they were strolling behind Nolla and Beryl toward the music room. Cobb was feeling expansive. Nolla would play the piano; he would smoke his cigar and look at a pair of beautiful women through an aromatic haze. He would listen to music not controlled by a dial but produced by a loved one's skill from an expensive instrument earned by one's own efforts. And all this would happen in a room of unmatchable taste, warm, well lighted, secure against the elements. This was what life came to if you were strong and good and lucky. What if the beloved cheek *were* a too sensitive tambour—a man couldn't always be thumping away like a kettledrummer.

The room they were entering had a calculated effect of bareness, achieved by good dimensions and a severe ban on furniture. A black Steinway with a half-raised top was the first focus of attention; later there appeared a Récamier divan, some full-length curtains dark green in color and with a classic hang. Four or five gilt chairs invited cordial sitting but no lounging. In a small grate at one end of the room some short logs were slowly being consumed to lizard-red ash.

Roddy lay on the rug near the fire; the others took chairs, while Nolla walked with neither haste nor urging to the piano. It was her hour, and she took it as naturally as Laimbeer had accepted the cigar. She pressed the palms of her hands together thoughtfully, rubbed her fingers for a moment, then began to play.

Her first mood was whimsical, humorous. Turning her head to glance at Roddy, she imitated with bright fidelity the celesta-like quality of his music box. Halfway through the "Czarina" she dropped the musical mimicry and entered upon the precise simplicities of a Mozart rondo. A pure and classic design emerged delicately under her fingers, creating an air of light repose for her listeners. This, Cobb knew, was played for him. He happened to like Mozart. The music posed no insoluble problems, it came round in a circle, whipping briskly as it came. You could actually see it turning, and the completion of its design could be viewed at the halfway mark.

He savored his cigar, smiling as Nolla curved into the coda. "Thanks, darling."

Nolla picked up her cambric handkerchief, rolled it walnut-wise between her palms. It was a signal of indecision: her family devoirs fulfilled, what would she now play for herself? Apparently she could not decide, for she rose from the bench and turned to her little audience.

"Any requests?" Her gaze was shared between her husband and their guests.

"Play some musical portraits," suggested Cobb. "Show the people how you tell fortunes on the piano."

"Yes, yes," echoed Beryl. She turned to the painter in brief explanation. "Nolla improvises for a few minutes, then we guess whose character she's describing."

"Amazing," said Laimbeer. "I've never heard that done."

"Watch out," warned Cobb. "She'll read you to the pelt."

The little audience settled back for a display of Nolla's pianistic clairvoyance. After the briefest of introductions, she began weaving a lyric tapestry in E-major. The chief figure in the tapestry was a young roebuck with golden antlers barely budding from his forehead. He was stepping through a primavera landscape, nuzzling at leaves and fruits suspended just out of reach above his head; the sky and foliage were part Italian, part Greek. With her left hand Nolla made little blue waves break against a sun-drenched shore. The young deer came to a pool and, bending over it, saw, his own graceful reflection in the depth. Like Narcissus, he brooded over the beauty of his own image but was suddenly drawn away from the pool by a flutelike call from the deep wood. Half timid, half eager, he bounded into the protecting shadows, whisking his bobbed tail in a presto passage with grace notes as he went.

"Roddy!" exclaimed everyone all at once. The success of the portrait was instantaneous and complete. Roddy blushed a little at the attention that clung to him while his mother prepared to execute her second portrait.

This time she struck a series of major chords legato, full-throated but darkened by shadows—then modulated abruptly into the brightness of A major with a theme warm and coaxing. She followed these with a double handful of merry runs borrowed from Chopin's C-sharp-minor Valse—a passage that might be interpreted either as laughter or coquettish flight. Laimbeer could not suppress a cry of amazement and delight.

"Beryl!" he exclaimed. He arose and moved toward Nolla as if to touch the maker of this delightful and penetrating entertainment. Standing over her, his dark face crinkling with pleasure, he struck his big hands together in *vivas* of applause.

Nolla glanced upward, warm blood petaling her throat and face. "My next one will be more difficult," she said, half turning to catch the expression of pride that she knew would be on Cobb's face. Laimbeer quietly took his chair again, and a bridge of suspense arched the room.

It was clearly Nolla's intention in her third portrait to catch the identity of one of the two mature males in the room. A massive bass motif rolled up from the depths of the Steinway; blunt triads of power were layered against hard-edged fifths that seemingly climbed in orderly progression up the keyboard. For a moment, as a melody of gentleness emerged, it seemed that the musical portrait was that of her husband. But this brief singing passage soon changed to a troubled dissonance, ugly, dark, and clashing, as conflict thrust iron wedges between the notes, endangering and finally destroying their harmony. The piano seemed to expand, then threatened to fly apart under the hammering. In a final torrent Nolla poured a cruel heap of discords over the picture. Her hands dropped to her side.

Laimbeer's voice repeated the bass motif of Nolla's first phrase. "A portrait of the artist," he said, "as a disorganized and no longer young man."

Nolla's only disclaimer was to rise from the piano and take a cigarette from a silver box. As she accepted a light from Laimbeer, her lips were dry with excitement. He spoke only to her.

"You have shamelessly exposed everyone else. Won't you reveal something about yourself?"

The challenge was frontal. Nolla could not meet it. It was Beryl who came to her rescue.

"Nolla's tired," she said decisively. "Dragging all those heavy personalities up and down a keyboard would wear out a longshoreman. Let's go into the living room and sit in front of the fire. It'll cool us off."

"Good idea," said Cobb, thumbing Roddy upstairs with an off-to-bed gesture. The boy made a pretty performance of saying good night. To Laimbeer he gave a man-to-man handshake and a cheery "See you tomorrow." On Berry he pinned an impulsive hug, conveying just the right suggestion that if he were older, manlier, more removed in kinship—well—— Coming to his father next (saving Nolla for last), the boy leaned forward in the half-embrace of a Saint Cyr cadet receiving a schoolboy's medal from his colonel. Filial, disciplined, respectful. The role in which Roddy temporarily cast himself did not, to Cobb's way of thinking, quite come off. But the devotional kiss planted on Nolla's cheek—*that* was no play acting. The boy murmured something in his mother's ear, placing his mouth very close to its fragile lobe. The endearment won the reward that Roddy had planned.

"I'll come and tuck you in."

Cobb observed the not uncalculated effect of this mother-and-son business on the painter. Here was a woman (Laimbeer was thinking) who could jack you out of your chair with her music, then, before the piano wires stopped vibrating, become a very Cornelia of maternal givingness. Rich, complex color here. Waiting to be mixed on a fresh palette, maybe?

A wry flavor, very much like the taste of crab apples, puckered the membranes of Cobb's mouth. Laimbeer would find out for himself how rich and complex the colors were. Yes, and how difficult to mix!

Everyone's eyes followed Nolla and Roddy as they mounted the stairs. By the slowness of their progress they managed to convey the shared pleasure of the tucking-in ritual that lay ahead. Not until they disappeared from view did Berry offer an unconscious comment.

"How's for a Deane's Golden Mixture?" she suggested, a hint of coarseness in her voice. "Four parts Scotch and one part soda."

"Why flood the tissues with water?" Cobb was at the cellaret tumbling whiskey and ice cubes into tall glasses. He found himself wishing that alcohol would affect Nolla as it did Berry—loosen her up, act as a plectrum on her yes-saying strings. He handed stiff drinks to Berry and Laimbeer and was making one for himself when Nolla came downstairs. For her own good he would try getting some alcohol into her.

"A Deane's Mixture," he smiled, handing her a glass.

They sat crescent-wise before the hearth, more relaxed in seeming than in fact, but with quietness deepening into a reasonable facsimile of repose. Tranquillity was the only direction that could be taken now; the slow fire, the sense of isolation created by the falling snow, the sedative effect of good whiskey—all these operated on the senses of the little group, plus a subtle addition never wholly forgotten when paired men and women spend an evening together. Cobb felt the glow deepening into an almost fusible warmth that was melting Berry, Laimbeer, and himself. About Nolla he could never tell; with her there was never any midnight certainty. And yet as the ice melted in her drink, some part of her frigidity seemed to thaw too.

Laimbeer had dedicated himself, for this hour at least, to the task of being engaging. Sensing Nolla's interest in matters French and of-the-studio, he was doing very well with some semi-psychologic reminiscences about Left Bank personalities—artists, poets, musicians he had known in Paris before the war. He told several stories about American exiles who had either committed suicide or gone on the beach rather than return to New York. Cobb felt that a vein of autobiography throbbed very near the surface of Laimbeer's recital and that his last-time-I-saw-Paris note was, after a lapse of seven years, unnaturally stressed. He could see, however, that Nolla, utterly gripped by all this, was reliving her own brief year of music in Paris (that frightful period before they were married) and was identifying herself, by some unreal but passionate process, with the characters in Laimbeer's memory play.

Occasionally, when the artist would mention a café, a street, a person she had known, a pathetic catch of assent came into her voice and eyes. She would nod, murmur, "Yes, of course, that was in the Place Pigalle," or, "Mellnitz? Wasn't he a pupil of Busoni?" Gradually it developed that Laimbeer had been in Paris while she was there in 1928, that they had lived not far from each other, had some acquaintances in common—indeed, had probably sat beside each other at the round marble-topped tables of Les Lilas and the Dôme.

"Why, you're practically buddies," scoffed Beryl, pouring herself another Deane's Mixture and handing one to Laimbeer. He ignored the jibe but took the drink.

Nolla wrinkled up her nose in an effort to recall something. "Do you happen to remember a strange person—oh, a very strange character indeed—I can't remember his name exactly, but he used to drive around in a barouche drawn by horses painted like zebras."

"Do I remember him!" laughed Laimbeer. "How could anyone ever forget Raoul Farceur?"

"That's the name," exclaimed Nolla. "He used to fascinate me, though I never spoke to him. Did you know him well?"

"As well as anyone could." Laimbeer settled back in his wing chair and pulled the *recitativo* stops way out. "Raoul Farceur was the character to end all characters, a mortal verging into myth. He was the symbol of a whole period—wonderful, morbid, futilitarian, call it anything you wish—between Versailles and, say, the Reichstag fire. After that little blaze, Paris went political. But until then . . ." Laimbeer gazed into the hardwood embers like an exiled Templar who knows that he will never see the true cross again.

Nolla prodded him gently. "This Raoul Farceur . . . ?"

"Was a Rumanian, tremendously rich, an intellectual dandy, a creative eccentric in the manner of Villiers de l'Isle Adam. He knew everyone in Europe—Picasso, de Noailles, Gide, Joyce—the whole crowd. Farceur was himself a painter, poet, philosopher—though somehow he was unable to get his talents down, either on canvas or paper. No matter. He had plenty of other gifts—very strange ones— and some extraordinary energy which he expended in rather bizarre forms."

"What, for instance, besides the striped horses?" asked Cobb.

Nolla was having a little spasm of laughter and excitement. "Well, for one thing, he used to lead a monstrous deep-sea turtle along the boulevards with a silk thread."

"That's right," roared Laimbeer. "And, when anyone asked him why he chose such a pet, Raoul would say, 'He knows the secrets of the deep.' Ha, ha, ha!" Laimbeer and Nolla were off in gales of merriment.

Cobb wanted to ask, "What's so funny about that?" but chewed his Hoyo instead. Laimbeer went on. "Raoul kept other creatures in his garish, overstuffed apartment in the Rue Boetie. One of them was a female beetle of a peculiar species—an Egyptian scarab found only in the region of the third Nile cataract. This beetle was the ultimate reach of the devouring female. Her pleasure took the form of"—Laimbeer tried to put the matter as delicately as possible—"of not releasing her mate after she had granted him the priceless boon of *Merci*. The poor male spent the rest of his life being dragged around—a ridiculous and pitiful situation even for a beetle. Raoul would lecture us on the moral of it all, but he always seemed to enjoy the male beetle's shabby discomfiture and the triumph of the queen."

Laimbeer paused reminiscently. "The queen concept fascinated Raoul. He was a brilliant chess player—probably the best amateur in Europe. I saw him defeat Edelmann once for a side bet of ten thousand francs just so the Prussian couldn't say he wasn't trying."

"Come, really now!" Cobb rallied his guest good-naturedly. "Amateur chess players, no matter how good they are, just don't go around beating Edelmann."

Laimbeer refused to become defensive. "Believe it or not," he said, "I saw it happen. Edelmann may have had an off-day, but he told me afterward that he never knew where the checkmate came from."

"Do you recall any details of the game? What kind of an opening was it?"

"I'm not enough of a student to give you a play-by-play account, but I remember that Raoul was playing the white. He made a Queen Pawn opening, and the Prussian countered with a Slav Defense. Then Raoul seemed to skip the middle game completely. His queen broke loose, hooked up with a knight, and simply massacred Edelmann."

Cobb shook his head. "Hard to credit. However . . ."

"Chess people swore that Farceur was a frightfully unorthodox player but admitted that some curious psychic energy gave his game a fearful attacking quality. 'That damned queen of his' was what they always complained of. I once asked Raoul how he happened to develop such a peculiar style of play."

"What did he say?" asked Nolla.

"Oh, he fobbed me off with some cryptic remark about his mother being a blond Muscovite more beautiful than the day."

Laimbeer, sure of his audience, went on with the Saga Farceur. "The queerest part of the story came when Raoul was about forty years old. His father died rather suddenly, in Rumania somewhere, and, would you believe it, Raoul lost not only his skill but even his interest in chess."

"Why, in your opinion?" Cobb's voice had an attorney edge.

"Well, for one thing, the king was dead. No need to keep killing him on the chessboard once he lay buried in his coffin."

"What became of the scarab?" asked Nolla.

"Raoul got rid of her. Apparently he was no longer interested in humiliating the proudful male. But after that"—Laimbeer's voice threw a new loop around his listeners—"our friend went in passionately for Tarot."

"Sounds like a religion," said Berry, distilling her alcohol into acid. "Let's skip it. This Farceur guy bores the pants off me."

"No, no!" cried Nolla. "It's fascinating. Please," she turned to Laimbeer, "please go on about Tarot."

As if his whole previous discourse had been merely a warm-up, Laimbeer rose from his chair and took an expository stance before the fireplace. "Tarot," he said, "is the sum of alchemy, cabala, magic, and metaphysics—a compendium of occult wisdom—all set forth in a pack of playing cards. In twenty-two picturized symbols, most of which resist too literal analysis, the Tarot deck is a repository of the ideas that have always gripped the human mind."

"You mean ideas like justice, liberty—things like that?" Cobb lighted a fresh Hoyo.

"No, Tarot undercuts all such transient jingle-bell notions. It's concerned only with the really permanent things, such as fate, temptation, death." Laimbeer ostentatiously threw the stub of his cold cigar into the fireplace, but Cobb did not offer him another.

Punctuating the snub with a brief silence, the artist went on: "Tarot also depicts the constant types into which human beings fall —Miser, Fool, Juggler. The figure on the first card, for instance, is the Juggler. And since we're going in for character analysis this evening"—Laimbeer bent his head slightly in Cobb's direction—"I'd say it represents our host."

Scarcely knowing whether to look pleased or not, Cobb compromised by looking puzzled.

"The Juggler," Laimbeer explained, "is the successful extrovert— master of the sword, cup, coin, and ball—really the four elements of fire, water, air, and earth—which he keeps suspended by his skill and energy. He is, in a word, the man of resource and invention."

"An evening of crystal gazing," said Berry. "Say, Eddie, after you get all this chop-chop wisdom rolled into little pills, what do you do—smoke it?"

Annoyed by the "Say, Eddie" approach, Laimbeer brought his forehead down hard against his eyebrows and addressed himself to Nolla and Cobb. "Properly understood—and Raoul Farceur was the only person I ever knew who understood all of it—the Tarot pack is a kind of abacus or counting machine for working out philosophic problems. At least, that's the way oversized thinkers used it in the Middle Ages."

Cobb puffed amiably at his cigar. "You don't actually believe this stuff?"

"The world," said Laimbeer dryly, "is full of fascinating ideas that one doesn't necessarily believe. I wouldn't base a life on Tarot any more than I would on yoga, romantic love, or the reformed calendar. But for a winter evening's conversation piece, or in the hands of a gifted fortuneteller, Tarot is reasonably diverting."

This fellow can turn on a dime, thought Cobb. The next thing he heard was Nolla's voice: "Where," she was asking, "could one get a Tarot pack?"

"There probably isn't one in the whole United States," said Laimbeer. "The only deck I ever saw was made in Provence shortly after the Crusades."

"Couldn't you *make* a pack?"

Laimbeer looked at Nolla as if her idea held more than casual attraction. "I never thought of it before, but I suppose I could. Raoul certainly dinned the stuff into my ears, and the figures themselves are strangely memorable. When I go back to town, I'll do a few sketches."

Berry, finishing a Golden Mixture, double strength, made a stab at getting the conversation around to herself. "How about first making some sketches of that portrait you promised to do of me?"

Polite irony glazed Laimbeer's reply. "Sketches shall be run up, whenever madame is ready. *Servant*. Madame is as good as hung." He turned to Nolla, preserving his exaggerated tone so that the affront to Berry would be softened. "And the Tarot pack—or a remembered version of same—will be in the mails next week, in homage from one clairvoyant to another."

The clock with the sun and the moon on its face struck twelve and ticked on for some minutes before Cobb arose with a comfortable yawn. The signal was accepted without protest. It was time for bed. They said good night with the affection that friends use upon each other after a long evening together. Cobb, trying not to look at Berry and Laimbeer as they ascended the staircase, said to Nolla, "Go to bed, darling. I'll fix things up down here."

Alone in the living room, Cobb took a final proprietary look around the premises, placed the fire screen in front of the dying embers, and dialed the thermostat down to fifty-eight . . . no, fifty-five. . . . Must save fuel till the oil truck comes. He snapped off the light switch, stood for a second in the darkness, then, neither buoyant nor weary, put his hand on the familiar balustrade and climbed the staircase, loosening his necktie as he went.

Another day, another dollar——

On either side of the carpeted corridor, doors were closed. On the north, Beryl's room adjoined Laimbeer's; to the south, Nolla's door, then his own. Triumph of civilization, refuge and barrier, the separate room! Typical invention of modern times, the latched door! Privacy unassailable. Loneliness, with a knob on either side.

In his own room Cobb commenced the ritual of going to bed. A simple routine: take off clothes, put on pajamas. Hang up clothes. Brush teeth, wash face, rub face and back of neck with a heathery toilet water. Brush hair. Look at teeth in mirror. Admire same. Drink half glass water. Glance at outside thermometer (30° F.). Inside thermometer (67° F.). Marvel at difference a few degrees make. Inspect desk barometer (falling). Listen for sounds from Nolla's room. Open window from top. Leap from center of room into bed (very hard on springs). Snap off night lamp. Lie on back in darkness, listening.

Listening . . .

To Nolla performing her much more painful and complicated rites in the next room.

Nolla's ritual of preparing for bed, begun when they were first married, had by this time taken on worrisome proportions. Originally it had centered upon a small pot of maidenhair fern that Nolla kept on her windowsill. Cobb had noticed that she took the fern off the windowsill and placed it on the floor before getting into bed. "Why do you do that?" he once asked. "Because a wind might blow it off the sill and break it," Nolla had explained. The single pot of maidenhair had grown to two, three, then half a dozen small plants—ivy, cactus, a miniature orange tree—all of which had to be placed in various "safe" parts of the room before she could settle down. In disposing her plants, Nolla would be in and out of bed three or four times—very disconcerting to a young husband. When Sicely came, there had been a dropping off in the plant ritual for a time, but it returned, with complications, after a few months. Nolla had begun to fear for the safety of her jewelry—and not only for its safety but its cleanliness. After polishing her rings, she secreted them in hiding places all over her room, then would get up several times to make certain that the jewelry was still there. Cobb, protesting, finally installed a small wall safe in Nolla's room. But the old hiding and cleaning obsessions persisted. Indeed, the cleansing rites multiplied, spreading to Nolla's clothes and person, until she was obliged to spend nearly an hour getting ready for bed.

Finally Cobb had dragged her off to a psychiatrist, an expensive soul curator who possessed enough vision and insight to recommend the deeper treatment of psychoanalysis. At this Nolla had balked. "I won't have my psyche pawed about." "Then try having another baby," urged the psychiatrist. Roddy was the result—a happy all-absorbing result for a few years. But gradually the old ritualistic trouble had crept back, bringing with it the grim outrider of kleptomania.

Cobb lay listening to the sounds from Nolla's room. Faint though they were, he could follow her ritual in every detail. He heard her nervous footsteps to and fro as she deposited the plants in various corners. The running of water . . . now she was scrubbing her hands. The heavy click of the closing wall safe. Open again. Closed again. More water running. More rearrangement of the plants.

God help her.

No use, Cobb knew, to interrupt the ritual. Remonstrance, counsel, only irritated her. Nolla's obsession had to exhaust itself first. Then, occasionally . . .

Patiently Cobb waited for the sounds to abate. The illuminated dial on his night clock said one-ten as Nolla got into bed for (he hoped) the last time. Cobb, shivering slightly—was it the cold? no, he was always tremulous when approaching Nolla's bed—turned the brass knob, opened the door to her room. The bluish night lamp brought Nolla's cheekbones into deathly relief, scooped out the hollows of her deep-set eyes. Why must she choose such a ghastly color? Cobb crossed the room, knelt beside her, switched off the blue light.

"Nolla," he murmured, finding her mouth gently in the darkness. She lay passive under his kiss and hands, neither encouraging nor rebuffing them.

"Darling." He chose not to press harder either with word or caress until she should give him a sign. The sign came feebly, like a small imprisoned bubble struggling upward through layers of fear and reluctance. Never had that bubble risen joyously to the surface or caught even for a moment the lightburst of shared love.

It did not now.

Loneliness and pity were all that Cobb brought back to his own room. Neither was enough to nourish a strong life or fill a heart longing to overflow with love. He asked himself what he might do that he had not done. Wherein had he failed? He gazed out of his window at the dark world of night and snow, heard the wind like a caped traveler rushing past his house. To summon the angel of domestic love, to cure his wife of her frightening compulsions, Cobb would have gladly walked naked into the storm. But no such heroism would be required of him. All he could do—all that anyone could do—was to be patient, cheerful, and steady-going in a world falling apart with guilt and grief.

He peered through the double panes of his window into the darkness of the storm. Snow was falling over the Dutchess hills, the ice-piled Hudson, and the great cities of the Northeast, covering with a fleecy shroud the houses, streets, and fields of men. It was falling on the alleys of Harlem and the broad lawns of fine Westchester houses. On the just and unjust, the rich and the poor, the living and the dead.

In a montage of unspeakable sadness, Fuston Cobb saw the snow sifting down upon a bunch of small pink roses on his mother's grave.

He opened his window from the top, took a few deep breaths of the gale. Then he leaped under his blankets and ten minutes later was fast asleep.

CHAPTER 5

Cobb's Patek-Philippe wrist watch was pushing nine next morning when he arose to bathe and shave. The rest of the house was sleeping; a hush of hibernation lay on the bedroom floor. Cobb put on a lumberman's shirt and a pair of heavy gray woolen trousers, which he tucked into high snow boots; he liked country clothes, wore them with a casual flair. On the way downstairs he passed Beryl's door, wondered how much of the night Laimbeer had spent with her. A fantasy of Berry—nightgown pulled up, rosy knees wound about the painter—smote him like a glimpse of a French postcard. Cobb tore up the picture savagely, trampled the pieces underfoot all the way downstairs.

Attars of coffee wafting from the kitchen told him that Mrs. Rollefson was up and around. He stuck his head in the kitchen door to give her good morning. The housekeeper, a professionally cheerful woman, ample-waisted but very tidy about the hair and ankles, had been with the family nearly six years now. She had marvelous forearms, a Dutchess County notion of her own value, and a Maya-like patience mildly flecked with martyrdom. Cobb suspected that she carried a private cross in the shape of her husband, a Norwegian seafarer who had broken his leg in a fall to the deck. Mr. Rollefson's sporadic bats made him the typical male liability to an otherwise satisfactory couple. Even when sober, Njals Rollefson was not exactly an Admirable Crichton, but he was a fair gardener and a good household mechanic, going about his duties in a pleasantly half-stewed condition. No one ever saw him actively drunk, because Mrs. Rollefson always kept him in the cellar at such times. Cobb genuinely admired the reticence that prevented her from complaining of her husband's tippling, but he wondered what kind of revenge she practiced upon him in private.

Emma Rollefson had a vividly picturesque turn of speech which she exercised chiefly on the weather. She would never say, "Warm. isn't it?" A summer day to her was "hot as a dog's tongue"; in winter the wind was "sharp as a briar." Her weather epithets delighted Cobb. To start her off now he said, "Quite a storm we're having, Mrs. Rollefson."

She did not fail him. "I thought I was being pelted with marshmallows when I stepped out for the milk this morning, Mr. Cobb. Some of them flakes were bigger'n cup cakes."

Cobb smiled. "Mail come yet?" Not that he expected anything important, but the R.F.D. mailman also delivered the *Times,* which he wanted for further news of the storm.

Mrs. Rollefson glanced at the kitchen clock. "Jim Fegley's late," she said placidly. "He can clash his gums all he wants about swift couriers on their appointed rounds, but that ain't saying the weather's obliged to listen. . . . How'll you have your eggs this morning, Mr. Cobb?"

"Sunny side up." He watched her slide the cast-iron frying pan onto the forward lid of the big coal range. A fine, intelligent woman with the rare knack of knowing when to drop a subject. "What do you hear from your son?"

"His squadron's due in any day, Mr. Cobb. Eighteen months in the Persian Gulf, he's been. I'll be all porcupine quills inside till I see him again." She broke the large brown eggs deftly on the rim of the frying pan, looked at Cobb queryingly. "You won't mind if he visits me here?"

"Not at all, Mrs. Rollefson. Have Gunnar up as long as you

want. After eating Flying Corps chow for eighteen months, he deserves some of your cooking."

Cobb took his breakfast at the end of the kitchen table. Munching his eggs and bacon, he kept hoping that either Nolla or Berry would join him. How pleasant if Beryl were to come trailing downstairs in a confectionery negligee and sit at the corner of the table drinking coffee with that intimate beginning-of-the-day air. But he had to content himself with the pleasant sense of having her in the same house. Doubtless he'd have her alone for a few moments some time during the week end, either at table tennis or possibly a walk in the snow. Then he'd catch up on the details of Berry's private life, ask her about Laimbeer. Was the guy a phony or not?

His breakfast over, Cobb put on an old felt hat and Mackinaw and let himself out the front door. The snowflakes, though not as big as Mrs. Rollefson's cup cakes, were certainly large and plentiful. He stood for a moment on his terrace gazing across the white expanse that rolled virginally toward Brompton. By the storm's white trickery, long familiar things—the dark stand of pines on the slope of Gresham's Hill, even the slope of the hill itself—seemed oddly distorted and misplaced. Exactly how did the road curve around that clump of firs? What had happened to the hollows in the wide meadow across the road? The strangeness of the landscape was intensified by some queerly threatening aspects of the sky. Low gray rags of cloud stood motionless overhead. Nor had Cobb ever seen such an odd sun; it had the leaden color of an old buffalo nickel burned to a half-glow in an ashy fire.

Cobb's intention had been to shovel a path from the front door to the mailbox, but why attempt to bail out the ocean with an eye dropper? He decided to take a walk instead, and struck out across the lawn, wading knee-deep through soft drifts toward the old gristmill that marked the northern boundary of his property. Summer or winter, he walked to the mill at least once every week end. Its smooth tumble always lulled him; the water sliding over the eight-foot drop into the pool below seemed a small symbol of the inexhaustible reservoir from which nature drew her energy. In summer dawns he often slipped down to the waterfall and stood under its green cascade for his morning bath. There was a little brick fireplace by the bank where Cobb broiled hamburgers and hot dogs for family picnics. In autumn, the pool was choked with oak leaves, brown and black; deer stopped to drink there on their way up from the lowland pastures to the daytime refuge of the hills.

Today, Cobb would have liked a companion on his expedition—someone to buck the snow with him in heads-down fellowship—but there was no one in the house who would venture out in such a storm. Roddy was too fragile, and it had been a long time since Nolla had walked with her husband. Berry might have come if journey's ending meant hot toddies and bed, but Cobb doubted that a mere walk in the snow would appeal to her. As for Laimbeer, there was something about him that didn't quite jibe with stuff like snow. Passing a gnarled pear tree, Cobb saw that the snow had primed its wood with patient juice. The gaunt bluestone ridges of the encircling hills were tempered to northern hardness by the snow. Even the rabbit leaping past had a pelt of thick gray fur. Cobb realized that only winter could give to trees, rocks, animals—and to human eyes, voice, and bones—a hard, boreal character that Laimbeer lacked.

There was really only one person in the world who would have enjoyed this brisk tussle with the weather. Sicely! How excited, how companionable Sice would have been, bounding along at his side, taking the snow like a northern caryatid tirelessly breasting the waves. On her vacations they sometimes walked a dozen miles a day, her young energy mounting higher than her father's during the first half of the jaunt, her dogged stubbornness matching his as they trudged out the last, tough mile. Cobb longed for his daughter now, but even in the spasm of longing he knew that Sice had all but passed out of his life and that whatever joys they shared in the future must be briefly snatched from her companionship with other men.

From the elevation of Gresham's Hill he turned to gaze backward to his home, substantial, wide-chimneyed, surrounded by the dark stand of evergreens. He remembered his first view of it ten years ago, recalled his determination to own the big Georgian seat with its twenty-five acres of fields, woods, and pond. The asking price had been forty thousand dollars. What a huge sum of money it had seemed! By shrewd dickering he had run the price down to thirty-four thousand—eighteen thousand dollars cash, a mortgage of twelve thousand, and his personal note for the remaining four thousand. Quite a scramble for a few years, meeting interest, amortizing the mortgage, furnishing, repairing, and landscaping the place. But now —furnished, painted, landscaped, and paid for, down to the last butterfly hinge, the house was his! Or Nolla's rather, for, like most men in his set, he had deeded it to her the day after gaining title to it.

Usually the sight of his home cheered and sustained him, but today the spell failed to work. He stood stock-still and let the white melancholy of the falling snow seep through the varnish of his city skin till it penetrated to the core of a lonely man, companionless on his own property, rejected in his own home. Was it for this that he had exerted himself so mightily at the tasks of building a business and a family? Was there never to be exaltation any more, no glimmering inebrieties of thought or feeling—but only the routine, careful discharge of custodial duties? If Cobb had been asked, "What else do you want to do?" or more pointedly, "What does your life lack?" he would have been hard pressed for a reply. He was, and he knew it, quieter and abler than most other men, less troubled by their chronic discontents and better adjusted to the world of private frustration. But the sparkle had gone out of his life, like the grape that seeps away from a wine corked too carefully, too long.

Above him, shrouded in a veil of snow, a great bird was wheeling across the dull bluestone sky. Cobb recognized it as one of the region hawks, a broad-winged plunderer of the upper air. Flying low, it made a steep-banked turn, then coasted with fixed wings over the bare fields, reconnoitering for a sparrow or rabbit. The hawk's absolute surety in its own element filled Cobb with envy and wonder. As the bird stooped like a feathered plummet to snatch a rabbit from a chink in a stone wall, Cobb broke into a murmur of admiration. How acquire a similar touch, an untamed dash even remotely comparable? How educate oneself, one's son, for that?

Somberly he plodded through the drifts toward the gristmill, seeking the special solace it always gave. Today it was a grotto of winter; a faery shell of ice encrusted the wheel, but underneath its glaze a broad ribbon of unfrozen water still fell against the dark paddles. The desire to flow like the millrace in a full steep drop, to discharge his accumulated need for love, was unrequited in Ruston Cobb. Nor was there any likelihood that the wheel of mature love would ever turn for him again.

He had renounced all that when he said good-by to Lucy Foederis.

* * *

The date of his first meeting with Lucy, inscribed on no tablet save Cobb's memory, was June 22, 1939.

He had driven the station wagon into the village to order some lumber and hardware after a long day of superintending repairs on the barn. It was late afternoon, and he wanted a drink badly but scarcely knew where to get it. The village tavern was definitely unattractive, yet it seemed to be the only place in town where one could quench a thirst. Cobb decided to wait till he got home and was climbing back into his station wagon when he looked at his watch. Only 5 P.M. A bad couple of hours yet to go before dinner. He decided to drop in on the Battens; Freddy and Gretchen would be on their stone terrace at the end of the lime-tree alley, shaking up something with a clink to it. Driving slowly down the best street in Brompton, he came to the Batten place—a remodeled colonial fortress hedged with privet, not too impressive from the front, but definitely well-done after you got onto the grounds. He crunched into the pebbly driveway and took a flagstone path to the back of the house. And there were the Battens at the far side of the croquet lawn, raising hands and voices in welcome extended only to one of their own kind.

Another figure, a girl, was sitting in a low rattan chair beside the swimming pool.

The pool was a natural basin, irregularly oval, dammed at one end by pretty gates and fed by a small brook. Fringed by a superb line of poplars, stocked with carp and sown with water lilies, it was a pleasant if somewhat conspicuous triumph of the landscaper's art. Gretchen had planned it, and Freddy had paid the bill. Both were proud of their joint product and were quite willing to let it serve as a backdrop for the technicolor scenario of their lives. Cobb had the feeling that Gretchen in particular was awaiting the happy day when a *Harper's Bazaar* photographer should arrive to take pictures of the layout.

Freddy came across the lawn, balancing on croquet balls as though they were stepping stones. A card, Freddy—rich, indolent, good-tempered, now working on his third wife and second inheritance.

"Leech and blister me if it ain't old Patents Pending!" cried Freddy. "Find any rubber hinges in the mail this week? Say, I've been thinking up patents for a lot of things." Freddy rattled on. "What this country needs is a good five-cent boutonnière. Get it? Five *scent*—rose, harebell, harelip, petunia, and garlic. Odor selected by a tube passing down the sleeve, ending in a rubber bulb, squeezed by hand. Or better yet, under the armpit. Say, that's good! Armpit adds homely strength." Freddy illustrated the idea by pumping his arm, bellows-like, against his side. "What's it worth to you, Rust?"

Cobb was taking Gretchen's hand. "Nice," she was saying, while Freddy chattered. Cobb's glance moved to the girl seated in the rattan garden chair. Her eyes, a shade deeper than amethyst, matched the tall iris screening the dolphin fountain. "I am inviolable," they said. Gazing, Cobb could not answer Gretchen or Freddy.

"Ruston, you don't know our guest, Lucy Foederis," said Gretchen. "Lucy, this is Ruston Cobb, prematurely worn out by an addiction to marriage and patent law."

Cobb felt himself sinking into the orchid quicksands of Lucy's eyes. He heard Freddy asking, "Scotch? . . . You take ice, don't you? Say, that reminds me of a wonderful idea for a patent—a thermostat attachment to a highball glass. Rings a bell when the ice cubes melt beyond a certain point. Works on batteries—*wet* batteries. Ha, ha. Do a search into it, will you, Rust? Where's Nolla?"

"Home, taking care of Roddy. Mastoid, I think. Roddy's my young son," he explained to Lucy, trying to be scrupulously careful that everything about him was quite clear.

"Bring him over when he gets well," said Gretch. "Freddy'll play with him."

The iced Scotch cooled the parched membranes deep in Cobb's throat but could not relax his swallowing muscles when he looked at Lucy. She appeared to be about twenty-three years old, yet ageless with the repose that comes early to women who contemplate perfection every time they glance into their mirrors. Her skin had the grainless texture of a gardenia, stained with the faintest of olive pastels. Noticeably she lacked ferment; her conversation and movement had the quality of a still wine. No rings were on her fingers, and Cobb wondered how such a woman could possibly remain unattached.

He remembered almost nothing about that first afternoon except the game of croquet that Lucy had played with him and Freddy. Innocuous pastime! But this game of croquet was etched with deep fidelity on his memory as one of the loveliest recollections of life. Lucy had played the purple-striped ball—he could see it now, rolling across the emerald lawn in a slow diagonal toward the side wicket. The game had given him an opportunity to watch her walk, bend over, lift her head, turn around, make all the commonplace movements that everyone makes while playing croquet. How could these movements be invested with such sensuous delight—a delight at once acute and lulling? Lucy was an excellent player; she had beaten them both while Gretchen jeered and Freddy clowned, and Cobb watched this girl with olive-gardenia skin bend, turn, and tap her purple-striped ball with the mallet. What was so wonderful about it all? Cobb could not say, then or now. But he had felt the oncoming holiday in his blood, joyous, calm, hasteless, secure, and had wished that the game might go on forever.

Seven o'clock had found him finishing a highball, his third, and looking at his watch with a start of remorse. While he dallied through the late afternoon with whiskey and croquet, Nolla was at home with a sick child. He got up hastily, shook Gretchen's and Freddy's hands first, so that he might come at last to Lucy's. She gave it to him without accent or pressure, but a lift of her amethyst eyes had said, "I'm not so inviolable as you think."

The next days were a time of pain and petty subterfuge for Cobb. Getting away from his house in midafternoon, riding over to the Battens, became the chief business of his life. At lunch he would invent some pretext for going to the village, and when he returned he would have some casual story about what he had done to occupy himself. He detested this lying; it was unlike him, yet he could do nothing else. Once he had risked asking Nolla to come with him to the Battens for a drink. But she, overborne by worry about Roddy's mastoid, had refused. She seemed not to notice her husband's absence and accepted, without hearing, his accounts of where he had been and what he had done that afternoon.

He began taking Lucy for long afternoon drives in the station wagon; the glens and woods along the bank of the Hudson made outdoor canopies for their meetings. One day they chugged up the Hudson in the *Chip,* Cobb's little outboard motor skiff, carrying a picnic basket packed by Lucy for the outing. She sat in the bow among kapok pillows, wearing a muslin dress sprigged with a strawberry pattern, and a leghorn straw hat with an expensively flexible brim. Her skin seemed to absorb the bright sunlight griddling the water and throw it back without heat; under the two-o'clock sun her complexion was flawless, with a pink underflush shining through her gardenia pallor. In midafternoon Cobb anchored the little boat at a neglected wharf and together they climbed a knobby hill thickly sown with wild strawberries. Lucy took off her hat and lay on her back, her arms outflung, Cobb bending over her like a man drowning in an enchanted pool.

Filaments of milkweed floated like summer snowflakes through the air.

A passion to explore this girl's heart, mind, and body—to discover, if possible, the terms on which he could have her—consumed Cobb. The facts of her life, though not ordinary, were simple enough. Her mother was English, of a good county family; she had married Lucy's father, a Danish-French commercial baron not quite of the international banking class but with holdings in many European countries; directorships in middle-sized mines, railroads, steamship companies; a solid house in Copenhagen, a flat in London, a villa at Biarritz. Lucy had lived in all these places, had been bred in a convent in France till she was thirteen, then was sent to an expensive girls' school in Switzerland till her eighteenth birthday. Without her saying so, Cobb got the definite impression that her parents had bred her up for an *haut-monde* marriage, that she was one of those highly milled products intended for the limited luxury market in which a small number of buyers bid briskly for top-cut merchandise. Lucy's exotic beauty, buttressed by a handsome *dot,* would certainly have landed her as the more or less cherished chatelaine of a continental establishment. She had been saved by the debacle of her father's fortune just prior to the war. He had escaped the Nazis

with a whole skin and about one-sixth of his money, to become one
of the first wave of *émigrés* to New York.

"And now here I am," said Lucy, with neither pathos nor an undue sense of strangeness in her voice, "lying with a married man
in an American strawberry patch on a summer afternoon."

"Would you change any part of it?"

The exquisite slow lift of her eyes was a prelude to her thought.
"Yes."

"What then?"

Her reply was an incredible mixture of naïveté, sureness, and hon-
esty. "I would have you unmarried." She was not smiling; her eyes
were level liquid, fed by inner springs of choice and desire.

The valve of a terrible flame-thrower opened suddenly, cindering
Cobb with a violet-colored blast. Lucy had burned his fantasies to
the root. Whatever flight he would now make toward her must be
made on the wings of reality. Divorce, remarriage, a settlement on
Nolla. He could not gather himself for the lift. He was silent as
they drove homeward, steadfastly resolving not to see this girl again.

For two days he had remained away from the Battens—days of
wretched desolation accompanied by almost total physical collapse.
He could not get off his bed; it seemed that the great muscle
sheaths of his legs had been severed and that his intestines were full
of concrete. To hide his agony from Nolla he pretended to be ill
and permitted her to go through the mockery of calling a doctor.
Anything to spare her. On the third day his desire to be with Lucy
broke away from his moorings of conscience and resolve. He drove
over to the Battens', asked Gretchen to invite him for dinner so that
he might be with Lucy when daylight merged into darkness. He
wanted to walk with her across the deep-piled lawn of evening.
"I've never been with her except in daylight," he explained to
Gretchen.

The Battens had charitably gone away after dinner leaving Cobb
and Lucy alone on the flagged terrace. Up from the carp pool came

the mixed scent of pond lilies and fresh-water grasses—a damp, ferny odor, oldest and strongest of aphrodisiacs. As the twilight deepened, Lucy's dinner dress of white voile grew luminous in the shadows, throwing her face, throat, and shoulders into a luminous chiaroscuro. Cobb had never touched any part of her but her hand; the desire to take her arm in his proprietary keeping led him to say, "Shall we walk?" She stepped off the terrace onto the grass, slipped her arm through his. A caress. Without speaking they walked toward the carp pond. The damp perfume of the mid-June night rose from its sedgy borders. The splash of goldfish nibbling at water flies, the throaty gulp of a bullfrog, were the only sounds in the world.

A compulsion taller than any barrier, deeper than any supporting pile of his life, welled up in Ruston Cobb's throat. Unexpectedly he had found a love that equaled his own. Lucy's fastidious heart, her honest mind, and all the serene bodily tributaries they governed, were spread before him. The possibilities of full-bodied emotion opened in a vista of fulfillment, no snatched idyllic fantasy but a life of depthless satisfaction. All this he saw in the mystical flash which at high moments lights the whole valley of one's life, from loftiest crag to lowliest pebble, with the blinding knowledge, "This is the promised pass between the years."

He wanted to say, "I love you," to the girl beside him. How pure the satisfaction of revealing to the loved one the mortal ache expressed by no other words. But he was silent. He knew the three words that men have chosen to convey their dream of immortality were too heavy with promises that he could not fulfill. Even with the perfume of Lucy's hair in his face, the curve of her breast docile to his hand, he knew he could never abandon Nolla and his children. No need to go home and put his hand on Roddy's feverish forehead, or comb with his eyes the curls of Sicely's hair. Useless to think that he could brave the hollows of Nolla's cheek and explain that a new and fresher cheek possessed him.

It was not duty or obligation or Queensbury sense of form that blocked him off. Nothing so superficial or acquired as these. What then? Cobb believed, without piety or paranoia, that he was one of the irreducible quartz crystals of the column that held up the world. If he crumbled, all was shattered; the world would collapse.

He had felt it by the carp pool with Lucy on that June evening. And now, knee-deep in snow by the frozen gristmill, he felt it again. Not that it made him happy to remember the strained good-by or stilled the longing to see the renounced face again. Not that it seasoned legitimate love with the flavor of deeper enjoyment. No. For ten years Cobb had realized almost hourly that when he said good-by to Lucy Foederis he had deliberately forsworn all the gifts of love. The realization did not make him happy—nor did he particularly mourn at forty-two the life that might have been his. Yet on this day of falling snow he remembered how once he had burned like an asteroid and even yet was glowing at the core.

*   *   *

Back in his house, Cobb found breakfast over and various small activities well afoot. Roddy was working on his jigsaw puzzle; Berry and Laimbeer were in the game room playing table tennis. Nolla, suffering one of her periodic migraines, was still in bed. The mail had come, and Cobb sat down in his lozenge-paned study to the ritual of reading the *Times*.

A curious staleness lay on the headlines; Cobb had the feeling that he had read them a thousand times before. "Soviet Diplomats Charge Bad Faith at Suez." "Race Riots Flare Anew in St. Louis." "White House Breaks with Senate Leaders." "Superliner Crashes into Utah Peak." "Clergyman a Suicide in Midtown Hotel." "Dog Saves Mistress and Three in Organ-Loft Fire." The usual grist of world confusion, conflict, and cross-purpose. "When," thought Cobb, "shall we ever read good news again?"

On the subject of the weather the great journal seemed moderately unperturbed. A single-column story noted that an unusual quantity of snow had fallen, and would, according to the Weather Bureau, continue to fall. Street Commissioner Timothy J. Fidd had issued a call for twenty thousand volunteer snow shovelers to augment his regular corps of street cleaners. "Everything," a spokesman for the Commissioner declared, "is under control." On the editorial page Cobb read one of those homespun vignettes for which the *Times* was deservedly famous. It was entitled "Woodpile Wisdom" and discussed in nutty, flavorful prose the blaze-value of oak vs. hickory on a winter hearth.

Remembering the ominous leaden sun of his morning's walk Cobb had the feeling that the city-room boys had somehow muffed their storm signals. Understandable. Who knows of country weather who only Times Square knows? He switched on his television set, hoping to pick up some spot pictorial news of the storm-ridden city. A series of street scenes showed busses lunging through white drifts while snow-removal machinery struggled desperately to keep the streets clear. Duffy Square looked like a Siberian tundra; pedestrians clung to their hats as a high wind shrieked down the triangular canyon. Seeing no snow shovelers at work, Cobb wondered why these loose platoons of the unemployed were not on the march. Where were they?

His question was answered by the next television shot. A mass meeting in Madison Square Garden was being harangued by a voice that had all the subtlety of a plumber's torch.

"Volunteer snow shovelers of New York City," the voice was saying, "pay no attention to Street Commissioner Fidd's call for gang labor. [*Applause*] His proposal that you shovel the sidewalks of New York at the slave wage of a dollar and a half per hour is a kick at the groin of the American workingman. [*Loud cheers*] Do not fall for Tim Fidd's capitalist-inspired crap. And no matter what he or anyone else says, don't shovel snow for more than six hours a day." [*Ovation*]

Cobb groaned. His sympathies were certainly not with Fidd,

whom he personally knew to be a cheap finagler, but he couldn't help being alarmed by the raw menace in the organizer's voice. Hate-filled, unappeasable, it struck, louder and clearer than any headline, the keynote of the age.

The Age of Foreboding.

Disquieted, Cobb cut the televised scene and began fishing among his pipes for the meerschaum with the cherry-colored bowl. He tamped home a load of Parson's Pleasure, and walked slowly up and down his study bringing the fine tobacco to a garnet glow. The motor release of handling the richly colored pipe, of circling the familiar round of accustomed things—his maroon leather chair, the mahogany table with its brass ship's lamp—somewhat restored his sense of security, but could not altogether still the trumpet insolence of the labor leader's voice.

The staccato clicking of a ping-pong ball drew him to the game room. Berry, in a sports skirt and white cashmere sweater, was giving a display of shot-making that had reduced both Laimbeer and Roddy to vanquished pulp. From the door, unseen, Cobb watched the stresses of her ungirdled torso revealed through her sweater as she reached for a shot or bent over the table. He recalled his morning thought of Lucy bending, turning, stroking the purple-striped croquet ball across that distant lawn.

How glorious the movements of women! The swiveling of their hips as they walked toward you, the fascinating business of hands as they drew off a glove, the delicate play of fingertips among wisps of hair at the nape of the neck! Cobb wondered whether women were comparably affected by the movements of men. Probably not. No masculine business could be as exciting as the crosshanded pattern of a woman's arms lifting a dress over her head. No male motion could be half so sweet as that semi-turn of a woman's torso as a nightgown fell, always too quickly, around the meeting place of thighs and waist.

Merely to observe these things, how good it was! To wait for such movements in a woman you loved (watching Nolla brush her hair was one of the rewards of life) or to see them coming smoothly off a silken spool of energy, as Berry's movements were now, created fresh hope in a world of grief and foreboding.

As he entered the game room, she waved her paddle at him challengingly.

"I've taken them both," she cried, "and now I'm going to take you."

"I can be had."

He ranged himself opposite her at the table for a warming-up volley. It was fun to absorb her wicked shots, smack them back at her without mercy. With the ball clicking in metronome cadence, a dancelike rhythm sprang up between them, and they began to move in a magnetic field generated by the game and their own polar tension. When Roddy dragged Laimbeer away on marionette business, the voltage increased, became almost unbearable to Cobb. Dismayed by the keen pleasure it brought, he accompanied his shots with a volley of banter.

"Do you play this vicious game often?"

She smashed one at his forehand. "Whenever I can find a victim."

Cobb chopped it back. "You like your victims passive?"

"On snowy Saturdays I prefer them a little on the rough side."

"Like this?" Cobb nailed a rising ball and cut it hard at Berry's backhand. The ball glanced off her paddle, struck her an eggshell blow above the eye. She dropped to the sofa with a stifled little moan and Cobb was beside her brushing back her hair, seeking the hurt with his hands. The cashmere sweater was a scented flag of invitation, provocatively flung out as she held up her face for his scrutiny. For a moment she played the game of doctor-and-patient, then her arms climbed around Cobb's neck and a warm clamor of passion opened under his mouth.

"I've wanted this so long," she murmured. Her fingers traveled across his face. *"God,* it's good to kiss you, Rusty."

] 81 [

Cobb had forgotten how warm and consoling a woman's mouth could be. Berry's kiss, her roving fingertips, and the warm perfume of her hair tipped him off his accustomed balance. He cupped his hand over the swelling commotion of the cashmere sweater, closed his eyes, and felt himself being sucked down into a funnel of poppied warmth.

"Berry—dear Berry . . ." Gently he disengaged her arms from about his neck. The forgotten paddle clattered to the floor as he rose and stood looking down at her. "It's sweet"—his hand was in her hair—"but we mustn't."

"Who says we mustn't? Not the man who makes the keys for my apartment. Locksmiths laugh at love, you know." She moistened the corner of her handkerchief with a vivid tongue and scrubbed tenderly at the lipstick on his mouth. "Do you realize, darling, that I live only six blocks away from your Sutton Place bear cave, yet you've never rung my doorbell *once?*"

"I've thought about it often enough."

"Have you?" Simple believing was in her throat. How tenderly different she seemed when Laimbeer wasn't around, or when she wasn't drinking. "What do you *do* with yourself nights, Rusty?"

"Oh, I follow the advice of an old traveling salesman—stay in my room and out of trouble."

"I see. The prudent type." A compulsion to give pain, to punish this man who had always rejected her, ruled her for a moment. But the danger of frightening him softened her. "I won't get you into trouble, darling. All I want to do is cook you a dinner, light your cigar from one of my bayberry candles, and embroider your monogram on a couple of nightgowns I brought back from Paris." She lay back on the sofa, settled her head on a cushion. "Does it sound too dangerous?"

"No."

Overflow of longing moistened Berry's lashes, "Oh, Rusty, why don't you take me over? Fix me good. God knows I need it. I'm sick of punks and phonies." The weariness of the battle overcame her. "I want a man, not necessarily a husband—I wouldn't know what to do with a husband. I just want someone to love me a little" —her eyes were brimming now—"and help me stay away from that fifth Martini. You could do it with one hand behind my back."

"How about Laimbeer?"

"Trial and error Number One Hundred and Sixteen. Or maybe Two Thirty-nine. I've lost count." Her full lower lip, pink without lipstick, came forward in vexation. "You'd rather talk about *him,* instead of you and me?"

"Talking about him might help me understand you. How'd you happen to take up with him?"

"The usual way. Big party, half pansies. Strange man, broke-but-proud type, standing off in a corner. Four quick drinks. Then he caricatured a couple of fagots on the back of an envelope. How that guy can draw—line feathery but clear if you know what I mean. First thing I was telling him he could clean up on fashion stuff. Brought him back to my apartment to show him what I meant." She broke off. "Well, I showed him."

"And now?"

"I'm fed with him; he's fed with me." Anger and desperation claimed her. "Laimbeer's a real painter, but he can't work or rather, won't work—he could make a thousand a month if he would— talks too goddam much, mostly about art and that kiss-of-death stuff, and oh, what the hell, he's just a wrong guy. When I dump him at Lexington and Forty-ninth Street Sunday night, that'll be the last of that."

She lay very quietly looking at Cobb through eyes strangely marine in color and depth. She seemed a changeling now, an Undine-creature condemned to spend her life gazing from sea caves at the only mortal who could give her a soul. Her need to be made whole, to be valued by one man, to light his evening cigar from the flame of her candle, to sew his initials onto her nightgown at a spot where they would cover the rim of her heart—to be saved from the fatigue and humiliation of successive Laimbeers—all these were in her eyes and voice as she pleaded, "Why don't you do something about us, Rusty?"

Affection, pity, and plain hunger for this passionate creature he had known since childhood broke to the surface of Ruston Cobb's life. Why not do something about it, indeed? He was tired of living with ghosts, no matter how beautiful, weary of loyalties that no longer sustained the weight of loneliness. His gaze traveled from Berry's lustrous hair spread fanwise on the pillow, past her full-lipped mouth, lingered at the curves of her cashmere sweater, and slipped along the middle secrets of her woolen skirt. The comfort a man might have here—the fulfillment, the release.

If only . . .

Berry heard the scruple as clearly as if he had uttered it. The old cry, familiar, unanswerable: Nolla, the children, the gospel according to Saint Husband. She avoided an argument that she could not win, and, with Cobb's eyes consuming her, chose to misread their scrutiny.

"What's the matter, darling? Is my torso screwed on wrong or something?"

"Your torso's wonderful. It always was." His glance changed key as if to recapture the time when her handsome limbs were only twigs. "It began to be wonderful when you were fifteen."

"And you began to be wonderful when I was twelve." On surer ground now, Berry laughed. "I remember everything about you since you first came for Nolla. Your wild brown hair, that checkered suit you wore, and the bucket seats of your old red Reo. You gave me a ride in it once."

"Did I?"

"Uh-huh. Afterward I went home and wept. Oh, I was a desperate little girl. And then I dried my eyes and did a very funny thing."

"What did you do?"

"I killed you."

"Killed me? How? Or rather, why?"

"Because you loved Nolla instead of me. There was nothing I could do about it except put you out of my life. I went about it very cold-bloodedly. First I took a snapshot of you that I'd snitched from Nolla and drowned it in the bathtub. Held you under with my own hand. Then I took a tennis ball of yours—remember how you used to let me bat them back to you before a game?—and flung it into a sewer grating. That hurt. But the last thing I did was even worse."

Memory of childish sorrow dogged her. "Once in a game of for-feits I clipped off a chunk of your hair and slept with it under my pillow for weeks. Then when I realized that you didn't love me, I *burned* it!" She shivered. "I can hear it sizzling now in the kitchen stove. 'There, Ruston Cobb,' I said, 'that finishes you. As far as I'm concerned, you're dead.'"

Double pity, half for the forlorn child, half for the grown woman, stirred Berry's voice. "The only hitch was, you didn't stay dead. I guess I can't burn you out of me, no matter how the flame sizzles. . . . Or drown you," she added miserably, "no matter how many Golden Mixtures I pour for myself."

Graceful as a mermaid trailing a dory, she rolled onto an elbow and gazed up at the man standing over her. Her posture brought the luscious heft and contour of her breasts into full relief. Ruston Cobb wanted to kneel beside her, roll back the cashmere sweater, and bury his face in responsive warmth. He did kneel; his hands reached out. This was reality. Not a dimming idyll by a lily pond or the tambour of a timid cheek. This was a swelling answer to a swollen need—an answer as simple as bread, as direct as a hawk's plunge, as satisfying as the fall of water on a turning wheel.

The house was quiet; Beryl's eyes were closed. Cobb bent over her, forgetting where he was, aware of nothing but the pulsing sweetness spread before him. He would take as much of this sweetness as his two hands could hold. His lips brushed scented wool, soft-tipped.

"I need these, Berry," he murmured at her breasts. "I need them so."

"Take them, darling. They were always yours."

His hand reached for the hem of her sweater. But between his need and its satisfaction, a shadow fell. Shackles heavier than the proprieties of time or place stayed his hands. Deathly guilt paralyzed Ruston Cobb; the cashmere sweater became a stone that he could not roll back.

Miserable, he rose from his knees, walked to the window and gazed out upon a desolation of snow.

Who had laid these crippling shackles on his life? Of what stuff were they made? Ruston Cobb could not answer these questions. He simply did not know. Nor could he find words to soothe Berry's anger as she got off the sofa and swept contemptuously past him out of the room.

CHAPTER 6

SLIPPERED AND HOUSE-JACKETED, Cobb lounged deep in his red leather chair, his whole posture suggesting the householder at ease on a Saturday afternoon. He was reaching for his meerschaum when Laimbeer slouched in. Boredom subtracted from the painter's face the compelling tension that usually gave an edge to his features. He brought into the study a whiff of Beryl's scent, and Cobb judged from the painter's listless air that he was surfeited, temporarily at least, with Berry's favors.

Quite clearly, Laimbeer was longing for tobacco, a drink, and an hour of male companionship. Cobb, more than disposed to dispense all three, silently extended his pouch to the painter.

Laimbeer shook out a palmful of the tobacco, held it to his nose. "You're amazingly in one piece," he said. "Constable in the dining room and Parson's Pleasure in the study. How do you manage it?"

"Any objection to trying for the unities? I had an idea that the well-balanced composition was what you artists were especially interested in." Cobb poured two glasses of straw-colored Scotch and diluted them with water. "Not that any of us have much chance of achieving it."

"Your chance is as good as mine." Laimbeer glanced over his shoulder like a man pursued by Furies wearing cashmere sweaters.

Cobb felt subtly cheered. If he himself couldn't float buoyantly on Berry's wave, he was glad that Laimbeer couldn't either. He lifted his glass, swallowed a large mouthful of whiskey. Just a dog in the manger. With the meerschaum warming his hand, surgical curiosity claimed him. Perhaps now was as good a time as any to nick Laimbeer's talking vein and let him bleed.

"I've always wanted to ask you a question, Laimbeer—that is, ever since I saw one of your early shows in the Hummel Galleries." The lift of the painter's eyebrows said, "Tell me more," and Cobb lengthened out his conversational stride. "About ten years ago I happened to be in a—well, let's say an emotional state, and was working off some of the overflow by looking at pictures."

"Did it help?"

"Yes, it did—I really don't know why." How could he explain that his longing for Lucy Foederis had been somehow assuaged by the contemplation of ideal color and form? "Well, one day walking along Fifty-seventh Street I saw a painting of yours in Hummel's window. It was an apple tree—a kind of pink snowstorm just at the moment when the blossoms explode. Remember the picture?"

Laimbeer's sardonic glance asked who should remember better.

"I went in and asked to see more. Hummel led me down a corridor and opened the door of a darkened gallery. 'Hold your hat,' he said. Then he snapped a light switch and I saw four walls hung with your canvases."

Cobb's thick eyelashes met in his retrospective effort to recapture the moment. "I almost lifted my hand to ward off the blows that rained down on me from those pictures. That room was a wind tunnel; the walls roared with power. It was like—like standing too near an express train as it whizzed past you."

Laimbeer nodded like a dead man corroborating a eulogy. "So?"

"That's just the question I want to ask. What happened to you after that, Laimbeer? What became of all that energy—those luscious nudes, those lyric trees and flowers? You jeered at my Constable, yet ten years ago you were catching the American landscape just as he caught that of haycock England." Cobb toned down the inquisitorial note. "Of course, you don't have to answer if you don't want to."

Laimbeer's gaunt hulk was motionless; his long arms hanging over the sides of his chair and the foreshortening of his knees gave him the appearance of an abandoned half-god sitting dejectedly in a lonely Pantheon. No worshipers, no faith, and small hope of regaining either.

The painter revived himself with a long pull at his glass. "It's hard to know where to begin with a chap like you, Cobb. First off, I can't decide how much you know, or care, about art. Oh, I don't mean taste. This house of yours is crawling with it. But what I must ask myself before sounding off is this: can you, or anyone like you, really understand what the artist tries to do?"

"Don't expect too much," laughed Cobb. "Just think of me as the well-tempered amateur with a little money to spend on a picture now and then."

"Fair enough. But there's something else I must warn you about." Laimbeer was chillier than a Jesuit superior advising a pimply stutterer not to go in for Holy Orders. "To explain what happened to my painting, I'll have to rip off those tweedy blinkers you're wearing, Cobb. When the light hits you, you're going to scream. Before I'm through, you'll be a disturbed, frightened, and oh God, what an angry man! Five gets you ten that I'm right."

"You've got yourself a bet."

Laimbeer held the glass of amber whiskey reflectively between his eyes and the fireplace. "We'll begin our little discourse with a merry glissando on how art is *not* produced. There used to be a school of painters—the Düsseldorf boys—that could have painted this whiskey, your nut-brown meerschaum, and me lifting a toast to good taste in all weathers, with undeniable charm and fidelity. You've seen their pictures: tables heaped with wine bottles, crimson cheeses, blue-black grapes, calabash pipes, and cherry-colored fiddles—all to the life. Usually the picture had some such title as 'Bachelor Joys' or 'Fruits of Leisure.' It was a pretty school, and those fellows certainly knew all the tricks of surface representation. Learned them from better painters than themselves, Vermeer among others."

"Whatever happened to the school?"

"Oh, it got mowed down along with a lot of other venerable simplicities—such as Lawn Tennyson, Euclidian geometry, the gasoline engine, and the economics of Herbert Hoover. All, all gone, the old familiar faces, giving place to the schizoid-making new. Newness complex, baffling, insecure, and unfathomable, all canopied over with confusion, alarums, and flight." Laimbeer fell into his deserted Pantheon stance. "Can't you imagine, Cobb, that it might knock a painter into a paralyzed mess?"

"How different or worse a mess than the one a patent lawyer's in?"

"Patent lawyers aren't obliged to make statements about the universe every time they open their mouths. They can roll with the punch, or even take it lying down. But the artist is obsessed by the need of stating his case. Every time he sees a brick barge or a bunch of bananas, his whole nervous system itches to organize them into a design that will express everything he believes, hopes, and dreads about the world he lives in. And it can't be mere visual representation. That's camera stuff. No, it must be a blast out of the artist's unconscious—a statement in terms of color, space, and tension—that verifies his inner knowledge." Laimbeer broke off contemptuously. "I suppose this is all Kurdistani to you, Squire?"

"Not at all." Cobb brought his meerschaum to a Düsseldorf glow. "But if you're an artist, what's to prevent you from making such a picture? You've got your canvas, paints, and a world teeming with material. Where's the block?"

"The block, as you put it, is the pitiful lack of any unifying idea big enough or strong enough to support the weight the artist must heap on it. Our age hasn't any *symbol* to nourish the creative soul." A Gallic shrug. "No eggs, no omelet. No symbol, no art."

"I don't quite see—"

"Then take a good long backward look at the Cross. *There* was a symbol—concrete, elastic, mysterious, nourishing—everything a symbol should be. It began to shape itself in the shadowy region where myth merges into the craving for ideal form. Primitive artists seized upon it, developed and enriched it. By the time Titian got hold of it, he could hang Christ and everything else on that priceless sky hook, and the audience would understand his message because the Cross was the biggest, most familiar truth in their lives. Half Titian's work was done for him before he stepped to his canvas." Laimbeer's voice trailed off. "But today the Cross is dead as Kelsey's nuts. Even if it weren't, Titian's treatment of it isn't likely to be improved."

Cobb took in the argument. "There are other symbols."

"Name one."

"Nature. Hills and streams, spring rain, summer clouds, winter snow." Cobb gazed through the lozenged window as if to renew his belief in the blue-white poetry falling in silence over the world.

"Noble, kindly nature, eh? A bountiful mother stuffing a rosy-nippled tit into Little Boy Blue's mouth while he lies under a hay-cock, fast asleep? Sorry, Cobb, but the whole idea has been upset by everything that's happened in the past fifty years."

"For instance?"

"What about the big city bank that holds the mortgage on Little Boy Blue's hayfield? Or the corporation that'll repossess the tractor if he doesn't pay up? Or the fission-bomb horror hanging over the whole landscape? How are you going to get those into your picture? They're part of it, you know."

"And don't forget Jeannie, the Nude Farm Girl, who wants him to wake up and make love to her." It was Beryl, flushed with alcohol, swaying in the doorway.

The wrinkles in Laimbeer's forehead crashed down on his eyebrows like metal stampers. "Not interested," they said. "Go way."

"Now, don't get creatively nasty, Eddie," cooed Beryl. "I just dropped in for my quota of Scotch. Pour me a dram, will you, Rusty?" She ran her fingers combwise through Laimbeer's thick hair, but her intention to sit on the arm of his chair was rebuffed by the painter's motionless elbow. With the flounce of a faro queen, she took a highball glass from Cobb and sat down on a chair of her own, crossing her handsome knees as though posing for a steamship-company ad. Then she began sniping with calculated shots at the man who had just rejected her.

"Watch J. Matisse Laimbeer button up like a deacon's vest," she said. "Go ahead, Eddie, I understand picture talk, even though I'm not Rosa Bon*hoor*"—she purposely mispronounced the last syllable. "Tell us all about the pangs of the art life and how it hurts"—she indicated the back of her neck—"up here."

She had the ring in his nose now and twisted the iron cruelly.

"Make with that patter about the nude as an outmoded symbol. How you can't paint busts and derrières any more because woman is in flight from the Provençal attitude and you haven't figured out a new position for her yet." She addressed Cobb. "It's *vurry* interesting, if you haven't heard it yet. But me, I'd rather take to the hay —in the same old position—for that twilight hour known to the profession as the matinee."

She drained her glass and held it out to Cobb for a refill. Part of the torment was intended, he knew, for him. But Berry's behavior was so clearly an exercise in pique that he had to smile at its transparency.

"Come on, Berry," he coaxed, filling her glass, "give up and settle down. I don't hear talk like this every day and I want to hear more. It ties in with a lot of things that've been bothering me; maybe Laimbeer knows the answers."

"Eddie knows a lot of answers, but not to the right questions." Berry, set on being difficult, was succeeding beautifully. "What's the *matter* with you men these days?" she flared. "Here we are on a country week end, snow falling in perfect *quilts,* and seventeen double beds upstairs in the twilight. But what do you guys do? You mooch around playing word games with each other, while fresh hot goodies go to waste. I *ask* you—no, I'm telling you—it don't make sense."

Berry's tirade, Cobb felt, was powered by unanswerable logic. Sympathy for her undisciplined energy, regret that he himself was barred from enjoying it, prompted Cobb's soft answer: "It'll keep, honey child."

"The hell it will." Wrath, not petulance, filled her now. She rose with the fury of a Goya come to life; a passionate ultimatum swung in her hips as she passed between them. At the door of the study she focused her large eyes on the artist. "Coming, Eddie?"

Laimbeer put his glass to his lips, made no reply. Swishing imaginary sequins, Berry mantilla'd away. A second later a crash of crystal was heard, then Nolla's puzzled face appeared at the door.

"What in the world did you say to Berry? She was so unnerved that she dropped her glass."

"Dropped it?" Cobb couldn't help laughing. "Flung it down, more likely."

Laimbeer was on his feet, sliding a chair under Nolla. "It was my fault, really. I was making quite a melancholy clatter about the special griefs of the artist. Beryl wasn't amused. I imagine"—Laimbeer was being very humble and endearing—"she's heard it before from this station."

"*I* haven't." Nolla's intonation said, "Won't you go on?"

Laimbeer made a brief résumé of the discussion. "We had disqualified religion, nature, and the nude as symbols no longer serviceable to the artist. We were about to plunge into the pit when you entered."

"I'd like to hear more about the disqualified nude," smiled Nolla.

Laimbeer rolled his fingers like a chalk talker playing with a crayon idea. "Have you ever been to Pinsky's?"

] 93 [

"Pinsky's?"

"A burlesque show. I used to go there to make sketches of a strip-teaser called Dora La Porte. You might say," he smiled reminiscently, "that Dora was the Disqualified Nude in person. The last time I saw her in action, I got quite an insight into the nature of the great American illness—an illness that prevents the nude female from being of much assistance to the artist, or, all too often, herself."

· Laimbeer, trying to recapture the exact mood of Dora's performance, reminded Cobb of the taxi driver whose eyes had been riveted to the tip of the spahi's pointer.

"There stood Dora," the artist went on, "splendidly formed and reasonably young—a big teasing coquette, taking off her clothes bit by bit, and with a superb technique, I don't mind telling you. The spotlight, deepening to mysterious purple as more and more female gear came off, picked up Dora's anatomical treasures and held them at last utterly exposed for her audience of goggling males."

The imaginary crayon in Laimbeer's fingers was busy with remembered contours. "As she lowered her shoulder straps, Dora was contemptuously aware of what was happening. She alone saw the mama-hunger in the eyes of her audience, pitifully looking up to be fed. That staring compulsive attention, that rabbitish quivering of their lips! What was it all about? What infantile needs did such a spectacle satisfy? Is the longing for the sight of the female secrets perfectly normal, or was it, in the Pinsky setting, a psychic illness seeking satisfaction in a dream closet?"

No one answered. By the pat fall of the questions, Cobb had the feeling that Laimbeer had said all this elsewhere, many times.

"There's a malaise hanging over the whole business of the female, both in life and art," Laimbeer continued. "Painters want to go on and say something further about the most fascinating of themes, woman. But what? Our statements are tied up with our attitude toward women, and that attitude is confused and exhausted. We no longer regard women either as madonnas or odalisques; they are neither chattels nor chatelaines. What, then, are they?"

Laimbeer's big fingers dropped the imaginary crayon as though it had broken under his pressure. "The nude is merely a footnote to the general situation. The whole contemporary text, wherever you examine it, is blurred and illegible. Like a letter found on a garbage pile, all smeared with filth and hen tracks."

Dark now. Cobb pressed the button of the brass ship's lamp; its inverted emerald shades threw saucers of gold upon the polished table. Laimbeer held out his great hand, let some of the lamp's diffused gold fall into his open palm.

"Monet once said that light was the central figure in every picture. A pretty aphorism, useful and valid in Monet's time, but no longer serviceable for ours." He spread his fingers as if to show the impossibility of scooping up the yellow quicksilver of light. "Something has fractured the rays of our sun; they come brokenly to the artist's eye."

Gloom, cold as seaweed, settled over the artist's shoulders. "Well, Cobb, that should answer your question of what happened to my work. Those luscious nudes and lyric landscapes, four hundred of them, were all painted before I was thirty. They sprang from sheer glandular exuberance and were good enough in their way, I suppose. A hundred collectors and museums thought so. But no artist can go on being merely exuberant. The time comes when he must stop leaping and *land* somewhere. And when that time came for me"—Laimbeer's voice was springless—"I discovered that the modern artist has no place to take off from, let alone any place to land."

Acute distaste for Laimbeer's orgy of self-pity smote Cobb. The circling flight of a defeated ego around its own beloved image— was it a rationalization of the painter's private weakness or an act to win sympathy from Nolla, as he had doubtless won it from other women in his time? Were these the famous burdens of the artist? If so, Ruston Cobb had no patience with them.

"I've always thought," he said, "that the artist was the special champion of life, a tireless celebrator of its freshness and beauty. But according to you, Laimbeer, he's nothing but a professional pall-bearer, lugging an idiot to his grave."

Serene egotism radiated from Laimbeer's features. "If there is death in the world, the artist feels it first—and strongest." As if to share his superb sensitivity with an emotional equal, he turned to Nolla. "Do you doubt what I say?"

The duet between them, half confessional, all counterpoint, went softly forward. "How can I doubt it," she murmured, "when I find such fearful symptoms of it in my own life? Cleavages, flaws, chasms—oh!" Her voice was pure plea. "How do these deathly faults enter the soul?"

"They are spawned by a sick idea of love," said Laimbeer in a flat declarative. "And they flourish because of love's failure in our lives."

"That is a horrible thing to say."

"Horrible but true. Merely in terms of dynamics, what other emotion could generate so much energy? Didn't Dante say that love makes the world go round?" Irony tempted him. "Which probably accounts for the stagnant mess the world is in."

A dangerous runner, loose in a broken field. Cobb felt obliged to throw a body-block into him. "Can't you, out of the goodness of your heart, say a kind word for *anything?*"

Laimbeer grinned. "Sure. If you want greeting-card sentiments, I can give you the standard canvas on love. It's the great purifier, the strong man's inspiration, the solace of the afflicted, et cetera. Men are ennobled by the love of a good woman, and women sing at their household tasks because they're in love. You know the build-up; it's crooned by crooners, gelatinized by the movies, and puréed by the women's magazines in flavors ranging from tomato to cream of spinach. Yet while all this romantic hubba goes on, the deathworm of guilt feeds at the cheek of love, burrows into its breast and belly."

He looked up fiercely, as if to nip off objections. "Can you deny it?"

A murmured "No" was Nolla's acknowledgment that the artist had caught a true likeness of love's diseased body, and that the likeness was a portrait of herself. Desperately, she put in a faint demurrer.

"Is love any different now than it ever was? Was it ever happy, anywhere?"

"I don't know how it prospered in the Piltdown cave," said Laimbeer. "But long ago on the Aegean, Sophocles brought the note of sadness in, with choric accompaniments *and* some really troubled characters. You don't see many husbands and wives as miserable as Jocasta and Swellfoot."

"Swellfoot?" The name was new to Cobb.

"Oedipus then. They crippled him in infancy by putting shackles through his ankles—made him clubfooted, you know."

"Oh." To Cobb came a vision of a college amphitheater: a chorus wailing in strophes of commiseration for guilt that could never be atoned. The Queen's face was buried in her hands, and the fingers of the King, her limping Son-Husband, sought out his own eyeballs.

"But all that," he faltered, "was only a—myth."

Huge, hideous laughter burst from Laimbeer. "Only a myth!" He laid back his great head, lifted his rump off his chair like a man suffering from meningitis, and roared at the ceiling. "Ho, *ha, ha, ha!* Only a myth!" He stopped laughing. "What in hell do you think I've been talking about for the past hour? Titian's Cross, Monet's Light, Dora La Porte's strip-tease are all myths, symbols—whichever you choose to call them. The Swellfoot myth is one of the juiciest gobbets ever spewed out of the human soul. It's got everything—timelessness, universality, *truth*. It's as true today as it was three thousand years ago in Thebes. And energy! Why, it streams right out of the unconscious—"

"If it's got so goddam much energy," Cobb interrupted angrily, "why don't you hitch some of it up to your canvas?"

Laimbeer's reply had the tired courtesy of a chessmaster about to say checkmte to a not particularly bright opponent. "Why doesn't a man with leukemia hitch up the power of the white corpuscles that are consuming his blood?"

"You make life, love, and everything else sound pretty pathologic."

"Well, *isn't* it?"

"No, by Christ!" shouted Cobb, rising to his feet in anger. "It isn't!"

He launched into a passionate defense of love. He would cut it free from the cerements of defeat and death in which Laimbeer had wound it. But as he tore into the fabric of the painter's argument, an amazing thing happened to Ruston Cobb. He discovered that a winding sheet, endlessly long and very much like a shroud, enwrapped the body of his wife, binding her from the roots of her hair to the spread of her toes. To orient his argument anew, Cobb turned to the image of Beryl, only to see her in the posture of the matinee. He heard her say, "I'm not Rosa Bon*hoor,* but I can do it better than her." And when he could pluck no weapon from this sheath to defend the glory of love, he turned to his dream of Lucy Foederis —exalted, mysterious, a wreath of birch leaves crowning a virginal trunk. A trunk made for climbing, nevertheless, a wreath graspable if he had but stretched out his hand.

Why couldn't he stretch out his hand, either for Lucy Foederis or Beryl Deane? Had he interpreted as virtue something that was only fear? Could it be that the winding sheet that shrouded Nolla bound him too?

Could it be?

And who had done the shackling job on him? Who had pierced his joints with a crippling ring?

He heard himself lamely ending on a note of duty and obligation.

Laimbeer was laughing cruelly while he held out his hand. "Give me my five dollars."

Nolla nervously twisted her fingers as Mrs. Rollefson came in to announce dinner.

CHAPTER 7

A ZINC-COLORED SKY, low-ceilinged, hung over the Sunday-morning world. From his bedroom window Cobb could see only an undulating blanket of snow silently deepening as the fleecy bolls continued to fall. The round knobs on top of the gate posts were almost buried now, and that orange-colored blob just visible over the top of the blue spruce must be the cab of Bart Waley's oil truck, he "Fanny B. Belcher," bogged down in the deepening drifts. Vaguely disturbed, Cobb strode to the telephone at the end of the hallway and gave the operator Bart Waley's home number.

"What's the story on the oil, Bart?" he asked.

Bart Waley had a post-nasal drip and a poorly fitted dental plate (upper), a combination that gave a jews'-harp buzz to his speech. Heartbroken apology was in his twangy voice as he embarked on a circumstantial saga of woe.

"Darn sorry about this, Mr. Cobb. I was on my way to your place last night when the 'Fanny B.' got stuck in a drift this side of your pines. Like to've blown a gasket walkin' back to town for the comp'ny snowplow." Bart wheezed retrospectively. "If 'twas *my* plow, Mr. Cobb, I'd 'a opened up your road right off. But the comp'ny manager—well, he had his hands full up in the Leechmere section till twelve o'clock last night, and was just about plumb nuts with calls, so you can't really blame him in a way." Waley's loyalty, torn between boss and customer, parted in the middle.

"I understand all that, Bart. I'm not the only customer in the township. But do you think you'll be able to dig that tank of yours out by tomorrow?"

Bart was rueful. "I sure hope so, Mr. Cobb. But you see, it's this way: Tod Brower, the darn-fool driver of the snowplow, went and snapped his blade around one A.M. this morning and we're waitin' for the county plow to dig *him* out right now."

The futility of whipping this particular dead horse overcame Cobb. "Well, see what you can do for us, Bart. . . . I've got a nice quart of Bourbon here with your name on it, any time you come around."

Shaking his head at the folly of getting angry with innocents like Waley, Cobb went downstairs. The living room was chilly; he turned the thermostat up to sixty-eight degrees and was reassured by the prompt hum of the motor pumping fuel into the burner. He'd go down cellar after breakfast and read the oil gauge himself. Probably there'd be at least five hundred gallons in the reserve tank —a week's supply, anyway. Why get hysterical about a dinky snowplow? He'd look at the Sunday *Times* while Mrs. Rollefson put on some of her good toast and coffee.

Usually the Sunday paper was in the front vestibule, delivered at some ungodly hour by the Brompton News Shop. This morning the paper wasn't there. Cobb opened the front door a crack and peered out. No tracks in the snow; no sign of the newsman anywhere. For the first time since the storm began, Cobb had the definite feeling of being shut off from the outside world. A gust of wind whirled a powdery column of snow through the open door; he slammed it shut, and slid the hand-wrought bolt into its groove as if barricading his home against an invader.

While Mrs. Rollefson whipped up breakfast, Cobb twisted the radio dial to a news station. Crackling silence was broken by the grave voice of an announcer:

"We have just received a special bulletin from the Federal

Weather Bureau with the request that it be broadcast from all radio and television stations. I will now read the bulletin:

A steady sheet of snow has been falling for three days over the entire northeast quadrant of the United States, and as far as this Bureau can predict, will continue to fall for some time. There seems to be no adequate explanation for this unprecedented and, it must be admitted, threatening condition. We believe that prevailing westerly winds are blowing fog banks inland from the Atlantic Ocean, and that this fog, encountering unusually cold currents in the upper air, is being precipitated in the form of snow.

The public will be well advised to remain in their homes, if possible, thus preventing further strain on railroad transportation, which is being seriously affected by the storm. Motorists are warned that snow-removal machinery has broken down in several states, and that automobile travel is impossible.

"Stay tuned to this station for further announcements. Your announcer is Osgood Clayborne. And remember: You can be a 'regular fellow' with Duz-Mor Branflakes."

A curious sense that all this had happened somewhere before came over Cobb as he snapped off the dial. The morning sky was dark as twilight; unbidden, a line from an old school verse crept into his memory.

> The sun that brief December day
> Rose cheerless over hills of gray.

Why, Whittier's "Snowbound," of course! He hadn't thought of it for years. Grand old poem. Those people up in New England, snowed in for a week, had a wonderful time telling stories, playing games, going about their chores. And what about the Penobscot Indians, the Hurons and Iroquois in their deerskin tepees? Hardy bastards. Lived off jerked venison and gnawed a few grains of corn for dessert. Cobb's spirits revived. If the Hurons could stand it, he could. Living out the storm would be a nice challenge to resourcefulness and ingenuity—virtues too rarely exercised in these button-pushing days.

Cobb remembered once being gale-bound for a week on Lake Erie with his father and mother aboard the *Gyrfalcon*. Provisions had to be stretched; even the champagne had run low. No radio in those days, either; the little steam cruiser had bobbed like a chip in the enveloping mist, completely cut off from the world—just at a time, too, when his father had wanted to get back to New York to wind up some merger or other. Cobb remembered how tranquilly the King of Strength had taken the whole affair, and how his deep instinct for rule had asserted itself. "Batten down the hatches, and let her ride!" was the only command the elder Cobb had given. But it had seemed to young Ruston that the very anchor cable drew strength from his father's serene courage.

The only unhappiness about that memorable week was the vast amount of time that his father and mother had spent together in their cabin. What are they doing in there? the boy had wondered. Why don't they let me come in too? He had solaced his loneliness by standing in his oilskins at the wheel, pretending to guide the *Gyrfalcon* through the storm. First command! Something of that commanding joy possessed Cobb now. While the house slumbered and the snow swirled, he swallowed his second cup of coffee and laid plans for riding out the storm.

Almost gloatingly he descended the cellar stairs to take inventory of fuel and provisions. The cellar of Ruston Cobb's house—deep, coolish, damp—extended under the entire building. Part of it was wall-boarded; the rest stretched off into a labyrinth of wine closets, woodbins, laundries, vegetable cellars. The ceiling was supported by whitewashed columns of brick resembling masts in the hold of a great ship.

Inspection of the oil gauge showed that a scant fifty gallons remained in the big tank, but the five-hundred-gallon auxiliary drum was full. He patted the container's cold flank. A week's heat and hot water! By regulating the furnace at half speed he could stretch his fuel out to ten days. He moved toward the deep-freeze unit, opened its insulated door, and peered into its compartments. He counted a dozen hams, twenty-five chickens, several joints of lamb and beef, twenty pounds of hamburger—enough to feed a platoon of infantry for a couple of weeks. He opened the door of the preserve closet and saw shelves loaded with jars of fruit, chiefly peaches, put up by Mrs. Rollefson last summer. On the opposite wall were rows of canned goods—the usual assortment of baked beans, tinned soup, and corned-beef hash—about twelve dozen cans altogether. A half-barrel of wholewheat flour stood in one corner, and a fifty-pound sack of cornmeal sagged in a covered bin. Some rice and potatoes, a small sack of bean coffee, six canisters of tea, and an odd lot of ketchup, pickles, olives made up the pantry's supplies. Altogether, a consoling array of food. How those Penobscot sachems would have grinned at such a heap of provender!

Roddy's voice from the head of the cellar stairs brought him back to the upper world. "Long distance calling you, Daddy. I think it's New York."

Ross Lufbery was on the phone. "Hello, Rusty," he said with false heartiness. "How's the Dutchess County patroon weathering the storm?"

At the thought of the cornmeal, hams, and canned goods stored snugly in his cellar, Cobb's voice climbed two notes at a time. "All set for a month's siege here, Luff. Got enough provisions in the cellar to feed an army."

"Smart Mr. Ant. A million grasshoppers salute you." Lufbery, terse and troubled, went on: "Things are getting worse by the minute here in Manhattan," he reported. "Makes the blizzard of 1888 look like a feather fight. Snow removal completely broken down. No surface traffic moving; railroads, cabs, busses all tied up. The Mayor's declared Disaster Rule, and has called out the Red

Cross to distribute food. It's a white hell and no relief in sight."

"How's the hotel fixed?"

"Jammed. Cots in the hallways and all that sort of thing. Half portions all you get in the cafés. The snow's got to lift soon or there'll be chaos."

"Any new dope on the snow shovelers' strike?"

Lufbery groaned. "Say, is the world falling apart or not?"

The operator cut in. "Please limit your conversation to five minutes."

"Don't take my question so seriously, honey," Lufbery snorted, "and stay the hell off this wire till I get through talking. Listen, Rusty, let me give you a piece of advice. You and your people stay put, see. Don't *think* of coming back to town."

Shop, sweetest of subjects, thrust itself even at this crisis into the talk. "Say, Luff, Oliphant of the State Department sent me some drawings just before I left Friday. Said he wanted a report on them the first of the week. Maybe you'd better call him up and say there'll be a couple of days' delay."

"To hell with Oliphant. If this snow keeps on a couple of days more, there won't be any State Department." A clucking sound on the wire warned that the nervous operator was about to cut in again. "So long, Rusty. I'll try to keep in touch with you."

"So long, Luff. Pecker up, old man."

Cobb hung up the receiver and tried to reconstruct the scene in the great hotel: the milling lobbies and crowded bars filled with desperate penned-in people, storm-bound, stranded, with no means of getting anywhere and nowhere to go. Came a vision of Lufbery imprisoned in a bedroom with a bad-tempered dancer—a modern Paolo and Francesca whirled endlessly, tiresomely, on winds of fatigued lust. Inferno twentieth-century style; two thousand rooms with two thousand baths, deluxe and damned.

He walked slowly into the dining room, where Berry, Nolla, and Laimbeer sat smoking after-breakfast cigarettes. Beryl in her satin peignoir looked like a fresh peach cobbler; the olive tints under Nolla's eyes told Cobb she had not slept well. Laimbeer, having eaten a man-sized breakfast, was slowly coming to life. A Sunday-morning tableau very pleasant to look at, an authentic replica of a thousand other Sunday mornings in ten thousand other country homes.

"Hey, Rusty"—Berry poured him some coffee and dropped his customary one lump into the cup—"what's our chances of getting back to town through all this?" She thumbed in the general direction of outdoors.

Cobb decided to give it to them gently. "The radio advises, 'Stay where you are.' *Must* you get back?"

Berry dabbed marmalade onto a hot muffin, laid it on Cobb's saucer. "Ginzburg'll have a miscarriage if I don't show up with the spring sketches. Otherwise"—one shoulder went up with silken indifference—"I'm all set for a midwinter vacation at Chez Cobb." A special forgiving smile. "I like it here."

"And I'll go crazy having you here," thought Cobb. Something in the way he dunked his buttered muffin told Nolla that reserves of information were being withheld.

"Who was the call from?" she asked.

"Lufbery."

"Things bad in New York?"

Cobb nodded. Why shouldn't he tell them? They were grown people, able to hear the truth. "Very bad," he admitted. "The whole city's chin-deep in snow, and the tide's still coming in."

Between Nolla and the painter flashed an inexplicit glance. "'On dead volcanoes only lies the snow,'" said Laimbeer quotingly.

"Who said that?" asked Nolla.

"Oh, some minor American versifier; can't remember his name. Bartlett's will tell you. Then there's that other cheerful thought—how does it go? Oh, yes: 'The snow has a ghastlier whiteness every year.'"

Cobb looked coolly at the man. "You've forgotten the best line of all," he said.

"Well?" asked Laimbeer. "How does it run?"

"It's from the Old Testament. Job, I believe." Cobb's voice was very low and quiet as he quoted the mighty lines: " 'Knowest thou the ordinances of heaven? . . . Hast thou entered into the treasures of the snow?' " He grinned back at Laimbeer. "I've forgotten the exact verse, but you'll find it in the chapter where God convinces Job of his ignorance and imbecility."

*   *   *

The principal excitement of the afternoon was the news that Laimbeer had finished the Tarot pack of cards he had promised Nolla. The painter, having gracefully accepted the fact that there was no getting back to New York, borrowed some of Roddy's water colors and shut himself up in his room for the day. At five o'clock he came triumphantly downstairs and with a self-possessed flourish presented a small rectangular package to his hostess.

"A staying-over gift," he smiled.

Nolla gave a low exclamation of pleasure as she examined the cards. "Look, Rusty, aren't they exquisite? A real Tarot pack!" Flushed, excited as a girl, she spread the cards on the living-room table to admire their intricacies of color and design.

Inspecting the cards, Cobb had to admit that Laimbeer had done a remarkable job with the materials at hand. Augmenting Roddy's water colors with red, black, and gilt inks, he had inscribed on pieces of vellum writing paper the strange symbols of the Tarot arcana. Then, cropping these pieces, he had glued them to the faces of ordinary playing cards, with the result that Nolla possessed one of the few Tarot packs in the world.

"They're beautiful," said Cobb ungrudgingly, as he examined the illuminated surfaces. Then, in an after-challenge: "What can you do with them?"

"He tells fortunes with them," exclaimed Berry. "He's going Swami on us any minute now."

Laimbeer riffled the cards expertly. "These things work better on a table that food has been eaten off," he said.

"Is that why gypsies always rap at the kitchen window in dreams?" asked Nolla, leading the way to the dining-room table.

"So they rap at your window too, do they?" smiled Laimbeer. "Well, that decides your card, although there really wasn't much doubt about it." He selected a card from the pack, laid it face upward on the table. "This is you," he announced. "The Seeress."

The card revealed the figure of a veiled woman enthroned between two columns of a temple, one of white marble, the other basalt black. On her knee she held a locked book, and about her neck hung two crossed keys. Mystic symbols glittered on her green robes, and behind her throne a tapestry was sprinkled with moons and constellations.

The face of the Seeress was a portrait of Nolla.

"You will now cut the cards." Laimbeer's voice was trance-keyed, impersonal. (If he's trying for a mystic effect, he's certainly getting it, thought Cobb.) Nolla cut the pack, then docilely handed it back to the artist, who proceeded to lay the cards face downward in a fan-shaped design. He placed the Seeress, facing upward, at the point where the ribs of the fan converged.

"This was Raoul Farceur's favorite layout," he explained. "There are other arrangements—triangles, circles—but Raoul maintained that the fan"—Laimbeer made an accordion movement with his hands—"was the perfect symbol of the female." He glanced apologetically at Cobb. "All this hocus-pocus is strictly traditional, you understand. Any resemblance to logic or common sense is quite incidental."

"Go right ahead. Don't mind me," said Cobb.

"Do begin," Nolla murmured tensely.

Laimbeer's hand went to the left side of the fan. "Sinister omens first—and card Number One is all important." He turned up the outermost card. "Ah, the Witch Empress."

A powerful female figure, lowering and heavy-breasted, lay half crouched over a flat altar stone. Her hair and shoulders were loaded with trophies. In one hand she held an upraised hatchet; in the other the severed heads of children. At the corner of the card were the four sacrificial emblems—the ram, the dove, the turtle, and the goat—all trussed and skewered.

"Does this card," asked Laimbeer, "suggest to you any particular person?"

A shudder racked Nolla; her frightened eyes flashed to her husband. No help there, only puzzlement and a creased forehead as if to ask, "What goes on here?" She shifted her gaze to Berry, but her sister's eyes, terrible with recognition, were fixed on the card.

"Well?" asked Laimbeer.

"It's my—my mother," said Nolla in bitter syllables.

"God," breathed Berry, "how like."

Laimbeer turned the card over quickly. "I imagine," he glanced at the sisters, "that I shan't have to tell you about the Witch Empress in any great detail."

"Skip it," said Berry. "Or we'll be telling you."

"No need. I must point out, however, that since the figure was upside down, her influence lies well in the past. Shall we go on to the next card? Hmm, amusing. The Phoenician Sailor."

They surveyed the pale drowned figure of a man. His eyes were open.

"What does the sailor mean?" breathed Nolla.

Laimbeer fumbled for an emollient phrase. "Oh, it has to do with gnostic wisdom—the secrets of the deep, like Farceur's turtle. Suggests either adventure, tragedy, or a visitor from far places."

"Could it be something about Roddy?" asked Nolla.

"Scarcely. The sailor is a youngish man but not a child. Perhaps the next card will explain the sailor's meaning."

The third card brought a smile to everyone's face. It was a young girl standing in a leafy bower, fertile with plants and foliage, birds and flowers.

"Why, that's Sicely!" exclaimed Cobb. "My daughter," he explained to Laimbeer.

"So-o." The painter nodded with mock solemnity. "If this were a gypsy tearoom, I'd predict a wedding between the Phoenician Sailor and your daughter." Laughingly he held out his open hand to Nolla. "You must cross my palm with silver before I go on. What, no silver? Then I'll go on anyway."

All very gay and playful. To erase the image of the Witch Empress, no doubt. Cobb valued the painter's sensitivity, admired his dexterous handling of the two sisters, each maimed differently by the ax-wielding mother. And how skillfully Laimbeer disguised, under a veil of banter, his real emotions about the Tarot pack!

At an increasing tempo he turned up the next few cards. "Ah, the Hanging Man. No doubt that's the tall dark artist in your life. . . . And here's the Juggler again, resourceful and energetic as usual. Hmm, the whole gallery. . . But what's this?" Laimbeer laid down the last card. It was the picture of a hooded skeleton striding rapidly across a bare, flat terrain. The figure carried a scythe across his shoulder and a terrible wind blew out his hood behind.

"Death," said Laimbeer casually. "There's never any mistaking him, is there? He gets around. Pops up in the queerest places."

Elaborately unperturbed, he gathered up the cards, riffled them coolly, then handed the pack to Nolla. "Practice with them over a pot of Souchong," he advised. "I daresay you'll find that the readings will compare favorably with those obtained from the best tea leaves."

*   *   *

Roddy had taken over the music room for the performance of his play; he had set his box of marionettes on a table at one end of the room, and had arranged chairs in a double row facing the stage.

All afternoon there had been an excited plugging in of electric cords and much experimenting with bulbs for lighting effects; the atmosphere reminded Cobb of those distant Sunday nights when he had given magic-lantern shows to the dearest of audiences, his father and mother. That enchantment was living again in Roddy as he undertook his complex task of being playwright, producer, actor, and manager all at the same time.

"All ready," he announced to the grown-ups in the living room after supper. "Better get your seats. The curtain goes up in five minutes." He darted into the kitchen to repeat the announcement to Mrs. Rollefson; in Roddy's book she stood on a parity with any other member of the household. Then, hastening back to the music room, he ducked under the black baize portière hanging at the back of his miniature theater and stood like a photographer about to take a picture.

"Turn off the lights, please, Daddy." When the room was in total darkness, Roddy snapped on a bulb to illuminate the marionette stage. A murmur of applause rippled out of the little audience.

Roddy's eager voice piped out the *mise en scène.*

"Good people," he began, "this play is called *The Dragon Slayer.* And it is a true story. It all happened in Thebes a long time ago— not quite like this, but pretty close."

"The child is a very historium of knowledge," breathed Mrs. Rollefson into the darkness.

"The characters of the play," prologued Roddy, "are the King, the Queen, a Soothsayer, and a General. Oh yes, there's a Town Crier, too. He tells what's happening in different places. Act One shows the King and Queen talking in their palace."

Cobb saw Nolla's face like a dim cameo, expectant, rapt as she gazed at the empty stage waiting for her son's mime to begin. Slowly, from opposite wings a king and queen jiggled toward each other and struck postures of royal colloquy. Now the dialogue began.

KING

For twenty years our land has been at peace,
Our gold and population show increase,
And all within our country goes so well
It doth remind me of our wedding bell.

QUEEN

Yes, Sire, your reign has been most fortunate thus far.
For twenty years we have not had a war.
Even the ravenous dragon comes not back
To eat our children and make us cry, "Alack!"

KING

The King of Crete is now my only foe.
I hear he's cooking up a warlike blow.
But who is this that enters on our sight?
Why, 'tis the Soothsayer with his beard so white.

SOOTHSAYER

Oh King, please listen to this wondrous news:
While I was walking by the salt sea mews
Seeking a certain shell of magic charm
I came upon a fire, still burning warm,
Where mariners had cooked some strange sea gulls,
And in the ashes were blackened bones and skulls.
Some of this ash I gathered and was grinding
With sulphur, when a flash most loud and blinding
Dazzled my sight and broke the altar rock
And threw me earthward with a fearsome shock.

QUEEN (aside)

Methinks this sea-gull powder hath much harm.

KING

Didst thou work further magic with this charm?

SOOTHSAYER

I did, my lord. I blew a rocky cave
To smithereens, killing some fishes in the wave.

KING

Good Soothsayer, tell no others of this power.
Go mix another batch within the hour
And keep it hidden in a secret place.
With it the King of Crete I will efface.

"That's the end of Act One," announced Roddy.

"Shades of Pearl White," murmured Cobb, reaching for Nolla's hand.

"You've got us hanging from the rafters," said Berry.

"Act Two!" cried Roddy. "The plot thickens."

The King and Queen sit on their thrones. A General stalks across the stage, bows, and speaks.

THE GENERAL

Against our shores the Cretan armies turn.
I come, great King, to get your counsels stern.

KING

E'en so. (*Hands him a sack of sea-gull powder.*)
Take this magic dust whose might
Will hurl the Cretan armies into flight.
Lay waste their city, let me hear the sighs
Of Cretan bastards rending earth and skies.

"You mean 'dastards,' don't you, darling?" said Nolla.

"Sh-sh, mother." Roddy, refusing to let the interruption throw him, went on:

THE GENERAL

'Tis done. This wondrous dust will blast their state.
Expect me back, Sire, at an early date.
(*A messenger tumbles on stage, panting.*)

MESSENGER

Most royal King, dire tragedy I tell.
The Dragon, swimming in the ocean's swell,
Draws near to Thebes. Half bull, half serpent he,
And soon upon our shores will landed be.

] 113 [

QUEEN

Oh beast of doom! He comes to eat our young.
Will nothing save us from his greedy tongue?
Hold, King! *(She turns to her husband.)* Suppose, instead
    of war,
Which this strange powder was invented for,
We use it to destroy this cruel beast
And save our children from his bloody feast?

KING *(enthusiastically)*

A good idea, Queen. General, give me back
The warlike powder in the precious sack.
Soothsayer, ho! Go parley with the Dragon;
Meanwhile we'll plot to fix the monster's wagon
And free our kingdom of its crawling bane.
It must not ever bother us again.

The bulb in the marionette box snapped off, and Roddy's voice came from the darkness. "End of Act Two. Can everybody hear out there?"

"Perfectly, son," encouraged Nolla.

"We're practically covered with goose pimples," said Berry.

"The third act is very short," explained the young impresario. "It's practically all done by the Town Crier."

Now the stage lights were on again and Roddy's play fairly whirled to its dénouement. In true Greek fashion he used the messenger to describe the action off-stage.

TOWN CRIER

Thebans, let's celebrate this happy hour.
The state is rescued from the Dragon's power.
It happened thus: the monster, making an unholy noise,
Was clamoring for his meal of girls and boys,
When one brave youth, the fairest of the land,
Walked straight up to the Dragon. In his hand
He held the sack of fiery dust and threw it
Straight down the monster's throat. The powder blew it
Into a hundred thousand little pieces.
Now that the monster's dead, our trouble ceases.

] 114 [

Huzza! Hurrah! The Dragon's dead! Here comes the King.

Roddy's King was pounding toward a grand finale in which royal wisdom and justice were giving lumps to the powers of evil, when the stage suddenly darkened.

"Damn!" said Roddy irritably. "Something's happened to the lights. Just when everything was coming to a happy ending." Still the showman, he addressed his father. "Turn on the house lights, will you, Daddy?"

In the darkness Cobb groped for the wall switch, pressed it with his thumb. Instead of the usual brilliant flood from the crystal chandelier, there came only a feeble glow, a dimness more shadow than light.

"Something's wrong at the powerhouse," he said. "Bring some candles, please, Mrs. Rollefson."

The company sat in eerie gloom while the housekeeper went to fetch the big candelabra from the dining room. Roddy, balked of his triumphant curtain, was attempting to explain to Nolla how his play was supposed to end; in his excitement he was biting his fingernails terribly. Who does he remind me of? thought Cobb. Suddenly he had a vision of the cinnamon-haired florist clerk; the resemblance between this pitiful creature and Roddy struck the father like a slap in the face.

"Stop biting your nails, Roddy," he snapped. "You can tell us all about it when the lights go on again."

The boy's lips closed tightly. He thrust his hands behind his back; tears sprang to his eyes.

Mrs. Rollefson came in with the candles. They punctuated the gloom with flickering apostrophes, and their flame shivered violently as a fierce wind stampeded the windows of the music room.

"All right, Roddy." Cobb attempted an apologetic heartiness.

"Now you can tell us what the King was saying when the palace lights went out."

The boy made a trouper's effort to obey his father and pull together the broken skeins of his poetry. "Well, you see, the King of Crete was sending a peace offering to the King of Thebes, because the same dragon was eating the Cretan children too. So the two kings promised not to make war on each other, and only use the powder when something bad, like another monster, came back to trouble them." At this summing up, Roddy's nerves snapped and he burst into sobs.

Nolla took the agitated child in her arms, comforting him with words and kisses. "It was wonderful, darling, the whole thing—the idea, the characters, the poetry. It just *couldn't* have been more perfect."

Unashamedly Roddy buried his head in Nolla's bosom. She stroked his silky hair, murmuring endearments. Seeing and hearing the caresses, Cobb turned away, pretended to tinker with a floor lamp. Now Mrs. Rollefson was bringing in more candles, Beryl was hovering over Roddy, and Laimbeer stood moodily gazing out of the window into the black wind. At length the three women led Roddy out to the kitchen for some hot milk, more endearments, and bed.

"Quite an allegory the youngster cooked up," commented Laimbeer.

"Yes. Do you suppose he realized the full implication of his story?"

"You'd be surprised," said Laimbeer, "what a thirteen-year-old kid can figure out. Anyway, he gave his own generation quite a play when he made one of them throw the powder at the dragon."

"Quite." Cobb tried to smile, but was remembering too vividly the resemblance between Roddy and the florist clerk. "Have a night-cap?"

"A short one."

Cobb mixed a couple of highballs, handed one to the painter. "There's something I'd like to ask you, Laimbeer," he said, cooling his throat with a long swallow. "Have you noticed anything—peculiar about Roddy?"

"He's remarkably bright. Precocious even, I'd say."

"Yes, but anything—queer? Over-effeminate?"

Laimbeer nodded. "A touch, maybe. Still, many creative artists are that way."

"But suppose he were to become more so?"

The painter shrugged. "Then that's the way he'd be. It's not the sort of thing that'll win him his 'Y' at Yarwash. But there are other careers, you know—acting, writing. He has unusual gifts for both."

"I suppose he has."

Laimbeer turned advisory, comforting. "You know, Cobb, other cultures than ours—older, wiser ones—weren't morally disturbed by this kind of thing. Aztecs and Egyptians honored beauty and fragility in their young men. And in Thebes—quite a town in its day—a boy with Roddy's grace and talent would have been wreathed at festivals, celebrated with songs." He shook his head consolingly. "You've no need to worry, Cobb. Roddy will find a place, his own place, and be happy in his own way. After all, it's *his* life, not yours."

The wind was lashing at the great house, driving snowflakes hard as pebbles against the windowpanes. Its strophic wailings dwarfed the whimpering griefs of man, and each snowflake, like a falling moment, signalized the burial of present hope and sorrow under the piling drifts of time.

Cobb broke the silence with a question. "Whatever became of Thebes?"

"It fell apart; got snowed under by enemies, plagues, one thing and another. Malaria helped as much as anything, I think." Laimbeer was meditative. "Once on a trip through the Peloponnesus, I saw what remained of the old town."

"Ruined towers and all that?"

"Not even ruins." Laimbeer finished his drink. "Just a muddy crossroads."

A dull pipe and a strained "good night" brought Cobb to his bedroom. With no desire for sleep he took off his clothes, put on his dressing gown and slippers, listened for a moment at Nolla's door. Her ritual had begun; there was no stopping her now. Aimlessly he walked about his room, peered through the whitened windowpane into the night, struggled to master the unmasterable truth about his only son, his only wife.

What flaw was in his life? What curse lay upon him? What must he do to be saved, or save those he loved?

His desperate eyes fell on his brief case lying on top of his desk. Thank God for homework. He sat down at the desk, drew out the long envelope bearing the green wax blobs of the State Department, broke the seal, and spread the drawings on his desk. Restraining his curiosity to examine the diagrams, he first read the letter from Oliphant, Under Secretary of State.

My dear Cobb:
    The accompanying sheets recently submitted to us by an American inventor describe, as you will see, a device of utmost significance. It is the Department's intention—in conjunction with the General Staffs of the Army and Navy—to proceed with the manufacture of an experimental model. First, however, we should like to be protected against infringements on existing patents, and would appreciate your studying the matter with this end in view.
    I need not emphasize that the enclosed material is highly confidential in nature.
                                    Sincerely yours,
                                        Jared C. Oliphant
                                        Under Secretary of State

With pulse-quickening curiosity Cobb scrutinized the India-ink drawings before him. He saw what appeared to be a massive electromagnet coil wound over a nickel-alloy core, all contained in a kind of oversized bakelite drum. There were no moving parts; the whole device was nothing but a tool for hurling electrons along a spiral path, then shooting them out of an aluminum tube in the fashion of an atom buster.

But what were they to be shot at?

The small hairs on the back of Ruston Cobb's neck grew hot and prickly as he studied the drawings. Could it be? Was this *it*—the last and deadliest of the machines that every scientist dreaded, predicted, deplored, yet frantically tried to invent?

He turned to the typewritten sheets accompanying the sketch and read the first sentence:

"The purpose of this device is to disarrange the photons of light. . . ."

He read swiftly, skippingly. "Law of Lawrence . . . has established that if electrons (units of matter) are speeded up to velocity of 186,000 miles per second, they are transformed into photons (units of light). . . . By controlling speed of electrons, this device can disarrange entire spectrum . . . intensify light rays to burning power over a large area of earth surface . . . or . . . induce total darkness. . . ."

So here it was. Fracturer of the sun, cyclotron of darkness, logos of the death wish, sin of inventive presumption that would destroy the world.

Down the hallway a telephone bell was ringing.

CHAPTER 8

COBB'S HEAD went up abruptly. Who could be calling at such an hour? He opened his door, heard the bell throbbing through the darkened house, and started down the corridor. As he passed Nolla's door, she opened it and glanced at him, her eyes wide with questioning.

Cobb lifted the instrument off its hook. Through a confused murmuring like distant surf, he heard the metallic clink of coins falling into a pay-station box. "Hello? Hello?" he cried. Then, very small and panicky, the voice of Sicely came through.

"Daddy, it's me, Sice."

"Sice? Where in the world are you?"

"I'm in the Albany railroad station. Oh, Daddy, it's—it's terrible here."

Cobb clamped a calm falsity over his voice. "Why, Sice, how's it happen you're in the Albany station? I thought you'd be back at school by now."

"It's the storm. We've been on the train all day, coming down from Middlebury. The tracks were piled with snow and the engine broke down and had to be dug out with shovels because the snow-plow broke down too." A little wail entered Sicely's recital. "The station is full of people, lying on the floor and everything. I'm frightened. Tell me what to do."

"Aren't any trains leaving? Have you asked the station master?"

"He says everything is stopped."

Cobb's brain was confronted by a white barrier thick and high, a barrier that he could not pierce or leap. His words came stumblingly as he tried to reassure his daughter.

"Now, Sice, there's no cause for alarm," he said soothingly. "I know it's a bad storm and things are all tied up everywhere. We're practically snowed in here, too. But it's bound to lift tomorrow. The railroad plows will be out and the tracks will all be cleared. Just go into the station lunchroom and have something to eat. It'll help keep your courage up."

"But there's no food there," said Sice. "It's all gone."

"Can't you get a cab to a hotel?"

"I tried, but there's a blizzard howling and the streets are choked with snow. It's worse than anything I've ever seen." Her voice broke completely. "Come and get me, please, Father."

"Of course, darling." Even in giving the promise Cobb wondered how he could fulfill it. Terrifying calculations oppressed him: darkness and wind reigned over the night world; Albany was a long sixty-five miles away and all roads were blocked solid with snow. It would be impossible to start out till daybreak. By that time, perhaps, the storm would be over.

Cobb's words were like a finger under his daughter's chin. "Sice, dear, hold on till morning, can you? If the storm hasn't broken by then, I'll come and get you. Meanwhile, bundle up in some extra clothes and hold on tight. . . . And oh, Sice, say the 'Our Father' over and over." He gave her a jollying, "We aren't afraid of a little old snowstorm, are we, Sice?"

"No, Daddy, I'm not afraid any longer. I'll do just what you say."

"That's the big girl. Remember, Daddy's coming."

"I'll remember. Good night, Daddy."

"Good night, Sice."

Two whistling blows struck the house with giant fists; the wind was a boxer trying for a quick knockout. The whole wing shivered as Cobb walked back toward his room.

Nolla's door was open. She had been listening, and fright made her eyes phosphorescent in the bluish light.

"How are you going to do it, Ruston? How can you possibly go for her? Even if the snow stops, the roads will be blocked for days."

"I know, darling. But I had to promise her something. She was all panicky, like you are now." Cobb put his arm comfortingly around his wife, stroked the tendrils of hair at her temples. He felt closer to her than he had for years; a wish that he might spend the rest of his life comforting her filled him with protecting strength. "Look, dear"—he held her off a little, pretending to marvel at her lack of faith—"haven't you always said I was at my best when the going was toughest? Do you really *believe* I can't get to Albany tomorrow?"

"Please don't be masterful, Rust. I know you can get there if you make up your mind to. But how? You certainly can't drive the car."

"That's true." His mood of buoyancy was gone now.

"And it's too far to walk."

Cobb nodded as if he had never intended to walk anyway. Then he asked very deliberately, "Have you forgotten the River?"

"The Hudson? But it's frozen, isn't it?"

"Yes, but they keep a channel open for tankers." Cobb was pacing up and down Nolla's room now, one fist clenched in rising excitement as he talked to himself. "I can get down to the River on skis. Then"—the rest of the plan was tentative—"then I could either hail a passing tanker, or better yet, break the *Chip* out of the boathouse." He whirled on Nolla triumphantly. "That's it! The *Chip!* Its outboard motor makes eight miles on a gallon of gas—ten with the tide. I could snake through to Albany in about six or seven hours"—he steadied the excitement in his voice—"grab Sicely, and be back here by tomorrow night. Nolla, Nolla, I can *do* it!"

He threw his arms around his wife, hugged her deliriously. "This is going to be an *expedition*. Wake up Mrs. Rollefson. Tell her to make a dozen sandwiches and a thermos jug of coffee."

"When—will you start?" faltered Nolla.

"As soon as everything's ready. The quicker I get there, the less danger for Sice."

Nolla lifted the curtain, peered through the crusted pane. "It's pitch black out there. You can't go out in that darkness."

"I'll take the big flashlight. It throws a beam like the headlight of a locomotive." Cobb's rising glance caught Nolla as she stood holding the parted curtain. Again the Greek posture, the sadness of a weak lamp throwing its helpless ray against the brawling dark. Pity for her lostness, a renewed determination to pillar her frailty with supporting strength, teemed into Cobb's open heart. All his failures with this woman were forgotten as he took her in his arms.

"I love you, Noll," he said. "More than anything, more than all. Kiss me, darling. Make me strong enough for both of us."

She turned her face up, gave him almost the kiss he wanted. Then with a maternal firmness not to be shaken by her husband's impetuous energy, Nolla made a decision.

"You can't go till morning," she said. "Sicely can wait. I won't let you go till the light comes."

*　　*　　*

Dawn lay like a leaden casket over the fields as Cobb opened the living-room window—the front door was blocked with snow—and let himself out into the storm. The wind had died down, but snow was still falling heavily on a monotonous landscape barely relieved by steeps or hollows. The road was completely obliterated, and no familiar thing remained above the drifts.

Like looking at a compass that's lost its needle, thought Cobb. He turned his back upon the smudged glow in the east—the Hudson lay directly west—tested the snow by inching forward on his skis, then, poles gripped firmly in his gloved hands, pushed off toward the river.

Ruston Cobb was wearing a ski suit of wind-resistant gabardine and a visored cap with furred ear flaps. On his feet were stout square-toed boots harnessed to hickory skis. Strapped to his back were a shovel and a small ax. In a knapsack he carried a dozen sandwiches, a thermos jug full of coffee. A flat checkbook and three hundred and twenty dollars in cash—all the ready money in the house—were in his billfold. Anything additional would have been mere baggage, fatal impedimenta on a journey that was going to tax his last reserves of strength and endurance.

On skis Cobb was barely average—nothing exceptionally graceful or skilled about his performance. The snow was far from ideal; no matter how he tried to skim across its surface, he sank into the fluffy matrix, and the task of lifting the snow-covered skis with every step was a strength-sapping job. Snowshoes would have been more fitting to the assignment, but he had no snowshoes. After a half mile of struggling he was so exhausted that he had to rest against the trunk of a tree until the good second wind came.

Advancing against the snow barrage he came to the main road, unplowed and tumultuous with drifts. Another thousand feet, and Cobb felt the ground sloping downward in a slow descent to the River. He had traversed this terrain countless times on his way to his boathouse; every hillock and hollow was balanced in his unconscious like little counterweights keeping the scales of memory even and steady. But now the snow had hidden all landmarks; it was as if a huge eiderdown mattress had been dumped over a workbench, burying the tools, blueprints, the desk itself. Cautionary prudence halted him; he knew there were dangerous gullies and deep ravines flanking the narrow path leading down to the River. If he fell into one of them . . .

Cobb drew a small compass from his pocket, lined up his course with the position of the sun and the known location of the boat-house. Hmm, a couple of degrees off his beat. Rather than change his course as he walked (the risk of falling into a crevasse was too great), he climbed back up the slope and began the familiar descent again. He discovered that the tiny counterweights of instinct located in the soles of his feet were trustier guides than all the powers of intellect. So it was true that a flier's brains were in the seat of his pants! How much men had forgotten from walking across smooth floors, sitting in plumb chairs, sleeping in level beds.

The River! Cobb could see it now, an icy tundra quiet as death. Somewhere, grooving its center, was the open channel, and once the *Chip* was in that channel, Sice was as good as saved.

Here was the boathouse, looking like an oblong igloo. Cobb un-strapped his shovel, laid aside his pack, and began to dig away the damp, heavy snow. He dug like a methodical maniac for half an hour, making a runway from the boathouse door to the top of the snowfield. With a blow of his hatchet, he broke the small padlock. And there, scarcely bigger than a bathtub, lay the *Chip,* varnished and glistening.

She was a clinker-built dinghy, tough and sturdy, but still fear-fully light for an ice breaker. Cobb remembered once carrying it bodily across a short portage; minus its motor, it probably weighed a hundred pounds. Now he patted its chubby prow, hefted it affec-tionately.

"You've got to come, baby." He took a big mouthful of brandy from his flask, glanced upward at the hidden face of the sun, then laid both hands on the *Chip's* anchor thwarts and heaved. The little boat slipped along the snowy incline like a sea sled, and Cobb found that by his tugging at her anchor rope she followed him like a small hippy duck eager to reach the water. Tugging, resting, nip-ping his brandy, Cobb reached the channel and shoved the *Chip* into the River with a final push at her curved rump. She floated like her name, taking her element with a bobbing grace. Cobb chortled as he buried the anchor in the snow, then raced back to the boathouse for his pack and the ten-gallon can of gasoline.

Returning, he settled himself in the *Chip's* stern and began the critical job of warming up the compact little motor, cold as a flanged icicle. He flooded the carburetor, turned the flywheel over and over, listening for the sweet, sucking noises of gas being drawn into the intake manifold. How were the batteries? *Bang!* A spark met a spray of half-volatilized gas. *Bang! Bang!* Cobb's heart exploded with relief. The plugs were firing! Patiently he teased the cold motor into popping warmth. *Bang, bang! Brrrrr!* The flywheel spun round for two seconds, went dead. Again he primed, coaxed, tinkered. Then, like a package of fusees touched off by a match, the motor roared into a connected chain of explosions. The propeller flew round like an egg beater in the icy river slush, and the little boat darted off like a waterbug for a huge ice cake in the center of the channel. Cobb barely had time to seize the tiller and deflect the waterbug's course. The *Chip* grazed the ice cake, headed northward along the only open road to Albany.

It was ten-ten by Cobb's wrist watch when he passed Canbuoy 233, a couple of miles upstream. From this buoy he knew it was exactly fifty-nine miles to the dock of the Albany Boat Club. By averaging ten miles an hour—the tide was coming in now, lifting the *Chip's* speed to eleven or twelve knots—he would reach Albany, barring mishap, some time in the late afternoon. Could Sice hold on till then? What would she eat till he came? Cobb supposed that the railroad would take emergency measures to feed the stranded throng in the depot. Still, one couldn't be sure. He tickled the *Chip's* throttle to get an extra revolution from the motor, and peered into the thick white curtain sweeping across the dinghy's bow. So much snow. Where did it all come from? He jockeyed the little boat past rafts of floating ice, holding her prow to the center of the channel. At noon he ate a roast-beef sandwich, swallowed a quantity of hot coffee from the thermos. Steady, Sice. Daddy's coming.

The weather grew colder. By 1 P.M. Cobb was slowly freezing at the tiller. When the little tank ran out of gas, he was glad of the chance to move about as he refilled it from the ten-gallon can. Another nip of brandy, some flapping of arms, and he was off again. Huddled in the stern sheets, wrapped in a tarpaulin, he piloted the *Chip* up the great water-course, under the bare span of Rip Van Winkle's Bridge, past buried towns, penetrating deeper along the mesial groove with the thick-flung seed of snow clinging to its fringes. Thoughts came like the snow, thick and churning, flake upon flake of old remembering, present fantasy, and future wish— a dream blizzard converging from all points of time onto the frosted windowpane of now.

A chip off the old universe, hexagonal and glistening like a six-pointed star above a fallen tower. Thousands killed as millions fleer. This is your Television Eye bringing you a pimp's glimpse of De Golyer's radioactivated sweetheart shrimps. The purpose of this machine is to disarrange by bombardment the non-ferrous metals contained in the object hereinafter guaranteed to cast eighty-six wedding rings. Springtime the only pretty ringtime get yours at Richter and Dehn's and place klepto-acknowledgment of indiscretion in discreet safety-deposit vault.

Jocasta with the light thin hair.

Promise me now upon this burning book, my heart (I promise, love), that never a commoner beat shall chill our blood unless Bart Waley doesn't come with the oil. Hasn't come yet, won't come ever, how can I make her come? Kiss? Only the cheek, ghostly lover, while that ghostly other stands by my bed with a hatchet in her hand. Whose mother? Not mine, sir. Then whose, sir? The mother of you, sir.

Don't put your daughter on the stage, Mrs. Worthington.

Nip.

Laimbeer? Inconceivable. Wouldn't dare right in the same house. Very attractive. Plenty of the old pezazz in a gloomy, Left Bank sort of way. *Beaucoup en rapport. Mais oui. Tu souffres, mon ami.* You have revealed us shamelessly by the light of your blue lamp. Will you not expose a little of yourself, madame? Indubitably well hung or Berry doesn't know her hangers. A coming young woman. Could strangle a man between hot, buttered muffins.

Cobb blinked his thick eyelashes like a windshield wiper to clear them of snow. On the west bank of the River he vaguely made out woebegone Athens, New York, looking like an Eskimo village. Two o'clock, and Albany thirty miles away. He stood up, flailed his arms, refilled the gas tank, and was off again, a solitary, stubborn mover in a stubborn, unmoved universe.

High on that headland he had picnicked with Lucy in a field of strawberries and milkweed. While May was making up to June, she had lain amid the tessellated leaves, face up to the cloudless sky, arms outflung, her mouth ready to give or keep, her nipples ruddier than the strawberries staining her blouse. Long ago and far away, sad as the cheap nostalgia of a hit-parade song. Into a roadstand juke box they had pushed nickels. "Others find peace of mind in pretending; couldn't I, couldn't you, couldn't we?" No, that wasn't the theme song for Lucy. Those strawberry pledges of love could not be happy at the nibbling game of snatch in the hay. This rick must burn with a leaping flame or not at all. If not, then not . . .

Cobb had the weary feeling of having gone over all this before, but he looked back at the strawberry headland till it faded in the snowy fog.

"Renounce," saith the Lord, in a very tired voice.

"I could conjugate that verb for you in all tenses,' replied Ruston Cobb, very cold now. "Test me on a new verb, Magister. Try me on *amo*. '*Amo te*, Sicely.' "

Nip.

The River was narrowing now. Across the bleak, townless stretch

] 128 [

south of Albany, an unimpeded gale blew from east to west, driving snowflakes like slingshot pellets into Cobb's face. Ice cakes piled thicker in the channel; to avoid crashing into them he throttled down the *Chip's* motor, threaded his way through the heavy floes. Twice he had to stand in the bow with a boathook, thrusting aside miniature bergs and coaxing his boat through narrow defiles of ice, slowing the forward motion of the *Chip* to three or four miles an hour. The dull wheel of the sun turned inexorably through the afternoon, wearing away the minutes like a cruel grindstone. At 4 P.M. the tide hung motionless, then turned to run seaward, hurling rough chunks of ice against the little boat. Minute by minute the cold blur of the sun dimmed into snow-filled darkness. At five-thirty Cobb knew that the *Chip* could go no further that night.

Only fifteen miles from Sicely! But he must wait till tomorrow.

It was imperative that he get the boat out of the river before the ice cakes crushed its fragile timbers. Cobb steered into a little cove, leaped onto the bank, and jerked the *Chip's* bow clear of the water. Only the immediate demands of survival shielded him from complete despair.

Cobb turned the boat over, making a shelter against the storm. He munched a sandwich, gulped lukewarm coffee, and began to feel indestructible again. Let the stupid elements rage. He had food, liquor, and shelter; he could last the night.

Up from the snow beneath him climbed a cold he had never known, the brutal rising cold of death. It bound his muscles with icy cords, chilled the red waterfall of his heart. The cold leaped upon a black trapeze and did a deathly giant swing. Feeling its fearful breeze, Cobb knew that he must have a fire or perish.

With his hatchet he chopped the seats out of his little boat, split them lengthwise, and stacked them in a tepee-shaped pile just beyond the curve of the *Chip's* gunwale. Then he hacked a big corner off his tarpaulin, chopped it into shreddy strips, and tucked them kindling-wise between the chinks of the firewood. Carefully he poured some gasoline into a bailing can and sprinkled a few tea-spoonfuls on the little pyre—not too much, lest the blaze rage itself out in furious burning. Striking a match, he held it to the soaked canvas; lickingly the little flame devoured the gas-soaked kindling, took hold of the broken wood.

Cobb had gauged to a drop the amount of gasoline that would make the fire serviceable to him. He leaned toward it to absorb its life-giving heat, nourishing it from time to time with a spoonful of gas, another shred of tarpaulin, another splinter of wood. When the *Chip's* seats were burned, he started on the floorboards; wet with bilge water, they needed more gasoline to coax them into flame. By ounces he doled out the inflammable liquid, nursed the miniature blaze through two hours of life.

The fire was like an infant putting its lips to a grown man, breathing into him the tiniest draught of life-giving warmth.

The baby's breath was failing. Only a few ounces of gas remained.

Now from downriver came a finger of light tentatively searching the tapestry of snow as if looking for a focus of interest. The low zoom of a fog-horn vibrated against Cobb's eardrums. His heart gave a double ruffle like a snare drum before music. Searchlight? Fog-horn? What other craft was on the river? *Zoom, zoom!* Two searchlights now, one steady on the course, the other freelancing along the riverbanks. In the penumbra cast by the roving light, Cobb saw a low, whalelike bulk plowing up the channel. *Zoom, zoom!*

A tanker! Albany bound. *Amo te,* Sicely. Daddy is coming. Blow, winds, and crack your cheeks, but the indestructible Daddy is com-ing for his Sicely. Cobb moved instinctively to the gasoline tank, dumped it all on his fire. A great flare shot upward, illuminating the dead waste like a flash bulb. Cobb placed himself between the flare and the oncoming tanker, waved his arms, danced, shouted maniac nonsense between megaphoned hands.

"Tanker, ahoy! No-*co*-ny! Stop! Hey, stop! Stop and pick me up."

A shrill toot answered yes to everything. The roving searchlight picked him up like a surgeon's probe, blinded him. Bells from the tanker's wheelhouse slowed down the propeller. The leviathan of the inland waterways slid alongside and a voice from the deck cried, "Douse that blaze or we can't come in."

Cobb threw armfuls of snow on the fire. Then a new direction from the tanker: "Grab the after ladder and make it snappy."

Standing on the edge of the ice, Ruston Cobb extended his arms as though to catch a chariot swinging low from heaven. He felt the plates of the tanker exuding cold as they brushed past him. How would he know when to grab? The beam of a small flashlight came over the side. He saw the iron ladder, gripped the handles, and swung himself up four rungs to the deck.

The propellers of Nocony Tanker No. 89, Captain Matt Gurley commanding, took up their northward churning once more.

* * *

"It's against company orders, and it may lose me my job," said Matt Gurley, "but I've a daughter myself and to hell with company orders. So give me the two hundred dollars and it's a deal."

Captain Gurley, a small man with a purple rudder of a nose and pale, triangular ears, sat on a chair with sawed-off legs and jabbed his forefinger at the world outside his wheelhouse. "Bad, bad—the worst in memory," he said with Calvinistic piety as Cobb handed him the roll of bills. "A judgment is falling on mankind," he sighed as he watched the rest of the money go back into Cobb's wallet.

"When do we reach Albany?" asked Cobb, interrupting the homily.

Gurley glanced at his chronometers, ticking four abreast. "We're due at Pier 13 in an hour—eight bells. Then four or five hours to pump out. Oil flows slower when it's cold." He spoke obliquely, like a deacon suggesting marriage to a rich widow.

"Have a nip of brandy," suggested Cobb.

"God's liniment for cureless aches," said the Captain, downing a precious two ounces.

"Cureless aches, indeed." Cobb took a drop and put the bottle in his hip pocket. "Must save some for my daughter," he explained apologetically. "And after you pump out—" Cobb shielded his anxiety with a casual lift of voice—"do you turn downriver again?"

"That," said Gurley, "depends."

"Depends on what?"

"On orders," said the Captain. "And maybe a few other things." Through the narrow wicket of Gurley's eyes, Cobb saw the man's weakness. "I could make it worth your while to start downriver as soon as your tanks are empty," he said.

Gurley got up from his low stool with sudden alacrity. "You must be hungry," he observed.

"I am."

"Could you eat a bowl of stew for ten dollars?"

"And tip the waiter five. In advance." He handed Gurley fifteen dollars. The Captain whisked off and returned a few moments later with a bowl of lukewarm lamb stew and two slices of bread.

"Free," he said pointing to the bread. "In honor of our unseen guest, Christ Jesus."

"His presence blesses our feast," said Cobb, wolfing the greasy stew. He ate a slice of bread and put the other in his pocket. "For my daughter, just in case."

Gurley nodded understandingly. "Some places charge extra if the food isn't eaten on the premises."

Cobb waited to let the oil of amiability rise to the surface of his voice. "Captain, just to save ourselves from undignified haggling about this, that, and the other thing—dockage, corkage, carrying charges, and whatnot—suppose I agree to give you all the money left in my wallet when you dump us at an appropriate place down-river."

"A God-marked and constructive idea," said Gurley. "It will, as you say, put an end to unseemly bicker and barter."

A commotion forward pricked Gurley's doughy ears to attention. "Heavy ice," he muttered, and started for the cabin door. A cautious thought made him turn for a last admonition. "When you bring your daughter aboard," he whispered, "take the midship ladder and go straight to my cabin forrard. What the crew don't see won't make them crosseyed." He was gone like a rat leaping through a porthole.

"A God-marked and constructive rascal," thought Ruston Cobb, moved to admiration by Gurley's unvarnished greed. His admiration mounted as he watched the Captain bring his craft into the harbor and warp it alongside Pier 13, nestling the tanker into its berth with a professional flourish that no amateur boatman could ever hope to equal. The man might be a text-mouthing hypocrite, but he could certainly handle this iron ark of his.

Through the swirling snow Cobb could see a few scattered points of light—all that was visible of the storm-bound city. His knowledge of the Albany waterfront was slight, but he judged that the railroad station lay about five hundred yards due west of Pier 13. All you had to do was follow a long street and turn to the right, barely a quarter of a mile in all. But how could a man without skis or snowshoes traverse that distance without bogging down? It would be like floundering through a marsh with a quicksand bottom—more a wrestling with the snow than a progress through it. Why hadn't he thought of tossing his skis onto the deck of the tanker?

Cursing himself for an unforehanded fool, Cobb cast his eyes along the iron decks looking for a loose board, a barrel stave, or anything else that would sustain his weight, shutter-fashion, on top of the snow. But the glare of the tanker's searchlight revealed only a bare deck, with a couple of fifty-gallon oil drums in the bow.

] 133 [

Cobb saw the oil drums, rejected them as unserviceable to his need, then in a double take came back to them quickly. A wildly ingenious plan was forming in his mind. He walked toward the oil barrels. He touched the rim of the nearer oil drum, rocked it easily with his hand. Empty!

Exulting, he tossed it onto the snow-covered pier and leaped into the drifts after it.

Now began a laborious progress up the long street. Pushing the drum ahead of him like a huge rolling pin, Cobb packed down a path sufficiently firm to bear his weight. Street lamps cast murky gleams over the senseless spectacle of a lone man pushing an oil drum through the snow. Tenement dwellers peeping out of top-story windows wondered what the man was doing out there. They did not know that he was putting to primitive use that greatest of inventions, the wheel. A window was flung up and a voice shouted drunkenly, "Hey, mister, got a match?" Cobb had no breath for drolleries. Gasping, rolling his barrel, he struggled on.

At the end of the street his strength was failing; his heart could not stand the strain. Exhausted, he lay panting across the barrel. This was the bottom of the pit. The tomb itself, and no one to roll away the stone. Cobb had no more life to spend, no more heart to pump with. In a confused blur he realized that it had been a mistake, this coming out to play at being God. Presumption. Sin that would destroy the world. Sicely. Find bread in pocket. Lungs bursting. Nolla with the thin brown hair.

Darkness.

He heard a roaring in his ears, felt himself being borne along on a powerful wave, lifted up, up, tossed like a chip in the air. Dazzling lights clawed at his eyeballs. Heavy machinery was grunting near by and the purpose of this machine was to disarrange the photons of light.

A man with a railroad lantern was standing over him. "Holy Jesus, he's alive," the man was saying.

Cobb sat up in the snow. "I want to get to the railroad station," he said.

"Well, in a funny ass-backward way, you made it, mister. You're in the station yard right now. You must have been on the track back there someplace, and the plow pushed you right into the station." The man turned to his companion. "We ought to collect a ticket from this guy, Beany. All passengers got to have tickets."

Cobb tried to remember something very important.

"Is Sicely in the station?" he asked.

The men looked at each other like trawlers who had pulled an unexplainable fish from the deep.

"She oughter be. No one's left the place for a coupla days. Our plow is the first thing through in forty-eight hours."

Cobb got up unsteadily. He wanted a nip of brandy, but he could not risk offering a pull to the plow crew. Must keep some for Sice.

"How do I get into the station?"

"Down the stairs and through the tunnel," said the man with the lantern. "C'mon, Beany, we ain't Saint Bernard dogs." Then he shouted after Cobb, "Hope you find her, mister! But damned if I know what you're going to do with her when you do."

* * *

The railroad station was a fetid shambles, jammed to the doors with a storm-bound throng. Luggage and refuse were strewn about the floor; the cold ammonial odor of clogged latrines was uppermost. Men, women, children, and infants sat or lay in attitudes of disorder or illness, huddled under coats, bedding rolls, or newspapers. The place had not been policed for days; it had the air of being on an hour-to-hour basis, waiting for something to happen—a train to take the people away, food supplies to come in, rescuers to arrive. But nothing had happened, and the temper of the inmates was a mixture of irritable suspense and mounting fear.

The black hands of the marble-faced station clock registered nine thirty-five as Ruston Cobb threaded his way through the disorganized crowd searching for traces of his daughter. He cast his eyes over heaps of baggage, looking for the pyramid of skis, ski poles, and snowshoes that would mark Sicely's crowd. But neither the sporting equipment nor the girls were to be found in the station. Frantically he buttonholed a forlorn colored porter sitting dejectedly on a heap of luggage—a Negro Elijah unfed by ravens.

"Have you seen a bunch of young girls anywhere around—school kids with skis? My daughter was with them."

The porter, recognizing the signs of an anxious father, waved an enormously tired, thin hand in the direction of the lunchroom. "They're all in there, mister," he said wearily. "I laid 'em kind of to one side, just in case." He lifted a pair of beagle eyes to communicate his meaning more exactly.

The sheer goodness of the man smote Cobb like a knout. He pulled a handful of loose change from his pocket, pressed it into the porter's hand. Slightly absurd.

The porter looked at the money as if it were something remembered from another life. "Much 'bliged, sir. But I don't know's this stuff'll be any use much longer." He gazed past Cobb, talking to him as though he were a shadow. "Seems I hear the doomwind blowin' through that snow outside. Doo—oom, doo—mm," he moaned through gray lips. "We's wronged Him, and He's bury'n' us for our wrongs."

Cobb started toward the lunchroom. He stepped across recumbent figures, avoided a puddle of vomit, and burst through the lunchroom door. The lights were dim here, but he could see a number of young girls sitting dejectedly on lunch-counter stools, others lying flat on the counters. In the half-light, Cobb could not distinguish his daughter from the others.

"Sicely!" he cried in a great voice. "Are you here?"

In a wild start of unbelief, the prostrate figure of a young girl rose on one elbow.

"Daddy!" She tumbled off the counter, leaped across the debris of tables and baggage, and threw herself sobbing into her father's arms.

He held her for a long minute, smoothing her blond hair, fondling her as a violinist might fondle an instrument saved from a flood. All intact. Pale, dirty, and tear-streaked, but undamaged. She had grown since Cobb had seen her last. In caressing her, his hands encountered unexpected fullnesses of breast and hips. At seventeen, Sicely was a full-grown woman, with promises of Berry about her lushness and traces of Nolla's pastel coloring in her eyes and hair.

She clung to her father ecstatically, kissing his face with the happiness of a child, bracing her body against his with the joy of a woman whose lover has come to take her away.

"I knew you'd come. They all said you couldn't make it, but I told them that nothing was impossible to my daddy." Overcharge of emotion shook her with sobs.

"Cry your eyes out, darling. Everything's all right now. Here, swallow some of this." He put the brandy flask to her mouth. "Another gulp, Sice."

She gulped bravely, stemmed her sobs. Cobb drew Gurley's piece of bread from his pocket. It was soggy and broken. "Eat this, Sice." He put it into her mouth. Between hunger and obedience the bread disappeared.

"Now grab your skis. We're getting out of here. Come just as you are, and don't ask any questions. No, we can't bring anyone with us. Get your skis and come."

From the heap of equipment on the floor, Cobb appropriated a pair of snowshoes. Then, leading Sice to the front door of the station, he fitted the shoes to his feet and stepped out into the snow-filled gale. Cobb broke trail, packing down the snow for his daughter. The brandy, bread, and the excitement of her delivery from the fetid railway station acted as stimulants to her bubbling energy. She was on a lark with her father, companioning him through the rough weather they both loved. She didn't even ask where he was taking her.

"Mush on!" she shouted against the wind.

The journey to the tanker took almost an hour. Powdered sleet cut their faces. There were no lights in the houses now; everyone had gone to bed leaving the outside world to wind and snow. Cobb could not see the green light of the tanker, but held his course toward the river until the marine searchlight came burning through the storm. From his thin reserves he managed to scrape up enough breath to cry, "Hurray, Sice, we've made it!"

Coming into the circle of the tanker's light, Cobb found the midship ladder. He would obey Gurley's orders: What the crew didn't see would never give them crosseyes.

"Up you go, Sice." He held her arm while she kicked off her skis, gave her a hand up the iron rungs, flung her skis after her. Then, taking off his snowshoes, he climbed up, snowshoes under his arm. Never had he felt anything so solid, so good as that iron deck.

Gurley's empty cabin was snug against the wind. Cobb and Sicely sat down on the two sawed-off stools, gazed at each other, and listened to the pumping engines. Suddenly the engines stopped.

"What *is* this?" she asked with humorous grimace.

"An oil-burning version of the Albany night line." Weary though he was, Cobb felt jokish, giggly, as he always did with Sice. She was the only person in the world he could habitually laugh with. Lucy had been grave, Nolla rarely smiled, Derry's passionate intensity turned to other things than laughter. But ten minutes with Sicely, and Cobb was giggling like a sundae-lapping freshman. They were laughing at nothing in particular when Gurley opened the door, letting in a mixed draft of blizzard and oil fumes.

The Captain had the look of a garage dealer about to palm off a defective tire on a stranded motorist. Obviously he had changed his mind about something, and Cobb waited for the new pitch.

"They'll be a little delay in shoving off," announced Gurley.

"Oh?"

"Fact is, I'm half expecting orders *not* to head downstream to-night."

Cobb saw a faint glimmer of intent. "But you haven't got the orders yet, is that it, Captain?"

Gurley nodded. "They're sure to come if I wait for them here. Sure as predestination."

"Hmm, a nice point of theology." Cobb decided to let this theologian develop his point further.

"But suppose," went on Gurley, eager not to be misconstrued, "suppose I was also predestined to receive, say, a piece of negotiable paper."

"You mean a check?"

"That's it."

"A check for five hundred dollars?"

Gurley shook his head. " 'Twouldn't outweigh the other."

Cobb wanted to find out how clear the Captain's theology was. "What other?"

"Getting orders not to start downstream."

"Well, then, a thousand dollars?"

"No-o." Clearly the Captain intended to put a high value on his orthodoxy.

Cobb looked at Sice. How tired and drawn she was. If only he could get her something to eat. "While we discuss this matter of predestination, Captain, could you have your steward serve up a sandwich and a cup of something hot for my daughter?"

"I'll get it myself. See if any orders have come yet." Gurley darted out the door.

Sice registered blank amazement. "What a horrid, sinister little man. Why, it's blackmail."

"Extortion is the word, dear. The act or practice of obtaining anything by the illegal use of fear, force, or threat, duress, torture, or any undue exercise of power or ingenuity. Incidentally, a crime in the state of New York."

"But I thought people always helped each other in times of disaster."

"Most people do, darling. The extortioner is a biologic sport, occurring once in a million times. You mustn't think that all Nocony tanker captains are like Gurley."

A new crease of bewilderment appeared in Sicely's forehead. "How does he know your check will be a good one?"

Cobb had to smile at Sicely's penetration. "Our captain is a rare mixture of cupidity and trust, darling. He knows exactly how much I'll pay to get started downstream, and he also knows that I won't give him a bad check or stop payment on the one I do give him. He reminds me, for some reason or other, of that fine old American Elder Brewster."

Elder Brewster Gurley came into the cabin carrying some bread and meat on a tray.

"No orders," he announced sententiously. "Seems the Lord's will is not yet revealed."

While Sicely devoured her sandwich, Cobb decided to reveal the Lord's will to Gurley at the latter's figure.

"Captain," he began, "I don't want you to labor too cheaply under the weight of your scruples. I know they're heavy: you should be paid well for carrying them." Cobb drew out his folding checkbook. "In terms of a National City Bank check, how much will you take to start downstream at once?"

"Five thousand dollars."

"Give me a pen."

Gurley, sorry he hadn't asked for more, produced a pen. Cobb wrote out a check and handed it to him.

"For a man who can charge ten dollars for a bowl of stew, I don't think your charges for a sixty-mile boat ride are excessive."

"Specially," said Gurley, "if you consider the weather."

The arrangements for the trip downriver were simple. Cobb and Sicely were to sleep in Gurley's bunk house and be routed out at a point specified as Canbuoy 233. Three miles south of that point, they were to be put over the side. " 'Twill be about dawn," said Gurley, stealthily closing the cabin door behind him.

Cobb bolted the door, grinned at his daughter. "Imagine, Sice! Home for breakfast! But we've got to get some sleep. You take the bunk and I'll sleep on the floor."

Sicely estimated the width of Gurley's berth. "No," she said decidedly, "you'll not sleep on the floor. We can both fit into the bunk. I want you near me." She pulled off her ski boots, loosened the waistband of her gabardine ski pants, and rolled in toward the wall. "Come to bed, Daddy," she cried, holding out her arms.

"Sice, you're a witch," laughed Cobb, unlacing his boots. "And me, I'm tired." He lay down beside her, pulled the blanket over both of them. Half child, half woman, she snuggled into him, stirring until she found a comfortable place. Then, warm and exhausted, they both fell asleep.

A banging on the door awakened them. "Canbuoy 233," announced Gurley.

Cobb leaped to the iron deck. "We'll want coffee," he said through the door. Then he shook Sice. "Wake up, darling. We're getting off in ten minutes."

It was 7:15 A.M. when they went over the side. "God be with you," called Gurley as the tanker slid into the powdery mist.

"*Et cum spirito tuo,*" shouted Cobb. "And may you live to cash that check."

The sun was a gunmetal balloon trying to get off the horizon as father and daughter faced each other at the edge of the River. Wordlessly, the girl clamped on her skis and Cobb laced the thongs of his snowshoes in preparation for the climb from the riverbed to the road.

"Two miles to go, Sice. The last mile will be a cinch. It's getting up this riverbank that's going to cost. How're your herringbones?"

"They've taken me up steeper grades than this." Sice squinted at the ascent. "I can do it on one leg."

"Well, take it easy. And mind you, follow exactly in my steps. I know the terrain here; it's full of gullies." His pause was a prayer. "But with luck . . ."

Cobb chose a course slightly south of east, and began the laborious climb from the bed of the river up the valley wall. His muscles groaned from yesterday's exertion, his left knee creaked, and the unfamiliar snowshoes were clumsy as mattresses on his feet. But a floating sense of triumph buoyed him up. In an hour he'd be under his own roof, hazardous mission completed, his daughter-bundle safe from the storm. From time to time he glanced backward at Sicely on the trail behind him. The exertion of climbing sucked at his breath; the ascent tore at his heart muscles. Once, utterly winded, he paused to rest on the ski poles under his armpits. From behind, he felt Sice's arm under him.

"Only a few steps more, Daddy, then we'll strike the road."

The few steps were taken, but no road came into view. Instead a sheer cliff rose out of the snow. Cobb came to a dead halt.

"I've miscalculated, somehow, Sice. This cliff—I don't remember its being here."

Sicely's younger eye recognized the place. "This must be the hawk's eyrie, Daddy. The place you showed us, remember, where the goshawks make their nest?"

"But that's a quarter of a mile south of the boathouse, Sice. We can't be *that* far off our course."

Cobb's instinct told him to go back to the river and start over again. But the desperate desire to get home, his awful fatigue of body weakened his judgment. "If we cut north diagonally—" he began.

"That's it, Daddy!" cried Sice. "We'll come out at the gas station on the Brompton Road. Let me lead for a while."

Before Cobb could halt her, Sice took a skimming glide along the base of the cliff.

"Wait, Sice," he warned. "Look out for gullies. No, Sice. *No!*"

Then it happened. It seemed to Ruston Cobb that an invisible hand reached up from the snow and pulled his daughter downward. With a scream she disappeared into a crevasse, and a loosened avalanche of snow poured in after her, roaring like a heavy sea.

"Sice, Sice!" Cobb threw himself face downward in the snow and hung over the ledge. He dug at the snow with his hands, tore off his snowshoes, and shoveled with them, blaspheming, shrieking, commanding. "Come back! Come back to me, Sice! I can't lose you now. We're almost home."

Snow fell.

A hawk banking over his eyrie saw a man lying face downward at the foot of a cliff. The man was striking himself in the head with both hands; the lower half of his body was writhing like a crushed worm. The hawk circling downward watched the man's motions grow feebler until they stopped entirely and the man lay as if dead by the brink of the crevasse.

A gunmetal sun climbed a full minute up the sky. Then a speck of red appeared at the edge of the crevasse. The man lifted his head, leaped to his feet, and began a series of rapid motions. The hawk could not know that the spot of red was Sicely Cobb's mittened hand struggling up through a loose surf of snow, or that the sight of his daughter's mitten sticking out of the feathery drift sent a torrent of hope flooding through Ruston Cobb's heart.

His first instinct was to throw himself into the snowy morasse and wrestle his daughter free. But a deeper wisdom bade him remain on the ledge. He whipped a jack-knife from his pocket, fumbled at the blade, dropped it in his anxiety, and cursed God's malice as he pawed frantically for the knife in the snow. Now the blue visor of Sicely's ski cap was pushing through the drifts. Her face appeared, purple, strangulated, the flares of her nostrils sucking at the air. Cobb saw her eyelids blink. She was alive.

"Don't move, Sice," he implored. "Not a muscle."

He found the knife in the snow and ripped open the blade with bloody fingernails. "Don't move, Sice, till I toss you a line."

He tore off his gabardine ski jacket, slashed it into ribbony lengths, tied the lengths together in quick, crude knots. At one end of this improvised lifeline he made a loop, then, lying on his stomach, he lowered the knotted cloth till the loop fell near his daughter's hand.

"Reach out ever so gently, Sice, and put your hand through the loop."

His daughter's hand caught at the knotted line. "Let it fall around your wrist now," commanded Cobb. Docile with trust and exhaustion, Sicely obeyed.

Like a man playing a carp that has swallowed a priceless pearl, Cobb fished for his daughter's life. By quarter inches he pulled her toward him; now her head and shoulders were free, her breath was coming back. Wordless, she kept her eyes on his, and the thong of confidence was stronger than the noose around her wrist. Naked from the waist up, drenched with the mixed sweat of exertion and anxiety, Cobb braced himself thigh-deep in snow and slowly pulled at the gabardine lifeline while Sice worked her body free. Now she stood on top of the treacherous gully, her head scarcely a foot below him. He lay flat on his belly, grasped both of her hands in his.

"Climb now," he said, and Sicely Cobb, hands locked in her father's, worked her skis free of the quicksand snow, and climbed into life once more.

CHAPTER 9

Entering the front door of his home was Cobb's sweetest triumph. Nolla, Berry, Roddy rose from their chairs and stood moveless, like figures fixed in the amber of unbelief. Then they rushed forward with delirious shouts and pummelings, swarmed over Cobb and Sicely like privateersmen boarding a fabulous prize. Everybody was kissing and squeezing everyone else. Berry, weeping blindly, threw her arms around Cobb's bare shoulders and clung to him in a wet suction of tears and kisses. "Rusty, darling," she kept saying, "I knew you'd make it." He hugged her in a full embrace. "Good girl." Then, disengaging himself, he turned to Nolla, standing white and paralyzed behind her sister.

"Look, Nolla." He tried to laugh as he kissed her wet lashes. "I've brought Sice home for lunch."

He saw Roddy gazing up at him as an Indian boy might gaze at a tribal totem come to life. In bearish play, he cuffed his son. Now all three—Nolla, Berry, Roddy—bore down upon him at the same time, smothering him with endearments spoken and bestowed.

Laimbeer stepped forward with a decanter of whiskey in one hand, a glass in the other. "I'll pour; you drink," he said.

Cobb had forgotten the man's existence. How proprietary of him to be dispensing drinks. "Thanks." He gulped the smooth corn liquor, the finest drink that had ever passed his lips. "Pour a girl-sized one for Sice," he said, "then give me another."

"Bottoms up, Sice." Father and daughter downed the whiskey together.

And now Berry was pulling off his boots, settling his feet on a hassock, while Nolla wiped his face with a towel and covered his shoulders with a blanket. A delicious warmth began to climb upward along Cobb's legs. Heavenly. Mrs. Rollefson came in carrying a tray of coffee, toast, poached eggs. Words fluttered up from her big bosom. "Some buttered toast, Sicely. And you, Mr. Cobb. You, sir, a cup of coffee, creamed and sugared like you take it."

So much kindness, so much love. Fire, food, family, all under one roof again. Cobb tried to eat a piece of toast, to drink some of Mrs. Rollefson's coffee. Halfway through the slice of toast a drowsiness overtook his nerves and muscles. "I'm sleepy," he murmured. "I think I'll go up to my room."

"Yes, dear." It was Nolla. She helped him climb the stairs, limpingly, one step at a time. "Does the trick knee hurt?" "A bit," he grunted. In his bedroom she undressed him, pulled down the blankets, arranged pillows under his head. "Shall I rub your knee with liniment?" Without waiting for an answer, she went to his medicine chest, brought out a squarish bottle. Pouring some of the fiery liquid into her cupped palm, she rubbed it into his knee joint with maternal strokings. "Mustn't rub too hard," she murmured. "It'll burn."

Now she was making tucking motions at the side of his bed. Then she bent over and kissed his forehead. "You're a wonderful man, Rust," she said. "No one else in the world could have done it but you."

Too tired to answer, Ruston Cobb fell off the edge of a high precipice into a feathery crevasse of sleep. Outside, over the entire northeastern quadrant of the United States, snow continued to fall.

He woke luxuriously six hours later and lay in a half doze, dreaming that he was stretched on a tropical beach beside Nolla while warm waves lapped a palm-fringed shore. He heard music softened by distance coming through walls and doors. Every muscle in his body was stiff and aching, but he no longer felt tired. He got up and with broken grunts walked toward the bathtub. He filled the tub with hot water, soaked in it until his flesh was a parboiled pink. Then he rubbed soap gently into his stubbly beard. A new blade in his razor, a cold shower, thick fluffy towels. God, how good he felt. And hungry. He put on some gray slacks and a cable-weave sweater and opened the door of his room.

Dear voices and laughter were coming up the stairs. Unseen, Cobb leaned against the upper railing and drank in the happy sounds. Nolla, in one of her rare gay moods, was telling a story about a wild baby-carriage ride she had given Beryl as a baby.

"It was a new baby carriage—they called them 'prams' in those days—Brewster green, with thick rubber tires and great jouncing springs. I must have been jealous of the luxury Berry rode in. Anyway, the nurse who was supposed to be taking care of us left Berry in my hands while she made park-bench romance somewhere. How I ever pushed Berry uphill in that heavy contraption—she was a fat butter-whelk of a baby—I'll never know. But I got her *up* all right. It was the ride down that almost killed her." Nolla stopped for breath. "Berry was gurgling and cooing innocent as a lamb. I gave that baby carriage a push and away it sailed, bumping over rocks and tearing through shrubbery like a jeep (of course we didn't know what a jeep was then) until it struck a tree at the bottom of the hill. Out popped Berry, like a round, rosy piglet shot from a barrel, and landed smack on top of a man sleeping off a drunk on the grass. Oh, was that man *surprised!*"

Shrieks of gleeful laughter filled the room. "Was she hurt?" asked Roddy.

"Not a scratch," said Nolla. "When I caught up with her, she was patting the man's face and drooling all over him with contentment. The carriage was in *toothpicks*." Cobb heard Nolla's voice modulate into gravity. "Did *I* get a trouncing from my mother!"

"You mean she really beat you?" asked Sicely.

"She was a very stern woman," Nolla started to say. Cobb knew that story by heart. Eager to join the group before the note changed, he came downstairs. Shouts welcomed him: "Daddy! Rusty! How do you feel now?"

"Fit as a grasshopper. Stiff, maybe." Cobb mimicked the brittle movements of an arthritic old man reaching for a chair. "But nothing that a stiff drink wouldn't unstiffen." He tousled Sice's blond hair lightly. "How's my wonder girl?"

A tall and very good-looking young man, wearing the uniform of a naval aviation lieutenant, was in the living room. The young man stepped forward with the respectful formality of a two-striper about to salute an admiral. By the planes and coloring of his face, Cobb recognized him as Emma Rollefson's son.

"Gunnar!" Pleasure at being greeted by his Christian name brought a flush to the young man's clear skin; his hand went out, not in a salute but in a delighted handclasp, as Cobb clapped him warmly on the shoulder.

"Happy to have you aboard, Lieutenant. But when did you get here and how?"

"He flew blind, Daddy," Sice explained. "All the way up from Bennett Field. Radar. You can land in an apple tree with it." Aware that she was being voluble on a subject she had just heard about, Sicely dimpled into embarrassment. "You tell him, Lieutenant."

"Nothing much to tell, sir," said Gunnar. "I had a ten-day leave, and hadn't seen my folks for a couple of years. So"—he was finding it hard to say that the DCNO(Air) had grounded all planes—"so I just stepped into a fighter job and here I am."

"You must be a snow hawk to fly in weather like this."

"From what I hear, sir, you're something of a snow hawk yourself."

Cobb laughed. Emma Rollefson's boy had a tongue in his head. "Where's the pursuit job now?"

"There weren't any apple trees around, so I set her down in the lee of your garage. Special ski landing gear." Unwillingness to take credit for a routine performance marked Gunnar's recital. "But you, sir—I'd like to hear how *you* navigated."

"Yes, yes, tell us all about it," urged Berry.

With his family grouped around him, Cobb recounted his adventures. He made a little saga of his journey upriver, spoke of the *Chip* as a person, praised the outboard motor's stubborn heart—"Mulish at first, but never missed a rev once she got started." The fierce loneliness of the River, the coming of darkness, his expedients for a fire, and his joy at seeing the tanker's searchlight—to these Cobb gave the quick narrative treatment of a modest Ulysses rehearsing his travels to the household at Ithaca. The incident of the oil barrel in the snow brought headshaking admiration from young Rollefson; his description of the Albany railroad station caused Sicely to start sniffling quietly. As the greasy scroll of Gurley's character unwound, the audience grew indignant. "Unbelievable," murmured Nolla. "A six-way bastard," said Berry. The false ascent from the River, the lost bearings, and the near catastrophe at the gully's edge were related without adornment. They were dramatic enough in themselves, the very stuff of survival, and when the tale was done, long gasps of marvelment supplied choric relief.

The commentary of silence was broken by Nolla. "What was the worst moment, Rust?"

Glad that he had not conveyed to his wife the real danger that Sicely had been in, Cobb assessed the question broodingly. "Two things really shook me, Noll. The first was Gurley's greediness. Under ordinary conditions, one presses an advantage, sure. But in an emergency, when the whole system is falling apart, men don't ordinarily haggle about the price of life. Gurley himself is almost certain to perish, yet he put a monstrous price on a bowl of soup and a sixty-mile boat ride. It was like asking a million dollars for a rope to toss to a drowning child."

Cobb paused, gathering up the form of his next thought. "But the thing that terrified me most—more than Gurley's greed and cruelty—was the sight of a modern city paralyzed by a single sideswipe from nature. Albany isn't the biggest or most important city in the world, but it's typical. And unless this snow stops soon"— Cobb made a thumbs-down gesture—"it looks as though that ingenious rodent, the city mouse, is dangling at the end of a thread."

"While his complacent cousin, the country mouse, isn't?" asked Laimbeer.

Cobb acknowledged the touch. "To a lesser degree, yes. Take our situation here. We're dependent for light, heat, and communication on a single strand of fourteen-gauge copper wire. When that wire breaks, or goes dead—as I momentarily expect it will—this house becomes dark, cold, and isolated."

"It doesn't seem quite bright, does it, to hang so much weight on a hair of wire," said Laimbeer mockingly.

"Well, that's what we've done. Here in the country we've got a few secondary defenses to fall back on: a fireplace, candles, reserves of food. But I put it to you, Laimbeer, how many people in Albany, Queens, or Manhattan have any such secondary line of defense?"

"You're putting it to *me*? My God, Cobb, didn't I win five dollars the other day putting it to you? The whole point of my argument was that the entire structure of our city civilization is an intricate extension of the death wish. Our celebrated technology merely repeats the old, death-loving patterns traced on the mollusks of love and art." Laimbeer halted for emphasis. "How otherwise account for such suicidal devices as the radar rocket or the atom bomb? Or how else explain that huddling death trap, the City?" Laimbeer's triumph rose to a taunt. "You got angry with me when I said all this before, Cobb. A little bit of snow hasn't made you change your mind, has it?"

For a moment it occurred to Cobb that Laimbeer really had the better side of the argument. All the evidence tended to show that somewhere, somehow, man's wonderful harnessing energies had gone astray and that his very inventiveness had made him fatally dependent on devices that the elements could crumple like a fifty-cent umbrella. But to call them "intricate extensions of the death wish"—that was further than Cobb could go. He made no rejoinder to Laimbeer's taunt.

His silence was a calculated mixture of courtroom strategy (how often he had clipped an opponent's wattles with the shears of silence) and a genuine pity for the painter's cheap gloating. He was content to let Laimbeer win all the word battles—score all the runs, jerk out all the neckties, say anything that gave him comfort or bolstered his ailing ego. Ruston Cobb knew that trials lay ahead in which verbal triumphs would count for nothing, and he was saving his strength for the coming battle.

The others in the room interpreted in various ways his refusal to join Laimbeer in argument. Beryl pulled her eyebrows together in sheer unbelief at Laimbeer's low punching. The long muscles in Gunnar's arms tightened involuntarily under his tunic. "Stinker," he murmured. Nolla, putting a truer meaning on her husband's silence, saw the impasse of character and logic in which the two men, so different, were locked. She gazed into the fire, said nothing.

"Well," repeated Laimbeer, "a little bit of snow hasn't made you change your mind, has it?"

And now a natural defender rose to protect Cobb. Teeth bared in an ocelot snarl, Sicely turned on the artist. "What are you doing to my father? Why do you sit there asking questions that don't make sense? *You* didn't come through the snow to save me. You wouldn't have dared—the wind would have blown you away. But *he* came through the winds and the snow, and brought me home safe." She was shrieking now like a young Clytemnestra. "Don't you dare bother my father when he's tired!" She struggled to loose herself from Cobb's grasp so that she could claw Laimbeer's face, tear his throat. "I'll kill you, do you hear?"

"Hush, darling." Cobb held her tightly in his arms, soothing her with words and kisses. He had no thought of apologizing to Laimbeer for Sicely's outburst; his only concern now was to comfort the sobbing, hysterical child, overstrained by tension and exposure. "Cry all you want, Sice," he said, holding up his hand to warn the others away.

Under his caresses she quieted; her tremblings ceased and the sobbing died away. Cobb took out a big pocket handkerchief, held it gently to her nose.

"Blow," he said smiling. Ruston Cobb was probably never happier in his life.

As he dried Sice's eyes and saw her half-ashamed smile, he knew the fearful satisfaction of having her for a daughter. Not that he needed her championing, not that he had been really confused by Laimbeer's question. But the knowledge that a passionately raging woman was ready to defend him, and would have killed his tormentor with her bare hands, filled Cobb with unutterable joy. He knew that the world would not fall apart while people like Sicely were in it. He knew that she carried in the lining of her ovaries a force that he had transmitted to her—a force that could overcome cold, darkness, death itself.

Mrs. Rollefson came in. "Dinner," she beamed, proud to be including her son in the announcement. "I've got pot roast and dumplings for you, Mr. Cobb. I said to myself, 'What would a man like after being out in the snow for two days?' And the answer came pretty as a June sunrise. 'Pot roast and dumplings with baby carrots, onions, and mashed potatoes.'"

"Emma," said Cobb, "without anyone's permission I'm going to kiss you." He put his arm around the housekeeper's waist and gave her a smack on the cheek. A wash of laughter cleaned the air of unhappy tension. The clatter of pulled-out chairs and busy forks drowned the ominous groaning of the wind.

The warmth of good food eaten at his own table lifted Cobb's psychic temperature to a cheerful norm, and the presence of so many glowing young faces—Gunnar and Sicely were almost incandescent with delight in each other—offset the dour creases in Laimbeer's forehead. Between Beryl and Cobb ran a secret electricity that crackled when their eyes met. Berry seemed calmer, but Nolla's external poise failed to conceal an anxiety that showed itself in preoccupation and silence.

Gunnar, unaffected by these crosscurrents of personality, was entertaining Sice and Roddy with stories of his awkwardness during flight training. His humor required that he make himself the butt of everything that happened, and Roddy, thoroughly enjoying the tales, broke out into uncontrolled spasms of laughter.

"What did the captain say when you pancaked onto the deck?" he asked at the crux of a comic yarn.

The Lieutenant's answer was interrupted by a heavy thudding against the French doors of the dining room. At first it seemed as though a branch had been blown against the glass, but the frantic beating showed that a live thing was at the panes.

"What's that?" cried Nolla, starting nervously.

"Must be a branch tossed by the wind," said Cobb. "No, it can't be—there it goes again."

"It's a bird!" exclaimed Roddy, running to the door.

"Open the door and let the poor thing in," suggested Berry.

A strange exaltation surged into Cobb as he lifted his voice above the clatter. "No, that would blow a snowdrift into the room. Come on, Gunnar, we'll go outside and see what it is."

Scarcely had he spoken when a terrific blast of wind drove the thudding object through the panes of the French door. Broken glass fell clattering to the floor as a fierce-beaked bird, broad-winged and mottled with brownish-red bars, was blown onto the dining-room table. One of its wings hung limply by its side, an air foil broken by the high gale. A glance at the creature's majestic head and baleful eye told Cobb that it was a red-winged hawk, wildest of the region

] 153 [

birds, untamable and haughty in its hatred of anything that looked or smelled like a man.

By its enormous size and wingspread, he guessed it to be a female.

Nolla, Berry, and the children were huddled in a tableau of terror at the further end of the room. The hawk, more frightened than they, made a futile, crawling attempt to rise from the table. It knocked over a candlestick and now its drooping wing tip lay in a pool of spilled gravy. A desire to spare the bird the indignity of soiling itself in the debris of human food lead Cobb to approach it.

"Easy, old girl," he coaxed.

A fierce screech, chorded of rage and contempt, came from the hawk. It was followed by a *whoosh,* and Cobb felt a splatter of hot birdlime strike him full in the face. It burned his eyes, filled his nostrils with a fearful reek. Blinded, he rushed from the room, the bird's contemptuous scream in his ears. He wiped his face on his sleeve, groped his way toward the kitchen sink, turned on the faucet, and doused his face to cleanse himself of the humiliating filth.

A terrible shaking anger seized him, churned his blood with acid more corrosive than the birdlime in his eyes. He steadied himself, gripped the edge of the sink with both hands till the trembling passed.

Nolla's voice was behind him: "Are you quite all right?"

"Yes, dear, I'm all right now."

"Gunnar has taken your shotgun; he's going to kill the bird."

Through blurred, smarting eyes, Cobb saw his wife, pale and anxious, Laimbeer behind her, close, protective, almost touching.

"No one will shoot the bird, Nolla. I have something else in mind for her."

Abruptly he left the kitchen, went to a closet under the living-room stairs, where he kept his sporting gear. He pulled out a landing net that he sometimes used for Florida fishing and walked silently into the dining room. The hawk had fallen off the table and was now crouched in a corner, beak high and menacing like a feathered cobra. Cobb advanced upon the bird and with a fowler's skill folded it gently in the strong silk net. The hawk's fright and agony were pitiful as it writhed in the captive mesh.

Roddy's face was a twisted puzzle. "What are you going to do, Daddy?"

"I'm going to put her down cellar in the old woodbin. It's dark down there, and she won't be frightened by things she doesn't understand. Then, after she gets used to me, I'll—I'll try to tame her."

He carried the bird down the cellar stairs, released it through the half-open door of an empty woodbin.

"Don't dash yourself to pieces," he said, latching the door. "I'll be back to have it out with you tomorrow."

CHAPTER 10

Aʟʟ ᴛʜᴇ instruments of time and weather were functioning perfectly on the seventh day of snow—a week without precedent in the records of meteorology. The column of mercury in the thermometer outside the lozenged window hung at a constant 31° F., and the indicator of the spring barometer leaned far toward the left in the region of "Storm." Ruston Cobb, smoking an after-breakfast cigarette, twirled the television dial and listened to the doleful summary of weather news as tabulated by the *Times* bureau. The announcer was doing his best to remain impersonal and scientific, but the melancholy facts at his disposal could not lighten the gloom in his voice.

"Continuing heavy snows throughout the East, Northeast, and Central regions of the United States," he reported, "have completely paralyzed all activity in the most heavily populated area of the nation. Traffic by motor, rail, and air is at a standstill for the third successive day. No food has entered New York City in the past seventy-two hours. The snow-removal program has broken down. The entrances to the Holland Tunnel, the Grand Central and Pennsylvania Terminals are blocked tight. Local stocks of food are exhausted and want is severe among all classes of population. If the snow lasts another day, famine appears unavoidable. Fuel companies are unable to make deliveries. Thousands of homes and apartments in the metropolitan area will be without heat tonight.

Electricity and telephone service are being maintained in the urban area, but in many rural districts all wires are down and power-house failures are being reported."

Short pause. "Please stand by for an emergency announcement from the Disaster Control Board of New York City."

"This," said Cobb, "I must see."

He sharpened the focus on the television screen and discovered, seated, a group of heavy-faced administrators of the third, or municipal, class, their expressions burgherish and worried. The Honorable Timothy J. Fidd, Street Commissioner, briefly introduced, arose and presented an officially grave mien to the shaving-mirror scrutiny of the camera.

"Fellow citizens," he began, "the seriousness of the occasion and our limited time on the air bid me be both frank and brief. I will be both." Whereupon he launched into a congeries of Hibernicisms, dangling participial phrases, non-sequiturs, and other oral elegancies, to wit:

"The storm which has now lasted a week, and which, according to advices from the Weather Bureau, shows no signs of relinquishing its grip on our city, is, as you all know, causing untold hardships among all classes. None of us is escaping the ravages of the elements. Rich and poor alike, employer and employee, every merchant, housewife, and salesperson, not to mention the members of the protective forces of our great city, from the lowest patrolman, ladderman, and street cleaner to the Commissioners themselves who will follow me in addressing you here—all of us, I wish to say at this time, are, in a manner of speaking, all in the same boat.

"No one is responsible for this storm; it is an act of God. But I stand here to assure you that despite the conspiracy on the part of certain Moscow-trained agitators (I call no names, I mention no individuals), I stand here to assure you that your Administration is doing everything humanly and mechanically possible to alleviate and if possible—er—um—abate the damage being wrought by the elements. I have before me [consults a paper] the latest reports from my departmental heads, who are at this very moment forming a civic army of 10,000 snow shovelers, armed with 3,426 pieces of mechanical snow-removal equipment and 9,821 shovels against the storm. All steps are being taken, every avenue is being explored, but unfortunately the great masses of snow that have fallen during the past week have overtaxed our equipment, broken some of it, and, what is more unfortunate yet, have buried a large percentage of the remaining equipment under snowdrifts, thus rendering almost—ah—nugatory, if I may use the expression, the—er—snow-removal attempts of your Commissioner to—ah—satisfactorily remove the snow."

"Pretty depressing." The doorway framed young Rollefson's lithe figure. Just looking at Gunnar's shining cheekbones and husky shoulders took the curse off Fidd's bastard rhetoric.

"Depressing or comical—I can't decide which. But come in, Gunnar, there' something I want to go over with you."

Gunnar sat down attentively in a straight-back chair. "I've been hoping you'd call me in for some leg work, Mr. Cobb."

"Headwork too, Gunnar. The fact is, we're down to our last thirty gallons of fuel oil. That's barely a half day's supply, even with the burners running at low speed."

Gunnar nodded, "I thought the house was chilly this morning." His bronzed fingers tugged humorously at the bottom of a thick sweater underneath his fatigue jacket. "So I put on one of these navy numbers. Worth fifty gallons of oil."

Cobb, intent on the problem of keeping the house warm, smiled absently and continued: "Down the road, not more than a hundred and fifty yards from the house, the 'Fanny K. Belcher' is buried in a snowdrift. From what Bart Waley told me, I gather she's loaded with a thousand gallons of fuel oil." He paused. "The three of us— you, me, and Laimbeer—making ten trips each with a five-gallon can, could haul in a hundred and fifty gallons a day."

] 158 [

"Let's go," said Gunnar. "What are we waiting for?"

"Buttonhole Laimbeer," ordered Cobb, "and bring him in here. He'll have to pull his weight in the boat, like anyone else."

A few minutes later the artist followed Gunnar into the study. He seemed uninterested but unresigned—a foul combination to work with at close range. Instead of sitting down, he began pacing the floor like a penned sladang, hating the walls, the snow, his companions, and himself. "Good God," he snapped, "how much longer is this thing going on?"

"Till it stops," said Gunnar curtly.

Laimbeer paused in his pacing, glared at the young pilot belligerently, then pulled himself together and sat down. Cobb, choosing to ignore the tension, explained the plan of action.

Laimbeer entered a realistic objection. "Sorry, but I'm not much good on snowshoes, Cobb. You'd have to spend your time keeping me on my feet."

"You won't need snowshoes. We'll pack down a trail, and after a few trips, the snow'll be firm enough to hold you up."

The artist made no further attempt to beg off. "Let me know when the trail is packed," he said.

It was in Cobb's character to keep the peace. "I shall. Come on, Gunnar."

The initial trip to the "Fanny K. Belcher" wasn't bad fun. Cobb breaking trail, with a shovel over his shoulder, and Gunnar at his heels, made the distance in a few minutes. They found the oil truck submerged like a black and orange submarine, with only her top structure showing above the snow. "We'll dig for her faucets first," said Cobb. Half an hour's work at the back of the truck exposed an array of frozen bronze spigots. Hanging by a chain was a hexagonal wrench. Cobb seized the tool, fitted it over a spigot valve, and gave a twist. A gush of oil leaped from the faucet.

"We're in!" he shouted. "Lieutenant Rollefson, break out the cans."

Digging at the side of the truck, Gunnar had dislodged a row of five-gallon containers and now tossed a couple of them, lightly as milk bottles, to his chief. Cobb hung them on the faucets, pushed back his ski cap.

"Strawberry or chocolate?" They both laughed.

The cans filled, they started back, balancing the oil on their shoulders. The weight of the fuel was considerable; Cobb was puffing when they reached the house. Then came more shoveling to uncover the intake pipe to the fuel tank, and finally a wonderful sense of triumph as the oil slid from the cans into the pipe.

A cigarette, then another sally for more oil. Timing the operation, Cobb figured that it took forty-five minutes for a round trip. Gunnar could have made it ten minutes faster. The young pilot seemed tireless, splendidly conditioned. Temperamentally he was cheerful and highly good-natured, except in one detail. His single irk was Laimbeer, and he made no attempt to conceal his dislike for the painter.

"That guy gets my nuts," he confessed to Cobb as they took a breather in the lee of the house after their third trip. "Why isn't he out here?"

"We promised to pack down a trail for him," said Cobb mildly. "He'll be out soon."

Not until the fourth trip did Laimbeer make his appearance. Cobb saw him standing in the snow, a curiously misplaced figure with his velvet fedora tied onto his head by a white muffler, and the tails of his belted French coat flopping about his waist in the wind. Laimbeer's hands were covered with thin suede gloves, but no overshoes or snowboots protected his city shoes. Altogether he presented a picture of pitiful unreadiness—a caricature of a man about to undertake a chore for which he had neither zest nor ability. Gunnar groaned when he saw him, but Cobb whistled a greeting: "Hey, Laimbeer. Follow us along this path to the truck."

The painter floundered awkwardly through the snow to the tail of the "Fanny K. Belcher," where Cobb gave him brief instructions in the science of filling an oil can. Laimbeer gingerly fitted the hexagonal wrench over the faucet, twisted it experimentally, and watched the oil gushing into the container. To Cobb that five gallons of oil represented an hour's warmth for his family, a glowing barricade against cold and death. To Laimbeer it was merely a weight to be carried laboriously from one tank to another. The painter, not lacking in physical strength, was realistic enough to know that the oil had to be carried and that the sporting thing was to help carry it.

The artist made two trips before Cobb found a reasonable excuse to let him off. The man's clothes were clearly unsuited to the work at hand. His shoes were sodden, his trousers soaked to the knees, and the belted ulster blew about his knees like a shower curtain.

"Look," said Cobb kindly, "you're not dressed for this business, Laimbeer. Go into the house and ask Nolla to find some country clothes for you." The artist hesitated. "It's all right," Cobb assured him. "We've got a hundred gallons in the tank now. That is, we will have after Gunnar and I make another trip. You can help us again tomorrow."

The painter muttered something vaguely apologetic and started for the house. Gunnar waited until the falling flakes veiled the retreat, then said scornfully, "Not much use, that guy."

"Not at bucking oil through the snow. But he has his points. Come on, young feller, let's get another ten gallons in before we quit for the day."

A terrible eagerness was mounting in Ruston Cobb. He wanted an interview with the winged creature in his cellar. He longed to begin taming the hawk.

* * *

Like all good cellars, the subterranean region under Cobb's house had a vaultlike quiet about it. Echoes of upstairs life never penetrated here. Only the whir of the deep-freeze motor and the intermittent drone of the fuel blower broke the silence. Those were quiet now as Cobb descended into the hold of his house to inspect the captive bird.

What was there about cellars that gave one mixed feelings of chilly guilt and furtive desire? Was it their likeness to a cave? The damp odors and accusing gloom stirred Cobb's unconscious; for the first time in thirty years he thought of the cellar in Jennie Nichols' house. An exciting girl, Jenny. Crazy erotic at thirteen. "No one's home. Come down to the cellar with me," she had said one day after school. Tremblingly he had followed her down the cellar stairs, into the little room behind the furnace. He remembered her coaxing smile, the lifted dress. Afterward, she had taken a signet ring from her finger. "Let's be engaged, so we can do it every day after school." He put the ring on his little finger, but took it off, fearful, ashamed, before going home.

A week later came the awful news that Jennie Nichols' mother had caught her down cellar with another boy. Everyone in school was questioned in the principal's office. Ruston's mother had accompanied him into the inquisition chamber.

"Now, Ruston Cobb," asked Mr. Wightman, the principal, "did you ever go with Jennie Nichols down into her cellar?"

"No, sir!"

"Never?" Mr. Wightman's paunch was rising and falling rapidly. "Never."

Mr. Wightman fussily consulted his notes. "Did she give you a ring with her initials on it?"

"No." Ruston had thrown the ring into the furnace grate that very morning. Would they rake the ashes to prove his guilt?

"Jennie says she gave you a ring."

"Ruston says she didn't," said Mrs. Cobb. Her regal weight came down hard on the principal.

"That is all," said Mr. Wightman.

A close squeak, a narrow thing. Next day Jennie was sent to a school for wayward girls. Ruston never saw her again.

A violent drumming came from the woodbin.

The hawk!

Cobb approached the bin softly, put his hand on the latch, and opened the door a bare half inch. As he peered into the murky half-light, he heard the feathery agitation of the bird's plumage, stiffening for attack. Then he saw the hawk hunched in a corner, one snathelike talon uplifted to strike. No compromise, no bargaining, only explicit hatred, was in the bird's posture. It said, "Come in here and I'll cut you down."

What did I expect? thought Cobb, closing the door. Fawning? Submission? This is no flop-eared beagle suckling a litter of pups. This creature is a queen, contemptuous of all suitors but one, her only mate. What chance have you in her affections? What are you doing here outside her chamber? Why are you so bent on taming her?

What does the hawk mean to you, anyway?

Cobb could not consciously say. But as he stood in the dim cellar, listening, guilty and indecisive, a noiseless shuttle began shaking out delicate webs of association. The first thread was the memory of a diplomalike scroll that Nolla had brought back from Paris— a Provençal *carte d'amour,* tracing the course of the *gentil* lover across the terrain of love. She had sought to coach him in the idyllic practice of Provence, to make him an adept in the love laws laid down by Eleanor of Aquitaine long ago and faraway. Law I: *The lover yields in all things to the wish of his lady.* Law II: *The cheek of the beloved is more to be desired than the naked body of any other.*

A quaint lore, not written by man but discovered by the Queen herself in the beak of a falcon perched on the rosebush of Merci.

What can ail thee, knight-at-arms, alone and palely loitering?
The sedge is wither'd from the lake, and no birds ...

Low rales of anger gurgled from the captive bird behind the latched door. Cobb recalled his vision of the hawk, winging in slow grandeur through clouds of snow, as he returned from the gristmill on that day of loneliness and renunciation. How regal and uncapturable, how high above him then, the hawk had been! How queenly and cruel!

Painful earlier associations came crowding now. As a boy of fourteen he had once taken an eyas from a hawk's nest high on a cliff of the Hudson, and had begun the arduous business of converting it into a falcon. He had smuggled the bird into the cellar of his parents' house, and was proving the ancient lore of hood and jess upon the young hawk, when his mother had discovered what he was up to. "Set the bird free," she had commanded. The boy had obeyed. *The lover yields in all things to the wish of his lady.* But Cobb's desire to tame the wildest and freest of nature's creatures had remained with him, and now was breaking out again with all the energy of manhood attached to it.

Falconers, Cobb knew, smoked a pipe in the hawk's presence for two or three days as the first step in training. Well, he would begin at the beginning; there was no other way. He loaded his briar, drew a nail keg to the door of the bin, and struck a match to the tobacco. "Take it easy, Queen," he soothed, puffing at his pipe and blowing the smoke through the crack of the barely opened door. The first pipeload was delicious. The nature of the bout, the tobacco blowing in slow, plumy clouds from his lips, made the man on the nail keg feel wonderfully elated. This coming to grips with a creature he had so long envied and admired brought Cobb's powerful taming instincts into strong focus. *Puff, puff.* There in the dark bin, hate-filled and proud, lay the feathered legend of untamability—no domesticated capon with spurs filed down to harmless buttons but a sun gazer, a wind climber, who, but for the accident of a snapped air foil, would have scorned the roofs of man.

The good Burley tobacco, specked out with Latakia and curly Perique, billowed fragrantly into the woodbin. But the narcotizing fumes were not an instant drug to the hawk. The smoke, cursed with the aroma of man, enraged the bird. Low, throaty growls, kin to the mastiff's, issued from a corner of the bin. "She feels it," gloated Cobb, drawing deeper draughts from his briar. The heel of his pipe was getting warm. Gurgling noises in the stem. Need a cleaner. Ah, here in pocket. He knocked the soggy dottle from the bowl, reamed the stem, loaded the bowl again. *Puff.*

At the end of the third pipe, Cobb's throat was parched, his forehead clammy. The touch of Perique in his tobacco, sparking the accelerator nerves of his heart, made it thump rapidly at a heavy pace. Peering at his wrist watch, he saw that barely an hour had elapsed. Yet he knew that his smoking must go on for three days and nights. "I'll need help," he thought, scraping the shreds of tobacco from the bottom of his pouch for the fourth straight pipe. Unsteadily he lighted up again, hitched the nail keg nearer the door, inserted the pipe into the crack. *Puff.* The tobacco was making Cobb deathly sick. Only by clenching the rubber bit doggedly between his teeth did he prevent the revulsion of his stomach nerves.

Through the smoke haze he heard footsteps coming down the cellar stairs. It was Roddy.

"Mother wants to know what you're doing down here."

"Sh-sh." Cobb held up a finger while the hawk whirred in its corner. "Tell her," he whispered, "I'll be up soon." He motioned Roddy away. Mystified at his father's abruptness, the boy tiptoed upstairs.

Cobb smoked on. The tip and edges of his tongue were raw and his head was an expanding ache. Yet he was certain that he noticed a slackening of the hawk's nervous twitching as the sedative smoke

] 165 [

poured into the bin. Impossible to stop now. If only he could get someone to spell him for a bit. Laimbeer? Too impatient. Besides, he wouldn't be interested. Maybe Gunnar. But then Sicely would have to come along, chattering, laughing, frightening the hawk. Berry might smoke a pipe or two, just for the lark. No, if she came down, the cavelike silence of the cellar might touch off that way-back thing.

Whatever became of Jennie Nichols?

At some distance through the nicotine fog, Cobb heard himself saying, "I'm sick." Dizzily he arose from the nail keg, reeled toward the cellar stairs, felt his way upward to the kitchen. Mrs. Rollefson was preparing food. She looked up from her mixing bowl in alarm as she saw her employer's greenish countenance. "Why, Mr. Cobb, you're the color of lemon custard," she exclaimed. "Can I get you something?" Cobb, too ill for pantry ministrations, wanted only to be alone, to lie down. With pinwheels whirling around him, he found the way to his room, threw himself down on his bed. The overdose of Perique had constricted his arteries, causing his whole body to throb like a boiler under too full a head of steam. Scotomas, discs of light, whirled in spirals from his eyeballs, and his smoke-disordered brain whirled in still wider spirals of fantasy.

The hawk swooped at him in power plunges from snow-filled clouds as he struggled for Sicely's life, while Gurley, the bargeman, haggled for more money. Jennie Nichols lifted her dress as Laimbeer slipped the Hanging Man card to Nolla under the table. Now he was at the wheel of the *Gyrfalcon;* his mother came out of her cabin, put her hand on the hem of her skirt, started to lift it. Writhing, Cobb rubbed out the image, just as he had rubbed away the birdlime. Now Sicely, in the iron cabin of the tanker, lifted her dress and said, "Come to bed, Daddy." Nolla played the piano, and Berry clung about his neck. The hawk plunged at his genitals, and the bird's talons became fingers with snathelike nails. Snow fell, formed dancing crystals in a black void, as Nolla murmured, *"Tu*

] 166 [

souffres, mon ami," and lay down on the sofa like Madame Récamier, but more on her back. Down a long alley of whitewashed
pillars, Roddy came tiptoeing timidly while the young man in the
florist's shop put a narcissus in Cobb's buttonhole.

From these toxic whirlings Cobb rose unsteadily, walked to the
bathroom, let the water gurgle down his raw throat and mouth,
then went back to bed. When he woke from a light doze, his head
was clearer and the pounding of his heart had ceased. Only the
dottleish taste in his mouth reminded him of the nicotine bout he
had just been through. He looked at his watch. 3:30 P.M. Just time
for a drink and a sandwich before picking up the falconer's burden
again. He opened the bottom of his writing desk, took out a pint of
Bourbon, poured a quarter-tumbler full, and whisked it off neat.
"Distillation rules the nation," he hummed. Cobb had no idea where
this line came from or why he was humming it. He only knew he
felt wonderful and that the task of conquering the hawk made him
feel still better. He took another nip of whiskey, brushed his hair,
and examined the burning tip of his tongue in a hand mirror. It was
bright red and its little papules were highly visible. "Must use
milder tobacco." Rummaging in his desk he came across a red tin
of Velvet. Smooth as a baby's bottom.

It had been his plan to slip down the back stairs, take a piece of
cold meat from the ice chest, put it between two pieces of bread,
and continue down to the cellar. But a desire to know what was
going on in the rest of the house took possession of him. What was
Roddy up to? How was Nolla standing the strain? He opened the
door of his room, walked down the hallway toward the great staircase.

An afternoon hush, broken only by the sound of a piano, lay on
the house. It was Nolla's music. She was improvising on a Debussy
theme, creating a melancholy, icebound landscape. Each note was
the footstep of a lonely wanderer traversing a painfully lonesome
field of snow. From her music the whole house took on a film of

] 167 [

uncommenting sadness, as if touched by the lament of the piano player, sadder than a great hall filled with stifled weeping. Cobb hesitated at the top of the stairs, came down softly, and walked toward the music room. At the door he paused. The music had stopped. Cobb took another step, looked into the room.

There in the afternoon dimness he saw Laimbeer leaning over the piano, rapt, his gaze fixed on Nolla. Her head, bent forward, was resting on the music rack; one hand lay on the keyboard, clinging to its echo of loneliness. Cobb saw Laimbeer's large hand close over Nolla's and lift it slowly, confidently, from the keys.

Cobb did not want to see any more. Noiselessly he withdrew, passed from the dining room into the kitchen. The wonderful smell of fresh bread came to him; new loaves covered with a cloth lay on the table. He picked up a warm loaf, broke a heel with one hand. Chewing it absently, he opened the door leading to the cellar, hesitated as if listening for a music he knew would not begin again, then opened the cellar door and went downstairs.

CHAPTER 11

SOMETIME DURING the night the electric wires went down.

Not until he pressed the wall switch early the next morning did Cobb realize that his home was without light or heat. Dressing swiftly in the darkness, he went down into the kitchen. By candle-light Gunnar Rollefson was stoking the kitchen range with a hod of nut coal while his mother stripped bacon for the frying pan. The housekeeper's "Good morning" was cheerful, as always; if she felt danger, she knew how to suppress all outward signs of it. Gunnar spread the coal evenly with the lid handle, put back the stove cover, and set the drafts. The effect of so much quiet domestic business was reassuring to Cobb. In the coming struggle, it would be good to have this able, disciplined pair on his side.

"Not much light coming in today, Mrs. R.," he said.

"It's dark as a preserve closet, and that's a fact, Mr. Cobb. I'll have to dig out some of them oil lamps from the attic. Candles don't have the *beam* that lamps have." She got back quickly to the busi-ness at hand. "How'll you have your eggs this morning, sir?"

"Sunny side up." He sat down at the kitchen table, poured him-self a cup of coffee, beckoned to Gunnar. "Sit down, Lieutenant. Let's get some of your mother's hot biscuits into us, then we'll call a board of strategy."

Some thirty-five hundred calories had disappeared off each break-fast plate before Cobb asked casually, "Any idea what's behind all this snow, Lieutenant?"

The question was merely an academic starter, and Gunnar knew it. While he had no special information on the subject of the freak storm, his knowledge of meteorology, gained as a pilot, equipped him as well as anyone to discuss the big snowfall. He sipped his third cup of coffee. "How much do you know about the atmospheric conditions causing snow, Mr. Cobb?"

"Almost nothing. Snow is just frozen rain, isn't it?"

"That's the general belief, but there's more to it. Snow is water, sure, but not the droplets that form rain." Gunnar paused as if seeking the simplest way of putting it. "Water vapor—that is, detached molecules of hydrogen and oxygen floating about in the air—polymerize in special crystalline form. I don't believe anyone knows exactly the law that governs that formation, except that these molecules *do* rush toward each other and cling together, not as fluid or gas but as geometric crystals. Then they fall to earth, either singly or bunched together into what we call snowflakes." He halted diffidently, like a man in the presence of a mystery. "I suppose it's an attempt on the part of unorganized matter to take on solid form."

There was a small rustle at the kitchen door. Sicely, in a quilted robe figured with pink rosebuds, came toward the breakfast table. "Good morning, Mrs. Rollefson." She kissed her father, smiled at the young Lieutenant. "I heard the last part about the snow molecules rushing together. There must be quite a lot of them attracting each other like crazy up there, wouldn't you say?"

Sicely's suggestion that nature was up to her old tricks brought laughter from Cobb and Gunnar. Sice blushed just enough, then asked, "Is it true, Gunnar, that no two snowflakes are alike?"

Gunnar nodded. "Some American scientist, I forget his name, has taken micro-photographs of about five thousand snow crystals. They're all six-pointed, but no two are identical. But here's the funny part: though they're all different, they *do* fall into two main groups, one from the high, cold regions, the other from the low, warmer layers. High snow forms small, closely packed crystals, while flakes from low-hanging snow clouds make ferny, stellar patterns, full of air and water. With a microscope you might even determine the altitude from which the flakes are now falling."

Sice sat fascinated as the young aviator talked. It occurred to Cobb that no woman dislikes listening to strangeness from the lips of an attractive man. A twinge of jealousy prompted him to get the conversation back onto a more prosaic plane.

"I hate to be brisk," he said, "but when you've got billions of these snow crystals clogging up your front steps, the problem is how to get them off."

"There's *one* problem," put in Mrs. Rollefson, "that'll have to be taken care of right away. It's the food in the deep freezer. With the current off, it'll be spoiling down there." Gathering momentum, she barged forward. "And after that, someone'll have to dig a path to the woodshed. Cordwood's all we got to warm the house, and it'll take a power of firewood to keep them crickets singing on the hearth." She consulted an inner list somewhere. "Then there're the questions of stretching the coal and parceling out the provisions and getting the lamps fittened up."

"Quite an agenda," laughed Cobb. "We'll break it up into assignments. Lieutenant Rollefson, suppose you take the snow-shoveling detail and clear a path to the woodpile. Mrs. Rollefson, you break out the lamps, while I go down the cellar and look over the food situation. When the others come down, they'll all get jobs on Operations Snowbound."

"Any need to synchronize our watches?" asked Gunnar with mock gravity.

"Yes, yes," cried Sicely. "Let's set them to the very dot." She took Gunnar's brown wrist, twisted it so that she could inspect the face of his chronometer. Then, puzzled by the complexity of its dial with its many sweeps and figures, she held out her own wrist with its small, gold strap watch. "You fix them, Gunnar."

The faint echo of a remembered juke-box tune resounded in

Cobb's memory: "Your time is my time, My time is your time . . ."
The desire for oneness! Even molecules of water vapor felt it as they
rushed together.

"We must keep them synchronized to the very *second*," Sicely
was saying as Cobb went down the cellar stairs.

*   *   *

In a remote part of the cellar, Rollefson, the caretaker, had fitted
up a combined toolshop and bunk house. Here he sharpened the
lawn mowers, tinkered with household gadgets, drank his solitary
bottle, then slept it off. Cobb had no desire to intrude on the man's
privacy, but the breakdown of the deep-freeze unit made it imperative. He groped his way down the long alley of whitewashed pillars
and knocked at the door of the caretaker's retreat.

A voice hoarse from much whiskey and little use said, "Come in."

Cobb pushed open the door and entered the caretaker's hideaway.
How neat and shipshape the place was! A well-trimmed lamp with
a polished reflector burned in a wall bracket; an iron laundry stove,
its pipe fitted into a flue of a massive brick chimney, kept down the
cavern damp. On one side of the room was Rollefson's workbench;
rows of chisels and auger-bits were suspended in leathern loops;
three good saws hung on wooden pegs. Among some curly shavings
a handsome jackplane lay on its side; its metal sole threw back the
lamplight. The melancholy order of the place was reflected in Rollefson's somber face and dejected posture. As he rose from his carpet-covered rocking chair to greet his employer, he reminded Cobb
of a captive bear with a chain around his neck.

The heel of a pint remained in the bottle on the dresser; the caretaker had started drinking for the day but was not yet drunk.

"Sorry to break in on you, Rollefson," began Cobb, "but things
are pretty urgent. The meat and butter must be taken upstairs to a
cold room, at once." The man's silence was unhelpful. Cobb stopped
apologizing and came to the point. "I'd like you to make four

wooden boxes about five by five by three, with a lid on each one. We'll pack them with meat from the deep freezer and carry them to a cold room upstairs. Can you do that, Rollefson?"

The man was neither eager nor sullen. "I'll start right away."

Cobb tried to keep his eyes away from the pint bottle. "Well, just have it in mind." His hand was on the latch now, but before he left he wanted to say something human and cheering to this caged bear.

"That's a fine boy you've got, Rollefson."

The caretaker's bleak eyes came up a degree in surprise. It probably was the first time that anyone had ever mentioned his connection with Gunnar's existence. The taste of credit was enjoyable but brief. "Yes," he said, "Gunnar is a good lad. His mother has done a fine job on him."

Cobb's instinct was to let it stand at that. If a man felt guilty about his failure toward his own son, what could one do about it? He was closing Rollefson's door behind him when he heard the caretaker's hoarse voice: "That bird in the woodbin, sir——"

"Yes."

"The tip of her wing is hurt. It needs tending."

"I know. But how to get near her—that's the question. Last night I tried the old falconer's trick of pipe smoking, but she'll have no part of me."

"It'll take more than a pipeful to gentle *that* bird, sir." Old and special knowledge was in the caretaker's voice. "Five hundred pipes more like. And no haste. She wants a quiet man who isn't lazy. If you're restless or sudden"—Rollefson shook his head at the folly of such hurrying—" 'twill only ruff her up. She's a proud one, ah."

"You've handled hawks, Rollefson?"

Soiled bandages of servitude fell from the man's eyes; they filled with blue, northern light. "Handled hawks? I was an eyas among them. My father was the best falconer in Norway. 'Twas common known that at sixteen I passed him in skill and patience."

] 173 [

In time and place Rollefson was far from the snowbound cellar room. "On the crags of Norway's fiords, fierce hawks build their eyries," he said. "High on the face of the cliff they build. A man can't climb up. You must lower yourself on a rope."

"You've taken them that way, Rollefson?"

The man fingered a broad scar over his eyebrow. "A gyrfalcon gave me this when I was fifteen. My father sent me down a rope to take a brace of fledglings teetering on the edge of their nest. In a few hours they would fly, be gone. I had them safe in my pocket when the mother bird came back with food. She went for my eyes; her talons hooked like sickles."

"What did you do, Rollefson?"

"I had a pistol loaded with blanks. I snapped it at her twice. Hawks hate gunfire, but she kept diving at me while my father pulled me up." Rollefson sopped at the scar as though it were still bleeding. "A year later we sold those eyases, trained and furnitured, to an English lord. One hundred pounds for the pair."

Long ago and faraway . . .

"Would you care to look at the hawk with me?" asked Cobb.

Rollefson rose from his carpet-covered chair like an old sea-rover being asked to inspect a rich man's yawl. "Very much, sir." Together they made their way through the labyrinthine cellar; nearing the woodbin the caretaker took the lead. He put his finger to his lips, then listened at the door of the bin. At the sound of stiffening feathers, he nodded approvingly, motioned Cobb aside.

"She weakens from hunger. That is good. For still another day, two days, she must not be fed. Meanwhile we must spell each other smoking at her." Rollefson developed his program with decisive strokes. "I'll start making the boxes. You, sir, must smoke at the door till lunch. I'll relieve you at noon. For seventy-two hours, till the hawk is drugged and manned, we must smoke at her, watch and watch. Wait, I'll fetch a chair for you to sit on."

Cobb did not wholly relish Rollefson's proprietary lead in this business of taming the hawk. Almost curtly he took the chair from Rollefson, established himself at the crack of the door, and loaded his pipe. He wished to meet the hawk's challenge alone, but, realistically, he knew that Rollefson's help must be accepted. No man could smoke seventy-two hours at a stretch. He held a match to the milder tobacco in the pipe bowl.

"See you at noon, Rollefson," he said pointedly, blowing the first mouthful of smoke into the woodbin.

Doggedly Cobb puffed through his watch. Strange thoughts occupied his mind and the wheel of his mood turned slowly, quartering through a determination to quell this creature, to sympathy and pity for the bird under the terrible assault of smoke.

When Rollefson came up quietly at noon, Cobb was throat-sore, hungry, glad to see his cadgerman. They talked in whispers outside the bin.

"We'll be needing a hood for him," said Rollefson. "There can be no training a falcon without one. What the bridle is to the horse, the hood is to the hawk."

"You know how to make a hood, Rollefson?"

"I have made many." There was no hint of alcohol about Rollefson now. The shuffling chained bear had disappeared. In its place was a confident, sober man.

"Then start on one today. And oh, Rollefson, you might work some soft leather into strips."

"For the jesses. Aye." Agreement of spare language lay between them.

"Take over, Rollefson. I'll be back for the afternoon watch."

*   *   *

The upstairs household, newly organized for the siege, had the air of a fortress not too fearful of its attackers. Three antique kerosene lamps, scrummaged out of the attic by Mrs. Rollefson, made golden islands of light in the darkened living room. A fine sheet of flame rose from the hearth, and beside the fireplace Gunnar had stacked a dozen stout oak logs in tiers. Nolla, a quilt around her shoulders, was embroidering an oval tambour; her eyes, given briefly to her husband, seemed to say, "So you've found time to look after your family at last." Laimbeer and Roddy were playing chess; Gunnar, an atlas over his knees, was tracing out his voyages for Sice, snuggled close to him on the sofa. Only Berry seemed unoccupied, restless, bored. An empty glass was in her hand.

Cobb's appearance in the upper world of the living room was greeted with a mixture of curiosity and pique. Half the household (the grown-up) was puzzled by his absorption in the hawk; the other, younger half gave him a cheering demonstration of interest. Sicely, glowing with a special light that shines through a young woman beginning to be in love, rose from the sofa, hung on her father's arm.

"Have you tamed it yet?" she asked, as though the conquest of a hawk was no harder than that of an affectionate girl.

"No, but she's melting."

Roddy came forward with a fistful of pipe cleaners that he had rounded up from various drawers and compartments. "Sure and there isn't a pipe cleaner in the house except these two hundred," he cried, mimicking Mrs. Rollefson's Gampishness with a smack of Irish thrown in for no reason at all.

Cobb stuffed the pipe cleaners in his pocket with the air of a man receiving a priceless treasure. "Thanks, son," he said. "I'll be using every one of them before I'm through."

Nolla was silent. Unerringly she had divined the psychic source of her husband's interest in the hawk, and saw in it something to be guarded against, defeated with favors withdrawn, voice inert, eyes not given. Bending over her with a tribulary kiss, Cobb saw the oval tambour on which some heavily penciled lines had been drawn. Her embroidery needle was picking out the design with silken threads of scarlet and gold. He could not get a full view of her needlework, and she made no offer to show it to him.

"Starting something new?" he asked.

"A *carte d'amour*," she said coldly. "Laimbeer copied it for me on linen."

The universal roadmap, thought Cobb. Guides the faithful traveler right to the central foliage. Aloud, he said, "And you, Berry, what have you been doing?"

"Who? Me? Oh, I'm just getting in shape for the Bored Stiff Sweepstakes. Time on my hands, lots of yawning, plenty of good art talk, and a couple million tons of snow in the front yard. A perfect setup. For Eskimos. Another week or so and I'll be all ready to play the title role of Blubberwatha, Queen of the Igloos. If I don't take an overdose of nembutal first."

"Cabin fever," murmured Laimbeer.

"Well, what about it?" snapped Berry. "You're getting free heat and three a day with extras, so it's O.K. with you if we stay here until the Fourth of July."

"Berry, sh-sh," said Nolla.

"Don't shush me." Beryl was boiling over now. "I'm tired of this jerk's continental charm, or whatever the hell he calls it. When they put pants on sponges, they'll get the measurements from Laimbeer."

The children, frightened at Berry's outburst, pretended not to hear. Cobb came over to her soothingly.

"Berry, darling, you're all wrought up. Here, let me pour you a drink."

"She's had enough already," said Nolla.

"For Christ's sake," screamed Beryl, "stop squirting that big-sister vanilla at me! I'll drink as much as I goddam please. Other people have *their* little vices; I'll have mine." She thrust her glass at Cobb. "Here, Rusty, fill it up. If everyone around here is going to be disagreeable, I want to be so drunk I won't care."

"No one's trying to be disagreeable, Berry." Cobb saw that he must set and maintain the temper of the snowbound household, keeping it constant and level; otherwise the whole edifice would collapse. If he let Beryl flounce off the stage now, injured and contentious, the disease of bad temper would spread through the house, contaminate others. He put his arms around her, kissed her cheerfully.

"Wait a while, Berry, and we'll all get tight together. There's ten cases of Scotch down cellar, enough for a month if—if everyone drinks only a quart a day." He turned to the children, "Rod, Sice, will you settle for a pint apiece so that Berry and I can have an extra noggin?"

Sicely, shrinking closer to Gunnar, responded with an embarrassed, "Of course, Daddy."

"How about you, Rod?"

Roddy leaped into the breach like an understudy getting a Broadway chance. " 'You can talk of gin and beer when you're quartered safe out here, but when it comes to *slaughter,* you'll do your work on *water,* and lick the bloomin' boots of 'im that's got it.' " He stopped suddenly, blushed in mimicry of Sice's embarrassed manner, and said, "Sure, Daddy, Berry can have my noggin's-worth any old time at all."

Everyone laughed. "My little trouper," said Cobb, hugging Roddy in the crook of his elbow. The boy had pulled the house off the rocks. Life could go on.

It did, with lunch and a game of darts afterward. Roddy, eager to beat his father, tried to imitate the easy, overhand flick that sent the feathered darts quivering into the cork board. But the boy's thin arm lacked drive. "I can't give 'em the old *tzing,*" he complained as his darts struck the board weakly, or fell feebly to the floor. "You'll get it," encouraged Cobb. "Watch this motion." He coached his son patiently, gave him an affectionate Dutch rub when Roddy finally got a bull's-eye.

Chess, however, was another story. Eager to show his superiority in some form, the boy begged his father for a game. "Just *one*, Daddy." Cobb had a dozen chores waiting for him upstairs and down, but he could not deny Roddy the chance to prove his skill at the chessboard. "All right, young feller," he laughed, sitting down at the inlaid table. "If you want a fall guy, here he is."

"Watch out for his middle game," warned Laimbeer. "He knocked me off in eighteen moves."

"Thanks," said Cobb. "He'll probably pull a Scholar's Mate on me." Actually his games with Roddy were close things, but he knew that the boy enjoyed this kind of pre-game banter. He watched his son, poised and serious, make the first moves with the white—a Giuoco Piano opening that rapidly developed into a powerful array of pawns, bishop, and queen in the center of the board. To break up Roddy's attack, Cobb on his eighth move exchanged a knight for a knight. The play looked sound to him, but his son's quiet smile hinted at disaster. Sure enough, on his nineteenth move, Cobb found his king pinned by the white queen, as Roddy's knight whisked in for the kill.

"You fell into the Greco trap, Daddy," exulted Rod. "After your eighth move, the best you could get was a draw." He turned to Nolla, embroidering by the fireplace. "Mother," he cried, "I *check-mated* him. The third time in a row."

Nolla smiled across the room at her son. "I guess that makes you champion around here." Her glance met Cobb's, and she construed his nod as a happy acknowledgment of their son's competitive flair. "It's worth being beaten," the nod meant, "if it bucks the kid up." Nice to be able to communicate across a room like that. "Wait till I get you on the grass courts," he warned Roddy. Then, calling to Gunnar, "On your feet, Lieutenant," Cobb was off on a belated round of chores.

With Gunnar's help he transferred the meat and butter from the deep-freeze unit to the new boxes that the elder Rollefson had

] 179 [

made, then carried the boxes to an unused room on the northern side of the house. "The temperature's about ten degrees colder than the cellar," said Cobb. "Just right for meat. It'll keep here indefinitely." He took a satisfied look around at the improvised refrigerator, shivered in the chilly room, and started downstairs, Gunnar behind him.

In the kitchen Mrs. Rollefson's usually placid cheek was disturbed by the righteous, I've-been-expecting-it look of a woman wronged in an old place.

"It's the elbow, Mr. Cobb," she announced. "It's froze stiffer'n a blue huspedar."

Cobb did not know what a blue huspedar was, but this "elbow" was a familiar source of trouble even in ordinary winters. It piped gravity spring water into the house, entering the cellar at a badly exposed angle barely a foot below ground. Cobb had often promised himself to have it sunk deeper, but now—with the whole house depending on the frozen elbow for water—there was nothing to do but thaw the pipe out.

In the attic he found a portable oil stove that might do the trick. Filling the stove with fuel oil from the furnace tank, he lighted the circular wick and placed the heater on a tall packing box directly under the frozen elbow. Gentle heat waves rising from the stove thawed the critical bend of pipe and let water flow once more. The stove had to be watched constantly, else its flames would climb and set fire to the ceiling of the cellar. To his other tasks Cobb added this duty of inspecting the stove at regular intervals.

Three o'clock found Cobb eager for his stint at the hawk's bin. Descending to the cellar, he saw Rollefson's heavy shoulders hunched over his knee, his mouth pressed to the crack of the woodbin door. The caretaker's posture gave him the appearance of a primitive shaman celebrating some totemic mystery. So deeply was he absorbed in his priest-ritual that he did not hear Cobb's approach; yet he made no sudden start when his employer touched him on the shoulder.

The caretaker's center of surprise was indeed low; he turned his head slightly to acknowledge the tap, then rose stiffly from the nail keg, stretched, and said, "By her breathing, she is in pain. The broken wing is troubling her." Rollefson turned a somber eye upon his employer. "It must be mended at once."

A fine tremor of apprehension shook Cobb. He stammered slightly. "B-b-but she isn't tamed yet. Dare we go into the bin?"

"I dare," said the caretaker. "The bird will know I am easing her pain. She will not attack me. But first we must ready ourselves. Come to my shop."

On his workbench, Rollefson methodically assembled materials for the operation: a candle; a small penknife with an edge honed to scalpel brightness; two needles, one small, one medium-sized; and some black thread that he twisted through a chunk of shoemaker's wax. He threaded the small needle and stuck the other one into the cuff of his coat. Then from the bottom drawer of his bureau he pulled out a large cotton sock and rolled it into the shape of a doughnut. He handed Cobb a pair of gardener's gloves. "Put these on. They will give you some protection." Next he poured a small quantity of rubbing alcohol into a saucer. "We are ready now—no, we must have something for the patient to rest on." He took a worn sofa pillow from his armchair, tossed it to Cobb. "Carry this, the candle, and the saucer of alcohol."

Outside the hawk's bin, Rollefson briefed his assistant in low tones. "I will go in first, slip the sock over her head. You follow with the pillow. Place it on the table, then light the candle. After that, do exactly as I tell you—but with no sudden movement, understand?"

"I understand."

Noiselessly, Rollefson opened the door of the bin, listened a moment, and made a strange sound, half cooing, half chirping, deep in his throat. Then he disappeared into the darkness. Cobb heard a ruffling of feathers and a mild, squawking complaint, followed by Rollefson's almost inaudible words uttered in the voice of a lover: "My kestrel, my windhover, I have come to mend thee, pretty bird. See, I slip this weary mansock over thy proud head. Gently, over thy head and shoulders."

In another voice, he addressed Cobb: "Bring in the pillow."

Holding the pillow in front of his face, Cobb entered the bin. At his approaching step, the hawk screamed through the muffling sock about her head. Cobb's hand was shaking as he lighted the candle, jammed it into the neck of a wine bottle, and placed it on the table beside the pillow. By the candlelight he saw Rollefson holding the hawk, his palms downward, thumbs joined, the tips of his fingers toward the bird's tail, his forearms around her head. The caretaker set her gently on the pillow. "See how I have my hands," he said to Cobb. "Hold her just so. Do not be afraid; she is weak and drowsy."

Cobb placed his hands over the bird, felt the violent thumping of her heart directly under his fingers. As she struggled in his grasp, he pressed her savagely down upon the pillow. "No, no," whispered Rollefson. "Firm but not rough. Like a young husband with a wife."

His hands were in her plumage now. "Lie still, my proud saker, while I search thee. Ah, here is the broken wing. A swift stroke and I will make thee whole again."

With an oblique slice of his penknife at the exact point of the break, Rollefson cut the hollow wingshaft clean through. The severed portion of the wing fell to the table like a branch pruned from a fruit tree. Plucking the medium-sized needle from his cuff, he dipped it into the saucer of alcohol, then stuck it lengthwise into the pithy tube of the wing stump. Picking up the severed plume, he fitted it over the jutting end of the needle, till both edges of the quill-like shaft came together in a perfect jointure. Cobb, marveling at the speed and dexterity of the operation, forgot the struggling bird under his hands as he watched Rollefson take the wax-threaded needle and whip the spliced wing sections with a dozen turns of the waxed thread.

"There, skyling," he soothed, knotting and snipping the thread. "When the needle rusts inside the bone, your wing will be stronger than ever." He motioned Cobb to loosen his hold on the bird. "Give her to me now; she needs gentling." The caretaker blew out the candle, drew the sock tenderly off the bird's head. "No more smoking this afternoon," he announced. "I will gentle her here till the evening watch. Get some sleep. You will need it later."

Cobb had a feeling of dismissal as he left the bin. He knew that alone he would have been unable to mend the bird's wing, and that without the caretaker's help he could never have tamed her. But his admiration for Rollefson's skillful technique was mingled with frank jealousy. He stood for a second at the door of the bin, listening to the inarticulate conversation between the bird and the man. Then slowly he mounted the stairs to his room, and slept till dinnertime.

*　　*　　*

That evening the whole family played games. First, Dumb Crambo, at which Roddy was superb, then Musical Chairs, with Nolla at the piano. The games, begun in a desperately eager attempt to forget the snow, developed a wild gaiety in the players. Beryl was particularly high; her bleak mood lifted, floated away on three Golden Mixtures. All her natural affection surged into a flushed and amorous warmth. When all the traditional games had been played, she suggested a plate-kicking contest.

"You hold a plate—not a good one—at about the level of your chin," she explained to Cobb. "Then the girls—Sicely, Nolla, me, and Mrs. Rollefson if she wants to—try to kick it out of your hand. Loosen your stays, girls, for the plate-kicking championship. You first, Sice."

Grinning, Cobb held the plate at arm's length, shoulder-high. If the girls wanted to break up the crockery, why not? Sice, pushed forward by Berry, advanced hesitantly, a virginal shyness about her. How, in Gunnar's presence, and with skirts on—how could she kick the plate in her father's hand? Cobb saw the difficulty.

"Come on, Sice," he urged. "It's all in the family."

Blushingly, Sice started to make the old college try. But at the moment of getting her foot off the ground, her courage failed. The result was pretty much nothing at all. Jeers from Berry.

"I can do better than that," she cried. "Watch me, everyone. You, Rusty, just keep your eyes on the plate." (How did Berry know there was a touch of the *voyeur* about him?) She took up a stance about three paces away, toes together on an imaginary line, her dress lifted loosely above her beautifully modeled knees. A rosy heat radiated from her face and throat, glowed through her tautly gartered stockings. She estimated the height of the plate, took a couple of short steps, and aimed her right toe at the china target. Cobb saw a flash of white as Berry's skirt fell back, but her toe never reached the plate. There was a ripping sound and a disgusted "Damn" from Berry.

"Key-rist, there go my nylons. I should of loosened my garters. Give me another chance, Rusty."

"It's Nolla's turn," said Laimbeer quietly.

Ruston Cobb looked at his wife curiously. Would she enter the contest? Yes, there she was, drawing off sideways, like a pole vaulter appraising height and distance. What had come over her? For whose benefit was she about to exhibit herself? In silence she stood poised, then gathered up the hem of her dress, not as Berry had done but like a Watteau court nymph entering the measures of a Versailles minuet. Or a nun about to cross a stile. Cobb had always loved the fine-drawn tension of Nolla's insteps and ankles; now he saw the nerves and muscles readying under her satiny skin. She came forward lightly, smiling, a ballerina, a high-wire queen, balancing the excitements in her body till they struck an exquisite center. Then her foot flew up; her toe touched the center of the plate. It sprang from her husband's hand and broke in a dozen pieces as it landed on the floor.

Laughter from Roddy and Sice, bravos by Laimbeer, and Berry's disgruntled "Well, I'll be damned" washed the room in a rollicking surf. Cobb grabbed his wife, kissed her full on the mouth. "Nolla darling, I didn't know——"

Laimbeer was cutting in like a stag at a dance. "Zigeuner Feodorovna," he exclaimed, "a tambourine dancer lurks somewhere underneath——" He realized a husband's presence. "No wonder the gypsy woman peeps in at your kitchen window. She is looking for new talent."

Powerless to compete with the painter in compliment, Cobb released his hold on Nolla's hand. Laimbeer drew her to the fireplace, enwrapped her with smiles, words, and glances. Never had Nolla's personality seemed so rich and flowering. Rightly or wrongly, Cobb could not help laying it to Laimbeer's courtier attention. He remembered a Chinese proverb: "The wise husband is not alarmed by other men's attention to his wife; what concerns him is the way the wife accepts it." And how was Nolla accepting Laimbeer's attention? Beautifully was the only word for it. That lingering, slow closure of her eyelids as she finished saying something to the painter was, Cobb admitted, a caress that he had never received from her in all his years of marriage.

Never inspired it, probably.

He glanced at his watch. Ten forty-five. In fifteen minutes he would take over Rollefson's smoking detail. Just time enough to get Roddy to bed, then, without announcement, he would slip down the cellar stairs. If he told Berry where he was going, she'd be down after him. No, she must stay upstairs, be a third to Laimbeer and Nolla.

"Taps, Roddy. It's getting on toward eleven."

The boy lifted his delicate face for a kiss. "Wasn't it a lovely evening, Father?"

"It was, Roddy." He patted the boy's blond head. "And you helped make it so."

"I wish it would keep on snowing forever. Mother was so gay."

"Go over and kiss her good night."

Cobb watched his son cross the room, saw the good-night kisses exchanged between mother and son. Then he slipped into the kitchen, took two bottles of beer from the cold window sill, and hastened to his rendezvous with the hawk.

*　　*　　*

Invisibly screened by snow, red Aldebaran glowed at its zenith; pale Leda declined. More than ever, Cobb had the feeling that he was descending into the hold of a great ship.

His greeting to Rollefson was as sailing master to boatswain: "How goes it?" The caretaker rose from his corncob vigil. "She rests well," he grunted, then brought the back of his hand across cracked lips to wipe away a terrible thirst.

Cobb handed him a quart of beer. Rollefson stretched out his arm in a Viking gesture—a steersman taking a mead horn from his captain. With his jack-knife he flipped off the beer cap. "Skoal." He held the bottle to his lips and drained a pint of beer in a long gurgle.

"I'll wake you at three," said Cobb. "Turn in."

"Aye." Rollefson's footsteps echoed down the long trough between the whitewashed masts. The house labored like a heavy galleon through a world of storm. Cobb set a match to his meerschaum and the midnight watch began.

Smoke-ringed pictures came from his pipe of seafoam:

His mother was saying, "We are having tea this afternoon with a lovely girl, the daughter of an old friend from Boston. I want you to be nice to her. She is very fragile, plays the piano beautifully."

He was bending over a claw-footed, mahogany Ivers and Pond.

"Please keep on playing. Our mothers are having such a grand time chinning about their scandalous past. Tell me when to turn the pages."

Her hair was of the thinnest Rapunzel silk, bloodless gold. Fragile, very. "No need to turn the pages for me. I have Chopin by heart. But turn now, if you wish. Oh, *clumsy!*"

Puff.

His mother was unpinning a six-pointed brooch from her high, wonderful bosom. The brooch was sown with diamonds and seed pearls. "I am so happy, son, about you and Nolla. She is exactly the kind of a girl . . . Here, give her this. No, I'll give it to her myself."

The hawk stirred, red Aldebaran declined; atoms of oxygen and hydrogen rushed together to form six-pointed crystals and fall into a Lucretian void.

De rerum natura . . . Lachrimae rerum.

Anxieties heavy as myth-bales crowded the hold of the laboring ship. The unconscious world broke loose, raged on witch-broom winds through the rigging of the falconer's soul. Figures from old folk tales whirled on the winds. Nolla imprisoned in a glass casket awaited the prince who would break with his kiss the witch mother's spell. Rapunzel's yellow hair was too tightly plaited and she was afraid to pull out her combs.

Into the hold of the Walpurgis ship glided the figure of Beryl the Undine. What secret maim in her middle parts was she attempting to conceal? Strange that so beautiful a creature should make of her cloveness a hateful brand and punish herself so cruelly for possessing it. Only believe, Undine, this is no shameful cicatrix, to be hid beneath waves of alcohol or maltreated by any passing knave of hearts, to wit, to woo, this esthetico-tomcat tart stealer . . .

Laimbeer.

Canvass me his character. I have no palette for it, my lord. *Harrummph.* A slash-doubleted rogue, a well-hung, masterful varlet, a mutton-dagger dauber, a cocksman artist, a cloak-and-poignard **poet,**

] 187 [

a muff fancier (no doubt), a piece of luxury fabric, frayed *peut-être* by much handling, but withal imported stuff, not woven on your domestic looms, see the fine immortal threads, a lost art to weave *that,* your Excellency. God knows when we'll have any of it on our shelves again. Catch the drape! Can be made up in any number of styles. Prince Charming, van Gogh Redivivus, the Hanging Man, and Misunderstood Genius. All guaranteed to land wearer in bed with Lady of Choice.

Price?

Less than you think.

Cobb opened his bottle of beer, gulped off a throatful. Ears tuned to silence, he listened for a signal from the hawk—a rustling, a murmur, anything to show that the bird still hated him. Nothing. Not a sound in the bin. Not a sound in the whole world. Hushed all. Yet how different from the waterfall stillness the day he had dreamed of Lucy Foederis! Could silences vary so? That one had been holy, peaceful; this one was menacing, guilty. A sudden impulse bade him enter the bin, come nearer the beaked captive. He would show her who was fearful of whom. Hand before his eyes, he pushed open the door an inch. No protest from the bird. Gently, another inch . . .

The stillness, the danger, the aura of guilt, reminded him of another door that he had once pushed open.

Gyrfalcon fog-bound. A lonely boy on the afterdeck. *What are they doing in there?* He had put his hand on the knob of the cabin door, turned it ever so softly. Nose at the crack of the door, breathing in his mother's perfume. Not to spy. Just lonesome. Ah, they were murmuring inaudible things in a wonderful tone never used on him. He listens excluded.

Squaa-rrraw-kkk!

Cobb stood rigid, paralyzed by the hawk's terrifying screech. It seemed that the sound would awaken everyone in the house, that they would all come running to find him there, prying at the door.

Chill changed to sweat, drops of perspiration formed on his fore-head, drenched the small of his back. He drew the door shut. Trembling, he sat down on the nail keg.

Not mastered yet.

Revengeful anger spread through Cobb's vascular system. Adrenalin-soaked recollections of childhood defeat swelled his nerves. "You shall be tamed and like it," he promised the bird. "You shall sit on my wrist, hooded and belled, a mouse catcher, a tinklepaw, a lure carrier, chained to a stump when I am not using you."

Puff! *Je vous en merde.*

Puff, puff, puff, puff, puff . . .

CHAPTER 12

THE TWELFTH DAY of the siege (and the third day of the hawk taming) was a heartbreaker. Nothing marched right; the house-hold machinery clogged at every turn, refused to take the steepening grade imposed upon it by the storm. The portable oil stove under-neath the frozen elbow set fire to the ceiling—a close thing till Cobb and Gunnar got it under control with soda extinguishers. The cord-wood running low, it became necessary to decrease the number of logs burned each day, thus reducing the cheer and temperature of the living room. Tempers were jangled; the strain of the white ambush was beginning to show in snapped answers and taut facial muscles.

Fagged by his duties as trouble shooter and his watches at the hawk's bin, Cobb's strength and temper were seriously frayed. He caught himself barking orders at Gunnar, whose good nature was unwearied. Cobb laid his hand on the young Lieutenant's shoulder. "Sorry," he apologized, "I'm getting edgy."

"Forget it," said Gunnar.

On his ceaseless rounds of the house, Cobb kept three necessities —food, heat, and water—in the foreview of his mind. If these could be maintained at a decent level, he confidently believed that his household ship could ride out the storm. But across his calculation fell a new and graver menace—the crippled ventilation of the snow-smothered house.

The first hint of danger came when he noticed that he was breathing more rapidly after exertion. He mentioned it casually to Gunnar as they stacked wood in the living room. "Guess old age is creeping up on me." "No," said young Rollefson, "the thing that's creeping up on you, me, and all of us—is lack of oxygen." Cobb noticed that Gunnar was panting, too. "Normally," the Lieutenant went on, "oxygen comes in through doors, windows, porous walls. But the snow has sealed everything up tight." He pointed to the fireplace. "If it weren't for the chimney, this house would be like a submarine stranded on the bottom of a snow ocean."

"Quite a simile. But doesn't any oxygen seep in through the snow?"

"A little. But scarcely enough to support eight or nine people—especially when there's no movement of air inside the house." Gunnar's face was grave. "I wasn't worried as long as the air-conditioning fan sucked fresh air in and pumped the bad air out. But when the electricity went dead, the fan stopped. That was three or four days ago. By this time, our oxygen supply is pretty well exhausted."

Cobb imagined that he was beginning to feel dizzy. "We've got to start that fan working again, Lieutenant," he said, leading the way downstairs.

With Gunnar at his side, Cobb inspected the blower unit attached to the furnace. The fan was unpromisingly sealed up with its motor in a rugged one-piece housing, smooth and compact as an egg. Nothing on the outer surface. Nothing, that is, except an oil cup perched at the forward end of the blower shaft.

Gunnar tapped the oil cup. "By knocking this off, we might get an inch or two of driving shaft."

"Off it comes."

The oil cup, removed, revealed a scant two inches of shaft as thick as a man's thumb. Cobb's first idea was to attach a crank to it, then turn the crank by hand. But there was scarcely a foot of clearance from the floor. Besides the labor would have been grueling. The crank idea was out.

Gunnar, who never opened his mouth until he had something to say, was waiting for a spark to fall. It fell.

"Why not attach a gear to the shaft and drive it with an old bicycle?"

"Noble thought. Scout the cellar for bicycles. There's half a dozen of them lying around here."

Within the hour the sprocket of a bicycle was fixed to the end of the shaft; Gunnar's young legs drove the pedals furiously, but race as he might, he couldn't make the fan turn fast enough to blow a current of air through the house.

"Leg power isn't enough," said Cobb. "We've got to get a motor on there somehow."

Gunnar grabbed his shoulder in excitement. "What about my old Harley-Davidson motorcycle? Remember the goggles-and-gauntlet period I went through before the war? I used to think I was Superman"

Remembering the Superman outfit, Cobb grinned. "Sure, but where's your rocket machine now?"

"In the shed beside the garage. I left it there when I went away. We could dig it out in no time, sir."

The lad's enthusiasm needled Cobb's heart-wall with courage. "Wait a minute. We'll get Laimbeer to help us on the shoveling detail It'll do him good to flex his muscles."

Cobb found the artist in the music room making a pen-and-ink sketch of Nolla. She was reclining on the Récamier divan near the fireplace, embroidering her oval tambour with the gold and scarlet threads. An Arthurian story-book air, a Lady of Shalott atmosphere that Cobb hesitated to break, hung over the scene.

As he entered, a *moue* of vexation tightened Nolla's mouth. She held her profile pose, pricked out a scarlet thread on her tambour. "Well?"

"Sorry to interrupt the—ah—sitting, Laimbeer. But we've got a shoveling detail underway. Thought you might like to lend a hand."

"Important?" Detached in voice and manner, the artist refined a contour at Nolla's cheekbone.

"Rather." Cobb held back the news of the oxygen crisis. "When you finish your sketch," he said, "you'll find us shoveling toward the garage."

"Count on me," murmured Laimbeer.

A hot rash of irritation prickled the back of Cobb's neck. The painter's cavalier tone, his unwillingness to pull his weight in the boat, were no longer amusing. The guy would have to be disciplined. This, however, was no time for a showdown. Fresh air was the important thing now.

He joined Gunnar at the back door, picked up a shovel, and began tossing snow. The distance to the garage was a long hundred and fifty feet; by working steadily they made it in a couple of hours. By the time Cobb lifted the last shovelful, he was utterly fagged.

Laimbeer did not come out.

Gunnar pulled open the door of the garage, jerked the tarpaulin off his old motorcycle. "It's Superman!" he shouted. Scrutiny showed a tank half full of gas; enough for two days. Together they trundled the heavy machine back along the path to the house. By the time they got it into the cellar it was four o'clock—the hour for Cobb's session with the hawk. Much as he longed for his turn at the bird, he tapped the elder Rollefson on the shoulder and said:

"Spell me, bos'n. We're fixing up a blower contraption."

The Norseman seemed not to understand. "Blower?" he repeated vaguely. He, too, was wearying; incessant smoking and shortage of sleep had dulled the edges of his mind. "But tonight we man the hawk."

Cobb had no time to argue with his cadgerman. "Smoke for me, Rollefson," he said, and hurried back to the ventilator fan.

While he hammered together a cradle of two-by-fours to support the rear end of the motorbike, Gunnar linked the driving chain to the fan shaft. "Now for the big buzz." He vaulted into the saddle of the Harley, kicked off the starter. *Brrr-uppp, put-put-put.* On the second try the engine took hold racingly. Gunnar throttled her down, threw in the clutch. The chain took hold of the gear teeth; the fan began to turn. Gunnar accelerated the motor; the fan turned faster.

"Shall I let her rip?"

"Hold on!" shouted Cobb. "We've got to pipe these exhaust fumes out of here." He seized a length of garden hose, attached it to the exhaust manifold, then jabbed the other end of the hose through a window into the snow.

"Open her up!" he cried. Gunnar twisted the throttle; the blower fan revved up, the blades whirring in a low crescendo. Cobb dashed upstairs into the living room, put his hand to the ventilation grating near the baseboards. Cool air was coming through. The fire from the hearth felt the new draft, crackled more brightly.

"What's the matter?" asked Beryl, coming into the room.

His victory over the deathly gas filled him with kissing exuberance. "It's O.K. to breathe again," he cried, seizing her around the middle.

"How can I breathe," murmured Beryl, "when your mouth is all over me like that?"

*　*　*

That afternoon the roof of the music room caved in.

Cobb was at the door of the hawk's bin pouring pipeloads of smoke through the open crack when he heard a rending crash, followed by a thud, as though a gigantic boot had kicked the house. Then the sound of running feet and Mrs. Rollefson's voice bellowing down the cellar stairs.

"Mr. Cobb, Mr. Cobb! Come quick, the roof is falling in!"

Rushing upstairs, Cobb saw his family huddled around the kitchen stove. Nolla, Sice, Roddy, Berry. Thank God, all present and accounted for. Gunnar striding in from the dining room made the official report.

"Roof of the music room just gave way, sir. No one in the wreckage."

"Let's have a look." Cobb led the way to the north wing, opened the door to what had been the music room. Now only a mountainous pile of snow loomed in the twilight; the roof timbers had snapped like matchsticks. Above his head Cobb saw the jagged edge of a single six by six—the only structural evidence that the room had ever existed. Piano, chairs, divan, chandelier—all had been smothered under the cumulative burden falling flake by flake on the flat roof.

How many of these innocent flakes did it take to crack a roof, smother a city, bury a civilization? Somewhere Cobb had read that the number of snowflakes that fell in a great storm was roughly equal to the number of stars in the sky, and that the stars were as numerous as the sands of the sea, the leaves on all the trees. Cobb felt for a moment the identity of all totals, the magnitude of their sums, and the minuscule figure of man struggling not to be overwhelmed beneath their weight. He closed the door of the music room.

"Tomorrow we'll salvage what we can," he said.

The tensions inside the house were now jangling like instruments violently plucked and out of tune. At dinner, absolute pitch was lacking. Nolla was in one of her "private" moods—remote, inaccessible, difficult. She was making it clear to Cobb that she blamed the loss of her piano (and dearer yet, the privacy of the music room) on his failure to shovel off the roof. Cobb inwardly admitted the oversight; he should have had the snow removed. Under ordinary circumstances, he would have apologized to Nolla—she was waiting expectantly for his submission—but a glance at Laimbeer's broad shoulders made the apology impossible. "If she wanted the roof shoveled off, she should have asked Laimbeer," was Cobb's un-uttered defense.

Between Gunnar and the artist a fearful edge of antagonism was being honed. Accustomed to the fellowship and shared duties of military life, Gunnar could not understand, as Cobb did, the painter's exemption from common toil. He was spoiling for a fight with Laimbeer.

The spark that touched off the general explosion came from Roddy in the form of a question.

"Father," he asked innocently enough, "do you think it will ever stop snowing?"

Cobb resurrected the old Cal Coolidge crack: "It always has." The light touch fell heavily.

"God," gritted Nolla, "the roof caves in and he makes wisecracks."

Sice plugged the gap of silence with a bit of information from her favorite source. "Gunnar says that even if it should stop snowing in the next five minutes, it'd be a week before we were all dug out."

"Just the idle thoughts of an idle fellow," said Gunnar, trying to pitch the talk on the up and up. "Don't let it get you down, folks. As a matter of fact, nothing very bad can happen as long as the food holds out."

"We've got tons of food, haven't we, Daddy?" Roddy was gnawing his fingernails again.

Cobb tried to ignore the fingernail business. "Well, not exactly tons, Rod. But plenty. Our real problems are light and heat."

Emma Rollefson smoothed out her capacious lap as though brushing crumbs of heating trouble out of the picture. "The coal range will keep the kitchen warm," she said. "And as long as a house has a warm kitchen, we'll be as snug as currants in a bun."

Seconding his mother's cheeriness, Gunnar patted the fieldstone fireplace. "By keeping this saturated with heat—never red hot, but just nice and steady—the living-room temperature will stay around forty-five degrees." He enlarged the field of argument. "While the snow keeps falling, the outside temperature *can't* drop much below thirty. And when the snow stops—well, the worst will be over."

"Q.E.D., we're as good as saved," said Laimbeer dryly. "Great stuff, mathematics."

Gunnar took a slow, hard look at the painter. "It's better than a lot of cheesy art."

"What would you know about art?"

"More than you know about mathematics." Gunnar's anger was on the loose now. "It didn't take an Einstein to figure out, back there, that we needed a hundred gallons of oil to keep the furnace going. And how many gallons did *you* lug? I forget. Was it five or ten?"

"Five," said Beryl, as if consulting a memo.

"Mind your own business, Beryl," snapped Nolla.

"Shut your goddam face," said Berry.

"Be still, all of you." Blue anger crackled in Cobb's voice. He rose, put his hands on his hips like a first mate addressing a tough crew of whalers. "Wrangling is *out,* do you hear? We'll either get along peaceably, or"—he smacked the table with the heel of his fist—"or I'll slap everyone's ears back. One at a time, or all together, whichever you want."

He got himself under control again, stepped off his first mate's hatch. "I want to make one thing clear. No matter what we think of each other, we're going to keep it between our teeth." He wheeled on young Rollefson first. "Do you get that, Gunnar?"

The young officer's face was flushed, ashamed. "Yes, sir," he said penitently.

"And you, Beryl?"

"Sorry, Rusty. I'll try to keep my lip buttoned."

"Laimbeer?"

Hunched in his chair, the painter made no reply. Cobb walked over to him, clasping both hands behind his back and trying to keep undue aggressiveness out of his voice. "Laimbeer," he said, "once when I asked you for a hand on some necessary work, you didn't find it convenient to respond. You goldbricked, ran out, didn't even show up. You were too busy with your art—and other little matters." The painter's jaw was at a tempting level, flush with Cobb's fist. "Well, after you leave this house, you'll be quite at liberty to conduct your life as you see best. But while you're here," Cobb paused and falling snow hissed in the chimney, "you're going to share and share alike on work—and food. Briefly, Laimbeer, you'll do what I say, or you don't eat."

Nolla was on her feet. "Stop acting like a domineering fool, Ruston."

"Keep out of this, Nolla."

"I won't keep out of it." She tried to thrust herself between the painter and her husband. "People don't talk that way in my house."

"Oh, they don't!" Fatigue and accumulated burdens of the past ten days snapped Cobb's self-control. The thousand thwarts of his married life boiled in his blood. "You mean they never have." He lifted his hand in a hatchet gesture. "Well, they're going to now. Get back into your corner and stay there till I tell you to come out."

Nolla's face was a pale mask of contempt. "Don't lift your hand to me like that, you—mama's boy."

Cobb slapped one side of her face with the palm of his hand. Only the daze in his wife's eyes prevented a second blow.

"Look out, Rusty!" screamed Berry. Cobb turned to see his son jerk a dart from the cork board. Roddy's face was white, his mouth tight with killer fury.

"Don't you dare strike Mother!" He drew back his thin arm, hurled the dart at his father's head. This time it had the old *tzing* as it whizzed past Cobb's neck, an inch from the carotid artery. Roddy stood paralyzed, then, shaking with pale ague, ran out of the room after his mother.

] 198 [

Wind of desolation roared in the chimney, blew a flurry of snow-flakes into the room.

Laimbeer started to get up, but Cobb shoved him back into the chair. "Stay where you are, Laimbeer. All I want to hear from you is one little word. It'll be unesthetic and all that, but you've got to say it or starve. Do you, in the presence of these remaining witnesses, say 'Yes' to the work-or-eat proposition outlined above?"

"Yes," muttered Laimbeer.

"Good. Now if you need a drink as badly as I do, you can help yourself to some Scotch."

Rat-toothed regret was gnawing at Ruston Cobb as he descended the stairs to the hawk vigil in the cellar. The toxic aftermath of anger began to work in him; delayed poison seeped into his nerves, bones, and muscles, made him an aching gelatine of remorse. The recollection of Nolla's stunned gaze, the slow lifting of her hands to cover the white imprint of his fingermarks on her face, her stricken gait as she left the room fell upon him like a basketful of adders. No use to attempt self-justification. Cobb tried to tell himself that he was taut with worry, overborne with fatigue when he struck Nolla, that he was heartily sick of her languid queen-beeism, her frigid martyrdom. But his pleas were invalid against the accusation in Nolla's eyes.

"You struck me!" The desolate indictment echoed down the alley of whitewashed pillars as Cobb made his way to the hawk's bin.

Rollefson, hoarse and bleary-eyed from double shifts of smoking, was barely able to speak. By grunts and signs he indicated that the hawk was yielding rapidly to the pressure of smoke and starvation.

"You can go in tonight." The caretaker pointed to some strips of meat in a basket. "Hood the bird. Feed it." Heavy-heeled with fatigue, he staggered off to his bunk.

Eager for the knockout, Cobb lighted his pipe, opened the door, and sat down on the rickety sofa inside the bin. Not a ruffle from the hawk. The arrogant knuckles were loosening, the fierce eyes dimming with submission. Soon Cobb would slip a leather hood over those eyes; later, thonged and docile, the golden talons would wrap themselves around Cobb's wrist. This was the triumph the man had promised himself. It was real; it was good; it was close at hand.

He lighted a candle, jammed it into the neck of an empty beer bottle, and placed the improvised candlestick on the floor near the hawk. Disturbed by the light, the bird was unable to lift beak or talon in protest. How patient, how strong, how *cruel* one had to be! By candlelight Cobb slipped the leather hood over the hawk's eyes. The soft, red morocco harness gave the bird a sinister appearance as it clung to the falconer's wrist. To build up its strength, he took a thin strip of beef that Rollefson had prepared, touched the hawk's beak gently with the food. With a feeble peck the hawk managed to get the meat into its mouth.

"Eating right out of your hand," said a voice at the door of the bin.

It was Beryl. The candlelight scooped unexpected hollows under her cheekbones, and her perfume scented the foul-smelling bin. She came close to Cobb, so close that the curves under her cashmere sweater nuzzled his arm as he fed the hawk.

"How queer the hood makes her look."

"Doesn't it? What's going on upstairs?"

"Not much." Berry was obliquely meaningful. "After the row everyone went to bed."

Cobb fed a second slice of beef to the bird. "Nolla and Laimbeer in the attic, I suppose?"

"Search me. They've disappeared, that's all I know." She rubbed her lower lip around the rim of his ear. "Rusty darling." Her voice, a female conch, sang into his bloodstream, dissolved, and reappeared achingly at a new pulse. He set the hawk on its perch, and caught at Berry's mouth. Her living red tongue, passive for a moment, took hold of him like a charged magnet, then pulled him slowly toward the broken sofa in the corner of the bin. Big, perfumed, hot, and female, she braced her luscious body against him, loosened the zipper of her skirt, kicked it off, then pulled the cashmere sweater over her head and flung it away. In her haste she ripped the shoulder straps of her slip; the torn garment fell drapingly around her hips. The candle flame threw her breasts into stark relief; with fingers stretched octavewise for the full chord of feeling, Cobb caressed them from root to tip.

Squaa-rawk!

The hawk shook her bells in jingling fury, strained at her leathern jesses as if she would gash the softness in Cobb's hands. But the bird's jealous, prohibiting scream no longer frightened him. Nothing in the world could frighten or stop him now.

Weakened by rage and long starvation, the hawk clawed angrily at its perch. In a fit of anger the golden talons missed their hold and the bird tumbled in a flurry of wings, jesses, hood, and bells onto the pile of droppings below. Head downward, she hung there, smearing captive pinions in her own lime.

Je vous en merde. That score was settled forever.

In Berry's hair, spread fanwise on the rickety sofa, Cobb buried his face the better to shut out all sensations save the exquisite pleasure she was building for him. Her eagerness and the intensity of her requitals were almost incredible to Cobb. But her very eagerness was flawed by an anxiety that threatened to mar the tempo and pattern of the exchange. Gradually, and for a reason puzzling to Cobb at first, Berry's emotional surety began to ebb away. She became a panicky child running down a dark, terror-haunted alley toward a distant beam of light—a frantic little girl fearful that some ghostly hand would seize her by the hair, snatch her backward before she reached her goal.

In the candle-shadows Cobb read the pitiful secret in Berry's tormented eyes and anxious face. This seemingly passionate woman was unable to run the full love-course! So much else became clear now. Berry's endless succession of men, her moody drinking, and her deathly conspiracy to defeat herself in love, all sprang from this one crippling thwart.

Afterward, with quiet endearments, he tried to reassure and comfort her. "You do wonderful things for me," he said with simple male gratitude. Berry's eyes were wet with imperfect happiness. A sense of something shared, even a defective partial sharing, gave her strength to throw off her sadness and pick up the casual wear of courage. She smiled, shivered slightly. "It's cold here, darling. Or did we forget?" She rose from the sofa and started hunting for her clothes.

A sullen squawk came from the falcon's corner. Cobb lifted the bird from her fetid wallow and wiped some of the filth off her plumage, courting forgiveness by tenderly holding the remaining strips of meat to her beak. A curious realization of love's duality, its constant shifting from cruelty to kindness and back again, filled his thoughts as he removed the bird's hood, settled her for sleep.

Candle in hand he turned to watch Berry putting on her skirt How glorious the movements of women! Glorious beyond all failure, weakness, guilt, suffering, and disappointment. Glorious quite apart from the degree or kind of love you felt for them. But now, watching Berry lift her arms to shake the cashmere sweater down over her shoulders, a terrible sense of deprivation assailed Ruston Cobb. As she pulled the hem over her breasts he knew he would be lonely, restless, and unfulfilled until he could be at them again.

It was three o'clock when he reached his room. Undressing, he heard Nolla coming down the attic stairs, enter her room. Silently he got into bed, lay there in the darkness.

Listening . . .

Ruston Cobb listened for twenty minutes before he realized that his wife, for the first time in many years, was not performing her bedtime ritual.

CHAPTER 13

"THE FIREWOOD," reported Gunnar next morning, "is almost gone."

There had been something less than a cord of wood to begin with, and the drain of keeping open fires blazing in the study and living room had by this time nearly exhausted the supply. Cobb snatched a reading from the big outside thermometer. Still glued to 32° F. Lucky it wasn't any colder. The blanket of snow actually kept things from freezing. Ermine lining. Vision of Sir Long Fall. Heaven tries the earth if it be in tune and over it gently her warm ear lays.

"There'll be a lot of broken lumber in the music room," he said, "beams, joists, studding. Plenty of studding." The pun grimly amused him. "Let's have a look."

As a source of firewood, the music room did not seem at first sight promising. A high dolmen of snow, supported by the further wall, was vaguely silhouetted against lowering clouds, but the center of the room was an oval mound, a monstrous sugar loaf at the center of which precious roof timbers lay buried. Work, muscular and long, must be performed before those timbers could burn on the hearth.

"First the shovels, then the ax," said Cobb. He was a contractor estimating a job in terms of time and energy. "We'll be needing help." He salted special meaning into his grin. "And this time, we're going to get it."

Gunnar returned the grin. "That'll be something to watch, sir."

"It will, indeed. Lieutenant Rollefson, break out the tools and stand by. I'll be back with reinforcements."

Cobb mounted the great staircase to the sleeping floor, groped down the corridor to the second door on the left. He paused, gathered his knuckles into a fist, rapped three times, neither belligerent nor polite.

A shortish long wait. Then Laimbeer's voice, a pillow-smothered, ill-tempered grunt meaning, "What is it?"

"Firewood detail, Laimbeer. You've got exactly twenty minutes to make the eight-thirty roll call."

No response from within.

"You heard me, Laimbeer?"

The painter took a long thirty seconds to get his head out of the pillow. "Coming," he mumbled.

Cobb repressed the malicious urge to add, "Never mind shaving." Too obvious. Must be correct. This is your shovel; this is your ax. By the sweat of your brow.

At eight thirty-five, Laimbeer, having gulped coffee in the kitchen, reported for duty at the music-room door. He looked foggy and rumpled, but after all, this was no beauty contest. Cobb handed him a shovel, explained the simple strategy of its use. "Dig into that center mound until you strike buried timbers. Then yell out for the buck-saw. We'll cut up the stuff where it lays and stack it in the living room. Got it straight?"

Laimbeer nodded without enthusiasm. He knew he was on a spot, and that before the day was over he would be soggy, cold, and exhausted from traveling along the route that Cobb had mapped out for him. But he was intelligent enough to realize that the road had to be traveled. If he doubted that he was in good enough condition to go the whole distance, he gave Cobb no indication of his fear. Stoically, Laimbeer began to work with the slow and easy tempo of a man resolved to be on his feet at the finish.

O.K. with me, thought Cobb. He knew that a certain type of prize fighter could absorb a frightful amount of punishment before taking the count. Bat Nelson never knew when he was knocked out. Result, slug-nutty. Others, weaker jawed, took the count sooner, lived to fight another day. He hoped that Laimbeer was the Bat Nelson type.

While Laimbeer and Gunnar shoveled snow, Cobb kept the household machinery in running order. There was plenty to do. The motorbike, pumping air through the house, had to be kept going; the portable oil stove under the elbow must not be allowed to wane or climb. Food had to be carried into the kitchen, and above all wood must be fed into the fireplace, not wastefully but just enough to keep the hearthstones warm. A program to keep Satan at arm's length. A day's work for a day's existence.

Going about his chores, Cobb felt alternately elated and depressed. His passionate encounter with Beryl in the hawk's bin had blasted the dikes of his emotional life, and great streams of energy poured from hidden reservoirs within him. The fierce bellows of her desire had fanned him into animal warmth; the whole surface of his body glowed when he thought of her, and the knowledge that she had helped him break through into a new and freer dimension of love filled him with gratitude, tenderness, and strength. But the tide of exaltation would scarcely attain full height before it ebbed down the dreary shingle of Nolla's suspected infidelity, leaving him stranded and desolate in its receding roar. He tried to rationalize the affair between his wife and Laimbeer, to excuse her, even to be glad for her sake. He told himself that Nolla's experience with the painter might wrench her free of the fearful bond that had always constrained her. He understood, almost approved, what had happened. But the knowledge did not make him happy or soften his intention to revenge himself on Nolla's lover.

On his rounds of the house, a tormenting curiosity pulled him, against his better judgment, toward the little attic room that Nolla had fitted up as a studio retreat. In the darkness he climbed the attic stairs, turned left, and followed a narrow corridor till he came to the southern end of his house. Then he let himself into the little room, lighted a candle, and looked about. Peaked roof, snug with wallboard and insulation. Very cozy, with its writing table, studio couch, and armchair. He turned back the corduroy couch cover. Hmm, fresh linen, a smear of lipstick on one of the pillows. A diminutive drum-stove crouched like a small black dog against a huge whitewashed chimney. Cobb opened the door of the stove; soft wood, kindling, and newspapers were ready for the match. Could the fire have been laid long ago? No, the dateline on one of the newspapers was February 20th, the last day the paper had been delivered. Convinced?

On the table lay the oval tambour that Nolla was embroidering. Curiously Cobb picked up the tambour, examined the needlework intently. It was a *carte d'amour,* a love map depicting the landscape of Champagne, so piously traversed by the troubadours of Provence. Here, traced on fine linen in Laimbeer's flowing line, was the whole countryside of love, its topographical features delicately lettered in French. *"Le Sentier du Premier Espoir, La Forêt des Rêves Amoureux"*—all converging upon the central Tree of Love on whose topmost branch flowered the white rose of Merci. Nolla had told the artist what to draw; he had drawn these figurative paths, dikes, hillocks, and flowering forests as part of his cavalier servitude. And Nolla's needle had faithfully followed his lines with silken threads —scarlet, emerald, and gold—recreating for herself the role of love queen, a contemporary Eleanor of Aquitaine.

Cobb laid the embroidery down, a new question in his mind. Who was beguiling whom? In this advance upon the central bush, who gave, who took commands? Which was the fowler, which the captive bird? Cobb could not answer these questions; he pinched out the candle and closed the door of the attic rendezvous behind him.

When he came back to the music room, the painter was still shoveling. The Bat Nelson type. Only a hundred and forty-five rounds to go. Cobb seized a shovel and pitched in. Snowflakes hard as birdshot peppered the trio as they worked; their hissing impact against face and hands chipped away the traditional notion of snow as a soft coverlet protecting earth's vegetation. By this time the storm had taken on an implacable quality; it seemed as though Nature intended first to ambush, then to massacre the plants and creatures of earth. The face of the plot, disclosed at last, was sinister and merciless.

Grunts, labored breathing, curses were the only sounds made by the three men as they worked. The sheer mass of snow that had to be lifted, carried away, and dumped over the walls of the music room was appalling; the treacherous footing made movement difficult; one slipped and floundered waist-deep. The dirty zinc sky threw down about as much light as a roof of a cave. And in this darkness, under the gritty barrage of snow, three men heaved and labored to uncover a few sticks of wood.

Cobb, knowing that his physical presence was a goad to Laimbeer, remained on the job all day. He put the hawk in Rollefson's charge, and sent Gunnar to inspect the motorbike and oil stove. Such matters could be delegated, but the pressure on Laimbeer demanded the personal turn of the screw, the privy pinch of salt, rubbed well into the wound. To make the going tougher for Laimbeer, Cobb decreed no lunch. His excuse said, "We must get some of these timbers sawed before dark," but urgent as the reality might be, both men knew there was a deeper reason for the order. To wear Laimbeer down, to fatigue him past the point where he could make love to Nolla, then, having taken his strength, to ply him with derision and contempt—this was the pressure chamber that Ruston Cobb was fashioning for his rival.

It would require, Cobb saw, a bit of construction. Laimbeer was no psychologic pushover, no suety lump. His frame was as powerful as Cobb's, his basic muscular equipment just as good, his driving motive no less strong. In actual years he was younger. Barring the factor of condition (Cobb shaded him here), the match was about equal. A short fight would be an even-money bet. But if the duel lengthened out . . .

Cobb lifted the stroke to thirty-six, grim-faced as he shoveled past Laimbeer, flailing his way out of a timber jam.

By the middle of the afternoon, much of the music-room wreckage had been laid bare by the trio of shovelers. Then, with an estimated two hours of daylight remaining, Cobb sent the buck-saw into action. Gunnar began on the six-by-six ceiling beams and sawed half a dozen four-foot oak billets before his arm gave out. Cobb spelled him for half an hour, adding five more oaken lengths to the woodpile. Then wordlessly he handed the saw to Laimbeer. The painter picked up the saw gingerly, laid its toothed edge against a cracked beam, advertising by his clumsy actions that he was unfamiliar with the tool.

"Here, this way," Cobb explained. "Don't push. Just pull. The teeth do the work. But put two hands into it."

He stood near the painter, overhanging him with his presence, ruling him psychologically as he toiled through the thick oak. After the first length fell, Laimbeer got the hang of the buck-saw. It was almost dark when, panting and spent, he finished his stint. As the others had done, he carried his wood, a section at a time, into the living room and stacked it by the fireplace.

The day's work was almost over and Laimbeer was still on his feet.

The painter was picking up his last piece of wood when Cobb heard him exhale in a fierce gasp of pain. It was so dark that Cobb could not see what had happened until Laimbeer came into the house carrying his burden. His face was gray-blue; his lips, grayer yet, were pressed thin against his teeth.

Nolla leaped forward. "What is it, Ed?"

Laimbeer dropped the wood with a crash, the first crack in his morale all day, and thrust his right hand into the circle of lamplight falling on the living-room table. His square, handsome fingers were purple with cold and dirt, and from the root of his thumb a broad splash of blood was oozing.

"A splinter," he groaned, not at the pain but at the defamation of his hand. "God damn it, get some water quick."

"Take it easy, Laimbeer. We'll get it out." Cobb was the headmaster calming a jittery boy.

"Oh, we'll get it out, will we?" In his anger Laimbeer mimicked the schoolmasterish quality in Cobb's voice. "We got it in, so we'll get it out, heh? Like hell you will. I'll get it out myself." He swung to Nolla. "Get me some soap and hot water. I'll wash this muck off first."

Faces turned to Cobb. He did not countermand the order. He could see that Laimbeer was almost hysterical at the thought of danger to his hands. Reasonable. As though a singer should get an arrow in the throat.

"Fetch the soap and water," he said, "and some tweezers. If Laimbeer wants to operate on himself—well, after all, it's his hand."

Nolla's eyes were spitting, but Cobb was too weary to support another brawl. He wanted only to unlace his snowboots and lie down between blankets for a rest before supper. An evening of work and planning lay ahead; he must be fresh for it though the heavens fell. He fished in the credenza, pulled out a bottle of Scotch, and, for the first time in his life, drank without lifting his glass or eyes to anyone else in the room.

"Call me when dinner's ready," he said to the people at large, and started for his room. Halfway up the stairs, Berry was at his side, her hand under his elbow. She opened his door for him, and, on her knees in the dark, unlaced the rawhide thongs of his boots,

] 209 [

pulled them off by the heel. She peeled off his jacket, pressed him down upon the pillow. Passive with fatigue, he let himself be covered with blankets, kissed, and fondled.

"I'll bring up some hot water when I call you for supper," Berry whispered, and without further fuss left the room.

That evening, Thursday, March 8th, was a dragging repetition of all the other evenings since the snow had begun. After twelve snowbound days and nights, there was little that Cobb or anyone else could contrive in the way of variety; the game-playing phase had passed; no one expected Musical Chairs any more, and after Roddy's performance with the dart, that little game was taboo. Either you paired off like Gunnar and Sicely to play gin rummy in the kitchen—the warmest and brightest room in the house—or you huddled close to the fireplace and tried to read for an hour before bed.

On this particular evening, Berry, without apology, went upstairs to bed, while Nolla and Laimbeer remained in the living room to imitate the motions of social beings. Weary as the painter was, he pulled out a pad of drawing paper and fell to sketching Nolla's profile as she sat knitting a pair of socks (the tambour was reserved for more intimate hours in the upper room). Laimbeer's sore thumb was hampering him, and his eyelids were heavy with the need of an after-dinner nap, but he sketched on. Cobb felt a grim admiration for the man's shrewd handling of Nolla. The delicacy of his exquisite sketches were, in themselves, effective flattery. But obedience to her wishes—particularly that he abstain from open warfare with her husband—was an even more suitorish tribute that the artist placed at Nolla's feet. Cobb knew well enough that she had given Laimbeer explicit instructions based on the traditional docility of the lover as prescribed by Eleanor of Aquitaine. And it had become the painter's delight to observe the letter of his lady's injunction, thereby gaining a double victory over her secrets and against her husband.

In a strange way Cobb was grateful for Laimbeer's punctilio in his relations with Nolla. The gravest wrong that one man could do another (and in his own house) was being done with less cock-of-the-walk crowing than would accompany the making of a grand slam at a gentlemen's bridge club. "A single arrogance," Cobb promised himself, "and I will kill the fellow." But the artist made no blunders in deportment, and Cobb had no technical handle for revenge.

Tonight he knew that as soon as he went down cellar to take his turn at the hawk, they would steal away to the attic, light the little drum stove, and begin their Provençal rites. He saw Nolla glancing at the clock. Seven fifty-five. In another five minutes he was due to relieve Rollefson in the hawk's bin. Ten minutes thereafter the little drum stove would be roaring.

Why should he go to the cellar anyway, to license by his departure the illicit pleasuring of this pair? Cobb remembered enough of the Code of Provence to know that a husband who demurred at his wife's amours was not *gentil*—was, in fact, no better than a stable boy. Courtly manners required that a husband ignore these privy affairs of the heart—that he smile, and bow himself out to carry on affairs of his own. Love and let love, Eleanor of Aquitaine had decreed. Well, to hell with Eleanor. Cobb jammed a fierce thumbful of tobacco into his pipe and decided to sit it right out here in the living room till Laimbeer fell asleep.

To support his vigil with good manners—he had no intention of carrying on a conversation or hugging the fireplace like a surly bump—Cobb picked up his *Encyclopedia of Sports* and turned to the article on falconry. He wanted more information about the next step in the hawk's training. Manned and hooded, what happened next? Ah yes, here it was, a couple of longish paragraphs on "The Lure." Very important. Cobb spread the heavy book on his knee and settled down for a session of instructive reading. He could feel rather than see the desperation in Nolla's needle as he read:

The lure consists of a weighted leathern disc to which two pigeon feathers have been attached to give it a semblance of reality. The falcon is unhooded, food is placed in the center of the lure, and it is tossed a few feet away. The bird darts at this artificial prey and tries to fly away with it. But alas, she is doomed to disappointment, for the weighted disc is too heavy for her to lift. Repeated failure breaks her of the habit of "carrying,"—that is, flying off with the quarry that she must learn to deposit at her master's feet. It is a most important lesson; a falcon that "carries" is as bad as a bird dog that runs off with retrieved game and devours it in a secluded spot.

Gradually the lure is thrown further and further away. The bird is obliged to fly after it, first with a leash attached to her jesses, then—oh perilous moment in the life of the falconer— utterly free. The risk is that the bird, sensing its freedom, will elect to bathe its wings in a sun-washed cloud and never return to the dark captivity of the hood. This first unleashed flight is a great crisis with bird and trainer, but if the falcon's education has been properly managed it rarely flies away. The well-trained bird soars into its element; the broad regions of the sky beckon, and for a crucial moment she balances the temptation on her wings. Then, if she has the makings of a true falcon, she darts toward the lure with the speed of light. She is no longer a wildling; for better or worse, she is a winged projection of the falconer, another symbol of man's cunning domination of nature.

Looking up from his page, Cobb caught the full ray of Nolla's eyes turned on the dozing artist. Such longing attention he had never seen in any woman's glance. "My heart circles over you," it cried. "I would beak you with desire and carry you away to an eyrie of delight. Be docile; let me instruct you now. Be patient, so that I may learn from you later. Sleep a little, the more to solace me when you awaken."

Which was the falconer here, which the prey? Lure and beak, net and wings were so entangled that he would never know. But such knowledge was unimportant. What was important—painfully, flutteringly clear—was Nolla's desperate need to be alone with her lover in the little upper room where the drum stove waited for the match and the pillow her thrown-back head.

Never had Cobb felt such pity for his wife, or identified her more completely with the hooded creature in the dark bin. He saw that her whole being was poised for skyey flight, and that she longed for the testing race with an emotional equal. The knowledge brought sorrow that only the unsuccessful husband knows. But as if to hush the pain, a second wisdom spoke: "It is the due of every living thing to discover its special region of delight, its own altitude of love, and try its wings therein. This alone is freedom and life. All else is captivity and death."

The rights of husbands seemed very small to Ruston Cobb—indeed, scarcely worth mentioning—as he put down his book, kissed the net of fine wrinkles at his wife's temple, and went groping down the dark stairs.

CHAPTER 14

The struggle for firewood began again next morning; Cobb roused his men out with the first filterings of daylight. Gunnar's young energy roared like a Pratt and Whitney engine, but Laimbeer had to prime himself with three cups of coffee before the mists of fatigue began to peel from his eyes. Cobb, stiff as a piece of old harness, knew that the painter must be a mass of sore muscles and aching bones, and that his performance over the love jumps had set no records. Odd that a man should be concerned about *quantity!*

The painter's thumb was obviously bothering him, but he offered no excuses and claimed no exemptions as he glumly took his shovel and began tossing snow. Fresh blankets had fallen during the night over the music-room debris; the wind had piled up new drifts in fantastic shapes, and not until mid-morning were the big timbers uncovered, ready for the saw.

Cobb's slide-rule eye judged that twelve hundred running feet of beams and studding could be salvaged from the floor, walls, and ceiling of the ruined room. Sawed into three-foot lengths, this meant approximately four hundred substantial pieces of firewood—some pine but chiefly oak. Consume these at the rate of forty a day—old and well-seasoned, they would burn rapidly—and by simple arithmetic you could keep the fires going for ten days. After that? Well, after that . . .

The temperature had fallen during the night; the dry air was ammonial sharp as the men toiled amid the falling snow. Faithfully they spelled each other at saw and shovel; then, bucket-brigade fashion, they passed the wood from hand to hand till it was stacked inside the house. During this phase of the operation, Cobb noticed that the painter was using only his left hand. He kept his bandaged hand in his coat pocket, seldom drew it out, and then only to nurse it for a moment. In one of the breathing spells, Cobb said brusquely, "How's that thumb of yours, Laimbeer?"

Grudgingly the painter produced his bandaged thumb; Cobb unwound the gauze, found the inside wrappings covered with a greasy brown salve. "What's this stuff here?"

"Arnica. Your wi— Nolla put it on last night."

"Hmph." Cobb examined the thumb itself. Swollen and badly inflamed, it showed angry signs of infection. "Here's what you do," he directed. "Go in and tell Mrs. Rollefson to take care of this. She's famous for her home remedies. She'll probably put some Epsom salts in a basin of hot water and make you soak your hand in it. Good treatment, too."

Laimbeer hesitated. "The sooner you go, the sooner you get back," said Cobb pointedly.

Twenty minutes later the painter reappeared with his hand in a new and bigger bandage. "She put a wet dressing on it," he reported as he took over the buck-saw.

"The Mayo Clinic couldn't do more." They were the last words uttered for an hour.

Slowly the fuel pile grew. Alternately shoveling and sawing, the three men salvaged nearly a hundred pieces of firewood by late afternoon. Time was now measured in terms of stacked wood, and the horizon of the world became the music room's broken wall. Occasionally, amid down-swirling snow, Cobb's shovel dredged up broken objects from another life: a dented cigarette box, a chipped crystal from a chandelier, a sheet of Mozart music stiff as death. Once his shovel struck something densely solid; scraping away the snow he uncovered the keyboard of Nolla's piano. His first impulse was to cry out to her, "Darling, look, it's still here." But the cry was smothered by a weight heavier than the snow. He gazed at the frozen keys that had skipped and sung under his wife's fingers. He saw her turning her head as she rounded the bend in scherzo time, giving him his favorite music the way he liked it, trippingly gay. But this keyboard image of remembered happiness was overcast by another: the memory of Laimbeer's hand claiming Nolla's in his proprietary grasp.

To demolish the picture Cobb struck the keyboard with the flat of his shovel. The strings and hammers of the instrument, choked with snow, were silent under his blow. Sudden tears dashed into Ruston Cobb's eyes, puzzling him with their salt urgency. Why should he weep for dead music when the musician herself was still alive? Was it a premonition of life without her, a fear that he had lost her forever?

Standing in the ruinous cold, Cobb knew then that in spite of his defeats and failures with his wife, in spite of her frigidity, withdrawals, and queen-beeism, his love for her was the rock on which his life was built and that all the powers of hell, death, and infidelity could not prevail against it. Let towers fall, snow descend, roofs crumple, winds rage, and drum stoves roar—let Berry strip off her clothes and Laimbeer cozen with Provençal endearments— and Ruston Cobb would only love Nolla Deane the more. Not for reward or pleasure, or hope that she would change, but because——

"Hey, Mr. Cobb!" It was Gunnar's voice calling in agitation through the snow.

"Coming. What's the trouble?"

The trouble was Laimbeer's hand. Clenching a fist of pain the painter stood swaying in the snow, the buck-saw at his feet, sweat pouring down his face.

"It's his thumb," said Gunnar. "I told him to go inside but he won't go."

] 216 [

"Come along." Cobb took the man by the arm, guided him into the house, and eased him into a chair beside the fireplace.

"Get some whiskey, Nolla. Beryl, hold a lamp. I'm going to take a good look at this thing."

He helped Laimbeer off with his jacket and sweater, gave him two quick jiggers of rye, then rolled back the painter's shirtsleeve and examined the injured hand. Under the lamp the depth and extent of the infection were dramatically visible. Wicked streaks of red radiated from thumb to elbow; the whole forearm was involved in an ugly inflammation, and the pain extended up the entire arm. Examining the swollen lymph glands in the man's armpit, Cobb knew that these damlike sponges were struggling to prevent the infection from invading the general circulation. A dark speck deeply imbedded in the swollen thumb indicated that a piece of the splinter was still there. In Cobb's judgment it had to come out.

"Roddy," he said, "get me your taxidermy set."

Laimbeer pulled away his arm. "You're not going to cut my hand?"

"Look, Laimbeer, it would be a lot easier for me to wrap this up again in a nice white bandage and tell you to forget it. Not that you could. You're going to have trouble until the rest of that lumber comes out. Now, do you want me to make a small incision in your thumb and go in after the splinter, or don't you?"

Snow hissed in the fireplace as Laimbeer considered his reddening arm.

"Go in after it," he mumbled.

Roddy appeared with the taxidermy knives; Mrs. Rollefson fetched a basin of boiling water. Then, while the entire household watched, Cobb prepped his patient's hand for the operation. There was nothing remarkable about the performance; it was household surgery of a minor kind—nothing that a careful man with a clean, sharp blade couldn't do. Plenty of soap and water, a quick incision. Please God I don't strike an artery. Didn't. Tweezers probing for

] 217 [

the remnant of splinter. "Ah, here's the little trouble maker. . . . Now to squeeze out the pus. Hurts, eh? Too bad we haven't any sulfa powder, but I'll pour in some whiskey instead. Forty-five per cent alcohol, you know. Feel better?"

"Much better. Thanks."

The little circle broke up into relieved segments. Nolla hovered at Laimbeer's side, lighting his pipe. Roddy, snuffling with a cold, gazed at his father with thoughtful, red-ringed eyes. "The child should be in bed" passed parenthetically through Cobb's mind as Berry handed him a jigger of rye. "Nice going, Doc," she said. "I'd like to be a nurse in your hospital." Sicely aimed a kiss at her father's chin, then rushed out in the kitchen to help Mrs. Rollefson serve up dinner. Cobb drained off the whiskey.

A peculiar hush lay over the room. A sound was missing. What sound? Cobb's ear went up like a stag that has outrun his hunters. Where were the pursuers? He gazed into his empty whiskey glass, heard Laimbeer and Nolla murmuring. Beryl was chattering at his side, and a clatter of dishes came from the kitchen. But some constant accompaniment had faded out, died.

"The snow," he told himself, "is not hissing in the fireplace."

He pushed open the door of the music room, looked upward. The air was without motion, clear and cold. Above his head he saw a star shining, then dozens of stars, thousands of stars blazing like steel sparks in a bright black sky. A great shout rose from Ruston Cobb's heart and lungs.

"The snow has stopped!" he cried.

His voice echoed throughout the house. His people came running. There was a pile-up in the center of the living room. Pummelings, huggings, kissings. "The snow is over," they laughed. "The storm is passed," they cried. "We are safe," they rejoiced.

Beryl's arms were around Cobb's neck. "You pulled us through, Rusty." Pride in his accomplishment, secret glory in being this man's sweetheart were in her embrace.

] 218 [

Cobb wished that these were Nolla's arms around him. "We're not through yet, Berry," he said, and his words were both a warning and a promise.

* * *

Now began the heaviest part of the siege. The cold came in on heavy iron skates, blown by a brutal wind that cossacked down through a cleft in the hills and rode screaming past the top of Cobb's chimney. All through the night the mercury sank steadily until it reached five above zero; there, like a crippled horse, it halted. Next day the world was locked in a vise of blue-white cold that grew crueler by the hour. Into the stony orifice of the fireplace Cobb fed the precious supply of wood, two sticks at a time, keeping the temperature of the living room at a fairly level forty.

"This cold snap can be licked by a three-way defense," he said at lunch. "First, of course, we keep the fires going. Second"—he glanced at Nolla—"we break out all the sweaters, mufflers, and long drawers in the house. Don't mind how you look. And last"—he took a heaping forkful of mashed potatoes—"everyone stokes up with good old carbohydrates—heat-making, cheap, and plentiful hereabouts. Inner blankets, that's what they are. In a couple of days this cold snap will break, and I want you all to be on hand for the nice spring thaw that'll follow."

Despite the intense cold everyone in the household except Laimbeer was in top spirits. They laughed and talked with the exaggerated gaiety of passengers on a ship that has passed safely through a hurricane. Laimbeer's gloom was recognized as natural; he was in pain and couldn't be expected to join in the lunch-table antics. But Berry, wrapped in an old raccoon coat and a Paisley shawl around her head, looked very healthy and comfortable. It cheered Cobb to see that her spunk kept rising; the tougher the going, the better she looked and acted. Nolla's tone was up, too. Her affair with Laimbeer was an endocrine tonic that brought color to her skin, a glow

] 219 [

to her eyes The task of nursing the painter, of attending to his wants, stretched her emotionally, kept her pulse at a hyperthyroid tempo. At times Cobb was almost grateful to the artist for the miracle he had wrought in Nolla; from a listless, dispirited neurotic he had transformed her—temporarily, at least—into a feelingful woman, pretty, with assurance. Even though she was swathed in a bundle of skirts and sweaters, Nolla had never looked more feminine. Tucking away the last of her sausage and potatoes, she announced to Laimbeer: "Class in bandaging meets at one P.M. Mr. Edward Laimbeer has consented to the use of his right hand for practice."

"But Mama," complained Roddy, "you said you'd read to me after lunch. It's been days and days since Captain Ahab sighted the White Whale."

The boy's face was pallid, unhappy. Since the dart incident, Roddy had lost much of his sparkle. Was it, Cobb wondered, because the boy realized the frightful implications of his attack upon his father, or was it merely lack of sunshine and fresh air? Cobb couldn't tell. On his side he felt only pity for the boy's plight. Led on by his mother, and now about to be deserted by her—this was the classic trap designed for the special torture of boy children.

Nolla glanced at her son, troubled conscience in her eyes. She had planned to spend the afternoon with Laimbeer in the attic studio, and now this other claimant, this earlier favorite, was complicating matters by his importunate claims. Could she put him off?

"Read on by yourself a bit, Roddy. That's a good fellow. We'll catch up together later on, yes?"

Downcast, bewildered, Roddy laid the unguent of grave acceptance on his soul. Cobb knew exactly how the boy felt. Who should know better? Roddy was what Cobb long ago had been—the fobbed-off, rejected one, hurt by the rejection but loving enough to swallow the hurt. The boy's willingness to supply, out of his own brimming surplus, the deficiency of Nolla's love touched Cobb with pity and admiration. He wanted to stretch out his hand and say, "I'll read to you, son," but he knew that the gesture, even if accepted, would be but a poor, thin fill for the lad's real hunger.

In a world where only the mother can nourish, how many must go unfed?

He noticed that Laimbeer's deep-socketed eyes were regarding the boy with a kind of self-recognition, as if the painter too were saying, "There I stood long ago, begging for a love never to be granted. Thin, hungry, thwarted, longing for death. To go on living, this boy must harden himself, as all men must." The painter's eyes met Cobb's. Kinship of the rejected, the loved-too-late, flashed between them. So! Laimbeer was not the cunning fowler but only the captive bird, caught in the meshes of the oldest net—the net in which Cobb himself had struggled so long, the net that Roddy was struggling in now.

"The fire is awfully low, Father." It was Sice. "Can't we have another chunk of wood on it?"

"Sure, darling." Cobb's watch told him that ten minutes must elapse before another of the precious two-by-fours could be fed to the flames. Stalling for time, he busied himself about the hearth. As he poked at the fire, it occurred to him that if he glanced up the chimney he might catch a glimpse of the sky. He bent over the slow fire, craned his neck around till his eyes caught an oblong of cloudless blue at the other end of the chimney. The sensation was like looking at the sky from the bottom of a pit. He called out to the others: "Hey, come look at the sky."

They came on their hands and knees around the edge of the huge fireplace, twisted their eyes till they focused on the blue vision above.

"It's shaped like a flag."

"Sun, melt us out of here."

Sicely and Gunnar pulled and poked each other like young cougars. Cobb felt Berry leaning close to him, choking with wood-smoke. He patted her affectionately, then got off his knees and saw Roddy sitting disconsolately alone.

"Where's Mother?"

Roddy pointed in the general direction of the staircase. "They went up to the attic," he quivered, biting his nails. The boy's voice was trembling with inadmissible knowledge, and his eyes were those of a frightened peep-jack on whose retina an unbelievable image was being etched.

Ruston Cobb did the useless things, the only things that a father can do for a bereaved son. He ran his fingers through the boy's silky hair, pressed the wet cheek close against the muscular bulge of his chest (poor substitute for the beloved bosom), soaked up the stifled sobbings with rough tenderness.

"Father, Father—I love her so terribly."

"I know, son."

"If she stops loving me, I shall die."

"She hasn't stopped loving you, Roddy. She loves us—you and me—very much."

Fierceness flared like a torch. "Then why does she go into that room with him? *What are they doing up there?*"

The voice was Roddy's, but the cry was the cry of every forsaken man child who has seen the door of love's chamber closed against him. There was no answer that Cobb could make. He made none. For himself, he did not care what Nolla and Laimbeer were doing in that room. He was thinking of a lonely boy on the afterdeck of a fog-bound boat, and of the heartsick heritage that every mother bequeaths to her sons. With his own son sobbing out his grief and loneliness, Cobb realized that all yearning, all remorse, and all guilt are fruits of that mysterious Yggdrasill tree blossoming in the forbidden garden of mother love, and that the boughs of this tree had made a darkness in the world, a darkness that not all the powers of light had ever been able to dissolve or penetrate.

* * *

Laimbeer's splinter infection really began to rage that evening.

Cobb noticed the dull, bricklike flush on the painter's face when he came into the living room just before dinner. The color was certainly not the afterglow of lovemaking; it was a heavier, more toxic hue; Laimbeer's eyes were puffy and his lower teeth constantly reached for his upper lip as if to intercept complaints of pain. At dinner, Mrs. Rollefson accidentally brushed the painter's elbow while serving up a stout ragout. An involuntary "Goddam it, be careful!" burst from Laimbeer's lips, followed by "Forgive me," uttered grittingly between pain and apology.

Nolla, all tension, turned to her husband. "You'd better look at Ed's arm after dinner," she said. "The infection seems to be climbing."

The infection was indeed climbing. Since yesterday it had leaped in angry red streaks up the painter's arm, burning it to the shoulder in raging tongues of pain. Inspecting the arm by lamplight, Cobb recognized it as a case of threatened blood poisoning, still localized but attacking with virulence the lymph glands in Laimbeer's armpit. Swollen and tender, these saturated sponges could not hold back another drop of the seeping infection. If the dam gave way, systemic poisoning would overwhelm Mr. Edward Laimbeer.

Cobb felt a terrible responsibility. He had forced the painter into the manual labor of breaking up wood, kept him at it after the splinter had entered his hand, then had removed the splinter fragment with imperfectly sterilized instruments. Circumstances, of course, had compelled and extenuated. Still, here was the painter with an arm horribly infected, and getting worse by the hour. What could Cobb say? More important, what could he do?

"I know what you're thinking," said Laimbeer.

Cobb had difficulty lifting his eyes to the painter's face. "What?"

"You're heaping coals all over your head and shoulders. Well, skip it, Cobb. Let's go into this thing on a reality basis. You're the resourceful one—the Juggler, remember? In a world full of nothing but snow and ice, how can we save this arm of mine?"

The blunt edge of Laimbeer's voice sheared away Cobb's self-reproach. "I've got an idea," he said.

"No more taxidermy."

"No, this is another system entirely. Your words 'snow and ice' suggested it." He turned to young Rollefson. "Gunnar, get your father up here, will you? We'll be needing his help." He turned again to Laimbeer. "If your arm can be kept at a low temperature— the nearer to freezing, the better—the microbes causing the infection will be slowed down. It's not a theory; it's accepted treatment. There's a device just patented—Frigiderme. I O.K.'d it the last day in New York."

"Sounds reasonable enough."

"Reasonable?" Cobb fished in his pocket for a pencil. "Why, it's revolutionary. Here, let me give you a rough idea." With rapid strokes he drew a V-shaped wooden trough, notched with semi-circular openings at either end. Voluble as a salesman, he was explaining the sketch to Laimbeer when Rollefson entered.

Cobb seized the caretaker by the shoulder. "Look, Njals, can you make a wooden cradle like this, say about a foot wide, a yard long, and lined with tin?"

Rollefson asked the natural question. "What do you want it for?"

"I want to pack it with snow or cracked ice, then lay this man's arm in it."

Rollefson took out a metal tape measure, laid it along Laimbeer's arm, like a tailor measuring a sleeve. "Forty inches," he muttered. Then added, "There must be a plug, for drainage."

"Yes, a plug of course."

"In an hour," said the caretaker, shuffling out of the room.

"Good man," said Cobb. "He said an hour; he means it. Meanwhile we've got to get the patient bedded down." He turned to Laimbeer. "Where do you want this hibernation to take place?"

] 224 [

"The attic studio?" suggested Nolla, too eagerly.

A vision of Lufbery locked in a hotel room with his Brazilian bombshell added a diabolic touch to Cobb's quick agreement.

"Just the place. Nice, warm stove. Plenty of snow outside the window. Won't clutter up the living room. Take him up there, Nolla. I'll be along with the Frigiderme as soon as it's ready."

Laimbeer was in too much physical pain to protest. Feverish and irritable, he allowed himself to be led, scarab-like, up the staircase.

An hour later Cobb was in the attic room with the trough Rollefson had constructed—a V-shaped affair, light, tight, and lined with tin. He placed a chair beside the studio couch, laid the cradle on it, and filled it with snow and icicles broken from the eaves. Then he paused to figure out a detail.

"It doesn't seem sensible to put your arm right into this snow, Laimbeer. We want it cold, but not wet."

"I could cut up one of Roddy's rubber sheets," suggested Nolla, "then wrap it round the arm."

"Perfect, Noll." It was the first time that Cobb had used this intimate name since he had struck her. He wondered what Laimbeer called her in private. Something from the French, probably. (What was the French for "darling scarab"?) "Make it presto."

When Nolla slipped out, a tension sticky as glue filled the room. Cobb let the tension grow stickier. It was not his play. Let Laimbeer move. The painter's lower teeth were reaching for his upper lip again. The guy was really in pain.

Cobb's resolution melted. "Hurts, heh?"

"Plenty."

"The snowpack will check the pain. Ask Nolla to give you some of her nembutal. You'll be asleep in an hour." One could talk and still say nothing, like a nun making a sick call.

Laimbeer was trying to choke up a gobbet of something difficult. "Cobb . . ."

"Yes." Now it was coming. Not maudlin, please.

"I'm—sorry about all this."

"Sickbed repentance?"

"Call it that if you want to. But there's more to it. May I—may I tell you something?" Silence gave him leave. "You seemed like such a tweedy Van Rensselaer stuffed bib at first. The old Groton tie and all that."

"I can't change my caste markings to please a week-end guest. Why should they annoy you?"

"Because"—the painter's struggle to shrive himself was acutely painful—"because I damn soon found out that your caste markings, as you call them, were backed up by something else that holds everything else together. In painting they call it form. Rouault has tons of it." Laimbeer's whole face was wry, as though he had bitten a lemon. "It irked the pants off me to see that you had a big dose of it too."

"Do you think artists are the sole custodians of the world's design?"

"I used to." Laimbeer was very quiet. "Sometimes you frignten me, Cobb."

"In what way?"

"Your will to keep things going—it's so ferocious. It rides rough-shod over circumstances, people, events. It's insatiable, and in some cases—mine, for instance—goddamned unselective."

"Skip the coals of fire, Laimbeer. I pressed you as hard as I could when you had your strength. Remember the 'work or eat' show-down?" Laimbeer nodded. "The infection in your arm changed the picture, that's all." Eager to get away from the gratitude theme, Cobb went on. "Maybe it's vanity on my part. Just another chance to let the Juggler prove how many things he can keep going."

"Could be. The Juggler in you explains a lot of things: the hawk, the firewood detail, the blower, and all that." The artist hesitated. "But there's one thing it doesn't explain."

] 226 [

"That would be . . .?"

With his good hand Laimbeer picked up the embroidery tambour lying on the chair beside his bed.

Cobb's instinct was to chill the fellow with the gentleman's-club cliché. "Please keep my wife out of this." Ridiculous. The man was trying to tell him something. Cobb clamped a calm over his voice. "What's so puzzling about it?" He was asking, not giving, information.

"How can a man with your positive energy for life—how can you reconcile yourself to this kind of—of, let's say, 'negation'?"

Negation. A delicate way of putting it. Was Laimbeer gallantly hinting that everything wasn't as cuddly and cozy as it seemed in the upper room, or was he really trying to get something off his chest? Make test. Counterattack.

"She seems to have thrown quite a hex into *you*," Cobb said dryly.

Laimbeer acknowledged the touch. "We're very much alike in many ways, your wife and I. She's more than half artist. She has an amazing insight into esthetics."

Cobb's glance said, "You're not sleeping with her insight."

The barb splintered against the painter's complacent hide. "Really unique in many ways. Take her talent for suffering. She suffers in an intense, complicated, and fascinating way, not so much clinical as—as creative. Why, the perception and arrangement that go into her suffering would supply a couple of novelists for ten years." Pleased by his idea, Laimbeer smiled appreciatively. "That's it. She suffers like Proust writes."

"I suppose she's told you what she suffers about."

"Nothing explicit. The same old classic material. Fears and compulsions that all neurotic women have suffered since Electra's time. Fear of being successful as a woman, fear of expressing herself as an artist. She plays a superb piano, I needn't tell you, but if she had to get up a concert program, she'd fall apart." Laimbeer scrutinized the gold and scarlet embroidery of the *carte d'amour.* "She can't face the fact of being an attractive female, so she takes refuge in tambour fantasies."

"Sad, of course, the misery she inflicts on herself. But otherwise it all seems fairly harmless."

"Harmless as Clytemnestra's ax."

"Ax?" Surprise witness catches defense unprepared.

"What would you call the weapon she uses on Roddy, or you? Or, for that matter, me? I don't like to seem unchivalrous, but properly viewed, I'm nothing but a trussed-up victim here. Roddy is helpless, of course." Genuine puzzlement brought together the wrinkles in Laimbeer's forehead. "But what really baffles me is why a man like you . . ."

Nolla's step was coming down the narrow hallway. She entered, radiant as if the room were a stage. "Here's the rubber sheeting. I've cut it into strips."

Cobb took the pieces of rubberized cloth from his wife. Faint odor of urine filled him with pity for their last wetting. Babyhood prolonged. Revenge at the drainage level.

"Hold out your arm," said Cobb. Why did he feel no resentment at the painter's cavalier observations about Nolla? Truth, like a sharp razor, caused no pain at the moment of incision. The hurt might come later, but not now. Spirally he wound the strips of sheeting from Laimbeer's wrist to shoulder, secured it with a safety pin, then adjusted the V-shaped cradle across the chair and couch. Into the snowy coldness he lowered the painter's arm, packed fresh snow around it, then stood back to appraise his therapeutic devising. The chair end of the cradle was too low; he picked up a book—de Musset's *Les Nuits*—and placed it under the trough. *Tu souffres, mon ami.* "How's that feel?"

"Fine," said Laimbeer, eager for the cure to take hold.

Cobb explained the plug to his wife. "To drain off the melting snow, pull out this stopper on the bottom and catch the water in a

] 228 [

basin." He saw that his efficiency was beginning to irritate Nolla, that she was now ready to be alone with her patient.

"Be seeing you," he said from the doorway. His own desire was to get out of the room as quickly as possible so that the drum-stove might burn, the snow melt, the plug be pulled, and the pitiful, stale waters whirl down the narrowing vortex of the drain.

That night Cobb slept in Berry's bed. He came to her hoping that their embrace would be no hasty repetition of the night on the moldy sofa but a full and perfect satisfaction of the special hunger that was growing in both of them. Slowly the exchange began, asker and answerer revolving like binary bodies around a winter night's dream. Then the old note of anxiety came into Berry's voice.

"Help me, dear," she pleaded. "Only you can make me whole."

Exultant maleness filled Ruston Cobb. Powerful fantasies came to life as he coaxed her with secret words, plied her with love names he had never dared utter to Nolla. Docile and trusting, she listened, let him search the sick cleft of her soul, tend it with knowledge and strength, curing himself as he cured her, till they came to the brink of the hazard she must take alone.

"Now—*you*," he whispered, and when he heard her heart making drums of her breast, he let his own heart be a drum too.

* * *

When Cobb awoke next morning, a faint, benedictine light was poking through the bedroom window; the effect was that of a yellow liqueur seeping weakly through finely cracked ice. He knew that the natural power of the spring sun must be the source of that light. Cobb bounded out of bed, threw on his clothes, and ran downstairs. The living room was cavernously dark, the fire was dead on the hearth, and no seepage of light came through the snow-blocked windows. Cobb knelt on the stones of the fireplace, craned his neck till he could look up the chimney, and there, like a glittering flag above him, he saw an oblong of sun-filled sky.

] 229 [

An irresistible urge to see the outside world overcame Ruston Cobb. He thrust his head and shoulders into the shaft of the chimney and reached upward for a handhold on the knobby fieldstone of which it was made. The aperture, big enough to inhale the flames of four-foot logs, was big enough to take a man's body. The power of light drew Cobb upward; it was like clambering out of a steep-sided tomb. His hands were bloody, his face was a sooty mask, when he reached the top.

Half-fainting, he lay for a while on the chimney, gulping great breaths of pure, sweet air. Then he lifted his eyes to a world of snow glistening like diamond dust under the ray of a strong sun. Violet needles of light pierced his eyeballs; in agony he clapped his hands to his eyes. Then, through quarter-opened lids, he peered through slits of his blackened fingers until he could bear to gaze upon the silver grandeur spreading without sign of human life to the horizon. Nothing was recognizable; no landmarks of hill or hollow, no spirals of household smoke, no meadow and no village. The giant pines nearest his house, the only vegetation visible, seemed like dwarf cedars. Cobb estimated that the world was buried under thirty feet of snow.

The thought did not depress him. Lying there in the life-renewing warmth of the sun, it was enough for Cobb to gaze at the blue miracle of the sky once more. Its dazzle intoxicated him; he risked snow-blindness to gaze at it with fully opened eyes. And as he looked upward, he saw living creatures, birds darting and circling in slow glides seeking food. He blessed the birds with tears and upraised arms; their cawings were the truest antiphon to his prayer of thanksgiving. He slithered down the chimney, ran shouting through the house: "Rise and shine! The sun is out! Rise and shine!"

He beat on all the doors. "Get up, get up! The sun is shining." He shouted up the attic stairs, "Nolla, the sun, the sun!" He wanted to run upstairs, hug his wife, roll her over and over, pummel her with joyful hands. Only by forcible remembering did he keep his feet off the stairs.

Calmer, but still jubilant, he came down to the kitchen. Gunnar too had been up the chimney and they laughed and thumped each other over their coffee like black-faced characters in a minstrel show.

"Mr. Bones, will you kindly pass de cream?"

"Ah sho' will, Mr. Interlocutor, I sho' will, suh."

"An' permit yo'self to lay in another inlay of marmalade?"

"Suttinly, suttinly." They laughed and cuffed each other again.

To them entered Mrs. Rollefson in an unprecedented state of dressing-gown disarray. She whispered something in Cobb's ear. Abruptly he left the kitchen, the housekeeper following. In the darkened living room she said, "When he didn't come down, I went to his room to call him. He's a sick boy, Mr. Cobb." She paused for moral emphasis. "He's been getting sick a long time without anybody noticing it."

Without anybody noticing it! Ah, that hurt most.

At Roddy's door Cobb tapped softly, turned the knob, and went in. The room was damp, lightless; the sweetish odor of pubescence hung on its cold air. "Hey, young feller." Tone false-jaunty. Cobb lit a candle, lifted it to see his son's face.

A glimpse, then no more false jauntiness. Chills and fever, fighting for the boy's frail body all night, had rumpled his golden hair, blackened his lips, carved hollows in his cheeks.

By the look, pneumonia. "How do you feel, son?"

"Hot, funny. Where's Mother?"

"She's coming, Roddy. She'll be right here."

"Is she still up in the attic?"

"No-ooo, no. Just having a bite of breakfast. Say, Rod, guess what. The sun is shining."

"That's swell. I heard you beating on my door. But send Mother, please."

"Right away, Rod."

In the hallway outside his son's door, cold sweat cascaded down Cobb's face, streaking it into runnels of soot. If only he had paid more heed to the boy's condition. If Nolla hadn't—— No, don't blame Nolla. Just get her down here. He put his foot on the attic stairs, kicked heavily against the carpeted risers to give warning of his approach. Halfway up the stairs he stopped. How could he enter a room and see Nolla rising sleepy-eyed from another man's bed? The thing was monstrous, impossible. He pounded the stairwell with his fist.

"Nolla," he cried, "come out."

He heard the door of the studio creaking open, then Nolla's slippered steps coming down the narrow corridor. He climbed to the top stair to meet her, nightgowned, uncombed. Her mien said, "This isn't part of the bargain. Get out."

Cobb broke through her angry displeasure. "Roddy's sick. He wants you."

Inhalation between gasp and cry came from Nolla. Her hand went to her cheek, and she wavered slightly. Cobb put out his hand to steady her. "Get dressed," he said, "with as few histrionics as possible." If he didn't blame her, neither could he pity her. She would have to take this one standing up, alone.

Slowly Cobb went downstairs to do what he could against the invisible enemy gnawing at his son. Roddy's illness exposed the father on his flank of weakest knowledge. He could remove a splinter because he could see it, and he could even apply the physical principle of hot and cold, much as he would rig a lathe or insert a washer. But now, while his son breathed rapidly, choked, coughed, sweated, shivered, and burned with pain, Cobb could only stand by the boy's bedside fighting down his own panic.

Onto this disordered stage strode Emma Rollefson, sleeves rolled up, corners of her mouth down. She did not like what she saw (or what lately she had been seeing), but her morality was sent sprawling by the challenge of a "hard case." Her first action was to put her hands under the blanket and feel Roddy's distended belly.

"Just as I thought," she said. "Bowels clogged tighter'n cold goose grease. A soap-and-water enema will loosen him up, Mr. Cobb. Fetch a bed pan while I get the hot water."

"When is Mama coming?" moaned Roddy.

"Mother's here, darling." Nolla flew into the room, gathered the boy's feverish head into her arms with tender anguished whispering. It mattered little that her caresses were without plan, her coddling words belated. They were deep sedatives to the boy's restlessness. A cup of water from her hand, her voice near—this was all the medicine Roddy wanted. Good medicine, too, if the disease were not an entrenched killer, spawning furiously in lobes and tissues from which no mother love, belated or otherwise, could rout them.

When Cobb came back with the hot-water bottle and bed pan, Roddy's bed had been pulled together, his face washed, and his hair combed by Nolla's own hands. Mrs. Rollefson was content to let her do the mothering as long as she, Emma Rollefson, were allowed a free field for the exercise of her medical skill.

"Anything else I can do?" asked Cobb.

"Yes," said Emma Rollefson without taking her hands or eyes off her patient. "Yessir, someone here can bounce that artist gentleman out of the attic. The air and light are better up there. This cold bedroom would bring a Poland-china hog down with the bone ache." She snapped her final sentence like a volley of shrapnel over Nolla's bent head. "Have him out of that room in half an hour."

Nolla lifted her eyes to her husband's face. "You do it," they pleaded.

The task of getting Laimbeer out of the attic was not an assignment that Cobb would have sought. He found the artist in a chafing ill-temper, breakfastless and mystified by Nolla's sudden disappearance. The snow in his trough was completely melted, and his arm was sopping wet.

] 233 [

"What's up?" was his surly acknowledgment of Cobb's "Good morning."

"Roddy's sick. Mrs. Rollefson says it's pneumonia."

"No!" Laimbeer's exclamation carried a dozen overtones. Sympathy for Cobb, relief that Nolla's ministrations were ended, plus a realistic sense of what his lot would be without her care. "That's tough. I suppose"—he looked helplessly at his arm—"there's nothing I can do to help."

"As a matter of fact, there is." Cobb, fiddling for the right phrase, wondered why he should be so tender about Laimbeer's feelings. "Mrs. Rollefson thinks that the light and air are quite good up here, and says that Roddy should have this room."

"But of course." Laimbeer lifted his arm gingerly out of the slushy cradle. "Be out of here in no time at all. Say, by the way, this snow treatment is pretty good. Numbs the pain, anyway. Mind taking a look?"

Cobb unwound the rubber sheeting, inspected Laimbeer's arm. It was still a discolored, ugly thing, and the flesh had the pickled texture of a museum specimen. But the swelling had subsided somewhat, and the infection had certainly climbed no further.

"Seems to be holding its own," murmured Cobb. "When you get downstairs to your own room, we'll give you a fresh pack of snow."

"And a cup of coffee?"

"Easy." Cobb opened the attic window, dumped the slush out of the cradle, and gazed for a moment at the yellowish light that was now positively streaming through the snow. He was not thinking of Laimbeer's arm or Nolla's infidelity. He was estimating the number of hours, days, before the sun would melt the snow down to the level of the electric wires, restoring light, heat, communication to an ambushed world. Three, four days? Could Roddy last that long?

"I'm ready," Laimbeer was saying. No backward looks. No more regrets than a traveling salesman leaving a one-night stand in a cheap hotel. The artist's voice had a cheery sound that cut unexpectedly at Cobb's sense of decency. *Les Nuits* of Alfred de Musset lay on the floor. Laimbeer stepped over it.

Twenty minutes later, having settled Laimbeer in his own room with a new snowpack, Cobb was back at Roddy's bedside. The boy seemed clearer now. Eased by Mrs. Rollefson's ministrations, his face was less tormented by pain. He put on a shadow of his old Thespian self for his father's benefit.

"Who goes there? Friend or enema?" he murmured faintly.

The old pun delivered in the cold room shook Cobb. "Friend," he said. He wrapped the blankets about his son, lifted him lightly in his arms, and carried him up the attic stairs.

In the warm upper room, Roddy did not improve. Hard, deep chills shook him like a rattle, bringing a froth of rusty sputum to his blackened lips. After the chills passed, fever would drive the mercury in the clinical thermometer to a hundred and four degrees. Between racking coughs, Roddy battled for oxygen while his pulse raced like a metronome gone crazy. Desperately his hands clutched at the bony cage of his ribs as if to open a crack that would permit the rising fluids and crowding pain of pleurisy to escape from his lungs. He retched, he gasped and shivered, he grunted, he tried to rise from bed, then collapsed in a drench of sourish sweat and bloody phlegm. With a napkin Nolla wiped her boy's face, pity and remorse in her eyes.

"How long does it go on?" asked Cobb.

Nolla seemed not to hear. "The crisis," said Emma Rollefson, "comes on the sixth day." She laid her hand on his arm comfortingly. "If nursing can pull him through, we'll do everything we can. Icebags, forced fluids, hot-water bottles . . ." Courage concealed the meagerness of the weapons at her command as she urged him gently toward the door. "If we need you here, I'll call you."

"Fight for him, Noll," murmured Cobb, tiptoeing out of the benedictine haze of sunlight into the darkness of the house below. Aimlessly he wandered through the cheerless rooms, putting his hand to a dozen trifles as he tried to forget Roddy's battle for breath going forward in the upper chamber. On the dead hearth in the living room lay an ankle-depth of cold, gray ash; today's fire had not yet been kindled. Mechanically, like a man who has forgotten why he repeats a compulsive act, Cobb started to build a fire. He heard laughter in the kitchen, peeked in to see Gunnar and Sicely having fun with the unpromising material of soapflakes and dirty breakfast dishes. Laughing, tossing crockery to each other, they did not see him; he backed away quietly, unwilling to spoil their play. Standing by the living-room mantelpiece, he smiled at the sameness of the preliminary rites that were the source of life's miraculous secret: the feminine smiles and glances, the male response, the rites begun anew in eagerness and joy. Thus, and good, was happy love, busy at renewing the universe. For a moment Cobb forgot his choking son, the storm-bound house, the grievous ills that were smothering the world. "Gunnar loves Sicely." No wonder people scribbled it on billboards, traced it in seashore sand, or carved it on the bark of trees. It was the triumph of the life wish, the only guarantee that death should not prevail.

Into his meditations a hulking presence shuffled—the elder Rollefson, heavy of gait and spirit. The man's awkward stance, indeed his unbidden appearance upstairs, were signals of some nether-world disaster.

"What is it, Rollefson?"

"The hawk, sir." The man's eyes were downcast. "She's main sick."

"Sick? Let's have a look."

The caretaker led the way to the hawk's bin. There in the candlelight, wobbling on its perch with lifeless wings and eyes unhooded, sat the bird, a queen of shreds and patches. Confinement and dampness had given her plumage a tag-rag appearance; from her breast and the extremities of her great pinions, feathers had molted away. Cobb passed his hand over the creature, felt the lack of tone in her ruff, the lethargy in the striking muscles of her talons. How cruel the contrast between her condition now and when Cobb had first seen her wheeling regally through the upper air.

"What's the matter with her, Rollefson?"

The caretaker fell into the medieval language of hawkers. "It's called the 'falling evil,' sir."

"Falling evil?"

"Like apoplexy in humans. A determination of blood to the brain. They fall down from their perch and lie helpless on the ground."

"Any cure for it?"

"A purge of lard sometimes works." Momentary hope in Rollefson's voice was overcast by clouds from a new quarter. "But we can't purge her, because she's got another disease."

"What other disease?"

"Frounce. An inflammation of the nose and throat. Falcons are sensitive to bad air, sir, and the air down here is not good."

In his hour of greatest anger against the hawk, Cobb had never intended reducing her to this pitiful condition. Gazing at the bedraggled bird, he wondered what fascination the hawk had ever exercised over him. How had this creature ever tempted him to a revengeful test of strength? Disenchantment, sudden and complete, was mingled with pity for the subdued bird.

"What would happen if we set her free, Rollefson? Could she fly?"

"It's a poor hawk that can't take wing, sir."

"Could she fight?"

"The air would sharpen her."

"Could she find food?"

"Who knows what food is to be found outside?"

"She must take her chances. It's a better fate than rotting at this perch. Unleash her, Rollefson; I'll turn her loose."

The caretaker began freeing the hawk's jesses, soothing her as he worked, caressing her with a litany of names: "My kestrel, my windhover, my sky climber." He fondled her with his great square hand, smoothed her ragged wings. "Who mended thee, tended thee, pretty saker?" he asked, laying his cheek against her mangy breast. The hawk nipped at his ear like a faded coquette. Not once had she ever revealed to Cobb this nuzzling, flirtatious aspect of her nature.

The caretaker extended his arm; unhooded, the falcon gripped his fist with her golden claws, perching there in the last test of docility simply because it was her station and she liked it better than any place else in the world.

Knowledge of jealousy smote Cobb. Not for him the endearing peck, the voluntary perch. Aloud he said, "The bird loves you, Rollefson."

"She feels in me some likeness to herself."

"Would you like to keep her?"

For a moment Rollefson gazed longingly at the bird on his fist. Slowly curving in his arm, he drew the falcon toward him till her beak touched the scar on his forehead made by a sister hawk long ago in the fiords of Norway. In the curve of the caretaker's arm half a century was gathered up, drawn close for a moment of remembrance. Then the arm went out again.

"No, I will not keep her. In this cellar she would fail and die. Rats and men can live in cellars. But not falcons. I know these things. I know." He broke off his sententious musings. "Better put the gauntlet on, sir. Her talons are still edged; in her weakness she must cling hard."

Cobb drew on the falconer's glove, set the bird on his fist, and started upstairs. In the narrow stairwell the hawk swayed closer to Cobb's face, its damp, feathery odor penetrating his nostrils. As he opened the door of the roofless music room, the golden eye of the sun beamed in a blue and brilliant sky. The hawk heard the screaming of jays and crows as they circled over the snow seeking food. A stiffening tension passed through the hawk's body. Cobb sat on the edge of the piano and began unlacing the red morocco hood. He slipped it off gently and the bird blinked nervously as the sharp light struck the membranes of its eye.

In the life of the true falconer this should have been the moment of crisis. Game on all sides—sparrows, chipmunks, starlings—helpless prey to be darted at, retrieved, laid at the master's feet. The suspense of releasing the bird should have pitched the man's nerves to a singing question: "Will my hawk return?" But the question was not in Cobb's mind as he clucked at her in a poor imitation of Rollefson's manner and whispered, "Fly away home."

Weak from disease and dark confinement, the bird wobbled on Cobb's wrist. Had the dove, beholding the waste of waters, trembled so in Noah's hand? The sun poured down, focused its ray on the hawk's curved beak, urging it to seek the lost dimensions of light and freedom. But still the bird hung off, hesitant, tremulous, afraid to try its wings. And now a roof sparrow fluttered past, chirruping innocently in its small careering from eaves to treetops. The predatory instinct of the hawk, deep as the tubes of its heart and hollow bones, declared itself. The elastic leap of the salmon, the effortless dart of the cottonmouth, were in its take-off. It spiraled into the sun, banked in a steep turn, folded its yellow talons for the dive, and stooped in a screaming descent upon the unsuspecting sparrow.

It struck, then, for a tick of eternity, checked indecisively. Cobb saw the division in the creature's soul. "Is this prey mine or my master's?" The edges of the bird's divided heart sprang together. "I have no earthly master. My loyalty is to the upper air." With the sparrow gripped in her talons, the hawk wheeled, spread her magnificent wings, and climbed into the blue reaches of the sky.

Following the bird with his eyes, Cobb saw the silver-skinned reconnaissance plane glinting against the sun. He waved his hands and shouted as the plane passed overhead. A puff of colored smoke from a Very pistol in the glass nose of the plane told him that he had been seen and his location noted on the chart of early rescue.

* * *

With the household attention focused on Roddy, the care and feeding of Laimbeer fell entirely on Cobb. Marked changes had come over the painter; prolonged pain had gouged deep lines into his huge, yellowish features; dark concavities in his cheeks and the blue-black bristle of his beard gave him the look of a Persian monarch stricken by a palace poisoner.

On his fourth day in bed, he was notably restless, thrashing about and over-talkative as Cobb came in with the midday bowl of soup. A couple of books, a pipe, an ashtray, and a hand mirror lay in the folds of the disorderly bedclothes.

Laimbeer picked up the mirror, gazed into it for a second, and said grimly, "I look like the breaking up of a bad Rouault."

"How do you feel? That's more important right now." Cobb put the thermometer into the man's mouth.

Laimbeer's craggy head turned on the pillow so that his eyes traversed the snow-packed trough in which his arm lay buried. His expression was that of a man caught in a bear trap, downing panic while he waited for a rescue party to free him. "I feel all right," he mumbled. "Jittery, perhaps. Maybe I'm feverish. What's my temperature?"

"Normal," lied Cobb. Actually the thermometer registered 102.5. "Here, eat this. It'll make you feel better."

Watching the painter spoon up the soup awkwardly with his left hand, spilling it over his beard and bedclothes, Cobb almost surrendered to the impulse to feed the man. But he could not actually bring himself to put food into a mouth that had hungered over Nolla.

"Shall I get Berry up here to feed you?"

"I'll manage." Laimbeer picked up the bowl of soup, drank it off. Cobb handed him a cigarette, lighted it for him, then went around to examine the painter's infected arm. He scraped away the snow, pressed the discolored flesh gently, and lifted a noncommittal smile to Laimbeer's questioning eyes.

"Wonderful stuff, snow. Variety of uses. Makes houses for Eskimos, protects vegetation, and checks spread of infection in important members."

"Is the infection really checked?"

Cobb opened the window, dug out a basin of fresh snow, and packed it into the trough.

"It sleepeth only. But you'll sneak through while its eyes are still closed."

"How do you mean?"

"I mean that in twenty-four hours at the most, there'll be squadrons of C-54s flying low over this countryside, looking for just such emergency cases as yours and Roddy's. They'll whisk you both off to a hospital somewhere South—God knows there must be someplace in Florida or Texas that isn't covered with snow. They'll shoot some penicillin into you, and a week later you'll be out, walking up and down your studio floor wondering what to paint."

"I hope you're right about the C-54s, Cobb. But I can tell you right now, you're wrong when you say that I'll be walking up and down my studio wondering what to paint."

"You mean you're going to give up painting?"

"I mean," said Laimbeer, "that I'm going to chuck the neurotic baggage that's *kept* me from painting." A fierce fire glowed in the brazier of the artist's face. "I know you think I'm feverish, or hopped up with the convalescent coke that sick people jab into themselves. But the roots of this thing go deeper, Cobb. They drive right down to the basic deposit of energy that made me an artist—a special act of creation—in the first place." All the man's arrogance was flooding back now, whether on a rising tide of fever or on a wave of new energy rolling in from creative depths, Cobb couldn't tell.

"You've heard of shock therapy for schizophrenia," Laimbeer went on. "The idea is to dump the patient into the pit of death and hold him there until he decides that he wants to struggle up again. His decision to keep on living is made way down deep in the bottom strata of his being. You know, Cobb, the unconscious has a tough will of its own. Wanting to live, it overrules the flabby, frightened part of us that makes us think we want to die."

"I've heard about the treatment." Cobb attempted to get Laimbeer onto a more objective discourse. "If shock therapy has such a good effect on sick individuals, then a nice big general shock like this storm ought to work wonders with society, don't you think?"

"Maybe." Laimbeer was under the egoist's compulsion to get the conversation back to himself. "All I know is, the threat to my arm has touched off the old creative geyser again. The way I feel now, I could paint with a brush between my teeth."

"What would you paint?"

"It wouldn't matter. Anything with tension in it. Wheat under hail, trees against the wind, the moon over Staten Island, or the sandhogs under it. Lovers grappling for the lifelock, salmon leaping waterfalls, or men shooting the rapids in steel barrels. Railroad plows scattering snow like an electric fan scatters cornstarch, or abalone pearl divers glistening at the gunwhale of their scows. Anything, everything. Just let me squeeze those tubes of raw color again between my thumb and forefinger. I'll know what to paint." Laimbeer made an effort to rise from his bed. "Why, I'd even spray Duco with an airbrush if you'd let me out of here."

Cobb pushed the painter's shoulder back onto the pillows. "Steady as you go," he laughed. He couldn't resist the temptation to remind Laimbeer of an earlier statement. "Remember taking five dollars from me back there? At that time you were all for having the artist jump into the lake." He paraphrased the painter's taunt. "A little bit of snow hasn't made you change your mind, has it? Or maybe you want to give me back my money?"

Sheepish remorse softened Laimbeer's tense features. "Cobb, if I ever get out of here alive, I'll give you back your money, plus the best goddam canvas that I paint the next year." Embarrassment burned the painter's cheek. "It'll be cheap payment for the things you've taught me."

"You could have learned as much from any random squirrel."

"No. Squirrels do all right in their own way, but they aren't saddled with notions of guilt and death, as you and I are. I had to learn from some animal who was carrying a burden as heavy as mine. Heavier, for all I know." Reminiscence turned the painter's eyeballs backward. "I got my first lesson when you went out into that storm to bring Sicely home. That wasn't just Juggler resourcefulness. You fooled death silly for forty-eight hours, snatched his crossbones, and beat his skull with them. I couldn't have done it. The storm would have blown me to pieces, just as Sice said. But somehow you pulled it off. How?"

The vision of Sicely's red mitten thrusting through the snow sobered Cobb into humorless self-revelation. "I happen to love my daughter very much. It never occurred to me that death could want her as much as I do."

Laimbeer roared with fever-exaggerated delight. "Cobb, you're terrific. You sit there and tear off timeless truth as though it was a piece of cigarette paper. If I had two arms, I'd hug you. By God, I *have* got two arms." He pulled his infected arm out of the trough, scattering snow and slush all over the bedclothes. "Don't you see what you've done, Squire?" Laimbeer held up his big left hand like a stop signal to prevent Cobb's cutting in. "You've given me a glimpse of the symbol for our time—the symbol of harassed man struggling between compassion and fear, Eros and Thanatos, love and death. I was fumbling for it back there, but Householder Cobb, Esquire, had to supply it."

Laimbeer's agitation was increasing. "I see it all now, Cobb. The new painting won't be an abstract mystery, something remote from the life of the race. Just the opposite. A special contract will be written between the artist and the poor bastards that see his pictures.

] 243 [

The artist will say, 'Look, you jerks. I'll show you marvels you've never experienced in your own miserable lives. My pictures will be powerful projections of feeling, sensation, and character. Viewing them, you'll be alternately calmed and agitated. If you're weak, my pictures will strengthen you; if you're hungry, they'll feed you; if you're in darkness, my pictures will bring you light.'"

"Lie down," advised Cobb, "and put your arm back in the trough." He forced the painter onto the pillow, brushed the slushy snow off the blankets. "You may be reaching for a new esthetic, Laimbeer, but you'll never make it with your arm gone at the shoulder."

"Don't say 'esthetic' to me!" shouted Laimbeer. "I'm sick of the word. What does it mean, anyway?" He choked with anger as though the word had wronged, misled him. "*Merde* on this twaddle about significant design. Art is more than that. It's the vital distillate of an age—a powerful *aqua vitae* containing all the myths, heroes, dreams, fears, yes, and horrors of the people that produced it." He glared pugnaciously at Cobb. "Maybe you still don't believe me."

"No, no. I believe you. Don't get excited. It's not worth getting excited about."

"It's the only thing that *is* worth getting excited about. The people need something to float them over the limiting facts of life: some hero to support them in the battle, a voice on the mountain to remind them that there's a high pass up there. If the artist doesn't do it, it never gets done."

"Sure, sure." Cobb was wretchedly tired. "Let me freshen up your trough a bit." He went to the window, brought back a basinful of snow, and packed it around Laimbeer's arm. As he worked, the painter raved on. "Didn't you tell me, Cobb, that once when you were feeling pretty low, you walked up and down Fifty-seventh Street working off some of your misery looking at pictures?"

Cobb heaped the trough like an ice-cream cone. "That's right."

"And I asked you, 'Did it do any good?' and you said, 'Yes, it did.' Well, then"—Laimbeer shot a heavy forefinger straight out—

"that makes you the Johnny-in-the-stalls that we painters paint for."
His voice rose impassioned, as a missionary to the heathen. "The
people are like blinkered nags trotting over mean cobblestones—but
nags with a strain of the old Winged Horse in them still. The artist's
job is to remind them of those forsaken pastures on the slopes of
Helicon. He must tutor their limited senses, purge their appetites,
and teach them how to live, not at the base but at the peak of life."

Laimbeer spat out the taste of his own rhetoric. "No, that sounds
like something out of Burne-Jones. Too goddam exalted. It's got to
be earthier." He let out a manic laugh and made wriggling motions
with his fingers. "Look, the earthworm—your only epicure. Excuse
it, Squire, that's Shakespeare." Laimbeer made an effort to recapture
his wandering thought. "What I mean is these silent little buggers
just keep on eating their way through the earth, enriching it as they
go. The farmer doesn't see or hear them, but there they are all the
time, fertilizing and loosening up the soil, getting it ready to grow
things. Look it up in the Department of Agriculture bulletin sometime, Cobb. You'll find it's all true."

"I don't have to. Everyone knows that if the earthworm didn't do
his stuff, there'd be no crops."

"Well, it's the same way with the artist," cried Laimbeer. "Whether
the people know it or not—and they most certainly don't—the artist
is deep in their soil, working it up for the big crop next year. Or
maybe next century, what's the difference?"

The painter's excitement, whipped up by his own eloquence, was
climbing dangerously. Cobb had a terrible vision of a delirious
Laimbeer rising from his bed, raging through the house. If the C-54
didn't come soon that vision might be a reality. He must humor
Laimbeer, cajole him, somehow manage to get him off the fiery
track of art talk.

"How about a tall double Scotch?" he suggested. "You must be
thirsty."

Suggestible, Laimbeer passed his tongue over his dry lips.

] 245 [

"A drink would go good right now. But hurry back. I've got a lot more to say to you."

Cobb made two stops. One at the liquor cabinet, where he poured four ounces of Scotch into a tall glass. Another at Nolla's medicine chest, where he dumped the remaining half bottle of sleeping mixture into the whiskey—a dose that would keep an ordinary person heavily sedatized for twelve hours. He returned to Laimbeer's room, handed him the drink. "Polish this off," he said.

The painter downed it in thirsty gulps, lay back on his pillow. The single candle guttering in its socket threw a weird light over the hollows of his unshaven face. Physical exhaustion was presenting its heavy invoice, but the painter's delirious energy waved it aside. He fumbled in the bedclothes with his left hand. "There's a book in the blanket somewhere. Ah, here it is." He held the volume up as a trophy. "Sophocles," he announced. "Dramatist to the court of Thebes. I've been reading *Swellfoot the Tyrant* again—not for the usual reason, the mother-son business, though I'm beginning to think Jocasta is the real villain in the play—but for the much more important stuff Tiresias has to say."

"Tiresias?"

"The old soothsayer. Charged to the whiskers with wisdom. Blind, by the way. Why should they always represent wisdom as blind or nutty? Well, anyway, when catastrophe threatens the city, Tiresias gets the first tremor of it, warns the people, tells them of their impending doom. Neither the people nor the king will listen. But Tiresias speaks anyway. And what a blast."

Laimbeer moistened his thumb, riffled the pages. "Ah, here it is." He ran his eye down the page. "Shall I read it to you?" he asked, edging toward the candle. The small flame threw only a blurred shadow across the page. "Can't see it." He tossed the book aside. "No matter. The point is that the artist sees the doom hanging over the city, realizes the danger, announces it to the people, and keeps on announcing it whether anyone pays any attention to him or not.

His only job is to be able to say, at the end of his life, what Tiresias said: 'I go, having said what I came to say.' "

"A wonderful epitaph for an artist."

Laimbeer's agitation was disappearing under the touch of the sedative tumbler. "Wonderful," he repeated. "But how few deserve it. Most of us get discouraged, turn away, sheer off into aberration or compromise. The impure artist tries to dodge his own destiny and ignores that of the race. No fate is sadder than his. He becomes a treader in two worlds, master of neither."

Laimbeer gazed around the darkening room as if looking for a third person or the hidden source of a perfume. "I had a dream last night, Cobb."

"Can you remember it?"

Laimbeer's voice was drowsy. "I think so. Yes, I dreamed that I was watching a young man, handsome and godlike, playing an antique stringed instrument under a fruit tree. He played with melancholy energy and sang a song that was the final variant on the loneliest, saddest theme I ever heard. His song said everything I wanted to say, but never had been able to. I begged him to lend me his instrument, so that I might improvise a song of my own then and there. But the youth shook his head and said, 'No, you cannot borrow this rebec, or viol, or whatever it was he was playing, because this instrument is a small, stringed replica of my soul and you couldn't possibly strike music out of it. You've got to fashion an instrument of your own, and make such music as you can.' "

Laimbeer halted in his recital of the dream as if trying to remember exactly the words the youth had used. "It was a very clear and beautiful statement, if I could only remember it. But anyway that was the sense and color of what he said."

"It seems a very happy dream."

"It was." Laimbeer's eyes were closed, his voice like an echo heard under water. "It was a remembrance of things past—and a hope for the future. That's the valuable part. Art is concerned only with the future. Even though the artist is saddled with heavier burdens, and imposts of old habit, he must keep on. In spite of failing strength and fiercer doubts, he will be heard."

"He will go on with greater knowledge," said Cobb.

"No," breathed Laimbeer. "With greater necessity."

*　　*　　*

Lapped in the old fantasy of warm waves breaking on a pink beach, Cobb was dozing in the lozenge-paned study when Mrs. Rollefson tapped him on the shoulder. "It's here," she said, and he knew that Roddy's crisis had come. For the fiftieth time he caught himself listening for the whir of airplane propellers above the house. If that Very pistol puff had been a true signal, a rescue plane should be dropping medicines by now. Twice he had heard the drone of heavy motors in the night, and once he had seen a silver flash settling over the village of Brompton. Gunnar, stationed on an upper balcony, was searching the skies for a glimpse of a plane, but thus far had reported no message of encouragement from the outside world.

Silently Cobb followed Emma Rollefson to the attic room, its curtains drawn against the rays of the late-afternoon sun. A hush like a faded dust-sheet lay on the furniture. Nolla, haggard with days and nights of nursing, sat dully in the cane-bottomed rocker; her thin hair was unbrushed, and fatigue had crayoned dark wrinkles in her forehead and at the corners of her eyes. Looking down at the frail blond shadow on the bed, Cobb believed there was no hope for his son. A week of fever had burned all the moisture out of Roddy's flesh; his skin, heart, and lungs were pure tinder now, awaiting the final blast of the blowtorch before crumbling to ash.

A terrible indignation swept Cobb as he beheld the punishment that the disease had scored on the helpless body of his son. It had been an unfair fight! If only the boy had been supported in the battle by those cunning handlers—shrewd drugs and serums—he knew that Roddy could have beaten the pneumonia to a standstill. He had a vision of Sice's red mitten pushing upward through the avalanche of snow. His children were no pushovers for death! But now, gripped at wrist and hair by the black wrestler, Roddy was overmatched and alone.

Cobb put his ear to his son's chest; faint and exhausted, the heart was still beating, its weak echoes drowned by louder bronchial rales whistling through Roddy's clogged air passages. If only those passages could be opened up, the boy's last moments could be made more comfortable. He lifted his eyes to Mrs. Rollefson standing on the other side of the bed. She read his thoughts, and they matched her own.

"A congestion of pus in the tubes," she said. "If we could keep them open . . ."

Congestion of pus in the tubes. A midwife's locution; imperfect knowledge describing an obvious fact. Yet, by giving a thing a name, Mrs. Rollefson had covered half the distance between diagnosis and therapy. That gulf she could not leap alone.

"What does one do about it?" asked Cobb, probing her sickroom lore.

"Sometimes you poultice."

"What kind of poultice?"

"Flaxseed, oatmeal, mashed potatoes—they all draw good."

"Which draws the best?"

"Oatmeal is very hot and quick, sir."

Cobb rose decisively. "Emma, go down into the kitchen and cook up a boilerful of oatmeal. Berry, get some towels, pillow slips, anything to spread the poultice on." He turned to his wife. "You, Nolla, bring the bottle of liniment from my bathroom. And a big spoon."

"Big spoon?" Nolla repeated the words in a daze. "You aren't going to——"

"Please, Nolla, do as I say."

Like a departing chorus, the three women left the room. Kneeling again beside Roddy's bed, Cobb searched the boy's face for an estimate of strength, as a mechanic might test a failing battery for a spark. With his hands he explored the boy's thin chest, calculating the remnants of life in that flagging pulse of energy the heart. Under the search Roddy opened his eyes, fever-brilliant, but for the time lucid and unwandering. The boy realized that this was his father, and that desperate hands were sounding him for some awful test.

"Am I pretty sick, Father?" he asked in a choking voice.

"Yes, son, pretty sick."

"Am I going to die?"

"Not if we can help it, Rod."

A long silence. Then the boy looked straight up into the eyes above him. "It might be better if I did, Father."

"What makes you say such a thing, Roddy?"

The boy held up a weak hand, spread its waxen fingers. "I bite my nails. You don't like—nail biting, Father."

Cobb pressed the boy's gnawed finger ends to his lips. "Forgive me, son."

The agony of self-accusation went on. "I—I wet the bed. You don't like boys who wet the bed."

"You're getting over that, Rod." A stab at comedy. "What's a little bed wetting between friends?"

"There's something else, Father." Rod's fevered brain was losing direction now. "When the muskrats frightened me, the boys in school laughed and called me a name. Name of a flower." A wandering gaze. "Pansy."

As if dodging a gun barrel pointed straight at his eye, Cobb tried to avoid the tormenting vision summoned up by that name. In clairvoyant detail he saw the scenario of his son's life as a homosexual. If Roddy lived and was fortunate among his kind, he would become one of those exquisite creatures, parasitic as mistletoe, that flowered most brilliantly in the airs of decline. The rooms through which his son would pass, the voices of Roddy's friends and lovers, the murmured fidelities, the screaming jealousies of the disdained and the clipped cruelties of the disdainers, the special tones and language of these parody courtships—Cobb heard, saw them all. Had his son been born for this? Should such a life be valued, preserved? Everything in Cobb's experience and training, his masculine vanity, his contempt, pity, and fear of homosexuals, whispered a bitter "No."

For a moment he felt a quiet resignation at the prospect of Roddy's escape from such a fate. Life, even in its happiest and most normal aspects, was no cherishable prize. What did it amount to at last? A few hours of achievement or ecstasy, of glimpsed illusion and snatched happiness—tiny infrequent islands specking out the monotonous waste of the years. What then could be said for the kind of life that Roddy must lead, a life of barren fulfillment and ridiculous tears, pitiful whimperings and suicidal despair at the mirror's aging tale, concealed beneath a ghastly mask of rouge and mascara?

Oh!

Whips of guilt lashed Cobb's shoulder, whistled about his head. For the first time in his life he felt the flagellant quality of self-torment, the cruelest punishment that men can devise. Realistically he knew that he could not blame himself for the flaw in Roddy's soul, that it was a symptom of the death wish that was threatening the world. Still the whips descended. Was this the way Nolla suffered? Forgive me, darling. I did not know. Sheathed in ignorant health, I had no way of knowing. Now I am beginning to understand.

Memory of Roddy's pluck and trouper nerve swarmed over Cobb. How the boy had rallied to his father's side with that comic song-and-dance routine in an earlier crisis. And oh, the priceless killer fury behind the hurled dart that had barely missed Cobb's throat. All the lad's grace with rhymed language, his marvelous histrionic talent, his wit, his in-fighting courage—the stuff that in a burlier child would have been called guts—all these the father remembered.

"Roddy," he cried, "don't pay any attention to what the boys in school say. They don't know a damn thing about it. They don't know how much grit and pluck you've got. I didn't know myself until a few days ago. Before the storm, I wanted you to trap muskrats and play baseball and shinny up trees. But now I know you can do better things than that. You can make rhymes, and set kings and queens in motion. You can throw a whole roomful of people into tears or laughter, just as you choose. When you grow up, you will be a great actor-poet, an artist with voice and words, the greatest kind of artist there is. Like Shakespeare. And when you come on the stage, people will clap their hands and shout your name—Rodney Cobb, Rodney Cobb!"

A smile of utter peace was on the boy's face. "Would you be proud of me then, Father? Would you love me then?"

Terrible sobs shook the man's frame. "I would be proud of you— I would love you—whether they shout your name or not, Roddy. Only live, son, only live."

Rales, harsh as rattling glass, attacked the boy's breathing. His face turned blue as the frail bellows of his lungs snatched at thinning streams of air. As Nolla and Berry came into the room, a strangler froth was on Roddy's lips. Berry hid her face in the towel she was carrying, and Nolla gazed strangely at her husband as if to say, "Can you save him now?"

Faint but certain overhead, Cobb heard the distant vibration of powerful airplane engines.

Mrs. Rollefson came in, her face red and glowing, bearing the steaming pot of oatmeal. "Hurry, Emma," urged Cobb.

"It's too hot to be put on right away," she warned.

"By the time you spread it on the towel, it'll be cooler."

Emma Rollefson poured the porridge onto a face towel, fanned the air with it a moment, then covered the mixture with a piece of cloth torn from a pillow slip. "Bare his throat," she said. At the V-shaped notch where Roddy's windpipe entered the bony cage of his chest, she pressed home the steaming poultice.

Cobb expected a piercing scream of pain, but when only a low moan came from Roddy, he knew that the boy must be nearly unconscious. How long would it require for the fierce heat to do its work on the clogged passages? Would it work at all? Yes, the violence of the treatment was already producing an effect. With his ear to the boy's chest, Cobb thought he heard the harsh rales soften into a low bubbling sound as the phlegm in Roddy's bronchial passages began to loosen.

To fight off the strangler, Ruston Cobb covered Roddy's lips with his own, and by a kissing suction drew bitter pluggets of phlegm into his own mouth. He spat them out, sucked, and spat again. Then he breathed into Roddy's throat, trying to pump oxygen through the bronchial tubes until it reached the boy's lungs. No use, the tubes were clogged. They must be cleared.

"Hand me the liniment, Nolla."

She hid the bottle behind her. "No, no. It will destroy his throat, his voice."

"If it saves his life, what matter? Would you rather have him voiceless, or dead?"

At the alternative, Nolla slipped into shrieking hysteria. "You presumptuous God-struck fool!" she screamed. "Do you think you can breathe or burn life into everything? Have you no decency, no humility in the presence of death?" Her voice rose shrieking. "For God's sake, let something die around here once in a while. Let *him* die!" She pointed to Roddy's frail form.

"Hush," said Mrs. Rollefson, looking crosswise as if to avert the sight of a blasphemer.

"Let him die," implored Nolla, "so that I can die too. I have stayed alive all these years only for his sake. Yet when he needed me most"—remorse and guilt came in sobs—"I failed him, exchanged his love for a snatched shred of happiness. Oh, miserable!" She gazed about the walls. "In this very room." She pointed to the sofa on which Roddy lay. "On that very bed. Let me be punished here by his death."

. "No one will die to atone for another's guilt," said Cobb. "Give me the liniment."

He wrenched the bottle from her hand, uncorked it, poured a level spoonful. "Forgive me, Noll, if I am made monstrous by the wish to keep those I love alive. But now Roddy *must* live, so that you can keep on living, too."

Cobb brought the spoon down slowly to the level of his son's mouth. He did not know what the effect of the burning liquid would be. He hoped it would groove a course through the clogged bronchial tubes to the boy's lungs, thereby letting in a few more breaths of life-giving air. He was willing to risk Roddy's beautiful voice, to sacrifice his artistry with spoken words, if thereby he might save his son's life. Let him be dumb if necessary, a nail biter, a bed wetter, a faggoting, mincing pansy. But live he must.

Cobb put his hand under Roddy's head to support it for the fearful dose; the spoon, at tilt, spilled some of the fiery liniment over the boy's slack, blue lips.

"Open his mouth, Emma. He must get all of it."

The housekeeper put her left forefinger against the edge of Roddy's lower teeth, and with her right thumb gently pushed open the delicate jaws. Something about the way they came apart told her that Roddy was past the help of medicine.

"He's gone, sir," she said. "Liniment won't do him any good now." She took the spoon from Cobb's hand and emptied it into the basin.

The finality of her gesture needed no confirmation. Ruston Cobb knew that it was unnecessary for him to place his ear over his son's thin chest in the hope of catching one more heartbeat, one last breath. But he bent over his boy's heart once more, not for proof of death but to confess there in burning tears his failure to love Roddy enough in life.

] 254 [

So late to learn. So impossible to amend. So lonely to bear.

He lifted his head and saw Nolla sitting dry-eyed, moveless, in the cane-bottomed rocker. Berry and Mrs. Rollefson had gone sobbingly from the room, yielding priority of mourning to Cobb and his wife.

The male instinct to take leadership in consolation barely stirred in the weary, defeated father. "I am too tired," he thought. "I have failed too greatly ever to lift my heart again." Yet deep beneath old layers of failure and weariness, new knowledge of pity stirred.

"If remorse has made me lonely," he said to himself, "what must her loneliness be now?"

To comfort an affliction heavier than his own, he rose and went to his wife. Wordless, he knelt beside her chair, then, for no conscious reason, laid his head dumbly in her lap. It was a posture he had never taken with Nolla before—a clear regression to his own childhood, and a tentative offer to fill Roddy's place in her now empty life.

Her fingers wandered among the graying curls at the back of his head; he felt her tears falling on his cheek. Then imperceptibly she started rocking as she had once rocked Roddy, and as Ruston Cobb's mother had rocked him, long ago.

CHAPTER 15

FROM HIS office window, seventy-one stories above the teeming harbor, Ruston Cobb saw platinum bees of sunlight fretting the waters of the North River. Seaward, at an elegiac tempo, moved the debris of the great storm. The river, swollen by torrents of melting snow, stood at an all-time high and was still rising. Piers and warehouses on the Jersey shore were submerged, and tangled fleets of freighters, tankers, and barges, torn from their moorings by the pull of rising waters, drifted and eddied downstream. The streets on the West Side were sluiceways sweeping down to the river an accumulation of garbage cans, dead animals, shutters, shop signs, baby carriages, and human bodies.

Many such bodies were floating out to sea. How many, the *Times* did not venture to estimate. Coast Guard crews, with orders to secure drifting vessels and make them fast to the nearest mooring, had been instructed not to fish corpses out of the water. Persons floating in the river were doubtless dead, and to stack them in tiers for identification purposes would place an impossible strain on mortuaries already overtaxed.

It would take weeks, months perhaps, to sort out and bury the urban dead.

The bright morning sky above Cobb's head was dense with airplane traffic transporting the sick and injured to hospitals in Washington, Richmond, and points south. Cobb recognized a squadron of C-54s skimming north with medicine and oxygen tents. How well he knew the drone of this four-motored airmaster; he had listened for it so long, so vainly, during his son's last days. Finally, one of them had landed on the field in front of his house. "Places for two," the pilot had shouted. But there was only one to leave Cobb's house that day. Laimbeer, wrapped in blankets, was bundled into the plane. "Tough," he said, tears streaming down his yellow face as he gripped Cobb's hand in farewell.

"Yes, tough." What else was there to be said? The propellers kicked up a cloud of snow and the plane's nose headed southward.

Broodingly, from his high window, Cobb gazed at the river, sparkling under a sun too brilliant for his dark mood of worry and loss. Restless, he turned to his desk. Where was Ross Lufbery? Two days of search and inquiry had uncovered no trace of him. The Waldorf people didn't know. The police didn't know. So many displaced persons. May, of course, take some time. Quite. I understand. Still, the torture of waiting, the misery of not knowing, the desolate routine of opening Luff's door and seeing his empty chair were psychic imposts preventing Cobb from getting started on the job of—of, well, getting started again.

How did you begin organizing a life handed back to you after three weeks of catastrophic interruption? First things first, naturally. But what came first? Should he summon in the meek Miss Dunham of the no-colored hair, who had turned up pale and weak as a dormouse after a long hibernation in bed with her sister, and tell her to send out the monthly bills? Or should he commence going through the stack of patent applications that the swift couriers of the Postal Department had dumped at his door that morning? He opened an envelope or two: a vinylite handle (non-conducting) for electricians' screwdrivers; a broadcasting device that provided canned radio programs for the deaf when they weren't hearing anything else . . .

No, not that. Tomorrow perhaps, but not this morning.

] 257 [

He turned again to his copy of the *Times,* surveyed the banner headlines:

City Digs Out of Engulfing 20-Day Snowstorm;
  Rail, Power, and Lighting Services Approach Normal;
    Total Dead Estimated at 800,000; Suffering Acute.

After three weeks of suspended publication, the great journal was crammed with news and pictures of the storm. Reporters and feature writers were having a field day with the material, while from the editorial page rose the cadence of almost Biblical prose. The dominant note of the lead edit was that of a chastised people acknowledging the fierce majesty of the elements and the well-timed mercy of their Maker. "The devastation visited upon our city," burbled the editorial, "is humbling testimony to a power infinitely greater than man's."

"They've got something there," said Cobb.

On an inside page he found paragraphs and pictures dealing with freak aspects of the storm, human interest well forward. The family of Angelino Pascarotta, 211A Avenue B, had subsisted entirely on mushrooms grown in the cellar by Mr. Pascarotta. Six boxes of soda crackers and three cans of tomato soup, won at a Bingo party on the first evening in the storm, had sustained life in Miss Bedelia Fogarty, spinster, 875 First Avenue. There were several instances of communal sharing. Martin Timmins, the Bronx, owner of a flock of two hundred carrier pigeons, had divided his birds with fellow tenants. George H. Turkus, 556 West 188 Street, had killed and dismembered all the family pets—two dogs, a cat, and three canaries—boiled them into soup, and kept himself, his wife, and mother-in-law alive. Tragedy had overtaken Sidney Lefferts, 443 East 66 Street. Lefferts, an employee in the Rockefeller Hospital Laboratory, had stolen a brace of live rabbits from the lab cages. Unfortunately, they had been inoculated with Rocky Mountain spotted fever.

Red Cross workers had distributed 1,450,000 packages of foodstuffs during the first ten days of the storm, and were now establishing soup kitchens in the Morningside, Chelsea, and Washington Heights districts. The fire, police, and sanitation departments had written new chapters in their sagas of public service. The police had assisted at 336 emergency births; firemen had carried several thousand gallons of coffee and tons of sandwiches up extension ladders to cliff dwellers stranded in upper stories. Cobb marveled at the ingenuity of the people, the shifts and devices of a population determined to live.

A muted buzzer whirred on his desk. Cobb seized the telephone. "Luff?" No. "This is K. A. Bellinger of the National City Bank," said a well-framed voice. The manager himself. Cobb knew him well enough to drop the "Mister."

"Hello, Bellinger. Glad to hear you're alive."

"Thanks, Mr. Cobb. Same to you."

"Everything all right at the bank? No assets frozen? No embezzlement in high places?"

"All under control, Mr. Cobb." Pleasantry gave place to discreet politesse, bank style. "There's a man here, Mr. Cobb, presenting a check of yours in the amount of five thousand dollars. His—um—get-up is rather unusual, and the date of the check shows that it was issued during the early part of the storm. Shall we honor the check, sir?"

Gurley! So the canting rat had got through. For a moment Cobb was tempted to throw a nice stopper into the extortioner's game. Let him whistle for the rhino. But no. High as the man's price was, he had saved Sicely's life.

"It's O.K., Bellinger. Give him the money. He did me a rather handsome service at a critical time. And thanks for checking with me." As Cobb hung up, he had the feeling that fiduciary trust was in the saddle again and that the accustomed powers were again in control of the world. Life could go on.

First things first. A letter to Oliphant of the State Department.

He swiveled his chair a quarter-turn to the dictaphone, picked up the mouthpiece, and tried to marshal words on the subject of the light-smashing blueprint still in his brief case. But words refused to come. "Must talk it over with Luff," he said, starting out of his chair.

Bereavement caught him on the rise.

The need of talking to someone he loved, of getting the thin but positive end of a lever under this load of uncertainty and restlessness, goaded him back to the dictaphone. He lifted the mouthpiece of the machine and began speaking familiar, homely words in a letter to his daughter.

Dear Sice:
    Here I am back on the job again, trying to pick up what you girls might call the loose ends of my knitting, and not doing very good at it. Nothing seems to march, or rather everything marches in different directions. The city is still trying to dig itself out, but so far only the main avenues and big crosstown streets are opened up. I had quite a time getting down here—the train from Albany was four hours late—but the Rhinecliff station was full of people we know, so I had plenty to talk about while we were waiting. Most of them pulled through the storm in pretty fair shape, but three or four families were hard hit. Mr. Twombley, the stationmaster, lost one of his twins, and Charlie Russell—you know, the insurance broker—told me that his oldest son walked out into the storm hoping to get some rabbits, but never came back.

Solicitous not to arouse grief in his daughter, Cobb hung off for a moment, then continued with the thought uppermost in his mind.

    Everyone was sorry to hear about Roddy, and I got some warm handshakes from people I scarcely knew. Usually, they had lost a child too, so if there is any comfort in sharing grief with neighbors, we comforted each other plenty on the station platform that day.

    How goes the battle at Mrs. Langham's Fattening School for

Girls? Does she feed you as much starch as ever? And, in her high-minded way, what does she say about the storm? I can just see her taking off her pince-nez and reading the elements a good lecture for being so unmannerly. "Nothing in excess" is a grand motto, but, as Mrs. Rollefson points out, "The weather ain't obliged to listen."

The day before I left, I helped Gunnar get his plane in shape, and he took off about 4 p.m., heading for his home field. He doesn't know whether he'll be court-martialed or not, but he says that even if they send him to Leavenworth, it'll be worth it for having met you. A fine chap; I don't know what we'd have done without him.

Mother is very tired and I want to take her down South with me for a long rest soon. She has been through a terrible strain and is about due for a vacation. I feel pretty seedy myself, so I think it would be a good idea if we went away together, say to Florida or Nassau, just to thaw the chill out of our system.

Well, Sice, that is about all for now. Before I sign off, let me tell you once again how plucky you were during the storm and how you kept your guard up when the danger was greatest. I can still see your red mitten poking through the snow. The sight will be with me always. You've got what it takes, dear daughter, and plenty of it. This is the considered and irreversible judgment of your affectionate

Father

P.S. I almost forgot to tell you that poor old Rollefson died in his bunk the day after you left. Heart failure, I guess.

Cobb put the mouthpiece on its hook, his own last words still hanging on the air.

Heart failure? Well, in a way, yes.

On a round of final inspection, Cobb had gone downstairs to turn off the motorcycle and decided to look in on the old falconer. Down the long aisle of whitewashed pillars, he could see an edge of light through the crack of Rollefson's door. At the door of Rollefson's shop he had paused, rapped lightly with a friendly knuckle. No response. He rapped harder; still no reply. Pushing open the door, he had seen in the lamplight the caretaker stretched out on his bed.

Drunk again. Well, why not? Unwilling to embarrass his old colleague, Cobb started to close the door when at the corner of his eye he caught a note of strangeness in the tidy room. Not the pint bottle lying on its side by the bedpost; that was normal enough. The thing that seemed out of place was the black, snakelike length of garden hose hanging over the headboard of the bed. What was the rubber hose doing there? Cobb stepped nearer to investigate. In the murky light, Rollefson's face was dark blue. And scarcely three inches from his mouth was the end of the hose, odorous with the characteristic exhaust fumes of a gasoline motor.

Njals Rollefson's right arm was not yet stiff as Cobb lifted it and let it fall again over the man's dead heart. "If I had come an hour earlier, I might have saved him," mused Cobb. But the very thought carried a reproach. Why should Rollefson be saved? The wild sea-rover, the captive bear, had slipped the leash of his captors, broken the walls of his cuddy-prison, thrown down its gates, and limped forward to embrace that old freebooter Death. No tears were in Cobb's eyes as he brought Rollefson's lids together, closed his mouth, and arranged his body in an attitude of the casually dead.

Nor was there any question in Cobb's mind about the story he must tell his people. Emma and Gunnar must never know the manner of this death. Njals Rollefson had died in his sleep—of heart failure, of cerebral thrombosis, or a dozen other things. Wife and son must not blame themselves for failures in love and patience, if failures there had been.

Cobb turned down the wick of the caretaker's lamp, blew out the oxygen-starved flame. Then, feeling sickishly dizzy himself, he hastened out of the cellar, leaving behind him another casualty of the storm, another blot on the life ledger he had so jealously tried to keep clean.

And yet, viewing the matter now, Rollefson's death was no blot at all. Rather, an account scratched off, settled. When one really came to the foot of the column, all assets spent, all futures discounted, all credit gone, what other course had one but to pay up with dignity and dispatch, as Rollefson had done?

The trick lay in knowing when the till was really bare.

Disciplining himself, Cobb bent over his desk, worked doggedly at the heap of letters and documents before him. The dot of NOW stood at twelve-sixteen when he rose, stretched, and felt the need of food. He would walk to the Club and view with his own eyes the damage wrought by the storm. He called in Miss Dunham, gave a few covering orders for the conduct of such business as might come in during his absence. "If anyone phones about Mr. Lufbery, take the message. I'll call you after lunch." He put on his hat, coat, and heavy overshoes, took a final look into his partner's office, and a minute later was descending in the express elevator to the street.

The noon rays of a melting March sun fell straight down upon the city and a springlike zephyr felt good to his cheek. Cobb stood for a few moments at the entrance to his office building, absolutely idle and purposeless, watching the crowds of people moving along the sidewalk in the hurrying New York manner. How bloodless they all looked! A greenish pallor gave them the complexion of cellar-grown vegetables. Silently he praised the sun from whom all color flowed.

If that light should fail, be shattered!

Along the edge of the sidewalk a high barricade of snow was being breached by a huge machine, part dredge and part derrick. An endless chain of buckets tore into the snow and pitched it, irregularly chunked, into a waiting truck. Evidently the snow shovelers' strike had been settled; battalions of men in nondescript clothing, most of them wearing shiny new rubbers and sodden brown gloves, scraped and heaved at the slush underfoot or climbed like ants over the hulk of a beached whale. Powerful hydraulic nozzles were dissolving the base of the snowy leviathan—and the sun was doing its work, too. Under the combined attack of man, machinery, and the spring thaw, the thirty-foot snowfall was yielding. It had made its threat, spent its elemental force, and now was nothing but a dead glacier—dirtying, lumpish refuse that had to be carried away in carts or flushed down with a hose. Overhanging catastrophe had become merely a nuisance!

Like a visitor in a great shipyard or busy foundry, Cobb walked northward through the city, observing his fellow men digging themselves out of the storm. A Resurrection Day friendliness possessed the people, banded them together in a league of joy and gratitude always noticeable among survivors of a shipwreck, flood, or plague. 'One twitch of nature makes the whole world kin.' Too soon this kinship would vanish and the warm ray of friendliness fade into the light of common day. But for the present, the atmosphere was inspiriting, comradely, with a joshing Old Home Week kind of banter as the prevailing note. Commonplaces of greeting—"Well, so you got through!"; "Yeh, it might have been a lot worse"—were accompanied by grins, handshakes, and cigar swapping. New York had squeaked through, and its citizens were in a mood of thanksgiving.

Beclouded heaven electing, the city might yet learn something from the storm.

But not too much. No danger of that, Cobb discovered, as he entered a cigar store to buy a pack of cigarettes.

"How about a lighter?" suggested the clerk brightly. Did he really believe that he was carrying a sales manager's baton in his hip pocket?

"No, thanks," smiled Cobb.

"A nice pigskin billfold with a patented key attachment?"

"Just the cigarettes, please."

Outside the shop, Cobb was lighting up when he saw a young man with a walkie-talkie accost an undersized woman in a dyed muskrat coat.

"This is Danny Disbrow," said the young man, giving his portable mike the old personality stuff, "your Walkie-Talkie Inquiring Reporter, asking questions of all and sundry from Station WHIZ at the corner of Fifth Avenue and Fourteenth Street, still buried under six or seven feet of snow, snow, the be-e-yootiful snow, as the Storm of the Century hangs on the ropes waiting for the K.O. Before we pin our searching inquiries onto passers-by, or passer-bys (make up your mind, Danny), I want to ask each and every one of you a *personal* question. Did you enjoy your *second* cup of coffee this morning? If you didn't, why not switch to Gruber's Javacup, the coffee tailored to your taste from first-crop, *second*-cup Mocha and Java? Point to the big, steaming coffeepot at your grocer's or delicatessen dealer's, and ask for it by name: Gruber's Javacup. G-R-U-B-E-R'S. Say to yourself: 'Havacup of Javacup!' And now we're going to ask this little lady in the big muskrat coat to step up to the microphone and give us her undivided attention for exactly thirty-five seconds. . . . What's your name, madam? . . . Sally Berkowitz? Top o' the morning to yez, Miss Berkowitz. Ha, ha! The brogue fooled you, heh? Now, in your opinion, Miss Sally, what is the silver lining inside the big, black storm-cloud just leaving New York? A little louder, please, Miss Berkowitz. You say it'll give employment to a lot of snow shovelers? Ver-*ree* good, Miss Sally, and to repay you for your sparkling answer to the Walkie-Talkie Question Man, the Gruber Coffee people are giving you a certificate for one pound of Javacup, ground to your order in any store in Manhattan, Queens, Richmond, Brooklyn, or the Bronx. 'Bye now, Sally. . . . Our next question is addressed to the banker-type gentleman in the black Homburg. . . . Tell me, mister, did *you* enjoy your *second* cup this snowy morn?"

So it was beginning all over again.

Cobb looked straight into the brassy, inquiring face of Danny Disbrow. Vapid, self-assured. What could he say to the fellow? How tutor him in humility, point out the danger the City had been through? Useless. Danny Disbrow would never know.

"Well, make up your mind, mister. I only rent this gadget by the day."

Once, Cobb would have struck the fellow. But now a sense of helplessness and compassion oppressed him.

"You must excuse me," he said, and moved on.

* * *

In the Club foyer, the brethren were gathering for the ritual of the heavy lunch. At the center of the largest group Cobb saw the portly figure of Street Commissioner Fidd, face shining, arm pumping, as he accepted congratulations from a ring of his cronies. Well, the fellow probably deserved all that was being said. Not a *deus ex machina* by any means, but, like everyone else, he had done the best he could. That salesman from the Arion Plow Company—what was his name?—would probably sell him a hundred new snow-removal machines at lunch. Carbuncular Ed Griffiths; Honest John Lynch; Joe Travers, the gall-bladder invalid holding down the Collector's office. All present and accounted for. All good fellows. Ask you about your wife and kids. Give you the shirt off their backs. Cobb wondered why he hadn't gone to the Olympian for lunch.

The reason, of course, was the Metro's steam room. Just to soak in its tropical warmth would lull you into seemingness of repose.

He checked his hat, coat, and galoshes, and took the elevator to the third floor. The baths! No exercise today—just the hot nozzle, the cold nozzle, the needle spray, then the refuge of the steam room. Grateful for the moist relaxation, Cobb spread a big towel on the stone bench and stretched out at full length. Straw-slippered figures shuffled past; parboiled faces glistened through the wreathing clouds of steam. Security and calm caressed his nerve endings. The world had not changed. Everything was the same.

The voices of two men came to his ears—one voice prying, credulous, the other informative, cynical.

"What's this wife-trouble business that Joe Garrahan's been having?" asked the prying one.

"Wife trouble is only the beginning of it. Tuesday, before the storm—no, it was Wednesday—they took him away."

"Away where?"

"To the loony bin."

"No!"

"Fact. Been coming on a long time. You know what a dog Joe is for the skirts."

"Who the hell ain't?"

"Well, sure, but not like Joe Garrahan. He got so bad he was bringing the dames right into the house when his wife was out. So one day his old lady catches him in bed with some red-headed bimbo: 'At your age,' she says, 'and with a son a priest, too.' So she packs up and leaves Joe after forty years being married to him."

"No!"

"Fact. Well, in a few days Joe begins to miss her pretty bad, so he figures out a scheme to get her back."

"Did he now?"

The narrator laughed, slapped his leg at the mirth of it all. "Coo-coo like a fox, Joe is. He buys a lot of fancy drawers, silk stockings, and stuff like that. Then he washes them in the bathtub and hangs them out on a line in back of the house. His old lady sees them, just like he meant her to, and comes tearing into the house, 'Where's this red-headed slut you're buying corsets for?' she yells, and dashes into the bedroom." The informative one almost choked with mirth, "Ha, ha, ha! Guess what Joe did then."

"How can I, if he's as nutty as that?"

"Joe—ha, ha!—he locked her in."

"No."

"Fact. Yes, sir, locked her into her own bedroom and wouldn't let her out. His son the priest had to get the wagon up there and take Joe away."

Dying fall of sadness. End of the recital. A dog for the skirts . . . All as before.

Cobb lunched on a high stool at the oyster bar. Clam-juice cocktail and Lynnhavens, followed by a pot of coffee and a Hoyo. He felt his strength flowing back on a full tide as he walked to the phone booth to call his office.

"Any news of Mr. Lufbery?" he asked Miss Dunham.

"Oh," she gasped, "a policeman came in with a card."

"What kind of a card?"

Miss Dunham's weak voice faltered. "There's a number on it, and the policeman wants you to go over to Bellevue and identify the—the person with the number."

"What's the number?"

"22,989."

"Thank you, Miss Dunham." Cobb hung up the receiver.

At the cab rank outside the Club, Cobb took a taxi. "Bellevue," he said to the driver.

"Nothing's opened up east of Lexington, chief."

"Take me to Lexington and Twenty-second then."

Leaving the cab at the corner of Lexington Avenue, Cobb floundered across town toward the East River and the Morgue. Here the miracle of resurrection was taking place the hard way, as small shopkeepers toiled single-handed with shovels, brooms, and snow scrapers to clear their doorways. Because these streets had no slope to the river, the snow was covered with garbage, dead dogs, cats, and the noisome excreta of overcrowded human animals. Cobb saw the pallid faces of men and women taking a breath of springtime air at the upflung windows. Children and bedding, both filthy, crowded the fire escapes. Cobb marveled at the tenacity of a race that needed so little encouragement to keep on going. He recalled Laimbeer's statement, made in half-delirium: "The people are like blinkered nags trotting over mean cobblestones—but nags with a strain of the old Winged Horse in them still." Probably so. Whether the people knew it or not, some ferment of aspiration, some vital yeast of hope and beauty, must be working secretly in their bloodstream.

At the corner of Second Avenue, Cobb saw a peddler's pushcart hub-deep in a bank of dirty snow. A dwarflike man wearing a large velveteen fedora was bucking at the handles of his two-wheeled vehicle, trying to push it by main force through the drifts. The sight, at once comical and pathetic, aroused something of the sidewalk superintendent in Cobb.

"Hey!" he cried. "Don't you know it's easier to *pull* than push a cart through the snow? Here, let me help you get it pointed right."

He waded into the middle of the street, put his gloved hand under an almost buried hub. "Catch hold of the other wheel," he ordered. "We'll lift it out first."

"Always *poosha* da cart," objected the man in the big fedora.

"I know. But through snow, you *pull*," said Cobb. "Come on, grab hold of that wheel. I'm in a hurry."

Together they heaved. In their efforts to turn the cart around, it lurched sideways. A tarpaulin fell off, disclosing the body of a fourteen-year-old boy. By his hue and posture, dead.

"Wh—what's this?" stammered Cobb.

Unabashed, the pushcart man tucked the tarpaulin around the small body. "This my boy, Vittorio," he said in a natural tone of introduction. He took off the large fedora and wiped its drenched sweatband with his coat sleeve. "Vittorio, he visit his uncle on Westa Side. Catcha bad cold. Die in storm."

"Where are you taking him?"

"I taka him home. My wife ver' sick. She cry, cry, cry all night, mus' see Vittorio oncea more." Large helplessness brought his hands up, palms outward. "What else I do?"

What else indeed? "Come on," said Cobb. "I'll help you pull him."

Backing, tugging, each pulling at a handle, they got the cart onto

Second Avenue and turned south. One of Commissioner Fidd's snowplows had opened a narrow lane, and down this channel, high-banked on either side with snow, the pushcart cortege proceeded in panting silence. Cobb had no notion of how far he would have to pull the cart. The Biblical two miles? It made no particular difference. Time and place vanished as he threw his weight into the handle of the pushcart and became one of the nameless unnumbered billions of human beings whose duty it was to carry their tribal dead to a place of burial. Trucks with skid-chained wheels taller than the pushcart crowded the sweating pall-bearers into the snowdrifts at a steep angle; once the body of young Vittorio tumbled out of his mean hearse. Cobb helped the father stow him under the tarpaulin, then bent again to the handles of the cart.

The image of Roddy pale in his decent coffin filled the upper-right quadrant of Cobb's eye. The image, blurred with tears, then gave place to another image lower and to the left—the image of Vittorio jolting from side to side in the banana cart. Cobb wondered whether the images would merge, be superimposed on each other like identical letters on an oculist's eye-testing machine. They did not merge. Personal grief and universal sorrow were different emotions. The two fathers must themselves die before their sons could become undistinguishable letters of dust.

"This the house," said Vittorio's father at last. A tenement like ten thousand others, wearing the soiled uniform of poverty.

"Want me to help you to carry him up?" asked Cobb.

"Vittorio not heavy."

Clearly the man did not want to involve him in the hysterical mother-son scene that lay ahead.

"Then I'll be on my way."

For the first time, embarrassment of caste overcame the peddler. Cobb's black Homburg and Chesterfield, his speech and manner, unnoticed till now, became barriers between man and man. But the tutorings of natural dignity prompted the pushcart owner to do and say the right thing. He took off his oversized fedora, held it with both hands across his heart.

"God bless all gooda men like you."

To acknowledge the man's bared head, Cobb took off his own hat. Could he match the dignity of the other's utterance? Only by repeating it. There was no other way.

"God bless you too," he said, giving benediction to a fellow man for the first time in his life.

* * *

On First Avenue, desolate as a street on the outskirts of Moscow, a small throng was gathered at the iron gates of the City Morgue. Cobb pushed through the passive crowd until he came to a door marked "Entrance." As he turned the knob, his nostrils were assailed with the acrid odor of formaldehyde, and his eyes beheld sheet-covered tiers of the assembled dead, stacked to the ceiling.

"Number 22,989," he said to an attendant.

The man walked down a lane between two stacks, like a stockroom clerk looking for a catalogue item. "Here," he said, throwing back a sheet.

As though he were walking without legs, Cobb approached the cadaver, took a single glance at its features. Lufbery! Not the rubicund, violent Lufbery that had been his friend and partner for almost twenty years, but an emaciated, discolored Lufbery, all tension of life loosened, the wick of life quite doused.

"Where did you find him?"

The attendant glanced at the ticket attached to the slab. "Under a drift at the corner of a Hundred and Sixteenth and Morningside Drive."

How in God's name had he gotten there? What mad desperation could have driven Lufbery out of the beleaguered hotel? Yet how like him not to wait like a sitting bird for death to creep up with its crossbow.

"I'll take care of the funeral arrangements," said Cobb. He signed a paper the attendant thrust into his hand, and walked out into the snow.

Plodding up First Avenue toward his Sutton Place apartment, Cobb's thoughts were all of Luff. The usual thoughts at first—tender, regretful, reminiscent. Their first tiny office on Pine Street; Luff's eruptive rage when business didn't come in, his profane exultation when it did. What a man for the expletive, both in language and action! How free, impetuous he was in morals and appetite! What would life be without Luff's stallion hoofs splintering the stable door of convention? Easy enough to find another business partner, but not another friend, brother, alter ego. Compared to Luff, the bald and tarnished cherub, no one was so fearless, so passionate, so *uncensored*. That was it! Luff's refusal to heed life's pious, prudential nays; his eagerness to enjoy women, food, power, money, as good things made for fresh use every day—all these had made him unique and inimitable. Yet an overdose of this very recklessness had led him to his end. How delicately the contending powers of Eros and Thanatos were balanced on the thin wire over the abyss.

It was nearly six o'clock when Cobb reached Sutton Place; twilight was winding violet gauze around the tops of the apartment houses as he let himself into his flat. He kicked off his soggy overshoes, threw his hat and overcoat at a chair, and lay down on the divan in his living room. Weary, weary, he was, weary of cold and snow. The awful fatigue of the three weeks' siege had sapped his reserves of strength. He wanted to lie down not in a steam bath but in the warm sunshine, for a year, for the rest of his life. Yes, he would have to get away. Nolla must decide to come with him, else he would go alone. Or take Berry.

He loosened the buttons of his vest and the waistband of his trousers, eased his feet out of his shoes, and lay perfectly flat on the sofa. He needed a drink, but was too tired to fix one. For a few moments his half-closed eyes saw the square of purple light through the southern windows of his apartment. How many shades of purple there were! Like gulls with wings dipped in the ultra-violet end of the spectrum, his thoughts rose, crossed, and recrossed in counterpoint of purple. The stripe in Lucy Foederis' croquet ball, dim and faded now . . . the angry flames consuming Laimbeer's infected arm . . . the royal-purple thread of Nolla's embroidery tambour . . .

Nolla-associations surged in waves over his tired nerves. Made suggestible by fatigue, he felt her arms about his neck on the night he started on his desperate trek for Sicely. His fingers tingled again as he drew back his hand leaving the imprint of a blow on Nolla's cheek. He heard her plea in the upper room: "Oh, let him die, so that I can die too." Knees parted, she cradled his head on her lap, rocked him maternally in the cane-bottomed chair.

What a fathomless deep their marriage was, a sea warm with pity, dark with revenge, tidal with compulsion, salt with tears.

Tears. Of mutual grief and of broken vows. Tears old as their first wedding night, as new as Nolla's plea for forgiveness yesterday.

"Why did I do it, Rust?" She was sobbing on the pillow beside him. "Faithless under my own roof, before my children's eyes, while you struggled to save us."

He had soothed, consoled her. "Life was running out pretty fast, Noll. You took hold of it as it passed. It might have been your last chance at happiness."

"You are my last chance, my only chance. There is no hope for me, except in you. Oh, dearest," she whispered, "help me break the terrible death lock that is on me. Help me be warm and alive, instead of cold and frightened."

Her confession that Laimbeer had failed to free her for love was both sad and welcome to the husband ear.

"Do you really want to be warm and alive, Noll?"

"So much, darling. Be patient with me still."

"Always, Noll." His hands searched her for a secret sign. Not given. The keys withheld.

She shivered miserably in his arms. "Wait, dear, a little longer. Till we leave this guilty house. I will go to the City with you."

"Darling, come tomorrow."

"Not tomorrow, but soon." Even as she spoke, Cobb knew she would not come.

"I will see doctors," she promised. "There are treatments, medicines . . ."

"Good ones, Noll. They can help you. Tell me when you are ready." He stroked the thin hair at her temples, re-enacting the old ritual of postponement and submission.

"Kiss me, Rust. In the hollow of my cheek."

Obediently he kissed her.

Was it all a beguilement to win control of him again? Cobb could not tell. But as he lay in the darkness of his apartment, Cobb thought it strange that he, so tenacious of life in other forms, should accept in love—the greatest of life forms—a gravely imperfect thing. In his love for Nolla, there was, and he knew it now, some overhang of the death wish, some will to be put off, defeated.

So, even in the strongest, a remnant of the death wish persisted!

And well that it did, thought Cobb. For if man's will to life were not diluted with some admixture of death, his energy would rage in cruel and monstrous appetites—avid, ugly, and self-destructive. To preserve the race, the mothers of men had kneaded the death wish, by impalpable pressures, into the souls of their children.

Sometimes the pressure was too heavy, the admixture fatally strong.

As in America?

Ruston Cobb was too tired to say. He dozed. The health of sleep claimed him. He snored slightly.

He was awakened by the ringing of his telephone. In the darkness he arose and walked uncertainly toward the instrument, lifted it off its cradle. "Hello."

"Rusty, it's me, Berry. You sound sleepy."

"I just woke up from a little nap. What time is it?"

"Seven-fifteen. I've been trying to reach you all afternoon at your office."

"I was out looking for Luff."

"Did you find him?"

"Yes. At the Morgue."

"Oh!" Shock and sympathy, blending, touched him like a caress between the living. How comforting against the encroachments of death.

"Have you had dinner?" he asked.

"No."

"Can't we go somewhere? I'm hungry."

Her voice slipped into a special register. "Why don't you come over and let me cook a couple of chops here."

"Shall I bring anything?"

"Only a Hoyo. I'll light it for you at one of my bayberry candles."

"How soon do you want me?"

"I want you now, but don't come for half an hour."

Cobb showered and dressed without hurry, content to let the hours ahead fall into the new configuration his life must take. The old pattern of manacled negation was broken now. He knew at last that his love for Nolla was exactly what it had always been—a worshipful adoration of the dream mother, without hope of fleshly fulfillment. He could never leave her or be wholly free to love anyone else. But the deepening attraction that Berry held for him was proof that the body could be as imperious as the soul, as tender in satisfaction and as worthy of delight.

Slipping into his town coat, he paused for a final scrutiny of himself in the dressing-room mirror. The glass reflected a highly milled, expensively wrought human product, prime, or nearly so, in its ability to enjoy, suffer, and understand. The face was rich-blooded, disciplined in fortitude, lenient with pity—the face of a man prepared to accept the consequences of the thing he was about to do.

But not without a final scuffle of conscience. Between the mirrored image and the man himself an inaudible colloquy went forward:

"They will say . . ."

Let them say.

"She is a sick girl."

Who is healthy?

"She may not respond as in the storm."

I can be content with less.

"It cannot last."

There will be moments.

"Moments are not the answer."

I know . . . I know.

Sad. To know the good, to see far off the vision in spun samite, to be dolorous for its sake—yet driven by mortal loneliness to take the easier and nearer thing. Faint and lost came Nolla's voice: *"Promise me now upon this burning book, my heart . . ."* And fainter still, his own vow of constancy: *"I promise, love."* Pledge of young hope inscribed on life's dedication-stone. Look for it now, a broken tablet beneath the quarry-dump of years.

Slowly he walked to the large window at the southern end of his living room and gazed out over the great city. Compassion for his kind—divided, guilt-muffled hearts doomed never to beat in full unambiguous strokes of happiness—smote Ruston Cobb. "There are so many of us," he thought. "It is the commonest case in the world."

A sense of the troubled destiny in store for himself and his country flooded into him as he beheld the festooned brilliance of the city, lighted up like a carnival, a dream of promise and glory seemingly suspended in middle air. So rich, so bright, so powerful! Would this fail and fall at last, become a muddy crossroads like Thebes? Would the warning written in snow be forgotten with the first thaw? Would the arrogant, visionless city be overwhelmed at last by a ray, a gas, a fog, a siege, a plague—by some device not yet traced in blueprint, by some fury not yet begotten in test tube, by some dark glint of the death wish not yet measured by electric beam?

Who could tell? It would be a close thing, a near thing, as the storm had shown. Doubtless, final catastrophe would bring the city down. But before it fell Ruston Cobb believed that his country would enter into a long age of greatness in which the artist would find a living symbol, the people a worthy vision, and the lover a guiltless, happy love never yet enjoyed by the sons and daughters of woman.

ABOUT THE AUTHOR

HENRY MORTON ROBINSON began as a poet, publishing three volumes of verse, while acting as Instructor in English at Columbia College. In 1927 he became a free-lance writer and produced a succession of articles and short stories for leading magazines. During these journalistic years Mr. Robinson wrote a number of books—*Stout Cortez, Science vs. Crime,* and *Fantastic Interim* being the only ones he chooses to remember. More recently, he collaborated with Joseph Campbell on a monumental study of James Joyce's last and greatest work. After five years of scholarly research and sheer divination, Messrs. Robinson and Campbell presented a puzzled world with *A Skeleton Key to Finnegans Wake.*

The novel now exclusively claims Mr. Robinson's creative energies. Of his first novel, *The Perfect Round,* published in 1945, *The Saturday Review of Literature* said, "The inventiveness of this author never flags; his ability to lure the reader into the next chapter never tires." And Manuel Komroff declared, "*The Perfect Round* is the first genuine attempt to approach the problems of our postwar world in terms of creative symbols."

The Great Snow signalizes the development of a ripely matured novelistic talent. In this novel an artist-narrator dedicates himself to the double task of exploring new creative material and at the same time exercising his remarkable powers as a story teller.

Mr. Robinson is married, has three children, and has lived for the past twenty years at Woodstock, N. Y. An illusion that he is a descendant of Lief Ericson compels him to take long voyages in small open boats whenever possible, weather notwithstanding. This illusion proved serviceable in the writing of *The Great Snow.* The voyage of the twelve-foot *Chip* up the ice-bound Hudson in *The Great Snow* is based on an actual journey of this sort taken by the author.